# *HIGH RATINGS...*

"Do you see why I need you to help me select next season's shows?" Dash asked. "You're young enough to know what today's viewers want to see—and smart enough to pick a hit show."

"True," Cathy said flippantly. "Well, boss, when do we start?"

He wanted to throw his arms about her and kiss that sweet little mouth. He'd done it, by God. He'd beat Marc Monroe and won Cathy. Almost lazily, he said, "Maybe you'd better give it a little more thought. It's a hell of a tough job, sweetheart."

"Oh no you don't, you're not backing out on me!" She advanced toward him, eyes sparkling with laughter, and put both hands on his shoulders, pinning him back in his chair.

"I'm not backing out, but I'm a fair man. I just want you to know what you're getting into. Long, grueling hours poring over scripts, most of them shit, dealing with neurotic writers and temperamental stars...."

"You rotten prick." She laughed, bending to kiss him on the forehead. "You just love to torment me, don't you?"

"Cathy, you wound me deeply—" he protested.

"Stow it. You don't fool me. We're too much alike. And you know I'd kill for a chance like this—so, I'll ask you again. When do we start?"

"As soon as your show goes on hiatus. That soon enough for you?" He waited for her to mention Marc, but she said nothing, only grinned from ear to ear and stooped to kiss him again, this time on the mouth. Jesus, couldn't she see what she did to him?

### ATTENTION: SCHOOLS AND CORPORATIONS

PINNACLE Books are available at quantity discounts with bulk purchases for educational, business or special promotional use. For further details, please write to: SPECIAL SALES MANAGER, Pinnacle Books, Inc., 1430 Broadway, New York, NY 10018.

### WRITE FOR OUR FREE CATALOG

If there is a Pinnacle Book you want—and you cannot find it locally—it is available from us simply by sending the title and price plus 75¢ to cover mailing and handling costs to:

> Pinnacle Books, Inc.
> Reader Service Department
> 1430 Broadway
> New York, NY 10018

Please allow 6 weeks for delivery.

_____Check here if you want to receive our catalog regularly.

# The LOVE GAME
## NANCY BACON

PINNACLE BOOKS　　NEW YORK

This is a work of fiction. All the characters and events portrayed in this book are fictional, and any resemblance to real people or incidents is purely coincidental.

THE LOVE GAME

*Copyright © 1982 by Nancy Bacon*

All rights reserved, including the right to reproduce this book or portions thereof in any form.

An original Pinnacle Books edition, published for the first time anywhere.

First printing, December 1982

ISBN: 0-523-41400-5

Cover Photo by Mort Engle

*Printed in the United States of America*

PINNACLE BOOKS, INC.
1430 Broadway
New York, New York 10018

**For "Lady" Pamela Williams,
a royal friend**

# THE
LOVE GAME

## Chapter One

Cathy Curtis sat slumped in a chair, alternately doodling on her clipboard and chewing on the end of her ballpoint pen, as she watched the television monitor. Greg Bedford sat across from her, a look of pure disgust on his face, a glass of Scotch in his hand. They were watching the "Kane Winslow Show" from backstage as it was being taped on Stage Three a few yards away. The sound of the show came to them from both the monitor and the stage, a kind of eerie stereo.

"Jesus, what a turkey," Greg sighed, taking a swallow of his Scotch. He rubbed a hand over his eyes as if to wipe away the sight of Kane Winslow cavorting on the screen.

Cathy nodded silent agreement. The "Kane Winslow Show" was a real turkey, all right. Mundane, dotted with uninspired guests, given to cooking demonstrations and the boring reading of recipes, it was the lowest rated show on the KNAB network, merely a filler between the soaps and the five o'clock news. Even though Cathy had only been working at KNAB for three years, she knew the story of Kane Winslow. He had been a one-time great in the movies, dancing partner to the lovely and famous Jane Simon in those musical extravaganzas of the thirties and forties. They had once been lovers and still shared a close relationship; in other words,

Kane knew where the bodies were buried. (Jane Simon had her certain little peculiarities as do most living legends.) When the public grew bored with the old-fashioned musicals, Jane had moved on to television with her own variety show, becoming romantically involved with the president of KNAB, the dynamic and brilliant, David "Dash" Sunderling. Getting Kane his own show as well had been a piece of cake for the still beautiful star and rumor had it that it had also been Kane's price for his silence regarding Jane's nefarious activities off-stage.

"I don't remember Kane's show ever being anything *but* a turkey," Cathy said. "And I know all about the Jane Simon thing, but surely Dash Sunderling wouldn't give Kane his own show just because he, Dash, that is, was having an affair with Jane. Did Kane *ever* pull in an audience?"

"Yeah, when he first started the show, nine, ten years ago. He's never been great but he was good enough to hold his own in the ratings and attract some pretty heavy-weight sponsors. And he had his following from the musicals, middle-aged women and older, who still remembered him as a Fred Astaire type and were loyal enough to overlook the fact that Kane was now slightly paunchy and fifty, prone more toward Bourbon than love ballads."

Greg took a swallow of Scotch and a drag on his cigarette, keeping one weary eye on the monitor. "He had his moments—before the booze got him. Now and then the "Kane Winslow Show" was almost brilliant when he had guests on like Bette Davis or Jimmy Stewart. Big stars didn't appear on talk shows in those days— unless it was Carson's show. Not like today when you can see everyone from the First Lady to the first test tube baby on Merv, Dinah or Mike.

"But mostly the "Kane Winslow Show" was simply

## The Love Game

ninety minutes of background sound for housewives as they ironed, cleaned and cooked."

"But the viewing public has changed since those days," Cathy interrupted. "Those same housewives are probably divorced now and forced out into the job market. No more sitting around on the old tush watching afternoon television while they darn socks and fold clothes." Jesus, she thought, I'd give my left tit for a shot at getting my own show. I'd have the ratings soaring to the top of the Neilsen's in less than a month! It was so damn unfair that an old fart like Kane could screw around with his own show regardless of slipping ratings.

"Yeah, that's about the size of it," Greg sighed. "And the kids who used to be glued to the tube, hooked on afternoon TV, hell, they're no longer watching it; they're on it! In student riots, protesting the draft, marching for Gay Rights, expressing their views on sex, drugs and our government. The actors and actresses of the seventies are too hip and candid for the old-style talk shows. Shit, Kane looks like a relic from the silent-movie era alongside these new-wave stars. He's still living in the days of feather boas, discreet love affairs and slow dancing. It's a sight gag to see him up there next to somebody like Jane Fonda or Robert Blake, for God's sake. It's ludicrous. Pathetic."

"Christ, Greg, I don't see why we can't just drop him. His show's the biggest bomb on Channel Six."

"Can't. He still has two more years on his contract. The best we could hope for is that he'll have a little class and quit on his own."

"That isn't bloody likely. Why can't we just buy out his contract and get somebody else to do the show?" Like me, she wanted to say, but carefully kept her expression bland, knowing that timing was all important in TV land.

"Don't think I haven't given it a lot of thought." Greg

gave her a wry grin as he crushed out his cigarette. He stood, stretched, and went to the small bar in the corner of the office for a fresh Scotch. "But KNAB's always carried the rest of the day easily enough with game shows and soaps, and if the viewing audience switched to Dinah or Mike Douglas during Kane's show, we got them back at five with the news."

"And now?" Cathy prompted. She loved this kind of talk, discussing the intricate workings of television, how it all fit together and came to be. She had learned a lot from Greg, he being the daytime programmer at KNAB and the one to give her her first job as a model on one of the game shows. She was now his assistant but had no intention of remaining in such a lowly position. She had her eye on a job comparable to his or higher—preferably, hostess of her own show, And that was just for starters.

Greg sighed again. "And now we've got a problem. Both NBC and CBS have good lead-ins before the news and a lot of the audience are just leaving their sets tuned to Channel Four or Two instead of switching back to Six for the news. Even ABC has a better shot at grabbing an audience share, even with those ridiculous old B-class movies they run every afternoon."

They both glanced at the screen where Kane Winslow was smiling directly into camera one, a full close-up, as he read the day's recipe. He reminded Cathy of the Ted Baxter character on the old "Mary Tyler Moore Show"—full of his own self-importance.

"Poor old son-of-a-bitch," Greg said. "I feel kind of sorry for him. He knows his days are numbered, but he hangs in there like a fucking bulldog, ignoring the bad press, the dropping ratings."

Cathy's eyes narrowed as she watched Kane saying goodbye to the studio audience. She didn't feel the least bit sorry for him, only impatient that he wasn't willing to move over and make room for someone younger and better equipped to handle a talk show. He removed his chef's apron, swept off his tall chef's cap and sailed it into the audience. The lucky lady who caught it would have the honor of being his dance partner as the credits rolled.

"Strangers in the Night" (Kane's theme song) swelled in the studio, and a screaming, gray-haired woman leaped to her feet, waving the prize. Kane advanced down the aisle, bowed low, swept the delighted grandmother into his arms and danced her up the stairs and onto the stage as if she were Ginger Rogers. "Jeez, it's like a re-run of the old Arthur Murray show," Cathy said, disgust obvious in her voice. She went to the set and clicked it off. "Well, what now, boss? Want me to call him in and maybe we can kick around some new ideas for the show?"

"No, not tonight, Cath. I've got a bellyfull of Kane Winslow." He swallowed more Scotch. "Dash has had me re-running all the old shows for the past couple of days to see if we can't revive some of the charm that used to be there. Personally, I think it's hopeless. I'd like to see a new host entirely, but since we can't get around Kane's contract, and he sure as hell isn't about to quit, then I'd like to see a co-host, at least. Someone young and hip enough to pull in the twenty- to thirty-year-olds. But then I get this mental picture of Kane in his 1940s' tuxedo, patent leather shoes and that ridiculous blond toupee, standing next to some little T&A cutie who advocates the joys of free love and marijuana. It's too ludicrous for words." He lit another cigarette and leaned back in his chair, feet propped up on his desk.

Cathy's heartbeat quickened at the mention of a co-host but she suppressed her excitement, stood and went to the bar to mix herself a drink. "Why don't we play on his ego? Get some sharp lady exec at KNAB to take him on a shopping spree and outfit him in the latest styles, compliments of KNAB. He wouldn't look half bad in some of today's fashions. He's still reasonably slim."

He's a pompous old goat, she thought, as she poured vodka and orange juice into a glass and dropped in a couple of ice cubes. And he should be put out to pasture instead of hosting ninety minutes of prime afternoon time.

"It'd take a hell of a lot more than a couple of new outfits. Old Kane needs a complete overhaul, from the top of that bleached rug to the soles of his dancing shoes! Pour me another Scotch, will ya, Cath?" He held out his glass and she carried the bottle to his desk and poured, smiling down at him. "He's like Rip Van Winkle, for Christ's sake. He has no idea that drug permissiveness and sexual promiscuity have shattered the old Hollywood. It's dead and buried. There're no remaining barriers of exclusiveness for movie stars. The glamour is gone, faded into oblivion like a bad color print, bleeding at the edges. There're no surprises. No magic."

"Then if Kane can't show them magic, let him show them how the magic is manufactured," Cathy countered.

"Explain." Greg hunched forward, his steady gray eyes probing hers. "If you mean what I think you mean, this could be it. Go on, explain what you mean by 'manufacturing magic.'"

He watched her take a sip of her screwdriver as she moved thoughtfully across the office, a frown between her perfectly arched brows. She was barely five feet four, with a mop of curly blond hair and the biggest, bluest eyes he'd ever seen. Eyes that turned deep violet when she was excited about something as she was now. She tugged down the hem of her tee shirt, ran a hand down the side of her jeans as if wiping the perspiration from her palm.

She didn't weigh over a hundred pounds, but those

pounds were distributed perfectly over firm, high breasts, narrow waist and long, shapely legs. She had dimples in both cheeks that flashed whether she was angry or amused, but beneath the tousled golden curls clicked the mind of a computer. Intuitively aware, she was sharp and witty—nobody's dumb blond. She had a real feel for television, a grasp of the business end of it, and Greg knew that, given half a chance, she was going to go far. And if she wasn't given a chance, she had the balls to take it. He respected her opinion even as he remained a little in awe of her youth and beauty. She had the ability to get right to the guts of a situation, to hell with protcol.

"For instance, one day the theme could be a circus, say, and then we'd show footage of what goes on behind the scenes of the Big Show with voice-overs of the people who work there, interviews with circus-goers and performers alike. We could really get into it—show the audience how the magic of a circus is manufactured. The last fifteen minutes or so could be wrapped up in the studio with Kane talking to whomever is responsible for the circus."

"Another theme could be a television show—what it's *really* like to work in boob-tube land, how many people it takes to put on a half-hour sitcom or game show, the writers, grips, producers, contestants, stars and so on. You might even stretch that subject out for a week, covering a comedy show one day, an hour-long drama the next, then the news, the game shows, like that, you know?"

"Go on, go on—I love it!" Greg was plainly excited and Cathy felt herself caught up with the same emotion.

"And then, maybe a costume shop or something—where the movies get their different costumes—showing how they're made, the fabrics, what they use for animal heads, who makes them, who rents them, which ones are the most popular—in short, everything you've always wanted to know about costumes! And then: an automobile factory, making a car—from a block of metal to a sleek Cadillac flying down our nation's freeways!"

"Yeah, and maybe a dairy! Milk, cheese and butter—from the cow pasture to the grocery shelf!" Greg was clearly caught up in the idea and jumped to his feet and went to hug Cathy. "By jove, I think you've got it!" he sang in a Rex Harrison Professor Higgins voice. "Get on the horn and order us some sandwiches. I want to get these ideas down on tape." He hurried to his desk, set up the recorder, a wide smile on his face. "We can kick around a couple more themes—shit, there're a whole wealth of themes just screaming to be done!"

"Sure, and just to make old Kane feel at home, how about an afternoon with Gloria Swanson or George Raft—or take the minicam to some old silent film star's home and show the memorabilia, how lavishly they lived in those days." Cathy was exhilarated, more excited than she had ever been. This was the way it happened: a casual thought tossed out, kicking it around—then the indescribable joy when you knew that it could just possibly work.

They exchanged dozens of ideas as they munched cold ham sandwiches and drank coffe laced with Scotch, giggling at the more outrageous and silly themes; making up new, absurd ones, both of them high as a kite on the project and falling effortlessly into a total meeting of the minds.

A couple of hours later, Greg switched off the tape recorder, stood and stretched the kinks out of his back. "We've got a hell of a lot of good stuff here, Cathy. I'm really excited about it. How about you?"

"I think it's super." She, too, stood and stretched. It had been a long session. "I can't wait to see what happens next. What *does* happen next?"

"We let Dash listen to what we have, then wait for

him to tell us if it's 'go' or 'no show'—which shouldn't take more than five minutes. Mr. Sunderling is not one to mince words."

"Just like that? That fast?"

"Yep. The Man, he don't fuck around. Time is money and television is both time and money."

"What do you think, Greg? Do you think he'll like it?"

"Yeah, I think it's got a pretty good shot. God knows, we have to do something about Kane's show. And this theme idea is damn good. I can't see any reason for Dash to turn it down." He gave her a broad grin as he led her to the door. "And guess who gets the 'created by' credit, my number one assistant?"

"Oh, Greg, it was both of us," she protested weakly, but her heart pounded with excitement and pride. She knew damn well it was her idea and she wanted Dash Sunderling to know it as well. If he liked the idea he might even suggest that she work with Kane on the show—even behind the camera would suit her just fine.

"It was *your* idea, Cath, so don't try to play coy. I'll see that Dash knows and you'll have both the money and the accolades if it's a hit."

"And if it isn't?"

"Then you'll get the blame and the crapper. Welcome to television, Ms. Curtis!"

Dash Sunderling loved the idea—so much so that he called Cathy into his office to meet the "smart little gal" who had thought of the theme show idea. She went, legs trembling, her heart in her throat, to the inner sanctum. It was opulent beyond belief. A thick, plush carpet in chocolate brown showcased the soft, ivory crushed leather sofas and chairs. An inlaid ivory and onyx coffee table stretched for fifteen feet across the vastness and in one corner a matching bar with six crushed velvet bar stools held an impressive array of liqueurs, whiskies and wines—something to tempt every taste. Dash's desk, a great slab of teakwood with inlaid ivory around the corners in a pattern of ivy vines and leaves, was as large as Cathy's entire bathroom. There were six television screens, each one tuned to a different station but with the sound turned off. His telephone apparatus had so many lines that it, alone, took up almost a fourth of the huge desk. It was made of some sort of blue, shiny material that looked very much like sapphire—but, it couldn't possibly be. Or could it? That was definitely crushed pearl decorating the box where there weren't great, intricate scrolls of heavy gold. The telephone receiver displayed a gold shield with the name "Dash" in raised letters.

Dash Sunderling himself was as opulent and beautiful as his office. He wore a cream-colored silk shirt open almost to the waist, exposing a tanned chest laden with gold chains. His French jeans were a shade darker than the shirt and well-fitted to his slim hips and long, muscular legs. His soft, calfskin shoes were yet another shade darker and his flesh was bronzed darker still. His face was granitelike with its strong, chiseled jaw and chin, arrogant thrust of a thick neck, a nose that could have been fashioned by a sculptor and full, sensual lips. His eyes were a shock: pale, faded blue, like jeans washed once too often or the ocean just before dusk when the sun bleaches it colorless. Fringed by thick black lashes and topped with straight, no-nonsense brows, they were a stunning contrast to his dark skin and hair. Just a touch of silver appeared at the temples of his fashionably styled brown hair and the only wrinkles he had were slight ones around his eyes, as if he had squinted often in the sun.

"Cathy, my dear. Come in—come in!" He walked briskly toward her, hands outstretched, and she saw the flash and brilliance of diamonds on his fingers.

# The Love Game                                11

Greg, who had been sitting in one of the soft leather chairs, got quickly to his feet, then just as quickly sank back down when he saw Dash take Cathy's hands and lead her to the sofa.

"Sit down, my dear. I'm delighted to meet you. May I get you something to drink? A cocktail? Coffee? Soft drink?" His pale eyes raked her body taking in her braless silk blouse and fitted straight skirt with the side slit. His gaze lingered a moment on her legs before he turned quickly toward the bar, his strides long.

"No, thanks, Mr. Sunderling." Her mouth was suddenly dry and she had to cross her legs to still the quivering. Dash Sunderling was everything she had heard and then some.

"Please. I insist. A little something." When Dash insisted, you acquiesced. He was standing behind the bar expectantly rubbing his hands together.

"Well, all right—maybe a little white wine." Cathy glanced quickly at Greg and saw his almost imperceptible nod of approval.

"Great!" Dash boomed in his big, strong voice. "Let's all have a little white wine, shall we? Something worthy of our celebration." He browsed through the wine rack, reading labels, than said, "Aha, I have it!" and knelt to a small refrigerator and withdrew a bottle of Dom Pérignon champagne. "My favorite white wine," he grinned, whipping a towel about the neck and popping the cork almost simultaneously. Again he stooped, this time coming up with three chilled tulip glasses.

He poured all around and motioned for Greg and Cathy to join him at the bar. Raising his glass, he touched the rim of Cathy's and said, "To the *new* "Kane Winslow Show"—and to *you*, my dear—" Pale eyes burned into hers. "—for coming up with the winning format." He drank, keeping his hot gaze on her face.

"Thank you," Cathy said, meeting his gaze fully. "But how can you be sure it's a winning format?"

Dash's eyes blazed and he almost choked on his champagne. Greg cringed. "How do I know?" The deep voice thundered now, rumbling through the vast office. "My dear, it's my job to know!"

"Oh." She said it meekly, stepping a little closer to Greg's side. "I see." God, he was formidable!

"Sit down," he commanded, waving a bejeweled hand at the bar stools and both Cathy and Greg dutifully climbed aboard. "Greg and I were talking before you joined us, Cathy, about the possibility of a co-host for Kane. Someone younger and with a more, shall we say, liberal point of view. A sort of roving reporter, someone who can go out into the field and interview the different people responsible for whatever theme we're doing that particular week. The co-host would cover the location shooting and Kane would do the wrap-ups in the studio. How does that sound to you?"

"Fine," Cathy said quickly, wondering why on earth her opinion mattered.

"Good. I want you to do it." Dash drank the rest of his champagne in one swallow and refilled his glass.

"Me?" Cathy's mouth fell open and she could only stare at him, stunned and disbelieving.

"You. Can you handle it?"

"I—I don't know. I mean, God, I never thought . . ."

"Can you handle it?" His faded blue eyes were blazing right into hers and she could only nod her head dumbly, numbly.

"Good. Greg said you could." He tossed off his champagne and refilled all the glasses. "Have a little more wine." He raised his glass and Cathy and Greg did likewise, touching rims. "To you then, my dear, congratulations and much success." They drank. "I'll get the writers on it right away. Something snappy. An interesting, fast-paced format." He came around from behind the bar, putting his arms around both Cathy and Greg, leading them toward the door. Apparently the meeting was over.

"Report to me on Monday. Nine sharp. I'll have a script ready for you." He opened the door and held it, smiling broadly, warmly. He shook Greg's hand and kissed Cathy's cheek. "Great idea, honey. Nice meeting you." They were outside and the door closed. Firmly.

Cathy had never been more excited, frightened or exhilarated in her life. Even though she had worked in television for the past three years, she realized that she knew next to nothing about it. Were deals really made that fast? As a model on "Eureka!" she had had only to smile and look pretty. As Greg's assistant she had merely been a glorified go-fer. As Kane's co-host she would be about eighty-five percent of the show. On camera. Talking.

The first time she heard herself on tape she cringed and groaned aloud. Her voice sounded small and squeaky, the Oklahoma accent dragging several letters off the ends of her words. She couldn't work with the Teleprompter, that fascinating apparatus connected to the cameras that moved, snaillike, showing her her lines. She had felt awkward and it had been obvious to all that she was reading. Cue cards worked a little better, but after a couple of weeks of rehearsing she decided that she felt more comfortable just simply knowing her subject, learning her lines beforehand, and, if need be, consulting a few, small notes.

She worked with a tape recorder every night for at least two or three hours, reading poetry aloud, reading everything aloud until her voice was a hoarse growl. She would then play the tape back, listening to the small but steady improvement in the sound of her voice, the enunciation of each word. She took courses in public speaking three nights a week and one afternoon of voice lessons.

She worked every day for three weeks with the crew, learning all she could. She had found it almost impossible at first to know when to change cameras. Even though the directions to turn from one camera to the next were clearly stated in her script, she still goofed from time to time, finding herself speaking earnestly into the wrong camera.

Every afternoon she sat in Greg's office playing back her tapes, over and over, looking for spots that she could improve upon, listening to the sound of her voice. When she was "in the field," Greg had told her, she would be chromo-keyed—her image smaller and superimposed over the action footage she was describing. She would have to slow down a little more—she still tended to speak too quickly when excited or nervous—and synchronize her voice with the action.

Cathy practiced interviewing everyone: friends, family, strangers, pacing her questions, learning to be patient while they answered. She lost five pounds and found that she could get along very well on six hours of sleep a night, so anxious was she to get to the studio each morning. She had little or no time for Greg, but told herself that her private life would have to be put on the back burner for awhile. This was her big chance and no way was she going to blow it!

## Chapter Two

Within a month after the new "Kane Winslow-Cathy Curtis Show" aired, it was obvious to all that KNAB had a hit. The show leapt from last in the Nielson's to a staggering twenty-nine percent, easily wiping out the afternoon competition, even stealing away some of the other networks' loyal soap opera fans. They had opened their first show with a behind-the-scenes look at "how TV manufactures magic," taking the viewers not only backstage but into the make-up salons, the dressing rooms, anywhere that a minicam could be carried. Cathy saw to it that even the most minute of details were filmed. She herself was stunned at the literally dozens of people it took to put on one half hour of television—the pulling together of so many branches of talent, even to the executives in their offices going over the budget, figuring out the time slots and what other shows their show would be up against. All of it so crucial to the succes or failure of any show.

Cathy's own fascination with the subject made the show come alive and sparkle with her intelligent, probing questions. She definitely had a way with people, could draw them out, open them up, make them tell things that they would not have ordinarily thought of. The people she interviewed were struck by her fresh, youthful beauty, her quick wit, her obvious interest in their work. They *wanted* her to know them, understand their job, how important *they* were in the sphere of things. This intelligent, stimulating interchange reached into the homes of the viewers, turning them on, grabbing their attention and holding it.

Everyone at KNAB was thrilled, with the exception of Kane Winslow. When first informed of the format change, he had raged and cursed, and then gone off on a two-week bender, forcing the station to air re-runs of his old shows. By the time he actually met Cathy for a script conference he had his drinking under icy control—not drunk but certainly not sober, either. He openly patronized her, bowing sarcastically to her every suggestion until she wanted to kick his ass.

Finally, weary of the verbal fencing, she had faced him squarely and said, "Look, Kane . . ."

"*Mr.*" Winslow, if you don't mind. I hardly know you," he had sniffed haughtily.

"Right." She had successfully hidden her smile of dry amusement. "Okay, Kane, we have to work together, but we don't exactly have to be pals. Why don't we go our separate ways for the first few weeks? I'll be in the field; you'll be in the studio. There's no reason for our running into one another. But the least we both can do is try to do the best possible job for the show. KNAB has a lot of money riding on this new format; let's try not to blow it for them, okay?"

"*I* did not request a format change, sweetie. I was quite content with the way things were going on the *old* 'Kane Winslow Show!' " He had emphasized "old" with a barely disguised snarl and had gone at once to the bar to pour himself a fresh Bourbon.

Cathy had raised her eyebrows helplessly at Greg and he had answered with a weary shrug. Everyone was pretty damn sick of Kane Winslow's sulks. "Well, apparently Mr. Sunderling wasn't too content with it," Cathy had sighed, wishing like hell that she could tell the old relic what she *really* thought of him. "Look, let's just try to get along, okay? Give the new format a chance. Who knows? You might even like it." She gratefully accepted the gin and tonic that Greg had mixed for her.

"Not very bloody likely," Kane had sniffed, sinking into a chair and staring morosely up at her. "It's all gone—the charm, the warmth. Hell, it's not even *my* show anymore. Now we've got some pushy female out running around like Brenda Starr, nosing into things and bothering people."

The meeting had broken up soon after and Cathy, clenching her teeth to keep from telling Kane what intimate act he could perform on himself, had allowed Greg to lead her from the conference room and into his office. "That pompous old fart!" she had exploded as soon as the door closed behind her. "What a fucking prima donna! Jesus, if he tries to fuck up the show, I'll kill him!" She took a huge swallow of her drink, angry tears springing to her eyes.

Greg had calmed her down, told her he would handle Kane—and so he had. The first month had gone more smoothly than anyone had hoped for. Cathy found that she did not have to see Kane at all unless she happened to accidentally run into him at the studio, and then she took great, malicious pleasure in giving him her widest, brightest smile accompanied by an even brighter greeting. Just seeing his pursed mouth and angry, flushed face caused her to experience a tiny thrill of satisfaction. As the show improved, and she along with it, the thrill of satisfaction turned into a confident strut of pure pleasure.

She was so involved with the show that she hardly realized that it had been over two months since she had gone to bed with Greg. They still had dinner together regularly, but Cathy's studio call was often as early as five o'clock in the morning, which meant a reasonably early evening.

With some surprise, she discovered that Greg's kisses no longer turned her on as they once had. She was now impatient for him to release her so they could talk about her show. She had never been in love with Greg and they both knew it, but she had been attracted to him and had enjoyed their rather pretty, if slightly bland, love affair. Now, when she looked at him, she saw a man of average height and looks, with steady gray eyes and a slightly stocky body—someone too obviously under her spell to be very interesting in his own right. She had known for some time that he was in love with her, but it hadn't really bothered her until lately.

She puzzled over this sudden change of heart. He was still the same man she had once listened to, spellbound and enthralled, as he told stories of television, the history of KNAB and his role in it all. He hadn't changed, but she had. *She* was now a part of KNAB. *She* was responsible for a hit show, from birth to air time, and the knowledge thrilled her, caused a surge of power to sweep through her body like a sexual climax. She felt the hunger that a taste of power brings for *more* power. Cathy wanted the "Kane Winslow Show" for her own. Just as she wanted a more powerful man for her own. And not merely a daytime programmer but the head of the network. She wanted Dash Sunderling.

Just thinking of him brought a moistness between her thighs, and she had only to close her eyes to see him as he strode brisk and businesslike about the studio. She pictured him speaking on two or three telephone lines simultaneously, his pale blue eyes turning often in her direction. They had worked closely together the first month, Dash checking over each and every theme that would be shot, going over locations with her, making suggestions for the right slant on each particular subject, asking her advice, wanting to know how she would be most comfortable handling it.

He exuded a sexual power so overwhelming that Cathy often found herself slightly dizzy after a meeting with him. But never did he make an improper comment or gesture. Rather, he treated her like a friend, an equal, someone whose opinion he respected and whose talent he obviously admired. He often invited her to his office for drinks when the day's shooting was over; or, if they were in the field, he took her to dinner and then put her in a cab with a polite, perfunctory kiss on the cheek.

She knew that Dash was aware that she was definitely female. She had seen his pale blue gaze going slowly and appraisingly over her body when he thought she wasn't looking. She had started out wearing jeans, tennis shoes and any old blouse or tee shirt while doing the research for the show. She was required to "dress" only when she was actually on camera, but even then she had opted for comfortable, action clothes, nothing too fussy or dressy. Now, with the show going into its third month, she found herself being a little more choosy about what she wore, often silently asking herself if Dash would find her more attractive in the beige silk or the blue crepe.

She was confronted with that very problem this afternoon as she stood contemplating her wardrobe, wondering what to pack. She was flying to San Francisco tomorrow morning to do a report on Fisherman's Wharf so her choices would have to be casual, perhaps even a little sporty. She took a long, lavender gown from the closet and held it against herself for a moment. She had bought it last week while in Palm Springs covering the health spas and had yet to wear it. Maybe she'd take it along in case she found time to have dinner out somewhere fancy. The restaurants in San Francisco were world famous and she was looking forward to sampling at least a couple of them. She also packed a black jersey gown that she knew set off her blond hair and creamy skin to perfection.

She checked her watch. Three-fifteen. She would just miss the heavy freeway traffic if she left now, so she quickly closed her suitcase and made a swift inventory of her apartment to see that she hadn't forgotten anything. She was driving out to the San Fernando Valley to spend the night with her sister, Maggie, and her brother-in-law, Ken Edwards. When she was going to be away on assignment for longer than four or five days, she always had either Maggie or Ken drive her to the airport so she wouldn't have to leave her car there.

She maneuvered her sky blue Pinto through the traffic, turning onto Ventura Freeway. She was hot and tired. She had had barely five minutes to herself since the show began shooting and was looking forward to a few relaxing hours spent with her sister in the quiet and comfort of the sprawling ranch in Thousand Oaks.

Ranch life and Maggie and Ken went together like a horse and rider. Ken had been a budding wheat and beef rancher back at Atoka, Oklahoma before the devastating flood had destroyed everything his family had built. The same lethal flood had also wiped out the entire Curtis farm, taking with it not only barns, tractors and livestock but Margaret and William Curtis as well.

Hitting just after midnight, a wall of water from a rain-swollen, broken damn had lashed through the once pretty valley, killing almost everything in its path. All that had been visible the day before had been buried under a shroud of brown, muddy water, churning with debris: the bloated bodies of animals, crumpled automobiles, splintered sheds, barns and houses. It had killed old Ralph, the mongrel shepherd who had been companion and lifelong friend to Maggie and Cathy. The girls had been held back by state troopers; crying, screaming,

## The Love Game

clawing at the steellike arms that held them, they had seen their home crushed and consumed by the rushing brown water. Old Ralph, swimming valiantly, had whimpered and yipped as the strong waves covered his graying muzzle, and then swept him away never to be seen again. They had huddled together, tears blurring the horrifying scene, as their home—all they had ever known in their young lives—had been destroyed.

It had been a Friday night and Maggie and Ken had agreed to take Cathy to the movies with them as it was a special showing of some new Walt Disney film. (Any movie would do for Maggie and Ken since they always necked through the entire picture anyway.) Returning home just after midnight, they had been stopped by a hoard of policemen, state troopers, fireman and rescue units. Cathy and Maggie had clung wildly to Ken. Under the eerie searchlights of the flood patrol they had seen it all—the grotesque bodies, the destruction, the fear, the uselessness, and, finally, the emptiness.

They had gone with Ken to a flood control shelter and huddled with other victims, spooning down hot soup, drinking cocoa, numbly accepting blankets and condolences from strangers, wondering what in the world would happen to them now. They had slept that night in the high school gym with about a hundred others, rising stiff and still frightened, not knowing what the day would bring. It has stopped raining. Everyone had said that was a good thing. But to twelve-year-old Cathy that was not good. Nothing could ever be good again. Her beloved mother and father, the faithful, comical old Ralph, they were gone. Washed away in one awful, vengeful stroke of nature. Dead. Home, clothes, souvenirs, picture albums, just things—all gone. But the most awful thing, the one most dreadful, wretched thing that Cathy couldn't bring herself to understand or accept—no more Mama and Daddy. How could something like that happen so swiftly? So horribly?

Cathy shuddered in the sultry September heat, tears filling her eyes as they always did whenever she remembered "that night"—that terrible, black, wet night that had changed her life so drastically. Ken and Maggie had been just seventeen, high school sweethearts who planned to marry after both had finished at least a couple of years of college. Within a week they had married and begun planning their future, trying to fit together the pieces of a shattered life. Ken had seen California as the golden land of opportunity and had moved his new bride and young sister-in-law to Los Angeles. He had taken the only job he was qualified for: groom, riding instructor, all-round stable hand at the White Oak Stables in Reseda.

Now, fourteen years later, Ken owned his own stables—the Rocking K Ranch. Up in the hills of Thousand Oaks, nestled back in a grove of black walnut, eucalyptus and oak trees, the ranch offered twenty-six acres of riding trails, an enormous riding arena, lessons and rental horses; Ken had built up a very successful business.

Cathy pulled her Pinto into the long, winding driveway and was immediately met by wild, reckless barking and rushing bodies as the Edwards's four dogs flung themselves against the side of her car. Laughing, she rolled down the window. "Hello, you crazy mutts. God, how can you run in this heat?" All four dogs reared up on the side of her car, pushing great, friendly, salivating muzzles into the window as they whined and licked her bare arm. "Okay, enough already. Wait until I park the car, will you?" She eased along at five miles an hour because the more energetic of the four, Coalie, still clung to the window as she drove. Cathy always brought them a treat when she visited the ranch: new, silly dog biscuits shaped like mailmen or cats (which made Ken snort with disgust and accuse her of spoiling them for the table scraps and dry kibble that was their daily staple), and, always, she brought doggie bags from her frequent dinners out.

She stopped in the shade of a towering oak tree and gathered up her packages as she stepped out into the sweltering heat. All four dogs leaped upon her, their dirty paws leaving dusty prints on her white Levis, and she laughed and scolded them, holding the bags high as she ran for the front door. It opened before she could knock and her little niece, Staci, bounced out and threw herself into the melee. "Help, call them off!" Cathy laughed, trying to walk with the three-year-old clinging tight to her legs.

"Staci, for heaven's sake, wait until Aunt Cathy gets inside before you attack her!" Maggie stood wiping her hands on a dishtowel, a big smile of welcome on her pretty face. She flapped the towel at the dogs. "Lacey! Coalie! Shep! Barney! Scat now, all of you! Down!" The dogs dropped as if shot, burying their muzzles between their paws, sheepish expressions in their dark, loving eyes.

"Thanks, Sis. God, they damn near kill me every time I come out!" Cathy hurried into the cool, pleasant dining room and dropped her packages on the table. She hugged Maggie, and Staci tugged at her legs, shouting, "Me, too, Aunt Cathy! Me now!"

"Okay, sweetie." Cathy swung the child up into her arms and hugged her mightily, kissing the warm, sun-browned cheek, smelling the fresh baby-smell of Johnson's Baby Powder. "Did you miss me, honey? I sure missed you." Staci nodded and clung tightly to Cathy's neck.

"Come on in the kitchen while I finish getting dinner in the oven," Maggie said. "Then we can sit down and talk. How's the show going?"

"Just great." Cathy followed, shifting Staci's weight on her hip, then sat down at the kitchen table, "Why don't you get the doggie bags and go feed those starving dogs of yours, honey? And there's a little present for you in the small bag, okay?"

"Oh, goodie—a present!" Staci raced from the room, wondering aloud what was in the bag.

"Can I do anything to help?" Cathy kicked off her highheeled, backless shoes and wiggled her bare toes. God, she was hot and tired.

"No, thanks, Sis. I just want to get these vegetables on—the roast is almost done." She deftly sliced carrots and potatoes and placed them around a savory-smelling pot roast.

Cathy went to the refrigerator and took out a bottle of wine. "You want some?" Maggie nodded and Cathy poured two glasses, taking hers back to the table. "Man, am I ever beat. These past two months have been a real ball buster." She sipped the icy white wine, leaning her elbows on the table as she watched her sister. Already, just being around the homey atmosphere, she was beginning to relax and unwind.

"You look tired. And you've lost a little weight, haven't you?" Maggie slid the pan into the oven and took her wine to the table to sit across from Cathy.

"Oh, a couple of pounds, I guess."

"Wish I could say the same. I can afford it better than you can." She laughed, looking down at her plump figure in cut-off jeans and tight tee shirt. She had the same blond coloring as Cathy, the same blue eyes and lushly built body, but where Cathy was a real beauty, Maggie was just very pretty. She lacked that added extra *something* that set a truly exciting woman apart from a merely attractive one.

Cathy laughed. "Why don't you come along to San

Francisco with me as my assistant? I'll run a few pounds off you."

"God, don't I wish I could. I love San Francisco."

"Me, too, although I haven't been there in so long it'll be like seeing it fresh all over again." She sipped her wine. "Hope I get a chance to sample some of the night life."

"Is Greg going with you?"

"No, not this time." Cathy had asked Greg to join her on the first few out-of-town assignments as she needed the confidence he gave her. Now she found she didn't need such assurances.

"How are you two getting along? You're still seeing him, aren't you?"

"Well, sort of. We have dinner every so often but, God, I'm so damn busy with the show I hardly have a private life anymore." She did not meet her sister's eyes. Maggie, she knew, was very fond of Greg and had hoped that he and Cathy would marry or at least come to an "understanding." She was so much in love with her Ken, so complacent with her married state, that she wished the same happiness for everyone she knew.

"Well, don't let him get too far away," Maggie warned. "They say the climb up the ladder of success is lonely at best."

Cathy gave a snort of laughter. "How can it be lonely with a dozen horny jerks looking up my dress while I climb the ladder?" Even though her status at KNAB had been raised by several points since getting the co-host spot on the "Kane Winslow Show," she was still pursued by the more persistent men at the station. The chauvinistic ones. Not believing that anyone as beautiful and sexy as Cathy could possibly have a brain in her head, they tended to humor her, treat her rather condescendingly, while ogling her breasts and making passes. She seethed with anger at such men but grimly held her temper in check, knowing she still wasn't powerful enough to have things her way. But someday she would, she repeatedly told herself, and when she did—watch out!

Maggie arched an eyebrow at her as she went to the fridge to refill their wineglasses. "Still having to fight off the guys in the crew?"

"No, I've got them under control—finally. It's the big brass that give me a hard time. The so-called executives. Every time I turn around one of them is hitting on me. Very subtly, of course and with just the slightest veiled threat that I might do better at the station if I let them get to know me a little better." She took the fresh glass of wine and sipped. "Now, if it was Dash Sunderling making the pass, I just might go for it."

"Dash Sunderling? Good heavens, Cath, he's old enough to be your father."

"So? He's still one hell of a sexy hunk of man." Her heartbeat quickened a little as it always did when she thought of Dash Sunderling. She wondered if he planned to fly to San Francisco for the shooting and found herself hoping like crazy that he would.

"Well, at least your sights are high," Maggie laughed. "God, the president of KNAB, no less!" She went to baste the roast, then took out salad makings and began washing them in the sink. "Want to give me a hand, Sis? My old man's going to be home any minute wondering why dinner isn't on the table."

Cathy carried her wine to the counter and set to work chopping radishes and green onions. "How does he stay so thin eating your cooking every night?" Ken was tall and slender with lean, sinewy muscles in his arms and legs—built more like a swimmer than a football player. His many hours spent on horseback had given him a gracefulness of movement that belied the wiry steelness of his body. He was sandy-haired with a perpetually bronzed face and light green eyes as clear as a mountain stream. That he plainly adored his wife was evident in every gesture, every glance, every touch. Seeing them together always brought a feeling of warmth to Cathy and then—and only then—did she think that maybe this marriage business might be a little bit of all right.

"He works if off every night after dinner," Maggie answered smugly, intimating what Cathy already knew: their sex life was full and lusty.

"Braggart." Cathy flipped water on Maggie and the two sisters giggled like naughty children.

Later that night, lying nude under the blankets, feeling the cool breeze blowing through the open window, Cathy thought about Dash Sunderling. That he was married and the father of two children, she knew, although that was all she knew. She had heard rumors that the marriage was not a happy one and that Dash often helped himself to female companionship, but he was very discreet in such matters and even the most dedicated snoopers could find nothing much to gossip about.

Cathy rolled over on her stomach, trying to find a more comfortable position. She was too excited about tomorrow's trip to fall asleep easily. Covering Fisherman's Wharf would be great fun, and she wished she had someone she cared about to share it with her. Maybe Dash would fly up for a couple of days. He often did, staying as much in the background as possible, watching her work, nodding his agreement from time to time. Then he would always invite her out for a drink or dinner, discussing the day's shooting, sometimes offering suggestions, most often complimenting her on a job well done.

At first she had been so in awe of him that she had merely sat and listened while he spoke, too impressed with his knowledge to utter more than a few sentences, but as time went on and the dinners and drinks added up, she found herself talking animatedly with him, becoming confident under his obvious approval. She wasn't sure just when her interests in him changed from wanting to please the boss to simply wanting the boss, but the last few times she had run into him she was terribly conscious of her appearance and found herself wishing that she had taken more time with it. He seemed always to catch her when she was dressed in old jeans and tee shirts, rushing off somewhere, too busy to stop and talk without it seeming obvious.

She punched the pillow into a comfortable hollow and snuggled into it. No wonder Dash never made a pass. She always looked so harried on location when he was around—and glamorous and cool for the actual taping when he wasn't around. She sighed. Maybe she just wasn't his type. Still, she was glad she had packed her lavender gown. Just in case.

## Chapter Three

Cathy stood in a shaft of late afternoon sun, her mike held a few inches from the animated face of old Pops McCleary as he explained his life on Fisherman's Wharf. He had been a street vendor for thirty-years and knew all the ins and outs of that fascinating area. He had been expounding beautifully for almost an hour, completely at ease with the mike, hardly seeming to notice the circling men with minicams jutting from their shoulders and paying not the slightest attention to anyone or anything but Cathy and her questions. If only everyone she interviewed could be as relaxed with a camera on them and a mike stuck to their face, her job would be a hell of a lot easier.

"And where do you get these shell novelties that you sell, Pops?" she asked. "Do you make them yourself or do you buy them from local artists?" There was a long, agonizing pause—a complete silence that means certain death for an interview—and Cathy hurriedly repeated the question, trying to recapture Pops's interest. He was staring past her, his almost toothless mouth agape.

"She-it and Jes-ass H. Ker-ist! What the fuck kinda car is that?" Pops pointed over Cathy's shoulder, then began walking away, out of the shot.

"What the hell —?" Cathy spun around, her face

flushed with anger and embarrassment. Whoever had ruined her interview would get his ass kicked from here to the Golden Gate Bridge. She signaled the cameramen to stop running the expensive film and stalked after Pops, fury in every step. He moved with an agility that belied his seventy-odd years, and she lengthened her strides—then stopped dead still. Staring.

Parked at the curb, the gentle purr of its motor just dying, stood a gleaming Stutz Blackhawk VI Coupe—and stepping out of the sixty-five-thousand-dollar automobile was Dash Sunderling. He adjusted his Vuitton bag on his shoulder and flicked away a nonexistent piece of lint from his perfectly faded French jeans, glancing quickly down at his slim Cartier wristwatch. He was a stunning apparition. Dying sunlight caught on the diamonds on his fingers and the gold chains about his neck blazed into new life, seeming to set him aflame as well. His white teeth flashed, his Gucci loafers shone, his bronzed face was alive with health. He paid no attention to Pops McCleary, who was running his gnarled hands over the satiny finish of the Coupe's hood, but went directly to Cathy and took her hands in his.

"Hi, how's it going? I never could resist San Francisco so thought I'd just pop in and see if everything's under control." He smiled down at her, giving her hands an extra squeeze until he realized she was still holding her mike.

She said the first thing that come into her head. "Goddamn you, you just fucked up my interview!"

Dash's eyes widened and he glanced swiftly at the cameramen standing around, minicams lowered now, lights switched off. A small silent crowd had gathered, staring back and forth between the resplendent, handsome man and the small lady (obviously quivering with anger) and the incredibly impressive Stutz Blackhawk VI Coupe. Old Pops McCleary (whom everyone on the

## The Love Game 31

Wharf knew) was grinning his glee as he poked his head inside to gawk at the white leather interior. He was heard to murmur "She-it" again before their attention swung back to Cathy and Dash.

"I'm terribly sorry," Dash said quickly, stepping back a little from the blazing anger in Cathy's eyes.

"Sorry? Damn it all, *you* of all people should know when the camera lights are on, we're shooting film! How could you just—just barge in here in that—that ludicrous car and fuck up my interview?" She turned and tossed her mike to one of the crew.

"Hey, don't get upset, Cathy. You can finish up and I'll stay clear, okay?" He grinned down at her, giving her shoulder a friendly squeeze. "It must be the last shot of the day—no harm done."

She shook off the diamond-studded hand. "It *was* the last shot. Period." She glared angrily at the sky. "Sun's gone. Now we'll have to pick it up tomorrow and it won't match. Shit. I had over forty-five minutes of great interview on film, ready to go in the can. I was just wrapping up when you—you . . ."

"God, what can I say? I'm really terribly sorry." He looked properly contrite and did not try to touch her. "You're right. I should have known better." He adjusted the Vuitton bag a little self-consciously and patted its bulk. "I brought the new figures—thought you might want to know that your show is now number one in the Neilsen's this week."

"Really?" Some of her anger left her. "That's great." She stared at a spot over his left shoulder, embarrassed now at her show of rage, not knowing what to say.

"Yeah, it is great, but that still doesn't excuse me for barging in here like a blundering fool and lousing up your interview." His smile was warm, intimate, and he touched her arm almost shyly. "What can I do to make it up to you, Cathy?"

"Oh, it wasn't really your fault," Cathy mumbled. "If Pops McCleary had kept his mind on the interview instead of freaking out over your car and walking off, we could have gotten it wrapped up."

"Pops McCleary?" Dash laughed, looking in the direction of the aged vendor still blissfully inspecting his car. "What a great name. He one of the locals on the Wharf?" Cathy nodded mutely. Dash took a deep breath, exhaling nosily. "God, what a wonderful smell. I love this place." His pale blue eyes drifted to ships tied to the pier, to men and women busily cooking tasty delicacies inside glass-fronted cafes, to gaudily dressed tourists window-shopping. "There's no place like it."

"It's very colorful." Cathy now felt awkward and could have kicked her own ass for giving the president of the network hell as if he were some ignorant kid.

"You been getting a lot of good interviews? The locals cooperating? Any problems?" He always used a minimum of words when speaking, his voice clipped and brisk, but now he smiled warmly into her eyes and fell into step beside her as she turned back toward the crew.

"No—no problems." She laughed a little. "The only problem is getting them *off* camera when the interview is over. Everybody wants to be a star." She reached up to smooth down her wind-blown hair and licked her dry lips, knowing that she had long ago chewed off all her lipstick. Damn him for his bad timing, anyway! The sun had disappeared behind a cloud that looked suspiciously rain-swollen and a sudden breeze chilled her bare arms. She rubbed them briskly and called to the crew, "Well, that's it, I guess. We'll pick it up here tomorrow." She grabbed her sweater off the bumper of the mobile unit and slipped it on.

"Come on, I'll give you a lift to the hotel," Dash said, taking her elbow and leading her toward his car. "You're at the St. Francis, aren't you?"

"You should know, your office made the arrangements."

He gave her a cocky grin. "That's because it's my favorite hotel and I knew I'd be coming up for a couple of days." He gently but firmly brushed away the crowd gathered around his outrageously beautiful automobile and slid behind the wheel. He had hurried forward to open Cathy's door, but she beat him to it. As the big engine purred into life, he turned to glance at her perfect profile, smiling a little to himself. She was so damn cute and cuddly looking, but as prickly as a porcupine, as feisty as a tiger cub. Damn, but she had told him off in no uncertain terms for ruining her interview. He couldn't remember the last time anyone had given him hell for anything, and, to his surprise, he found he liked it.

Cathy stood looking at herself in the full-length mirror on the closet door. She ran her hands lightly over her hips in the lavender gown, moved her legs so the left one peeked provocatively through the high, sexy slit. She wore bone colored heels with narrow straps over the toes and ankles. The top of the gown was cut low but slightly loose so it fell in soft folds over her breasts, exposing deep cleavage when she leaned forward. She had had her hair done in the hotel beauty salon and it was swept away from her face in a casual, almost throwaway, style that looked as if it grew that way naturally. She clipped on large, gold hoop earrings, then took them off. The gown was so perfect in its simplicity, it needed no jewelry. She would have liked to see a large marquise diamond nestled between her breasts—the only gem that could possibly go with the gown—but that would have to wait.

She applied lip gloss and stared intently at her face. Was she wearing too much make-up? Too much mascara? She had agonized over false lashes for an hour and then decided against wearing them. Her own dusky lashes were long and thick and the smoky taupe eyeshadow she wore went well with the sable brown mascara. She knew she looked great. Her cheeks were so rosy with excitement that she had not bothered with blusher. She wished she had a mink coat or any good, expensive wrap but would have to settle for the beige beaded shawl. The telephone shrilled and she jumped a foot, grabbing it in mid-ring.

"Mr. Sunderling is waiting in the lobby, Miss Curtis," the voice informed her and she said, "Tell him I'll be right down, please."

He was standing at the magazine stand, glancing idly through the current issue of Time, when she stepped off the elevator. She paused a moment, taking in his rich appearance. He wore an off-white suit, white Gucci loafers and his silk shirt, opened precisely the proper number of buttons, was the same shade lavender as her gown. Gold chains glistened against the tan of his skin, and his chest hair curled enticingly about them.

"Well, I see we're color coordinated," she said lightly, stepping up to him and slipping her arm through his. "Did you send spies to my room, or what?"

"Cathy—hello!" His gaze ran quickly and appreciatively over her and she let the gown fall open a little, exposing a golden stretch of bare leg. "You look terrific!" He patted her hand tucked into the crook of his arm. "I think this is the first time I've seen you in anything but jeans and sneakers." His warm gaze caressed her from breasts to ankles. "And I would say it's a definite improvement."

"Thank you." They stared at one another in silence for several seconds.

"Well, we'd better get going. I've made reservations at the Blue Fox. Ever been there?"

"No, but I've heard it's wonderful." She gave him her

special smile, the one that showed both dimples and looked directly up into his eyes. Damn, he was tall.

There was a small crowd gathered around his extraordinary automobile but they parted respectfully, eyeing Cathy and Dash, wondering who they were. Your plain, everyday citizen did not drive a Stutz Blackhawk VI Coupe, nor did he squire a luscious blond as beautiful as a young queen. Cathy heard the low murmurings, saw the envious glances as she allowed Dash to help her into the Coupe. She loved it. It was great to be ogled like you were *somebody*. Great to sink into the luxury of a sixty-five-thousand-dollar car. And simply super great to be dining out with the handsome and flamboyant president of KNAB.

Dinner was a leisurely feast, accompanied by icy Dom Pérignon champagne, Dash's favorite. His second favorite was Moët et Chandon; he loved caviar but only the black, not the red; he hated liver of any kind whether they called it pâté de foie gras or simply chopped liver; he thought vacations should be spent in the sun, in Tahiti or Bora Bora and he did not much care for temperatures lower than forty-five degrees. Conversation was pleasant, and they both realized that they were taking the careful inventory of one another that strangers do upon meeting—finding out one another's likes and dislikes, listening to each other reveal a little more about themselves as the evening wore on. Even though they had worked closely together these past three months, they had never discussed anything more personal than the "Kane Winslow Show."

Tonight they were getting to know one another, and what Cathy saw unfolding was a warm, sweet, rather gentle man for all his flash and style, gaudy diamonds and almost vulgar car. He seemed to be hiding some secret sadness and when the bright, dazzling smile flashed, she noticed it rarely reached his eyes. In fact, he said very little about himself on a truly personal level but instead drew her out, had her talking about her childhood, her parents' death, her plans for the future. Even as she sized him up physically, unable to put the thought of what it might be like to go to bed with him out of her head, she couldn't help but see his game: the Great Man trying his best to put the Young Girl at ease. He had not tried to touch her, not even with his soft, pale gaze, but had kept the conversation on a strictly impersonal level, even as he seemed to be opening up to her. Even as he told her his likes and dislikes, she realized he was, in fact, telling her nothing of any real importance.

And she told him everything. The expensive champagne mellowed her and she heard her own excited voice saying all the things she had dreamed of until now but had never really verbalized. She told him she wanted to be a power in television—not merely a co-host on some silly piece of fluff like Kane's show—but a *real* power. She wanted to call the shots, have a hand in everything from the selection of shows to the juggling of time slots, to the knowledge of rating and sponsors.

Dash had grinned and said, "After my job, huh, kid?" and Cathy, the champagne making her bold, had tossed her head and laughed, "Why not?"

It was pouring rain by the time they finished dinner and Cathy was almost soaked through when the parking attendant brought Dash's car around and helped her inside. Now, if she had a mink instead of the flimsy shawl, she would be warm and dry. She must have said the words aloud without realizing it, for Dash reached over to squeeze her hand and say, "You keep bringing those ratings up on the show and I'll buy you one as a bonus."

Leaning back against the soft, crushed leather seat, smelling the rich fragrance of Dash's musky cologne and seeing the muted lights streak by the window, Cathy

## The Love Game                                    37

thought she had never in her life felt so incredibly good. She did not want this magical evening to end, but end it must. Tomorrow was a work day. Tomorrow was scrambling about on ship decks that reeked with the acrid odor of fish, trying to get the close-mouthed fisherman to open up for the cameras. Tomorrow was the wrap on the Pops McCleary interview and tomorrow Dash would probably drive back to Los Angeles.

He left her at her door, leaning over to give her flushed cheek a chaste kiss, telling her to get to bed and get some sleep, he'd see her tomorrow. Then, almost as an afterthought, he turned and said, "How about breakfast then we'll drive out to the Wharf together?"

She had mumbled something, keenly disappointed that he hadn't asked to come in for a nightcap. She went directly to the mirror and leaned in close, studying herself. What was wrong with her that he hadn't so much as made a pass? Damn, most men would have taken advantage of her inebriated state, her obvious need for company. She stripped off the lavender gown and hung it carefully in its plastic bag, then removed her pantyhose and turned to stare at her nude reflection. It had been far too long since a man had seen her this way: soft, creamy blond all over, skin as warm and ripe as a peach. "Piss on you, Dash Sunderling!" she swore, turning furiously away from the mirror.

The maid had been in earlier to turn down the bed and it stood in the glow of bedside lamps, soft and inviting and in one stubborn, sudden flash, she knew she was not going to sleep in it alone. She picked up the telephone and asked for Dash's room. "Hi, boss—it's me. I can't sleep." Her voice was husky, just a little slurred. "You wouldn't happen to have a bottle of that Dom Pérignon in your pocket, would you?" She stumbled over the pronunciation and giggled delightfully.

A moment later the soft knock sounded and she

walked, naked, to the door and opened it, reaching out her arms to him before he was even inside. "Cathy," he said with a groan and then gathered her close, his big, strong hands sliding down to cup her naked buttocks and draw her tight against him. They did not kiss but merely stood, rocking a little, pressed tight, just holding on to one another. Cathy's eyes were closed and she sighed, hugging him to her, standing up on the very tips of her toes to reach his neck. Then he whispered her name again as he moved his mouth around to kiss her, hot and hard, his tongue finding hers and sucking hungrily.

"I want you, Dash," she said against his nibbling lips. "I've wanted you for such a long time." Taking his hand she led him to the bed and lay down on it, her blue eyes turning almost purple with her desire. Her lips were parted and moist, her eyes heavy-lidded as she watched him hurry out of his clothes. Then she reached up for him and he was in her arms. At last.

"God, Cathy, I don't believe this—I've wanted you—dreamed about you, but I was afraid . . ." Her lips on his shut off further words and she pulled him greedily over her body, clasping him tightly to her hammering heart.

"Just love me, Dash, love me this one time . . ." Her hands moved down between their bodies to find and grasp him. She heard his moan of response, felt the sudden heat that filled him as he grew harder, bigger. "Oh, Dash," she panted, eyes opening to stare wildly, passionately into his. "God, I can't wait! I'm so hot—put it in me—now, my darling—please now!"

"Jesus." It was a soft cry then he was filling her, holding her so close she could hear his heart as well as feel it pounding like thunder against her own. His hands moved shakily over her breasts, trembling with thumb and forefinger over the ruby rosettes of nipples. A moment later his hot lips were on her own and she felt the shudder race through his body as he climaxed with a hurting, hard kiss that rocked her head on the pillow and her own orgasm streaked through her.

He did not remove himself from her moist warmth, but kissed her gently now, with infinite tenderness, moving slowly, deeply, bringing himself to rigid hardness again, still deep inside her. And this time it was a long, long time before he cried her name and filled her with his hot, wet sperm.

They awoke at dawn, almost simultaneously, smiled sleepily and a little shyly into one another's eyes, then Dash took Cathy's face between his two big hands and kissed her, "Good morning, darling. How did you sleep?"

"Like the proverbial log," she laughed, throwing her arms happily around his neck and kissing him again. She glanced toward the windows but the heavy drapes were drawn and she could not tell if it was yet light. "What time is it? Am I late for work, boss?" She teased him with one finger sketched lightly across his chest hairs, tangling playfully in his gold chains, then tweaking his nipples.

"I don't think you'll be going to work today, honey. It's been raining like a bastard all night." He trapped the teasing finger and brought it to his lips to kiss and nip it. "Didn't you hear the thunder last night?"

"I thought it was my heart." She flopped back on the bed, pulling him down on top of her. "Come down here and tell me good morning properly. . . ."

Much later, after they had showered together, making love yet again under the hot spray, Dash holding her slippery, soapy body up to his hard penis and lowering her upon it like an impaled virgin at sacrifice, she said, "I knew you would be good, but never, never as good as this. You are definitely a 10, Mr. Sunderling."

"Then you must be a 20," he laughed, bending his dark, wet head to kiss her ready mouth. "But you sure as hell don't take very good care of your men. Where the hell is my breakfast? If you expect me to keep up this pace, you're going to have to feed me."

"I thought I had 'fed' you." She laughed suggestively, reaching for his penis, but he grabbed her hands and tickled her, lifting her completely off the floor, then letting her nude body slide erotically down his own.

"Brat. What am I going to do with you?" His pale blue eyes were clear and laugh-filled as they gazed into hers.

"Love me," she murmured, slipping once again into his strong embrace, her mouth reaching for his.

"Again?" he cried in mock amazement. "My dear young woman, do you realize how old I am? I'm no young stud to be used and . . ."

"I know, I know," she interrupted, laughing. "You've got ties older than me. Shut up and kiss me." They kissed for a long, heart-hammering time, then she swatted his naked butt and turned to get dressed, calling over her shoulder, "Order me ham and scrambled eggs, hash browns, wheat toast, coffee and orange juice.

"Good God, woman, that's a lumberjack's breakfast." Dash was still laughing as the placed the order with room service. Never had he felt so young and vibrant, so full of love and life. His prickly little porcupine was as delightful as a new puppy. As delicious, soft and creamy as pie a la mode. As hot, passionate and bawdy as Mae West. He hummed as he slipped into his clothes and tossed the bedspread over the ravages of the night before. Christ, he had come no less than five times in a period of a few hours. What had this delightful, dimpled darling done to him? He felt fifteen instead of almost fifty. Already his cock was jerking inside the confines of his trousers, wanting to be free inside her.

## The Love Game         41

While Cathy did her face and hair, Dash made the necessary calls to the crew, telling them what they already knew; there'd be no shooting until the weather cleared up. All of the interviews had been set for outdoors, which was now impossible with the heavy rains and dark skies. He smiled with secret pleasure; that meant more time alone with Cathy. Time when no one had any claim on either of them. Time to explore her marvelous body at his leisure. Time to fall more deeply in love with her.

On the third day of their sexual odyssey, the skies cleared and bright, friendly sunshine spilled into her room. Dash raised his head to look hungrily into Cathy's face. It was sated and soft, her eyes filled with real happiness. He traced a pattern across one perfectly formed breast, then lowered his head to kiss the erect, rosy nipple. "This is why I didn't try to make love to you before," he whispered, his words barely audible against her warm flesh.

"Why?" she murmured, reaching her arms around him and arching her back so her nipple would fit more firmly into his mouth.

"Because now I never want to leave."

"Then let's stay."

"We can't stay here forever."

"Nothing is forever," she whispered, pulling him between her open, eager thighs.

## Chapter Four

They were sitting in the Bistro, Cathy and Dash, watching the lunch crowd thinning out. Several show business luminaries had stopped to congratulate Cathy on the show, telling her to get rid of that old fossil, Kane, and she'd have a real winner.

"God, Dash, I just don't understand how people can be so cruel," she said, leaning briefly against him then drawing away when she remembered where they were. The only time they could safely be seen in public was an occasional lunch—for business purposes, of course. "Not that I have any great love for Kane Winslow myself, but he's a human being, for God's sake, not yesterday's *Hollywood Reporter* to be tossed in the wastebasket. Don't these people realize that they will someday be old and perhaps not as beautiful as they are today?"

"Do *you* realize it, my pretty Cathy?" Dash's voice was soft, as it always was when he spoke to her.

"Yeah, sure, of course I do." She was momentarily angry. "Christ, Dash, you of all people know how I feel about getting by on looks alone. Why do you think I work my buns off sixteen hours a day, if not to prove that I've got more going for me than just a pretty face?" Even though she had been doing the show for six months, she still found herself warding off passes and

## The Love Game

constantly having to prove that she had a brain. Hollywood, which should have known better, was perhaps the worst offender of the "beauty but no brains" syndrome; male or female, if you were good-looking, you automatically were as dumb as a rock.

"Cathy, my darling girl, you're so very young. How can you possibly know how you will feel in twenty years?" He let his hand rest on her knee under the table.

Cathy's hand slipped under the heavy linen tablecloth to squeeze his. Her eyes were laughing. "In twenty years it won't matter. I'll have my own network by then and everyone knows that network presidents are notoriously ugly!"

Dash laughed with her, then quickly pulled his hand away when a mink-wrapped blond stopped at their table. "Dash—*darling!* How lovely to see you!" She leaned forward to kiss him, crimson-tipped fingers sinking into his cheeks, her dark ranch mink sleeve trailing across the table and almost upsetting Cathy's wineglass.

"Bitsy, dear—hello!" He removed the hand from his face and leaned a little away from her. "You're looking wonderful. Is that a St. Tropez tan you're wearing?"

"Silly." Bitsy dimpled prettily. "Côte d'Azur. I've just this week returned." Her wide, smoky brown eyes slid to Cathy.

"Say hello to Cathy Curtis. Cathy, Bitsy Bushore."

"Hi, Cathy!" The bubbly, high-pitched voice was now directed at her and Bitsy Bushore's big, brown eyes grew even larger, her smile wider as she gazed down at Cathy. "Oh, *darling*, I love your show! It's simply *marvelous!*" She extended a dimpled, tanned hand, the crimson nails at least an inch long, and warmly gripped Cathy's. "I *adore* the way you handle yourself on those 'in the field' interviews. You remind me of a velvet-wrapped Barbara Walters!" Again, the high, trilling little girl's laugh and her bejeweled hand with its expensive Côte d'Azur tan gave Cathy's an extra squeeze.

"Thank you—I think." A velvet-wrapped Barbara Walters?

Bitsy slid into the booth beside Dash. "Scoot over, darling, and I'll sit with you a minute. I'm waiting for Monte." She wrinkled her cute little bunny nose and stage-whispered. "He's gone to the sandbox."

Cathy knew who Bitsy Bushore was, of course, as did anyone old enough to watch television. She had been touted as the tube's first sex symbol in the fifties—a bouncy, bubbly piece of blond fluff who had starred in her own series, a lightweight sitcom about a backwoods beauty who goes to the big city and takes it by storm. Sort of a "Tammy Goes to Town"—entitled "Heavenly Hillbilly." Although the series had been off the air for over a decade, Channel Eleven still aired re-runs every afternoon at five-thirty, so now Bitsy had a whole new set of fans. She had to be in her late thirties, and yet she still looked as perky and sassy as ever. She had the angelic, perennially youthful face of a Debbie Reynolds or Sandra Dee, with soft blond hair curling in babyish tendrils about her still smooth cheeks, sooty false lashes setting off the smoky brown of her big, wide eyes and a soft, pouting mouth. The dark mink coat hid her body, but Cathy knew that she was stacked. She did an occasional cameo role in this or that television show or movie and still managed to grab space in the fan magazines.

Dash moved closer to Cathy, pressing his thigh against hers and giving her a brief, expressive glance, one eyebrow at a rakish angle. "So, Bitsy, how does it feel to be a lady of leisure—flying off to the Côte d'Azur in the middle of winter, for God's sake, while we peasants stay here and drown in a seasonal downpour?" It had rained almost steadily since Christmas, forcing Cathy to do indoor locations for the last six shows.

"I simply *love* it, darling," Bitsy trilled, sinking her sharp, red nails into his arm. She pouted in Cathy's direction. "I simply *abhor* the rain, don't you, luv?" Her wide eyes were guileless, warm and friendly, and Cathy couldn't understand why she didn't like her. Bitsy certainly wasn't the least bit jealous or intimidated by Cathy's beauty or youth, as most women were, but there was just something about her that made Cathy want to pull away from that direct gaze.

"I'm not too crazy about it," she said. "Particularly when it forces me to change my shooting schedule. I'd much rather do outdoor locations."

"Oh, but I simply *adored* the spot you did with George Raft last Thursday," Bitsy gushed. "Gosh, what a super old house he has—and just *crammed* with memorabilia!"

"Well, it's an apartment, really, but quite a lovely one. He's lived there for years." God, did the little twit always speak in italics?

"Maybe we should do a spot on you, Bitsy," Dash grinned, giving Cathy a wink that only she could see. "You've been in pictures, what?—twenty, thirty years!"

Bitsy squealed and slapped his arm. "Dash—you cad! I haven't been around *that* long!"

"You've been around since the Garden of Eden," said a husky, amused male voice and Cathy looked up into sad, brown eyes in an incredibly handsome face. Full, sensual lips smiled slowly. "Our Bitsy is the original Lilith," he said to Cathy. The dark eyes swept her, then moved to Dash. "Hi, Dash. How's it going?" He extended a long-fingered hand as sunbrowned as Bitsy's and just as bejeweled. Sapphires and diamonds winked as he shook hands with Dash and then took Cathy's and bent over it as courtly as an eighteenth-century cavalier.

"My name is Monte and, of course, I know who you are. I wouldn't miss your show." He kissed her hand.

"Oh, Monte, you stinker." Bitsy gave him a playful slap and turned innocent eyes upon Cathy. "Don't believe a *word* he says. He just *loves* to put people on." She gave a delicate snort, her tiny nostrils flaring. "Hah! As if anyone would *dream* of *me* being a Lilith—with *this* baby face?" But she squirmed a little and shot Monte a not-so-innocent glance.

He shrugged and turned his dark, morose gaze back to Cathy. "I'd love to dress you," he said.

"I beg your pardon?"

Bitsy giggled, leaning closer and squeezing Cathy's arm. "Monte's a designer, luv. The only man I know who gets a bigger kick out of *dressing* a woman than in *undressing* her!"

"Oh—I see." Cathy took a sip of wine, wishing they would leave. She had never been fond of the flamboyant Hollywood types, finding them too shallow and boring, a waste of her precious time.

Monte withdrew a thick, creamy card from his pocket and handed it to her. "I rarely solicit business from strangers, but I feel I know you as I see you daily in my home." The slow, sweetly sad smile almost touched his eyes this time. "And I really would love to show you my new spring line."

Cathy glanced down at the card. It was the color of old lace with raised gold letters spelling out MONTE, LTD. and a telephone number. No address. God, how exclusive can you get? "Thank you." She slipped the card into her purse.

"Monte's the best," Dash said. "Maybe you can find something smashing for the Emmy's." He gave her a private smile. "I have it from a very good source that your show is going to be nominated."

"Oh, Dash, that isn't for months." She ducked her

head, flushing slightly. "Besides, it isn't *my* show . . ." She, too, had heard rumors that she was to be nominated for an Emmy and had had to control the wild burst of elation every time she thought about it.

"Well, really, luv, Monte's things aren't just off the rack, you know." Bitsy stood and looped her arm through the tall, young designer's. "It takes countless fittings—and *everyone* who is *anyone* will be wearing a Monte gown to the awards. You simply *must* pop by the shop and have a look."

"Well, perhaps—but I'm awfully busy." God, she hated to be pushed.

"I have a splendid idea! Why don't I give you a jingle later this week and we'll pop by together? I must get something *devastating* for the Academy Awards. You're going, of course." She did not wait for an answer but rushed breathlessly on. "You would be *stunning* in that new burgundy that's all the rage this season. What do you think, Monte?"

"Huh-uh. Too heavy. Pearl or silver with that delicious, creamy skin." He was looking at her with a steady, penetrating gaze that made her feel like a butterfly impaled on a pin. "Or perhaps an ice blue—with just a touch of iridescence. I have a bolt of marvelous watered silk I'd like to show you." He took her hand again, his dark eyes gentle. "Say you'll come. It isn't often I find someone as lovely and perfect as you to dress."

"Well, I like that!" Bitsy flung open her mink coat to show off a voluptuous body encased in designer jeans a size too small and a wildly printed Pucci blouse. "What's this, buster? Chopped liver?"

Monte calmly closed the coat. "Yes, my dear, it is—until you lose fifteen pounds. And I've told you repeatedly *never* wear jeans unless they are a size five."

"These *are* a size five!"

"But *you* aren't, luv." He chucked her under the

chin. "Come, let us off and leave these good people to their lunch." He waved rather dispiritedly and Bitsy called over her shoulder that she would be in touch.

"If those jeans were a size five, then I must wear a pre-teen," Cathy said, more cattily than she had intended.

Dash chuckled as he tossed his American Express credit card onto the silver tray holding the luncheon check. "Isn't she something? God, I've known Bitsy since she was a little girl and she never changes." He shook his head fondly.

"Yeah, she's something all right, but *what*?" Cathy swallowed the rest of her wine.

"I'll admit that she takes some getting used to, but she's a great little gal when you get to know her. There's not a mean bone in her body." He signed the receipt and stood, helping Cathy out of the booth. "Why don't you go to Monte's with her, honey? She was right about that—Monte's about the best designer in Beverly Hills. You've probably seen his clothes on half the actresses in town."

"Is that why most of them make Mr. Blackwell's 'Worst Dressed' list?" She slipped into her morning dawn mink stroller (a Christmas gift from Dash) and they stepped out into a chill drizzle of afternoon rain. "Jesus, isn't it ever going to stop raining? I've had the Gray Eagle Academy lined up for almost a month now and have had to cancel so often I'm almost embarrassed to call them again."

Dash's Stutz Blackhawk VI Coupe eased to a halt, driven by a delighted and awed parking attendant who seemed reluctant to give it up. Dash helped Cathy inside. "They understand, babe." He pulled out into the heavy Rodeo Drive traffic, reaching over to squeeze her hand before turning his attention back to the road. "You're too serious, my sweet—lighten up. It's only a television show."

## The Love Game

She harumphed, then snuggled closer, slipping her hand up between his legs where she left it. "Well, one good thing about the rain. No one can see how close I'm sitting to you through the windows." She kissed his cheek and lay her head upon his shoulder. "I love you," she said softly.

"Not nearly as much as I love you, my little Cathy." He kissed the top of her head, expertly manuevering the big automobile with one hand and hugging her closer still with the other.

Their affair was in its fifth month and never had Cathy been happier. Her step had taken on a new lightness, she found herself whistling or humming a tune as she went about her day—and waiting eagerly for the nights when Dash would be with her. Not so much for the sex (even though their greediness for one another had not diminished in the slightest) as for the conversation. She loved to listen to him talk about television (still his first love) and would beg him for more stories long after he grew weary. She soaked up every scrap of information like a thirsty sponge, storing away the knowledge for future use. She now understood why he had said "yes" to her theme format; producers often had to say yes to new ideas, take a chance on newcomers. Dash had told her that studios and distribution companies only stayed alive as long as they had a product to sell.

That the success of the "New Kane Winslow Show" was due entirely to her made Cathy flush with pride— and seethe with wanting more. More control. More *power*. When she had learned that the show would most probably be nominated by the Television Academy for an Emmy for Outstanding Program Achievement she could barely contain herself. Her emotions had vacillated wildly from elation to despair; she could just see Kane Winslow proudly rushing up to the podium to accept the little gold statuette and taking all the accolades. Accolades that should rightfully be hers. She was carrying ninety-nine percent of the show, often doing the wrap-ups in the studio herself as Kane's drinking worsened. And these past few weeks, with the weather forcing them to shoot inside, she had both opened and closed the show from whatever location they were filming from. She sometimes felt a twinge of guilt for ousting the old lush from his own show but then would shrug it away; if he couldn't hold his own in the fierce competition of television, it was certainly no fault of hers.

She felt Dash's hand squeezing her shoulder. "What do you think, babe?"

"Hmm? Sorry, darling, guess I was wool gathering. What did you say?"

"I said, maybe we should do a spot on Bitsy Bushore. She was damn near as popular as Shirley Temple in her heyday. Then that awful series she did—what was it called?"

"Heavenly Hillbilly,' I think."

"Whatever. Anyway, she must have fans of all ages. My two kids grew up watching her and now my granddaughter watches all her re-runs." He turned into the studio gates, slowed, waved to the guard and continued on to his parking space. "Give it some thought. You can't do the Gray Eagle Academy as long as this rain keeps up." He opened his umbrella, held the door for her and they hurried inside the building, going directly to Dash's office.

"Jeez, it's cold." She shook the water off her mink and tossed it casually over the back of the sofa. "Is the coffee plugged in?"

"I think so." Dash went to the bar, checked the percolator, then poured two cups of the steaming brew.

"Thanks, darling." Cathy wrapped her hands gratefully around the warm mug and went to sink into the softness of the plush, leather sofa. "Let's see, we're airing the Hollywood Wax Museum and the Movieland Wax Museum tomorrow and Friday. I guess we could shoot Bitsy Bushore over the weekend and run it Monday." She sipped, leaning against his shoulder when he sat down beside her.

"Great. I'll get Clare right on it." He reached to the end table for a telephone and buzzed his secretary. (He had six phones scattered about the vast office, one always within his reach.) "Get Bitsy Bushore on the horn, Clare. I'll speak to her myself."

"Wow, I've never seen you take such personal interest," Cathy said, a little miffed. "Do you have the hots for her, or what?"

"My darling girl, you sound jealous." He drew her close and kissed her, leaving no doubt in her mind who he had the "hots" for. "Jesus, what a great compliment for an aging old cocker!"

"Aging, my ass." She ran her hand over his flat belly and down, gripping him shamelessly, feeling the instant response.

His voice was husky when he whispered, "You keep that up and I'll have you right here in the office."

"It wouldn't be the first time." She parted her lips for his kiss, snuggling against the warmth of his broad chest, wanting him. The muted buzz of the telephone drew them apart, and she reached for her coffee, sipping as she listened to his voice asking Bitsy Bushore if they could do an interview with her and take a tour of her home.

He was still speaking, his voice animated, interspersed with intimate chuckles and boisterous laughter as Cathy finished her coffee and stalked across the office to stand staring moodily down at the rain-soaked traffic of Sunset Boulevard. She did not like Bitsy Bushore one bit and she really couldn't put her finger on the reason. The blond had certainly been friendly enough; it was just a feeling Cathy had. Bitsy made her uneasy, reluctant to be drawn into the charmed circle in which she seemed to live. She had always hated helpless, fluttering women who wielded their femininity like a weapon, existing solely on their sex appeal. A mean little smile touched Cathy's lips as she remembered the slightly overblown body of the aging sex kitten, the fine lines around her carefully made-up eyes, the sagging of her plump chin. Ms. Bitsy Bushore was in for a rude awakening—and very soon.

"She's thrilled with the idea," Dash said, coming up behind her and slipping his arms around her. He nuzzled her neck. "They'll be expecting us Saturday, around noon."

"They?" She turned in his arms, locking her arms around his waist.

"Uh-huh." He kissed her nose, her lips. "Her husband will be there as well."

"I didn't know she was married. Surely not to Monte?"

"Lord, no—Monte's as queer as a three-dollar bill."

"I thought so, but I wasn't sure."

"You haven't been on the Hollywood beat long enough, my girl. Give yourself another few months and you'll be able to spot a fag a block away."

"Well, what do you expect? I'm just a little country girl trying to make good." She said it lightly but Dash's attitude sometimes grated on her sensitivities. He was awfully prejudiced about homosexuals, blacks, the working class—in short, anyone who wasn't as successful as himself. She moved out of his arms and went to pour herself another cup of coffee. "Who is she married to? Anyone I might have heard of?"

"Marc Monroe—the hotshot war correspondent. He was an anchorman for CBS news a few years back, then went to Vietnam to cover the war. Some say he's responsible for bringing the whole damn mess into America's living rooms. Remember, they were calling it the "living room war' because it was the first war America was involved in that was brought into our homes by television?"

Cathy nodded but she really didn't remember. She had been too young to pay much attention to the Vietnam conflict.

"Now he freelances. Sort of a roving reporter, I guess you'd call him." Dash chuckled fondly. "Globetrotting little bastard, I really envy him in many ways. He 'rushes in where wise men dare to tread'—taking his minicam everywhere from the fighting in Iran to Nicaragua, from Israel to Lebanon. If there's an earthquake in Biafra or a revolution in Cambodia, Marc's there."

"Sounds like he has a death wish," Cathy murmured. She was suspicious of men who had to prove their maleness at the risk of their own lives or that of their crew.

"Hell, he's an adventurer, that's for damn sure. I guess in the old days he'd have been called a soldier of fortune."

"Even today they still call them mercenaries." She said it rather tartly, not liking Bitsy Bushore's husband anymore than she liked the lady herself.

Dash smiled at her, at the grim set of her lips. His prickly little porcupine was such an idealist, seeing only the blacks and whites. She hadn't lived long enough to notice the shades of gray in between. "I always thought that type appealed to women. I know that Marc Monroe has left a string of broken hearts all over Europe, the Middle East, the Far East, and . . ."

"How comforting for his wife," Cathy interrupted. "He sounds like a jerk to me."

"Wait'll you meet him. You'll probably fall madly in love with him and leave me flat."

"Not very bloody likely. I detest macho men."

"What's that make me—a milquetoast?" He arched an eyebrow and she came quickly to him and wrapped her arms about his slender waist.

"It makes you the man I love. A man who thinks with his mind instead of his cock." She raised herself on tiptoe, tugging down his head to kiss him fully, sweetly upon the mouth.

Dash clung to her, buried his face in the fragrance of her hair. God, he loved her! His fiesty little Cathy, capable of so many moods: caustic one moment, demurely gracious the next; teasing, vicious, hardheaded, softhearted Cathy. His voice was husky, muffled in her silken curls. "When you're in my arms like this, I tend to think with my cock as well."

"Ah, but that's different—you're different." She wriggled against him, arms tight about him, loving the way he responded to her. "Will I see you tonight?"

"Can't, darling. It's Wednesday. Dinner with Grace."

"Oh, that's right—I forgot." She rested her head against his chest, feeling the cool metal of his gold chains against her cheek. "How's she doing?"

"The same." He signed, stroking her back through the thin silk of her shirt, delighted as always that she did not wear a bra.

The only cloud on the clear horizon of their love was Dash's wife, Grace. She was the doomed victim of Hodgkin's disease, keeping him tied to her with the strong bonds of pity and a long ago love. Every Wednesday and Sunday were "Grace's days" when Dash dined with her, read to her and tried to fill her pitiful existence as much as he could. Dash had told Cathy that Grace had asked only one thing of him: to stay with her until she died. She did not mind (indeed, she insisted) that he have a life outside of her and their marriage, but she could not face dying alone.

Their two children, David Jr. (a year older than Cathy's

twenty-six and the father of Dash's only grandchild, Suzy) and Joy (two years Cathy's junior) were frequent visitors. David and his wife lived nearby in the exclusive Holmby Hills estates and Joy was going for her masters, majoring in psychology at UCLA where she lived on campus.

"Tomorrow night, then," Cathy said softly, giving him one more hug before releasing him. She glanced at her watch. "Guess I'd better be going. I have a meeting with Greg in a few minutes." She collected her mink coat and walked briskly to the door. "Oh, darling, will you please have Clare send over whatever we have on Bitsy Bushore and Marc Monroe? I may as well do my homework tonight since I'm not seeing you. I'll be back in my office in a couple of hours." She blew him a kiss and opened the door. "Love you."

## Chapter Five

Cathy sat at the table in Bitsy Bushore's big, airy kitchen, watching the actress dimple prettily for the camera, her voice animated, her gestures eloquent as she talked about her early days in the movies. A fragrant filet of sole *meunière* grew cold on the delicate Spode dishes as Bitsy spoke. Earlier, Cathy had watched her prepare the light luncheon, dutifully repeating the recipe for her viewing audience. She had taken the perfunctory bite, declared it delicious, then steered the conversation back to Bitsy's career.

Out of the corner of her eye, she saw her cameraman, Frank, panning the vast ktichen, recording the huge hanging baskets of fern and geraniums; the triple row of copper-bottomed pans—so shiny they appeared never to have been used; the elegant Waterford pitcher filled with iced tea; the immaculate buttercup yellow and white squares of the tiled floor. Gossamer thin yellow curtains sprigged in a celery green leaf design were drawn back from large windows from which one could just discern a tennis court through the rain and a multitude of trees and scrubs.

A cut-crystal carafe of white wine sat on the table and Bitsy refilled both their glasses without so much as a pause in her nonstop description of a childhood spent working with the likes of Lana Turner and Cary Grant. The interview was proving to be better than Cathy had hoped. Bitsy needed no prompting whatsoever to reel off anecdote after amusing anecdote. Hot klieg lights circled the kitchen table, causing a fine sheen of perspiration to film Bitsy's dusky complexion, turning it luminescent and making her eyes sparkle like brown diamonds.

"May we see the rest of the house, Bitsy?" Cathy asked when at last the actress paused for breath. "I'm particularly interested in seeing your wardrobe. I understand you've kept at least one costume from each film you appeared in."

"Yes, that's right, Cathy." Bitsy laughed, turning her head toward the camera. "I've also kept each and every script, all of them signed by the actors who appeared with me." She sipped wine and leaned forward just enough to show her deep cleavage in the pearl pink hostess gown she wore.

"Okay, Frank, that's it." Cathy stood, a small sigh escaping her lips. She glanced down at the now cold lunch, the wilted salad and light, airy rolls, the ice cubes melting in the Waterford pitcher. Her crew loved it when Cathy's guests showed off their cooking skills as they were the ones who ate the results. Not a morsel of the delicious luncheon would go to waste.

Cathy unclipped the tiny microphone from her lapel and stood patiently while Troy, her make-up man, subdued the shine on her nose and straightened her collar. She was wearing a pale green silk blouse that buttoned down the front, forest green trousers and high-heeled cordovan leather boots. While Troy fussed with Bitsy's hair and make-up, Cathy glanced through the script. The next shot would be Bitsy's wardrobe closet, bedroom and bath, then they would wrap it up in Marc Monroe's study where, apparently, the great man was now ensconced. He had not as yet shown himself and

Cathy found herself sneering inwardly; obviously he deemed it beneath him to appear on a talk show like any other publicity-hungry celebrity—he was, after all, a *serious* reporter!

"I guess we'd better use the cordless hand mikes for the next shot, Frank," Cathy said, peering down the long hallway that led to Bitsy's boudoir. The walls on both sides were hung with portraits of Bitsy, publicity stills from her numerous movies and television roles, magazine covers and marquee posters. "You can follow us with the minicam and Bitsy can tell us what we're seeing as we go." She turned to her lighting man. "Leo, throw a baby spot down at the end of the hall and you'd better set up a couple of kliegs in her closet. I doubt there'll be any windows or natural light."

A few minutes later they were strolling down the thickly carpeted hallway, each holding an ice cream cone-shaped mike and pausing every so often as Bitsy explained different photographs, throwing in amusing and/or informative remarks about her fellow thespians. Cathy had to admit that Bitsy was a damn good interview, needing no prompting, always bubbling with enthusiasm. She kept up a running commentary as they entered her bedroom and Cathy was not completely aware of her surroundings until Bitsy gushed, "Oh, you're going to simply *adore* my bed, Cathy! It once belonged to Theda Bara, the great silent film star."

Cathy almost gasped aloud but caught herself in time. She could only hope that Frank had his camera on Bitsy because she knew that her own face mirrored shocked disbelief.

A huge, gold-guilt, swan-shaped bed sat in the far corner on a two-foot high platform, its half-spread wings curving protectively about a kingsize, round mattress, its graceful neck arched high. The carpet was snow white and ankle-deep, the walls, white flock on white silk with a narrow gold-gilt molding bordering them at the ceiling. The ceiling itself was like an enormous circus tent; hundreds of yards of pearl-white silk gathered in the center to form a luxurious Big Top, with a many-faceted, sparkling, crystal chandelier, its hundreds of prisms dripping their icy teardrops of brilliance upon everything below. Two marble pillars, six-feet tall, stood on either side of the swan bed holding urns filled with great lacy spills of delicate ferns. The columns, carved to depict a Roman orgy, featured heavy-breasted, naked nymphs and gleaming satyrs with hard, marble cocks interwined in frozen debauchery, their sightless eye boring directly into Cathy's amazed ones.

She could not help herself. "Good God!" she gasped, lowering her mike and remembering to motion Frank to stop rolling. "I don't believe it!" She advanced farther into the room, staring. A circular mirror with wide veins of antique gold was above the round bed and the twin lamps on either side were intricately carved ivory columns that looked suspiciously like erect phalluses. The shades boasted finely sketched scenes of naked, voluptuous woman languishing upon plush chaises while equally naked winged cherubs fed them grapes or combed their long, loose tresses. The bedspread was genuine chinchilla, a soft, pale gray, and there were a dozen silken pillows nestled against the swan's broad, golden chest. It was an X-rated Disneyland.

"I don't believe it," she said again, walking carefully about the bedroom. "Bitsy, you've *got* to be kidding! Surely you don't sleep in here?"

"Of course, darling. Isn't it a giggle?" The brown eyes danced with amusement and mischief.

"It's more of a gasp," Cathy murmured. "God, Bitsy we can't show this on television!"

"But, darling, it's *art*," Bitsy protested. "Surely you wouldn't think of covering up Picasso's *Blue Nude* or Ruben's delightful ladies, would you?"

"I'm afraid this is just a touch more—more—" She groped for the proper word, turning helplessly to Frank who was gaping at the marble pillars. The rest of the crew were crowded in the doorway, staring. "Frank? What do you think?"

"Uh, well, I guess we could use a soft focus. If I stay far enough away, we can show the bed and still keep the, uh, figures sort of muted, you know . . ." His voice trailed off and he grinned sheepishly. He had gotten some good footage before Cathy had motioned him to stop rolling and he couldn't wait to show the guys in the cutting room.

"Well, I guess we'll have to go with it. Just pan the room, do a close-up of the bed, but for Christ's sake stay away from the pillars and lamps!" She glanced up at the mirror and raised a questioning eyebrow at Bitsy.

The blond shrugged and smiled innocently. "I like to see how I'm doing," she said and the crew broke up, forcing Cathy into laughter as well. It was impossible to be angry at the childlike Bitsy, but now she understood what Monte had meant when he had called her the "original Lilith." She could not imagine anyone actually going to sleep every night surrounded by marble penises and breasts, held in the golden embrace of a ruby-eyed swan and snuggled under at least fifty thousand dollar's worth of fur. She wondered how many of the beautiful little creatures had given their lives so that Bitsy Bushore might wriggle her bare bottom upon their soft pelts. It was a little decadent.

"What's in here?" she asked, opening a handsomely carved guilt door. "I don't need any more surprises." It was Bitsy's bathroom, if that opulent expanse of white carpet, gold, crystal and marble could be called a mere bathroom. A huge, round, sunken marble tub sat in the center, surrounded by hothouse flowers and tropical plants. The faucets were 24-karat gold in the shape of swans. A golden wood nymph held a golden cornucopia out of which the water would pour to fill milady's bath. Twin columns of marble, exact replicas of the ones in the bedroom, stood guard on either side of a French bidet, and behind a silk screen stood a majestic, thronelike, Louis XV chair.

"I call it the 'Throne,'" Bitsy giggled, raising the seat of the chair to expose a porcelain toilet bowl. She poked Cathy in the ribs and Cathy couldn't help laughing. It was preposterous, ludicrous, and the only way she could handle it was with humor.

"Who's your decorator?" she deadpanned. "Roman Polanski?"

"No, the Marquis de Sade," Bitsy quipped and both women laughed.

The shooting of the wardrobe went without a hitch and they moved cameras and lights back into the living room where the crew took a cigarette break.

"Goodie," Bitsy said, going straight to the bar. "I'll take a booze break. Can I get anything for anyone else?" From the expressions on the crew's faces, Cathy was sure that Bitsy could have gotten them any number of things. They had all but fallen over themselves since arriving, asking politely if they could move this or that piece of furniture; being careful where they strung their numerous cords and cables; and, to a man, ogling her cleavage and following the suggestive sway of her hips. Cathy had to smile; she'd never seen her crew so solicitous before.

"I'll have a little Scotch if you have it, ma'am," Frank said, glancing quickly toward Cathy. Almost apologetically he added, "We'll be wrapping up after the next shot."

"Cathy, would you like something? Perhaps some nice white wine?" Bitsy poured Scoth and motioned for the rest of the crew to join them at the bar.

"No thanks, Bitsy. I'm not much of a drinker." She turned her gaze toward the solid oak door she knew to be Marc's study. Bitsy had pointed it out earlier, putting a crimson-tipped finger to her lips and whispering, "He doesn't like to be disturbed when he's working. I'll introduce you later." Well, it was "later" now and the last shot of the day lay behind that closed door. She needed to look at the room, decide where the lights should go and determine the best setting for the conversation between herself, Bitsy and Marc. She was curious about the man Dash so obviously admired. Could that fearless roving reporter be the same man who slept in the ludicrous swan bed? Would a war correspondent worth his combat boots be caught dead in a sunken tub with naked cherubs gamboling about his head? She strode briskly to the door and rapped sharply.

At his request to come in she opened the door and stepped inside. "Mr. Monroe, I'm Cathy Curtis, I—" She stopped dead still and stared into the most incredibly handsome face she had ever seen. Marc Monroe sat behind a large teak desk that was piled high with papers. His sun-streaked hair was mussed, his tanned face, weary. He wore a moustache and thick sideburns. His jaw was square and firm, the lips full and dusky rose, the nose beautifully sculptured. His broad-shouldered torso strained the seams of a blue tee shirt with the slogan WAR SUCKS, and his hands, clasped together on top of the desk, were strong and sun-browned and without jewelry. Not even a wedding ring. She felt as if she had been kicked in the pit of the stomach by a Kentucky mule. All breath left her. Her heartbeat faltered, fluttered, set up an erratic beating.

He smiled and it was St. Patrick's Cathedral lit by a thousand candles. "Hello." He stood and she saw lean hips in faded old Levis. No fancy designer jeans for this man. He came around the desk, his broad hand outstretched. His legs were long; *he* was long and lean and smoothly muscled. He took her hand, towering over her. "I'm terribly sorry I didn't come out earlier and say hello, but I've a deadline on a piece I'm doing for *Esquire*." Even, white teeth flashed beneath the dark moustache. "I hope you'll forgive me. Has Bitsy taken good care of you?"

She wanted to take a step backwards, away from this stunning apparition but instead she swayed forward. "Yes—yes, she has. She's been most helpful." Was that high, breathless squeak *her* voice?"

"Good. May I offer you something? A drink?" He motioned toward a small bar in the corner of his study.

"No, thank you. I—I uh, wanted to see . . ." She gestured vaguely, conscious of the pulse beating wildly in her wrists, her temples, her loins. "You know, the room—your study—where we can put the lights and . . ."

"Of course. How can I be of service?" He still held her hand and now drew her farther into the room. His warm gaze settled on her nipples, suddenly rigid through the thin, silk shirt, and he thought he could see the beating of her heart beneath the fabric.

An answering jolt streaked through his chest, momentarily confusing him. Jesus, she was the most lovely woman he had ever seen. Her eyes were enormous, the color of a Caribbean sea at sunrise, the long lashes tipped in gold. Her parted lips were an open invitation to be kissed and it was all he could do to keep from sweeping her into his arms and tasting the promised honey of her mouth. He fought to keep his voice normal, his eyes on her face when he wanted desperately to devour her body, drink in the sweetness of breast and hip.

"Well, I just wanted to get an idea of the room and go over a couple of questions with you." She was acutely cognizant of his nearness, his warm hand still holding hers, the musk of his cologne like a drug in her nostrils.

"Quite frankly, I don't know why I let Bitsy talk me into this interview. I'm not much for talk shows." He laughed softly, intimately, and she saw that his eyes were silver-gray, the irises ringed in a darker hue, smoky and smoldering.

"Oh, gee, well, if you'd rather not do the interview . . ." (She cursed herself for sounding like an unsure, giddy adolescent.)

"Oh, no—no! I want to do it—now." (Who was this golden-haired enchantress who could turn his blood to quick-silver with a single glance?)

"I mean, if you'd rather not, we have plenty of film—more than enough, really—I would understand." (God, those eyes seemed to be going straight through her, piercing her heart.)

"I wouldn't dream of letting you down—and you must have allotted time." (Her skin was radiant, the color of a sun-ripened peach and he could almost feel the heat from it.)

They both stopped speaking and simply gazed at one another. The air crackled with tension, a sexual electricity, an almost physical feeling as if something incredibly wonderful and dangerous were about to happen.

"Oh, *there* you are!" Bitsy's high, shrill voice washed over them, guiltily drew them apart. "I see you've met my husband, Cathy. Is he being a good boy or his usual caustic self?" She went to them, laid a hand on Marc's arm and looped her other arm through Cathy's.

"Really, Bit," Marc drawled, his gaze still on Cathy's

face, "you should have told me how beautiful our interviewer was and I would have agreed to do the show without a whimper."

Bitsy wrinkled her little bunny nose at Cathy. "You should have *seen* him, Cathy! When I suggested that he do your show with me he roared like a lion! You would have thought I had suggested we rape orphans and plunder the church poor box the way he carried on!"

"Now, Bit, I wasn't that bad." Marc chuckled and moved away from her toward the bar. "Besides, I didn't know it was Ms. Curtis's show—you told me the 'Kane Winslow Show.'" He poured himself a glass of Scotch. "That's why I didn't want to do it."

"Well, it is Kane's show," Cathy said quickly. "He does the studio interviews and—and—" (What else did he do? Cathy's mind went totally blank and she gazed, mesmerized, into Marc Monroe's eyes.)

"Oh, pooh, you're too modest, darling." Bitsy's parrot bright eyes crinkled at Cathy. "You *know* you run the whole show." She went to join Marc and poured herself a drink as well. "She's *only* marvelous, darling," she said to him, now crinkling the famous nose in his direction. "Now don't tell me you've never seen her show. You haven't missed a pretty girl in twenty years!" She said it with sincere good humor, with not a shred of jealousy in her laughing voice.

She's a better actress than I gave her credit for, Cathy thought. Jesus, if Marc Monroe was *her* husband, she wouldn't let him out of the house! What a hunk!

"Ah, but I didn't know it was her show—it's still listed as the 'Kane Winslow Show.'" He turned his disquieting gray eyes upon Cathy. "How long have you been with the show, Ms. Curtis?"

"Six months." She did not know what to do with her hands, so she stuck them in her hip pockets, cowboy-style.

"I've watched the show every afternoon since returning from the Côte d'Azur," Bitsy said. "And it's simply *marvelous*! The best talk show on the air, really. Cathy's a *super* interviewer, Marc darling, very easy and natural. She lets the guests speak and actually *listens* to what they have to say!"

"In that case, I'll make a point of watching it. Are you still in the same time slot?" (Her eyes were so blue, so clear, the whites startling against the pansy irises.)

"Yes, three-thirty to five—ninety minutes." (Jeez, dummy, she chastised herself, anyone can figure out that makes ninety minutes! Why did she blurt out such stupid drivel whenever he asked her something? She had always prided herself on being articulate.)

"Good heavens, it's a quarter of three!" Bitsy squealed. "I have to be in Beverly Hills at three-thirty!" She gulped her Scotch in one swallow. "Where on earth did the time go? Cathy, you said it wouldn't take over a couple of hours. I *especially* told you I had an appointment!" The sex kitten mouth pouted, the big brown eyes grew rounder, slightly accusing.

"Well, I guess we ran over a little," Cathy said, glancing quickly at her own watch. She shrugged her shoulders and smiled. "You're just a great interview, Bitsy, what can I tell you? We spent a lot longer than I had anticipated—particularly in your gym." (After seeing Bitsy in skintight pink leotards and four-inch high sandals, Cathy had decided to spend a little longer on the excercise segment knowing the public would love it; the crew certainly had!)

Bitsy dimpled at the compliment, happy again. "Oh, goodie, then you have enough on me so that I can just sneak away like a little mouse? Marc will finish the interview, won't you, puss?" She wrinkled her nose at him, eyes crinkling. "I have a fitting with Monte and you *know* how he is if anyone is late." She went quickly toward the door. "Goodness, he throws such a fit!" She paused to hug Cathy and kiss the air next to her cheek. "Ta, luv, and thank you *sooo* much! It was super fun, wasn't it? Shall I tell Monte to be expecting you, dear? You'll *love* his things! Marc, you behave yourself. She's a *nice* girl!" And she was gone in a swirl of pink, leaving a lingering scent of Joy.

Cathy looked up to see Marc watching her. Their eyes locked, held, then they were both laughing helplessly. "Well," Cathy said when she got her breath. "What do we do now?"

"I don't know, boss lady, it's your show." He added more Scotch to his glass. "Drink?"

"Oh, I may as well. Surely it's the cocktail hour somewhere." She went to the bar, looked at the array of liquors and selected a bottle of vodka. "Have you any orange juice?"

"Your servant, Madam." He stooped to a small fridge beneath the bar and came up with a bottle of orange juice and a tray of ice cubes.

"I don't usually drink this early in the day so I might as well get my vitamin C while I'm at it." She mixed a screwdriver, aware of his gaze. The physical proximity was overpowering; she could *feel* him.

"Seriously, will Bitsy's premature exit cause problems with the show, timewise?" He stirred the lone ice cube in his Scotch with one finger, his eyes drinking in the sight of her.

"No, not really. We have more than enough film." She tasted her drink, aware of his thoughts, *too* aware of him. "I did want to do a wrap-up, however—thank Bitsy for so graciously inviting us into her home, let her plug whatever she's currently plugging—that sort of thing." Thank God, she breathed silently. She would not have to interview Marc. She knew she could have never gotten through it with her new, sudden affliction of thick tongue and sluggish brain. "But I can wrap it up in the studio later. We'll get out of your hair and let you get back to work."

Marc pulled a mock hurt face. "What? You mean you don't want to interview me? I'm crushed."

Cathy laughed. "Sorry about that, fella."

"Cath? What's happening? Are we through for the day?" Frank stuck his head around the door. "I just saw Bitsy leaving."

"She had an appointment, but we have more than enough film, don't we? We can do the wrap up in the studio. Frank, say hello to Marc Monroe, Bitsy's husband."

Marc raised his glass in a casual salute. "Hi, Frank—nice to meet you."

"It's a real pleasure to meet *you*, Mr. Monroe. I've been a fan for many years." Frank hurried forward and shook hands, more animated than Cathy had ever seen him. She could not imagine laid back, slightly sardonic Frank being *anyone's* fan. "I loved that piece you did on the Jelgobe Fulani tribe in the Sahara desert. Christ, it's hard to believe that they are still that primitive in this day and age."

"Actually, they live in Sahel, the Sahara's southern rim, in the Upper Volta village of Oursi—" Marc began, and Cathy hurried toward the door, murmuring, "Excuse me, I'll just go tell the crew . . ." Relief washed over her the moment she was out of Marc Monroe's presence. She felt as if Frank had somehow rescued her, saved her from a fate worse than—what? She didn't know. She only knew that never before had a man had such a disturbing effect upon her.

She paused a moment in the hallway to pull herself together. Bless Bitsy for leaving so suddenly and giving her a chance to get out of this posh, overstated house, away from Marc Monroe and his intense silver-gray eyes. She went into the bar where the crew still hung

## The Love Game

around, drinking and talking. She told them they were through for the day, then quickly gathered together her own paraphernalia and was walking toward the door, putting on her jacket as she went, when she heard him call her name.

"Cathy—wait up a second." He didn't seem to be hurrying and yet he swiftly closed the space between them. The silvered eyes were hurt. "Were you leaving without saying goodbye?"

"Oh, I'm sorry, I thought I had." She got the coat on and extended her hand. "Bye, it was nice meeting you." She shook his hand briefly, dropping it the moment she felt his returning pressure. "Thanks so much for allowing us into your lovely home." She went to the door, grasped the knob and saw that he was still beside her.

"It was my pleasure." His hand covered hers on the door knob. "Would you like to have dinner some night?"

"I like to have dinner every night." She turned the knob, watching his hand on top of hers turning as well. He drew back his head and laughed, squeezed her hand, then released it.

"That's beautiful," he said, still chuckling. "I'll have to remember that line. But you didn't answer me. Will you have dinner with me? You name the day." His eyes held her even if his hand no longer did.

"I'm sorry, I don't date married men." Christ, she sounded prissy even to herself.

"Oh, I see." He stood looking at her for a long moment. Her back was to the driveway and even though it had stopped raining the air was still damp and cold. He drew her collar up around her throat and held it there, sighing. "How can I say this without it sounding like the oldest cliché in the book?"

"Let me guess. Your wife doesn't understand you and you have been separated for months even though you still share the same house but no longer sleep together." Her smile was tight. "Am I close?"

"As a matter of fact, you're right on." A slow grin spread across his handsome features. "Are you as well informed on other subjects, Ms. Curtis, or do you specialize in married men's excuses?"

"Good day, Mr. Monroe." She turned and ran lightly down the broad, wet steps, not looking back until she reached her car. Then, when she did chance a peek from the corner of her eye, she saw that he still stood in the open doorway—and had the audacity to throw her a jaunty salute.

She spun out of the circular driveway, aware of her car skidding on the wet pavement, angry and not knowing why. He was just so damn cocky, so cool. He had fully expected her to jump at the chance to have dinner with him! She turned onto the Nimes Drive with its huge mansions lining the street on either side, misty and ethereal, with muted yellow lights glowing from the windows. The posh and exclusive Bel Air Estates had long been a favorite place for Cathy to drive and think. She usually drove slowly down the tree-shaded streets, drinking in the peace and quiet beauty of the elegant neighborhood. But today she saw nothing; her troubled thoughts were on Marc Monroe. What had he done to her? She could not remember a time in her life when she had felt exactly this way. Except maybe the time she and seen Elvis Presley in concert in Las Vegas. Her body had felt shot full of electricity then, too, her head pounding in time with her wildly beating heart. There had been the same feeling of danger, the same shivery thrill, as if something fantastic were about to happen.

The rain had stopped the Saturday afternoon Cathy had met Marc Monroe, and now, the following Friday, all of Los Angeles lay in a golden bath of warm, spring

*The Love Game* 71

sunshine. Cathy's windows were down and the breeze ruffled her hair as she drove. She handled her small Pinto easily, expertly, maneuvering in and out of traffic on Sunset Boulevard on her way to Brentwood.

The Gray Eagle Academy was an exclusive private school for boys, set back a mile and a half from Sunset Boulevard and surrounded by five acres of lush Beverly Hills foilage, shubbery and manicured lawns. Only the very rich could afford to send their boys to such a school and still there was a waiting list for enrollment. Academically, Gray Eagle was one of the best schools in California, its curriculum varied and interesting. Many celebrities sent their sons and roll call sounded like a who's who of movies, television, sports and politics. The academy had an excellent equestrian program (several Gray Eagle students had gone on to the Olympics), and such old-world skills as polo, fencing and archery were still taught. (As many of the boys' parents were actors, the academy felt these skills would be useful if the boys decided to follow in their footsteps.)

Cathy stopped at the rather formidable gate and waited for the mobile unit to catch up. She had purposely waited a full week before doing the Gray Eagle episode as she wanted the ground to be sufficiently dry when she filmed the various outdoor sports in which the academy excelled. She saw the mobile unit, waved, and continued on through the gates to the parking lot. The school was an old, Tudor-style mansion, complete with turrets and alcoves, surrounded by immaculate green lawns and rose gardens.

The headmaster (looking exactly like Clifton Webb) greeted her on the broad, oak steps, both hands graciously outstretched. He bowed over her clipboard (she carried it in one hand, her briefcase in the other) and guided her inside. The moment the doors closed behind her, Cathy was aware of an "other world" sort of feeling. Antique chandeliers hung, seemingly suspended in space, thirty feet above from dark-beamed oak ceilings, and there were candle sconces on the walls in the foyer. Tasteful paintings in ornate, gold-leaf frames hung along the wide corridor, giving it the look of an art gallery, and underfoot lay a soft, spongy carpet in muted tones of dusky rose, faded blues, greens and yellows. Occasionally, straight-backed chairs, antiques all, broke the space along the walls, some accompanied by delicate tables with fragile, curved legs, seemingly too dainty and frail to support even an ashtray. The very atmosphere breathed wealth and taste.

The headmaster, Mr. Fitzsimmons, ushered her into his office and a moment later his secretary entered with a lovely silver service of coffee and small cakes. There were three Louis XV chairs, each with its own small, perfect Porthault pillow resting just so against the arm; a gorgeous Persian rug in the center of a hardwood floor that was buffed to a high sheen; and the few paintings on the walls were originals. Cathy was impressed.

"This is very lovely," she said, accepting coffee (served in an authentic Haviland china cup and saucer) and perching on the edge of a Louis XV chair. (Did one actually *sit* in such a chair?) "It's so gracious—I wasn't aware that anything like this existed in L.A."

"Brentwood, my dear," Mr. Fitzsimmons corrected her, pursing his mouth. "Yes, it is lovely—thank you so much for noticing. You'd be surprised how many people never notice all the lovely things the Gray Eagle Academy has to offer."

"What about the students? I mean, it *is* a boys' school and boys will be boys." She laughed but Mr. Fitzsimmons did not. "I mean, aren't you worried that they might start roughhousing and harm some of these marvelous antiques?"

## The Love Game

"My dear Miss Curtis, the pupils at Gray Eagle Academy are young gentlemen. They do not roughhouse, as you so charmingly put it, inside the academy. They have ample space outdoors for such activities." He bit into a chocolate petit four, his pinky finger properly crooked.

"I see." Cathy helped herself to a petit four, glancing down at her clipboard and the notes she had made.

"Of course we have a gymnasium as well where the boys can play when the weather is bad, as it has been most of this winter." He popped the rest of the small cake into his mouth and patted his lips with a creamy linen napkin. He finished his coffee, patted his lips again, and stood. "Well, are there any more questions before we get started, Miss Curtis? I'd like to—" He paused, chuckled dryly, "—wrap this up—isn't that what you say in show business?—as soon as possible. The wife and I are leaving for Newport Beach this afternoon for a weekend of tennis."

"How nice for you. It's certainly perfect weather for the beach." She, too, stood, tucking her clipboard under her arm. "I'll just run outside and see if the crew is ready and we can get started."

They moved down the long, wide corridor, Mr. Fitzsimmons gravely intoning the pertinent facts of the school as they went, Frank following with his minicam jutting from his shoulder. Every few feet, they paused while the headmaster opened a door and allowed them to film the classroom inside. Each room was identical to the last: rows of desks holding rows of boys all dressed in identical gray flannel jackets, black trousers, white shirts and black ties. A teacher (always a male; did the Gray Eagle Academy smack of sexism?) stood at the head of the classroom dressed in proper good taste, in what Cathy mentally labeled a "banker's suit," their expressions dour until they saw Cathy and/or the camera. Then wide, welcoming smiles lit their faces and they beamed proudly at their classes while every head on every boy turned toward the doorway to stare.

They filmed the boys eating lunch (The massive dining room was like somthing out of an old English castle with chandeliers, good bone china, starched white tablecloths and real linen napkins.), then moved outside to the dorms. There were at least a dozen scattered back among the oleander, lilac bushes and delicatley drooping pepper trees, each dorm having its own house mother (in some cases a couple) who lived in a separate apartment on the grounds. The women served as surrogate parents to the boys and saw to it that the dorms were kept clean, the maids were doing their jobs and the meals were on time. On the remaining property, as elegantly landscaped and choreographed as everything else, were tennis and badminton courts, swimming pools, ping pong tables, stables, riding arenas and jumping courses, a football field, tracks and a baseball diamond.

It was late afternoon by the time they arrived at the stables to do the last shot of the day: the equestrian course. Mr. Fitzsimmons had excused himself earlier, pleading the long drive to Newport Beach, and had assigned young Russell Strait (son of the famous Hollywood writer, Raymond Strait) as tour guide. Six horses were in the ring, cantering smoothly about in a circle while a tall figure stood in the center with an incredibly long whip that was flicked in time with the clip-clop of the horses' hooves. To Cathy's amazement, it was a woman—the first one she had seen who wasn't cooking or serving food, doing the laundry or cleaning—and what a woman!

She saw Cathy and the crew and came striding toward them, purpose in every step. Her long, lean, graceful body seemed made to order for the skin-tight, fawn jodhpurs, knee-high shiny black boots with three-inch heels, and white silk shirt open at the throat. Her hair was auburn, glinting like a newly minted copper penny in the sun. She wore it pinned casually atop her head in a loose, Gibson Girl-style with wispy tendrils escaping to caress her long, elegant neck. She had green cat's eyes, the nose of her aristocratic ancestors, a full, generous mouth, firm chin and stubborn jaw. Her shoulders were broad, her backbone ramrod straight, her legs slightly apart in the "at ease" stance of a general. She was the definite English equestrienne.

"Pamela Winters," she said, extending her hand to Cathy. Her voice was as crisp as a Maine fall. "Head riding instructor of the Gray Eagle Academy. How do you do?" Her grip was as firm as a man's.

"Hello, I'm Cathy Curtis from the 'Kane Winslow Show.'"

"Of course, I've been expecting you. How can I be of service?"

"Could you kind of show me around the place—you know, the stables and tack room, where you store the hay and oats, that sort of thing. I need to get an idea of camera angles and where we can set up any equipment we might need. Do you have an office where we can film the interview later?"

"Yes, just over there by the stalls." She nodded in the direction of a small, charming cottage partially hidden by lilac bushes.

"Frank," Cathy called, "want to come along with us and Ms. Winters will show us the layout?"

"Call me Pamela, please," the riding instructor said, leading the way across the lawn to the large white and red stable. The odor of horse manure drifted to them even though the grounds were immaculate and even then three grooms were mucking out stalls and corrals. The six riders in the arena continued to canter about in a circle, and next to the tack room three students were saddling their mounts. They were all dressed in gray jodhpurs, knee-high black boots, black, fitted jackets, white shirts and black hunt caps. Each carried a black leather riding crop.

"Maybe we can shoot some of the boys taking the jumps..."

"Some of these little bastards *should* be shot," Pamela interrupted with a chuckle. "Have you ever tried to teach a millionaire's pampered pet which end of the horse bites and which end kicks and shits?"

"No, I'm afraid that part of my education is sadly lacking," Cathy deadpanned and Pamela gave a hoot of laughter.

"Consider yourself well off," she said. "Well, here we are. On the right is the tack room. We have three grooms who keep the tack in good repair, the stalls mucked out, corrals mended, that sort of thing." She led the way inside and they were enveloped in the pungent odor of saddle soap and leather.

"This is great," Frank said, going to the nearest horse and stroking its silken mane. The horse raised his head, gave Frank a curious glance, then lowered it once more to the manger. "Good boy, you're a beauty," Frank crooned, then turned to grin at Pamela. "I've always been crazy about horses."

"Me, too." Cathy joined him and reached out to scratch the chestnut's ears. "My brother-in-law has a riding stable in Thousand Oaks and I sometimes go out and go riding with him."

"Really?" Pamela asked. "I've been looking for a good stable to board my horse. I have to get him out of the city before the smog kills him. Perhaps you'll give

## The Love Game

me your brother-in-law's number. Thousand Oaks would be ideal."

"Sure, remind me when we get to your office. It's really beautiful at the Rocking K—I'm sure you'll love it. There're miles of trails, and Ken even has a couple of creeks running through his property."

"It sounds wonderful. Do you think I could take a ride out tomorrow and have a look?"

"Sure, I don't see why not. If you'd like, I'll give Ken a call from your office and you can speak to him yourself."

"Thank you so much, Cathy. That's awfully good of you."

"Don't mention it," Cathy said, smiling. She liked Pamela. From the first moment she had shaken hands with her and looked into those humorous green eyes, she had felt an instant rapport. "Well, let's get this show on the road before we lose the light. I'm sure my crew is anxious to get home." They walked back across the arena. "This is really a great place." She shook her head when Pamela offered her a cigarette. "I wasn't aware that such a place existed in the fast-paced, jaded seventies. It's so old-world and rather Victorian, don't you think?"

Pamela tucked her slim gold Cartier lighter into her shirt pocket and took a drag of her cigarette. "Yes, it's Victorian—but perhaps not the way you mean. The Victorian era was severely moral and stuffy on the outside—and rampant with hypocrisy and degeneracy underneath—much as our own dear academy!" At Cathy's raised eyebrow, she chuckled and said, "I know of what I speak, milady. My father is the sixteenth and present Earl of Glendorshire and therefore I am well informed of Victorian skeletons in the castle closets!"

"An earl—you're kidding! Than that makes you—a what? Not a duchess?"

"A lady, if you please," Pamela answered, drawing herself up to her full height, gazing imperially down her nose and mimicking perfectly the drawing-room accent of British royalty.

Cathy dropped a dutiful curtsy and they both laughed.

It was after five before Cathy was able to call Ken. The shooting had gone well as had the interview in Pamela's office, and Cathy was more than pleased with the day's work. The crew had left and now Cathy sat with her feet propped up on a leather ottoman, a glass of Louis Roederer champagne in her hand. Pamela sat across from her behind a Queen Anne desk on a Sheraton chair, also holding a glass. During the shooting, the women had discovered that they liked one another, a rarity for both of them. Cathy had never bothered with women friends as they were usually jealous of her, and Pamela had been leary of most women as they were often fonder of her title than of her.

"Hi, Sis," Cathy said into the telephone. "How are you?" She sipped champagne, smiling softly as she always did whenever she spoke to sweet Maggie. It had been too long since she had been out for a visit, and she decided to go the next day. She asked about Staci and Ken, then her smile slipped and she silently mouthed the word "no," shaking her head. Her face went pale.

"What is it?" Pamela asked. "Is something wrong with your family?" She went quickly to Cathy and placed a hand on her shoulder.

"Kane Winslow committed suicide," she said, then spoke again into the receiver. "Oh God, Maggie, I don't know what to say. No—no, I hadn't heard. I've been on location all day—yes, since early this morning." She reached up to take Pamela's hand and squeeze it. "No one from the studio tried to contact me—yes, they had our location—God, I just can't believe it! Poor old Kane." She leaned her head back, sighing, listening as Maggie spoke. "Okay," she said at length. "Thanks, Mag, for letting me know. I'll be out tomorrow, okay? I'm bringing a friend—someone who wants to board her horse— yes, tell Ken, will you? Thanks, honey, see you tomorrow."

"Jesus, that's a shock. What happened?" Pamela refilled their glasses and sat on the ottoman at Cathy's feet.

"Pills and booze, apparently. The maid found him this morning. Jesus, why is it the poor old servants are always the ones to stumble upon the grisly scene? It's such a Hollywood stereotype."

"Did he leave a note?"

"Maggie didn't know. She just saw it on the news teaser saying he had committed suicide, film at five, you know."

"I don't have a television here," Pamela said. "But we could probably catch the news on one of the boys's sets."

"No, I don't want to see it—not yet. It hasn't quite soaked in—what this could mean—you understand. . . ?" Her voice trailed off and she sat staring into her champagne glass as if it were a crystal ball. Would it mean that the show was now hers?

"Yeah, I see what you mean. It could be a hell of a break for you, careerwise."

"Oh, I wasn't thinking that—I mean, God, I'm sorry he's dead!" She flushed guiltily. How often had she thought, "If only Kane weren't around, I'd do the show my way!" But she hadn't wanted him dead—just not around.

"Sure, you're sorry the old bugger's dead, but you're also a normal, ambitious career woman and you realized at once what his death could mean to the show." She lit a cigarette, squinting at Cathy through the blue haze of smoke. "Hell, ducks, it was your bloody show anyway for all intents and purposes. I read the trade papers. I know the network was just keeping the old boy around until his contract ran out."

"Well, sure, but I still wouldn't want the show at the cost of Kane's life. . . ."

"Stow the sentiment, luv, and take it any way you can get it. Everyone else does; you can be bloody sure of that!" She stood, pulled Cathy up with her and looped her arm through hers. "Now come along, ducks, you're going home with Lady Pamela and have a nice, lovely dinner and a hot spot of tea." She herded her outside and to the parking lot. "And after tea we'll have a couple of magnums of Louis Roederer and both get terribly maudlin and tell one another our life stories. Won't that be grand?" She was using her veddy, veddy British accent and Cathy couldn't help but laugh. "I shall regale you with the tale of my childhood, the sadly poignant epic of the poor little princess and all those wicked villains in the family castle. Kane Winslow's death will pale beside my stirring saga, I assure you!"

"I'm beginning to believe that you're some kind of English nut, Lady Pamela, but all right, I'll go for it." She slid behind the wheel of her blue Pinto and smiled up at Pamela. "Thanks for inviting me. I don't much feel like eating dinner alone tonight."

"Grand! Follow me!" She flashed a wide smile and strode briskly to her own car, a silver and black Bentley. Since they all looked alike to Cathy, she couldn't tell how old it was, but it was beautiful and well cared for.

As she followed Pamela's taillights in the early dusk, she couldn't help but think about Kane. She had never liked him or even pretended to, so why this heavy sadness? He was a chronic alcoholic who had been warned numerous times by any number of physicians that continued drinking would kill him. Perhaps it hadn't been suicide after all. Perhaps he had accidently taken too many pills (like so many other tragic Hollywood luminaries), washing them down with too much booze. Yes, that was probably it. Surely a man didn't kill himself simply because he was losing a television show!

## Chapter Six

Pamela Winters lived on Camden Drive in Beverly Hills in a Tudor-syle home perched atop a gentle slope of manicured lawn. Trees completely surrounded it, and on both sides hedges of Italian cypress separated her property from the equally elegant homes of her neighbors. The circular drive was cobblestoned and the double doors were at least twenty feet tall and arched at the top.

Pamela switched on the lights and shrugged out of her jacket, hanging it on a mahogany coat rack in the foyer. "Make youself at home, Cathy. I just want to get out of these trousers and boots and then we'll get dinner started."

"Thanks, Pamela." Cathy looked around the living room. It was small and cozy with a marble fireplace against the far wall and chocolate-brown shag carpet throughout. The chairs and sofas were arranged in such a way as to inspire conversation, and the wallpaper was French, depicting a turn-of-the-cenury rural scene. There was a wet bar in the dining room (dining and living room were combined) and plants everywhere; huge plants in big, bold urns sitting on the floor, on the fireplace hearth, great bunches of foliage spilling from hanging planters and wall vases. Cathy recognized a small Degas on one wall, a Monet on another, and the rest of the paintings looked real as well, even if she did not recognize the artists' signatures. Double sliding glass doors led out to the patio and pool area which was artfully lighted with amber, red, blue and green bulbs. It was gracious and unpretentious, a sort of understated elegance, the smallest detail of the decor perfect.

Pamela returned wearing an African caftan in bold patterns of black, brown and yellow, her long russet hair pulled back from her face and held with a tortoise shell clip. "Let's have a fire, shall we, ducks? It's a bit nippy in here." She stooped to start the gas logs and adjust the damper. "There, that will catch in no time." She flashed Cathy her wide, warm smile. "Well, shall we see what the pantry holds? What are you in the mood for? I know I have some steaks and perhaps a chicken breast or two."

The kitchen was equally tasteful and filled with plants and antiques. A butcher's block that looked to be well over a hundred years old stood next to the stove, and there was a cherrywood table and four chairs, their seats upholstered in handmade needlepoint cushions. The wallpaper was again French, this time depicting a scene from a seventeenth-century country kitchen, and instead of curtains on the windows, there were delicately carved shutters in natural cedar.

Pamela kept up a steady stream of conversation as she pawed through the contents of her freezer, and Cathy leaned against the table to watch her. The Englishwoman seemed to crackle with energy in everything she did, her movements sure and swift. At length she gave a triumphant "Aha!" and turned to show Cathy two Cornish game hens, each bird weighing no more than a pound each. "Perfect, what?" She tossed them to Cathy and bent to the lower part of the fridge and took out salad makings. "We'll have wild-rice stuffing and perhaps a veggie of some sort, okay, luv?"

"Whatever you'd like," Cathy said. "Anything's fine with me." She handed over the hens and watched her expertly strip the cellophane from them, remove necks and giblets and toss them into the sink. "Can I do anything to help?" She wasn't much of a cook, having spent her years after high school with Maggie (who was an excellent cook) and now was so busy she usually ate out.

"Why don't you pour us a spot of the bubbly? It's there in the fridge." She washed the hen's cavities and rubbed them with sage and salt.

Cathy found glasses (lovely long-stemmed, tulip-shaped ones) and filled them with chilled Louis Roederer champagne, wondering how Pamela could afford to drink such an expensive brand. She had noticed several bottles of it in her office and again in the wine rack in the bar.

They sipped their champagne as they cooked, Pamela preparing the giblets for the wild-rice stuffing and Cathy chopping the salad vegetables. There was a great deal of laughter as Pamela told amusing stories of her childhood and they both (by subconscious agreement) avoided the subject of Kane Winslow's suicide. They had finished the first bottle of champagne by the time the stuffed game hens were in the oven and the artichokes were simmering on the stove. Pamela popped the cork on the second bottle and carried it into the living room where she plopped down on the striped satin sofa.

"Ah, lovely, the fire is going nicely. Sit down, luv, and put your feet up." She kicked off her high-heeled mules and put her own feet up on the coffee table. "Mater would have a royal fit," she murmured, wiggling her toes. "She was quite strict about such matters as keeping one's feet where they belonged—namely on the floor."

"Growing up in a castle must have been some trip," Cathy said. While preparing dinner, Pamela had told her of her early life. Her father was indeed the sixteenth and present Earl of Glendorshire, the family going back to the twelfth century when Richard II had granted them lands and bestowed the earldom upon the first Peter Cecil Winters. Many of Pamela's ancestors had distinguished themselves in diplomatic service during the reign of Queen Elizabeth I and others stood out for military achievements down through the generations.

Pamela's father, Lord Peter Winters, a lifelong equestrian and riding instructor, had served for a time as the Queen's Master of the Horse before going into his current occupation as an antique dealer. Her mother, Lady Jane, was a distant relative of the Duke of Windsor and now worked with her husband in their London shop. Both enjoyed a close friendship with Queen Elizabeth and were frequent visitors at Windsor Castle. Pamela had fallen in love with horses at the tender age of three when she had seen her first race at Royal Ascot and had been taught to ride by Her Majesty's Master of the Horse, Lord Westmorland. She had grown up on horseback, cantering leisurely through the English countryside with other royal offspring and had remained true to the sport to this day.

Perhaps she would have married a duke, she had mused to Cathy, had not her father (as well as other members of Britian's gentry) faced economic crisis in this era of diminished empire and been forced to go to work for a living. (Other lords and dukes had turned their estates and castles into museums or parks to earn the money to keep the tax collector away from the castle door.) Lord Peter, however, was an enterprising sort with a love for antiques and had happily opened a small shop in downtown London, stocking it with many fine pieces from his own family vault. This explained the lovely antiques in Pamela's home as well as the Queen Anne desk and Sheraton chair in her office. Perhaps she still lived on a royal allowance of some sort that enabled her to drink Louis Roederer champagne as if it were Ripple wine. Cathy would not ask her, of course, but she couldn't help but wonder.

"We still have a small country cottage in Gloucestershire," she said now. "With horses, of course, and I visit as often as possible." She pointed a long finger. "There's a photo of it—Horse Neck Hall, Father calls it. It's really quite charming."

Cathy went to study the large, framed photograph near the fireplace and almost gasped aloud at the "small country cottage." It looked immense, a sturdy building completely surrounded by a yew hedge and sporting octagonal windows and a sod-covered peaked roof. Old brick walks and walls encircled it, and one could discern several horses grazing in belly-deep grass in a pasture beyond. "Is that a lake?" Cathy's voice held a touch of awe.

"Umm, yes, luv. We have a small, private lake on the property. Mum loves boating."

"I see." Cathy sat down, stifling a giggle at the absurdity of sitting with her bare feet up on the coffee table, drinking champagne with a real "lady" and discussing country cottages with their own private lakes. She, little Cathy Curtis from Atoka, Oklahoma!

"Feeling better, ducks?" Pamela refilled their glasses. (God, she drank the stuff like it was water!) "No more guilt feelings about Kane Winslow?"

"None whatsoever. Thanks to you, Pamela. You were right—Kane Winslow pales beside your royal antics."

"Ah, but I've barely touched upon the highlights, luv." She grinned wickedly and leaned forward, eyes shining. "I didn't tell you about old Uncle Percy who was constantly trying to get into me knickers, did I?" Cathy laughed and shook her head and Lady Pamela went into a lewd and hilarious account of being chased down castle corridors by the old lech who wanted nothing more out of life than to get young girls into the kip. Cathy's stomach hurt from laughing so much, that she wasn't sure she would be able to eat dinner.

She found she had no trouble, however, when the succulent little birds were served, golden brown and crackling with seasonings, their tiny cavities spilling out steaming wild rice and the savory aroma of spices. They ate at the kitchen table, the meal accompanied by the pot of tea that Pamela had promised and rounded off with a light and airy Danish torte.

"God, I'm stuffed," Cathy moaned, pushing away from the table. "Thanks, Pamela, it was excellent."

"It was nothing, ducks." She leaned back and lit a cigarette with her Cartier lighter. "You don't smoke, do you?" Cathy shook her head. "Not even pot?"

"Not even pot."

"Would you like to try some? I have an excellent stash of Koana Gold."

"No, thanks, but you go ahead if you'd like." She glanced at her watch and sighed. "Guess I should catch the eleven o'clock news and see what they're saying about Kane."

"You go ahead and turn on the telly. I'll be right in." Cathy went into the living room and switched on the set with the remote control and heard the pop of another champagne cork. She smiled to herself. Lady Pamela was certainly fond of the "bubbly" and she realized that she, too, could get hooked on fifty-dollar, imported champagne. She smiled her thanks when Pamela set a fresh glass before her and glanced at the TV to see if they were reporting Kane's death. It was George Fischbeck reporting the weather and a promise of sunshine for tomorrow. Good, Cathy thought, I need a little sunshine in my life, then was instantly guilty. She had more than enough sunshine in her life for a dozen people: her own television show, the possiblility of an Emmy nomination, a salary of $125,000 a year. Why then, did she feel an emptiness, a certain unhappiness when she least expected it?

Pamela reached to the table for a small but very beautiful Fabergé box and flipped open the lid to reveal a double row of neatly hand-rolled joints. She selected one and lit it with a gold Dunhill table lighter and inhaled deeply.

Christine Lund's crisp, no-nonsense voice brought Cathy's attention back to the television. "And now for our local news," the attractive anchorwoman said. "All of Hollywood is shocked and saddened by the apparent suicide of Kane Winslow whose body was discovered this morning in his Beverly Hills home." She went on to explain the pertinent facts and then told some of the highlights of his long and illustrious career. A montage of old footage filled the screen, scenes of a very young and dashingly handsome Kane Winslow dancing with Ginger Rogers, Kathryn Grayson and Jane Simon. Black and white turned to color and there he was on his last television special with a very young and gorgeous Ann-Margret and a perky, adorable Joey Heatherton. And then Cathy's heart stopped beating, and she couldn't supress a shocked gasp. There *she* was, smiling happily, seemingly so cozy on the studio sofa with Kane as Christine's voice droned on about the Kane Winslow talk show and his charming co-host, Cathy Curtis. "Ms. Curtis could not be reached for comment," she said, "but David Sunderling, president of KNAB spoke for everyone connected with the "Kane Winslow Show" when he said—" But Cathy did not hear what Dash had said. Her heart had resumed beating and had sunk like a stone to the pit of her stomach. God, she'd forgotten all about the news coverage. Of course they would want a comment from her. Her co-host was dead—and the show would undoubtedly go to her. She reached for her champagne and drained it in one swallow.

"Here, luv, take a hit." Pamela pressed the joint into her hand and Cathy drew in deep, gasping a little, fighting tears, but keeping the pungent smoke in her lungs as long as she could. "Come on—another." Pamela nodded approval as Cathy dutifully drew in another lungful of smoke. "That's right, luv, go with the high. Let it relax you."

"Thanks, Pamela. God, I wasn't expecting to see *me*. I mean, I guess I should have known that they'd show footage of the show, but, well, it sort of caught me off guard, you know?" She still wasn't used to her celebrity and seeing herself on the evening news had shocked her. "I guess I should call Dash. He's probably been trying to get a hold of me all day."

"Take a moment, luv. It's still early." She drew in on the joint and passed it to Cathy who did likewise. Pamela was right. It did relax her. She felt her heartbeat level out, resume its normal pattern, and the knots in her stomach unwound.

"There's nothing I can do—nothing I can say, really. Dash has already given a statement to the press. Of course, they are still going to want to talk to me, but . . ."

"It can wait until tomorrow, luv, I'm sure." Pamela refilled their glasses, emptying the bottle. "In fact, why don't you spend the night here with me? I have quite a comfy guest room."

"Oh, no thanks, Pamela. It's very sweet of you, but I'd better go home." She sipped her champagne, feeling the unfamiliar rush of marijuana course through her bloodstream, making her flushed and warm. She needed air and she needed to be alone. She stood, a little unsteadily, and smiled down at Pamela. "I don't know how to thank you for everything, Lady Pamela—the wonderful dinner and delightful conversation—and just everything. You've been marvelous to someone you barely know. Thanks so much."

"Pish, don't mention it, ducks. We royal folks are rather a likable lot." She stood and took Cathy's hand. The green cat's eyes searched Cathy's face, concerned. "Are you sure you're up to driving home? You're more than welcome to stay."

"I know, and thank you, really, but I'd better go home and prepare myself for tomorrow's onslaught. There're bound to be reporters on my doorstep in the morning." She slipped into her jacket and tucked her purse under her arm. Impulsively, she hugged Pamela and kissed her smooth, cool cheek. " 'Thank you' seems so inadequate for all you've done for me"

"Then don't say it, luv." Pamela grinned and looped her arm through Cathy's, leading her to the door. She took a card from a silver tray on the table in the foyer and pressed it into her hand. "Promise to give me a ring when you get home so I'll know you weren't busted for driving under the influence, all right, ducks?"

Cathy glanced down at the card bearing Pamela's telephone number and nodded. "Okay, I will—goodnight—and thanks again. Next time it's my treat, okay?"

The phone was ringing when she let herself into her apartment and she picked it up and said, "Hello, Dash."

"Cathy, where the hell have you been? I've been calling for hours!"

"I've been dining with the daughter of the sixteenth Earl of Glendorshire, Lady Pamela Winters, if you please." She giggled, still feeling the marijuana high as well as all the champagne she had consumed.

## The Love Game

"I'm coming right over." The receiver went dead in her hand, and she shrugged and replaced it in its cradle.

She had changed into a nightgown and robe and was drinking a cup of tea when the doorbell rang. She fell into Dash's arms and tears spilled down her cheeks as she sobbed, "Oh, darling, I didn't want him to die! Really I didn't! I didn't want the show that much!" Suddenly all her guilt feelings and frightened thoughts rushed over her and she clung to him and sobbed harder.

Dash patted her back, stroked her like a baby as he propelled her to the sofa and drew her down on his lap. "Shh, baby, shh—I know. God, sweetheart, nobody's blaming you."

"Yes they will." She gulped and snuggled herself in his lap, drunk and tearful and sick to her stomach. "Everybody at the studio knew how much I hated him, but I swear it, Dash, I didn't want him to die! And—and they're going to think I'm glad—and—and all those reporters tomorrow will find out and they'll ask me about the show—and, you know, they'll think . . ."

"They will *think* and *print* exactly what I tell them to think and print," Dash said firmly. He took his silk handkerchief from his breast pocket and wiped her streaming eyes. "Blow," he said and she did. "Now, what's all this nonsense about? Where's my tough little Cathy, huh?"

"Oh, Dash, I'm—" She hiccupped and wiped the back of her hand across her nose like a small child.

"You're drunk," he laughed. "Where in hell were you tonight?"

"I was dining with the Queen." She giggled, still weeping a little, peeking at him through wet lashes. "I mean, a lady—Lady Pamela Winters. She's the riding instructor at the Gray Eagle Academy and she's so neat, Dash, you'll just love her. She's so funny and nice and everything."

"And she must own a liquor store from the looks of you. I've never seen you so plastered. I thought you Okie broads could hold your booze."

"Oh, Dash, I couldn't help it. I was feeling so guilty about Kane and everything." She shivered and snuggled deeper in his embrace. "I feel like such a hypocrite. The first thing I thought when I heard about him—his suicide—well, I thought about the show and that now it would be mine and I didn't even care that he was dead. Not really, you know—you do understand, don't you, Dash?"

"Of course, it's perfectly natural. You're an ambitious woman."

Her eyes widened as she stared up at him. "That's exactly what Pamela said. I never thought of myself as a—as a..."

But he interrupted with a fond chuckle. "The first time I met you you told me you were after my job. Remember?"

"But I was just kidding!"

"No, you weren't, little Cathy. But that's okay. I see the hunger in you even if you don't yet. You want power, baby, lots of power." She started to protest, but he silenced her with a kiss, then continued in a softer voice. "But you are so young, my darling, so very young that you don't quite realize what you already have. You're smart and quick and shrewd and you have a way with people that's almost frightening. I've seen you operate, you know." He chuckled again, softly, intimately. "You've been operating on me ever since San Francisco..."

"That's not true! I love you!"

"Yes, I believe that you love me, but you also love who I am and what I stand for." He turned her face up and traced a finger along the dimples in her cheeks, her soft mouth. "There're not many women who want to discuss television sponsors and the Nielsen ratings two seconds after they've made love, you know."

"Oh, Dash!" She flushed hotly and squirmed in his arms.

"But that's all right, too. I hate boring, clinging women. I love your mind, sweetheart. I love your questions and your thirst for knowledge. I love your honesty and your intuitive grasp of the business." He stroked her arm and then closed one hand over her breast, squeezing gently. "And I love you so much, it almost breaks my heart. I wish I could be young for you, little Cathy. I wish I could be the man I was twenty years ago—Christ, we'd *own* this fucking town! But I'm getting old . . ."

"Don't say that, Dash, don't even think it! You're young and beautiful and wonderful and I love you so much!" She gripped his hand covering her breast, pressing it harder and closer.

"Well, if I am, sweetheart, it's you who makes me young." He kissed her fully, filling his arms with her softness. "Now I'm going to answer the question you've been worrying yourself sick about all day and then I'm going to take you to bed and make love to you until you forget who the hell Nielsen is!

"Yes, the show is yours. I've already had Clare type up a statement. I've also had her type a statement from you to the press about how shocked and grieved you are about Kane's death. They will both be released tomorrow morning. You won't have to meet with anyone you don't want to meet with. You won't have to say anything you don't want to say or don't feel like saying. I will protect you completely, my little Cathy. Understand?" He shook her gently. "It's all over. It's okay to be happy. You've got your own show. You were not to blame for Kane's death. Hell, his liver was shot and it just as well could have been an accident as a suicide. No one really knows for sure yet. It's not your fault."

"But I took his show away . . ."

"Bullshit! He threw it away—traded it for a lousy bottle of booze. You made the show, Cathy. It's yours and everyone knows it has been ever since you came up with the theme format." He stood, pulled her to her feet and hugged her close. "This is a tough business, baby, and you've got to toughen up as well or it'll kill you. There're going to be a lot of toes along the way that will get stepped on, a lot of feelings hurt—and a hell of a lot of people out there just waiting for you to make a mistake so they can shoot you down. Namely, the press. They love a loser almost as much as they love a winner and they're happier, still, if it's one and the same person.

"I'll keep them away from you this time, but I won't always be around as your mouthpiece. You're going to have to get a grip on yourself, a tough perspective of who you are and tell the rest of the world to take a flying fuck at the moon!" He shook her gently, his pale blue eyes boring into hers. "You got that, babe? You can do anything you set your mind to. You're the greatest. Okay?"

"Okay, Dash," she said in a tiny voice. She leaned against his chest, feeling his heartbeat, strong and firm. And as he led her toward the bedroom, a smile of pure triumph touched her lips.

## Chapter Seven

Cathy and Pamela were sitting in Maggie's comfortable living room after having spent the afternoon riding the trails and talking, getting to know one another even better. They had discussed everything from Kane Winslow's death to their sex lives and had been surprised at how much they had in common. One born in a castle in England, the other on a farm in Oklahoma and yet they found they had the same attitudes about most things.

Pamela had adored Maggie on sight and had threatened to steal little Staci the moment Maggie's back was turned. The child was in awe of her English accent and had giggled delightfully when Lady Pamela told stories of her childhood. Ken had agreed to board Pamela's horse, an Arabian gelding named Desert Fury, and had seemed as taken with her as his wife and daughter were. Both he and Maggie were delighted that Cathy had found a female friend, as she had always been such a loner, insisting that she hadn't time for girl pals as she was concentrating on her career.

It was a glorious spring day and the horseback ride had been more fun than Cathy had anticipated. Ken had given them two of his best rental horses and they were frisky and full of spirit on such a crisp, fresh day.

Pamela had set her mount expertly, her hand firm and sure on reins, while Cathy had had a bit of trouble getting the hang of it again. She hadn't been in the saddle for almost a year and knew she would be sore as hell tomorrow.

"Well," Maggie said now. "I suppose I'd better go and get dinner started. You're staying, of course."

"Yes, we're staying, but I'm buying," Cathy said. "I'm in the mood for Mexican food and ice-cold Margaritas. How about you, Lady Pamela?"

"All for it, ducks. I ate so much trail dust today my teeth still feel gritty."

"Sounds great to me," Maggie agreed. "But let's go Dutch. You don't have to buy our dinner, Cath."

"I insist. Besides, I'm a rich and famous television personality. I can certainly afford to buy my family dinner now and again."

They had gone to the Sagebrush Cantina, an enormously popular little Mexican restaurant in Calabassas that featured the latest craze, a mechanical bucking bull. The music was loud, the tequila one hundred proof and the food excellent. Maggie and Ken had left Staci with a sitter and were thoroughly enjoying a rare night out. Maggie loved listening to the sophisticated banter between Cathy and Pamela and was more than a little proud when someone recognized her sister and came to the table for an autograph. She was proud at how graciously Cathy responded when her fans commented on Kane Winslow's suicide, particularly when she knew how Cathy really felt about it.

It was a strange feeling, in a way, being related to a celebrity. On the one hand, she knew all there was to know about her baby sister and yet, when she saw Cathy faced with the reality of being recognized as a television star, Maggie felt she didn't know her at all.

## The Love Game

She was simply that very pretty young woman, Cathy Curtis, who had a talk show on Channel Six. She was the definitive woman of today—liberated, successful, smart, unafraid. But Maggie still hoped that Cathy would find a good man and settle down. Cathy needed a strong mate, Maggie realized, someone stronger and brighter than herself, someone she could look up to and admire. Maybe Dash Sunderling was that man, but Maggie didn't think so. Even though he was one hell of a good-looking man, virile and dynamic, he was still twice as old as Cathy, too great a distance, in Maggie's opinion, for the relationship to work.

She wanted her kid sister to be as happy as she herself was. But maybe she was reading the cards wrong. Maybe Cathy *was* happy going it alone, doing things her way. She had always wanted a career in television and hadn't had the usual daydreams about a white wedding and bouncing babies on her knee. Maybe Cathy didn't need a man to complete her life as she did. She silently chastised herself for being such a worrywart. She had always mothered Cathy, protected her, trying to make up for the loss of their parents. It was high time she cut the apron strings, she thought, but knew she'd never let go completely. She loved Cathy too much to ever stop worrying about her happiness.

"Come on, let's go watch the cowboys' getting their butts busted on that mechanical bull thing," Cathy said, dropping a hundred dollar bill on the dinner check. Their waitress, Tara, a bright-faced, perky little blond, recognized Cathy and led them to a front-row table, promising to return with a pitcher of Margaritas. Loud jeers and raucous laughter filled the room as another sucker hit the sawdust, and the victorious mechanical bull stopped bucking. Cathy looked at the huge slab of black leather and shook her head. It was incredible that such a ludicrous-looking machine could have captured the public's interest as astoundingly as this one had. (Concieved at Gilly's, the world-famous bar in Texas, it had caught on and moved west along with the current cowboy craze.) It had no head, tail or legs but was merely an enormous piece of tough black leather, vaguely resembling the torso of a bull, mounted on a metal frame that was electrically operated to buck in speeds from one to ten. Not many would-be cowboys could stay the distance, however, and were usually dumped at around six or seven.

"Well, Lady Pamela, are you going to show the peasants how it's done?" Cathy asked as another screaming customer hit the floor.

"Not bloody likely," the Lady of Glendorshire sniffed. "Royalty does not make an arse of itself by attempting to mount an electronic monster that has been programmed to bust one's arse. I'll just sit here quietly, thank you, and observe you Americans in another of your strange, native rituals." She shook her head as another young man mounted the bull. "Most odd," she murmured.

Tara returned with a pitcher of Margaritas and served all around. "The drinks are on that gentleman over by the bar," she said, grinning at Cathy and rolling her eyes. "Boy, is he ever a hunk!"

Cathy raised her eyes to gaze into the steady, silvered gaze of Marc Monroe. He saluted her with his glass and she saw the flash of his teeth beneath the golden-blond moustache.

"I say, luv, you Americans are beginning to look up if *that's* a natural resource. Blimey, I haven't seen a man that good looking since Errol Flynn o.d.'ed on teenyboppers!"

"Who is he Cathy? Do you know him?" Maggie looked at Marc and back at Cathy, almost feeling the crackle of electricity that flashed between their eyes. Uh oh, she thought, this one could be serious, and she looked again at the tall, handsome man leaning casually against the bar. He wore tight Jordache jeans, a blue and white plaid western shirt and lizardskin cowboy boots. And he was clearly the most incredibly handsome and sexy man she'd ever seen.

"Uh, yeah, that's Marc Monroe—you know, the reporter. He does news stuff." They were all watching her, so she lifted her glass in a brief salute of achnowledgment and, to her horror, saw him push away from the bar and start walking toward them.

"Of course. I knew I'd seen him somewhere before," Ken said. "Hey, this is some thrill. I've always been a fan of his. He's a hell of a writer as well as an interviewer."

"You, too?" Cathy mumbled. Was there no end to Marc Monroe fans? "Well, hello!" she said, glancing quickly up at Marc, her voice too bright and hearty. "What a surprise. How have you been?"

"Hanging in there. And you?" Marc took her hand and held it in both of his.

"Oh, fine—just fine. Working hard." She tried to withdraw her hand but he held it even tighter, his disquieting silver gaze moving over her face. She stammered a little as she made the introductions all around and then he pulled up a chair and sat down next to her.

"I tried to call you several times last week. You're a difficult lady to track down."

"I was swamped last week, catching up—you know. It's the first week we've been able to shoot outside and I had so many shows already lined up." She shrugged and felt her face flush, her heartbeat quicken as if she were a kid caught in a lie. She *had* worked overtime all last week but she had also gotten the messages that Marc had called and had deliberately not returned them.

She had her course all mapped out, her plans all made and there wasn't any room for detours along the way. Even one as charming as Marc Monroe. Besides, she loved Dash and would not sully their relationship for a fast roll in the hay. She had met men like Marc Monroe before—to damn good looking for their own good; spoiled because women had been throwing themselves at them since puberty; cocky because things had come too easily for them and bored with women and sex but feeling compelled to bed every eager female they met just the same. She had too much pride to be just another number.

"We did Pamela, by the way, just last Friday. She's the riding instructor at the Gray Eagle Academy for boys." She swallowed some of her Margarita and looked swiftly at Pamela for help.

"Yes, it was marvelous fun," Pamela drawled. "I'd never been on the telly before. Now I'm immortalized!" She laughed gaily, sizing Marc up, liking what she saw.

"I was sorry to hear about Kane," Marc said softly. He took Cathy's hand and looked deeply into her eyes. "Are you handling it okay?"

"Of course." She said it too quickly and flushed under his steady gaze. "Thank you for asking—we'll all miss him at the studio. He was a fine man." She almost gagged on the words and took another long pull of her drink. "In fact, I'll be doing a tribute to Kane next week, devoting an entire show to his memory. He was a show-business legend."

"Yes, he was," Marc agreed. "I grew up watching him in the movies and wishing I could be half that suave and successful with the ladies. Kane Winslow always got the girl."

"Yes, he was terribly handsome as a young man." She finished her drink and poured herself another. The idea of the tribute had just popped into her head, and she wondered why she hadn't thought of it before. It was a natural. She would devote an entire show, maybe two, covering Kane's career. She would show old film clips from his movies, invite old co-stars to appear on the show and talk about Kane. He had worked with the biggest stars in Hollywood and their names alone would guarantee a high rating. Stars like Bette Davis, James Stewart, Ava Gardner, Frank Sinatra (Just those two would make her ratings soar if they appeared on the same stage!) She would invite stars television viewers rarely saw. Stars who were *truly* stars. Kane's career had endured for almost thirty years, so he had worked with all the greats in show business. And they would appear too, Cathy knew, because big stars loved a tribute to one of their own. Never mind that they might have hated his guts when he was alive, had perhaps competed with him for that coveted perch called stardom, they would be the first to applaud him his longevity and fame. And it was also free publicity and good exposure for them.

"I think that's a wonderful idea," Maggie said. "I'm sure he still has many fans who would love to see a tribute to him." She was surprised at Cathy's announcement. It was the first she'd heard of it.

Marc had raised his eyebrows when Cathy had mentioned the tribute but had remained quiet. He was well aware of the gossip around town of the long-running fued between Cathy and Kane. "Yes, it would be a nice send-off," he said, still holding her hand and now squeezing it gently. She flushed, either with embarrassment or guilt, he wasn't sure.

"What say we drop this ghoulish subject of death, eh, ducks?" Pamela said, not concealing the boredom in her voice. "I for one am much too high to dwell on anything more to do with the old gentleman's demise!" She grabbed the waitress's arm as the girl hurried by and ordered another pitcher of Margaritas.

"I'm with you, Lady Pamela," Cathy said with relief.

She was sick to death of the subject of Kane's suicide. She lifted her glass to her lips and leaned back, watching the bull bucking its screws loose trying to unseat a leggy cowboy who was thoroughly enjoying the rough ride. "Hey, look at that one—looks like he might make it."

They all watched as the bell went off signifying that the cowboy had ridden the bull at the highest speed and for the time specified. A cheer roared up from the crowd and the leggy cowboy was lifted off the bull and paraded through the room on the shoulders of the jostling bunch of well-wishers.

"Hey, Ken, why don't you give it a try?" Maggie teased. "You're a *real* cowboy after all."

"No way, Jose," Ken laughed, holding up both hands in surrender. "I can get my ass busted right at home without having to pay for the privilege." He grinned at Marc. "How about you, buddy?"

Cathy tried not to listen to the conversation around her; the awe in Ken's voice as he questioned Marc about his work; Marc's quiet, steady voice when answering. She hated to admit it but she could well understand why women found him so attractive, why they fell in love with him. It wasn't just his incredible good looks or even the aphrodisiac of fame that attracted them. It was his warmth, his *niceness*. His smile was shy and sincere and he seemed to have a shade of humility—something all too rare in famous men. He spoke teasingly with a light touch of humor that seemed to draw everyone into his special aura of warmth. She saw Pamela gazing at him, her green eyes traveling slowly and appraisingly over the bulge at his crotch, and she felt a stab of jealousy.

"I've had enough of this joint," she said abruptly, tossing off the rest of her drink. "Besides, I have to work tomorrow, so I think I'll call it a night." She gathered up her handbag and ducked her head so Marc wouldn't see the flash of jealousy in her eyes.

"Tomorrow's Sunday," he said.

"There's no such thing as Sunday in television," she answered shortly.

"Oh, gee, Cath, do you really have to go?" Maggie asked, and Cathy felt guilty at spoiling her rare night out without Staci. "Yes, I do, honey. I'm sorry. I want to get started on the tribute to Kane so we can air it the first of the week. But why don't you guys stay? You can grab a cab—my treat."

"No, we'd better pack it in, too," Ken said. "Weekends are my busiest time with all the city folks coming out to rent horses."

"Pam, are you coming with me or would you rather stay awhile longer? Perhaps Marc would give you a ride home if you want to stay." She did not look at either of them as she stood and adjusted her purse over her shoulder.

Pamela looked at Marc and realized that further flirting was futile. He obviously had eyes only for Cathy. She sighed and stood. "Okay, ducks, let's go."

Marc fell into step beside Cathy as they all walked outside and stood waiting for their cars. "How about lunch next week?" he asked.

"No, thank you, I'll be tied up all week." She looked away from his gray eyes, silver in the moonlight, and felt a shiver of desire sweep her body leaving her knees weak and her heartbeat erratic. Damn him anyway, for being there to spoil her evening! She thought she had successfully put him out of her mind and had had no intention of ever seeing him again. She had instructed her secretary to tell him that she was on location should he call, and she had not returned any of the messages on her answering service. One would think he would have gotten the message that she did not want to get involved with him. But he was so used to women falling for his charms that he undoubtedly felt she would too, in time.

"You have to eat," he said lightly, quietly, looking down at her. "Surely you can spare an hour for a hamburger." He touched her arm, and the feel of her soft flesh beneath the fabric thrilled him more than most women would have stark naked.

"No—no, I really can't, but thank you anyway." Where the hell was her car? She had to get out of here before she gave in to the moonlight in those hypnotic, silver eyes and made a fool of herself. She was Dash Sunderling's lady and would not jeopardize that position for any pretty-boy type like Marc Monroe!

"I see." Marc's hand fell away from her arm and he drew in a breath that ended in a sigh of disappointment. "Well, it was good seeing you again, Cathy. I'll look forward to your tribute to Kane Winslow. Goodnight."

"Goodnight," she said curtly and turned to watch the parking attendant as Marc shook hands with Ken and bent to kiss a delighted Maggie on the cheek. There was her car at last, and she fairly ran toward it as if escaping. From what, she wasn't sure as she slid quickly behind the wheel and called impatiently for the others.

Cathy dropped Pamela off and went home, her mind a jumble of thoughts. She tried to concentrate on her tribute to Kane, but Marc Monroe's silver eyes kept swimming before her. The softness of them, the love that she couldn't help seeing there, the desire so plain it was almost embarrassing. She shucked off her clothes and stepped under a hot shower, almost viciously scrubbing the day's fatigue from her body. She felt exhausted.

The thought occurred to her that she would like to curl up on her mother's lap and suck her thumb and be rocked to sleep. But she had no mother. And she was no longer a child but a grown woman with heavy responsibilities of her own. Many people depended upon her so she couldn't falter or show any weakness. She was aware that the crew of the "Kane Winslow Show"—correction: the "Cathy Curtis Show"—would naturally be concerned about their future. She would have to call a meeting tomorrow morning and assure everyone that their jobs were still intact. She was suddenly struck with the realization of just how many people depended on her for their livelihood; everyone from make-up artists to the lowliest grip. If her show failed, they would be out of a job. She sighed mightily as she stepped out of the shower and reached for a towel. This business of being Head Honcho could be wearying as hell.

She slipped into a blue silk nightgown and padded barefoot into the kitchen to make herself a glass of hot milk. The tiny kitchen seemed alien somehow. She had spent so little time at home in the past six months. She supposed she should buy a house as Dash had often suggested. He hated visiting her in her apartment building, fearing that he might be recognized. She could well afford a home of her own (Dash had told her that a pay increase would accompany her new position as sole hostess of her talk show.) and had been meaning to go house hunting when she found the time. She carried the glass of warm milk into the living room just as the doorbell rang.

"What now?" she murmured as she went to the door and asked, "Who is it, please?"

"Western Union, ma'am. Telegram."

She opened the door a crack and peered up into those same silver-gray eyes that had been haunting her all evening.

Marc Monroe grinned sheepishly. "I'm sorry, but I didn't think you'd open the door if I said it was me."

"You were right." She leaned against the door, staring

up at him, knowing she should close it but feeling powerless to do so.

"May I come in?" She nodded mutely and he stepped inside, his eyes sweeping her body in the thin, clinging blue gown. "God, Cathy, you're so damn beautiful!" He took her two hands in his, gripping them hard. "I couldn't stay away—even though I knew you didn't want to see me. I had to talk to you—try to make you understand. I followed you home. I've been sitting outside for a half an hour, trying to get up the courage to ring your doorbell." The words rushed out, spilling over one another, and he felt his palms began to perspire.

"Cathy, you've got to listen to me—give me a chance to explain. You've got me crazy. I can't work or do a damn thing but think about you. Ever since I met you, I've been in a sort of daze, wandering around like some love-struck adolescent, oblivious to everything else. I watch your show every day, drinking in the sight of you like a man left too long in the desert, seeing you there on the screen, so close I can reach out and touch you.... God, Cathy, I love you! I know, it sounds stupid as hell—but there it is. I love you. But you wouldn't even give me a chance to tell you, to explain about my marriage—" He laughed shortly. "If you can call it that." The gray eyes, shining and intense, bored into her. "There is no marriage between Bitsy and me, Cathy. Hasn't been for the past couple of years. We're friends, roommates, if you will—nothing more."

"Spare me the intimate details, please." She pulled her hands free and turned away, but he caught her arm and spun her about to face him.

"You're going to listen to me. It took a lot of nerve for me to come up here tonight and face you and by God you can certainly have enough class to listen to me!" Anger flashed in those soft, gray eyes, and his hand on her arm burned like a brand. "I didn't intend for this to happen. I didn't come looking for you. You walked into my house and straight into my heart, and I'm honest enough to admit it and to want to do something about it. If you *really* weren't interested I would have walked away, never bothered you. But you *are* interested, Cathy. I know it. I feel it—here." He tapped his heart then spread his hand over it and she saw that his hand was trembling.

"You're wrong—I'm not the least bit interested." But her voice was weak and her own hand went to her heart, felt it fluttering like a trapped bird.

His voice sank to a whisper, husky with emotion. "Cathy, why are you doing this? Why are you denying how you feel? Christ, I'm not some green kid just off the bus. I *know* when a woman is attracted to a man . . ."

"I'm sure you do!" She jerked her arm free of his grip and walked swiftly to the coffee table where she had left the glass of milk. Her mouth was cotton-dry, her tongue oddly thick.

He came up behind her and asked softly, "Why, Cathy?"

"Because I'm in love with Dash!" she cried, whirling to face him. "And I don't have room in my life for some macho stud who thinks he has to bed every woman he meets to prove his masculinity! I'm not some empty-headed little Hollywood starlet to be fucked and forgotten! And I won't be treated as one!"

"Dash?" he said, frowning slightly. "You mean David Sunderling at KNAB?" When she didn't answer, he nodded slowly, thoughtfully. "Of course, why didn't I see it? Bitsy said she thought you two looked more like lovers than business associates when she saw you at lunch that day—but Bitsy thinks everyone is sleeping with everyone else, so I didn't pay any attention."

"Do you realize just how rude and presumptuous you are, Mr. Monroe? Where do you get off barging into my apartment uninvited and discussing my lovelife as if it were your right? It's none of your damn business whom I sleep with or do not sleep with!"

"Dash Sunderling is old enough to be your father. He's also married. You told me you didn't date married men."

Cathy trembled with fury. The gall of the man! Through clenched teeth she said, "I can't believe we're having this conversation. It's the most ludicrous, juvenile . . ."

"Then let's stop sparring and get down to the truth. Why won't you see me, Cathy, give me a chance . . ."

"Why the hell should I? I don't know you, and, quite frankly, I don't *want* to know you! My life is perfectly happy just the way it is and . . ."

"No, it isn't, darling. You're miserable because something very important is missing from your life."

"I don't believe this!" She rolled her eyes heavenward and sighed in great exasperation. "What do I have to do to prove to that gigantic ego of yours that I am not interested in you? Jesus, hasn't a woman ever turned you down before?"

"You're not just another woman, Cathy, you're my love."

"You're crazy!" She stared at him, at the tiny, half smile playing around the sensual lips, the almost pleading expression in the magnificent silver-gray eyes. Her anger subsided, was replaced by a sort of awe as she gazed into the depths of those eyes, now filled with a love so strong she could almost *feel* it.

"Crazy about you," he said softly and reached out both of his hands to take hers. She did not pull away but stood still and felt the touch of his fingers on hers, sending little thrills up her spine, causing her stomach to flutter, her heartbeat to quicken. She was powerless to pull her gaze away from his, even when she felt him drawing her closer, moving slowly against her so that through her sheer nightgown her nipples brushed against the cool pearl snaps of his western shirt. "Your eyes have shot arrows into my heart," he whispered huskily.

She swallowed and licked her suddenly dry lips. "That's—that's from Dante," she whispered just as huskily.

"Yes, and for the first time I know what it means." And he filled his arms with her, bringing his mouth down upon hers as gently as a rose petal. She did not struggle or raise her arms to hold him but merely stood and allowed him to kiss her. He felt her heartbeat against his own, felt the heat rise between their bodies, the slight trembling of her thighs pressed to his.

"Cathy," he groaned, wrenching his mouth away to stare into her upturned face. "Cathy—darling—I'm in love with you whether you like it or not!" He kissed her again and felt her sway toward him, heard the small catch of her breath. "Please like it, Cathy—please let me love you. . . ."

"I don't know anything about you," she said weakly, her body still bent toward his, arms at her sides, knees quivering.

"All you need to know about me you can read in my eyes," he said as he drew her once again into his arms and kissed her. He took her arms and placed them around his neck, and then she was straining toward him, holding him as tightly as he was holding her, kissing him with a passion that shook him to his very core. He became instantly erect and was amazed. He hadn't gotten a hard-on so fast since puberty. She felt it and pressed her soft belly against it, wrapped herself around it, holding him closer still. He wanted to crow in triumph, fling open her door and shout to the sleeping world, "See? She *does* love me!" His hands slid down to hold her slowly writhing buttocks and she sighed and wriggled closer still.

Without removing his mouth from hers, he bent and lifted her in his arms, pressed her against his hammering heart and carried her to the sofa. She murmured against his lips as he lowered her to the cushions, and he whispered, "Shh, my love—don't talk—don't say anything to spoil it."

He knelt above her, eyes now almost black with desire as he hurried out of his clothes, and she could not have stopped him even if she had wanted to. He drew her nightgown off and gazed at the beauty of her body, her heaving breasts and gently pulsating belly. She reached up for him as he lowered himself upon her, and then the incredible heat of naked flesh against naked flesh seared them both. He lowered his head to kiss one pink, erect nipple, and she groaned and flung her body upward, her hands going to his head to tug it down, down, to press her breast further into his searching mouth. Her hands moved between them and she lightly, timidly, touched his penis. He flinched as if he had been stung, felt the blood pounding through him, engorging him, and he lifted himself and fell forward, plunging deep and true inside her waiting warmth. His heart constricted, pounded in his ears like a deafening flood that sent wave after wave of passion careening madly through his bloodstream. He cried her name, buried his hot face in her hair and spilled wildly into her like a dam breaking all boundaries.

She stroked his hair, caressed his damp, warm body, held him lightly against her. Her legs tightened about his waist, holding him in place as she slowly began to undulate against him. Her fingertips played about his shoulders, tickled down his back and her hands cupped his buttocks closer for a moment before moving up once again to hug his neck. She kissed his closed eyes, his relaxed mouth, nibbled at his earlobe and felt the shudder of response streak through him when her warm breath tickled him.

His limp penis moved inside her, grew bigger until it filled her once again and then he was moving with her, fucking her with long, smooth, deep, satisfying strokes that brought a cry of pure joy to her lips. Her legs fell all the way open and he raised himself on his elbows and gazed with love into her passion-dark eyes. Her lips were parted, crushed and swollen from his wild kisses, and her hands rested lightly on his arms as she watched him watching her. Their bodies moved as one, slowly, sensually, with the same thoughtful rhythm. Like interlocking puzzle pieces they were joined, each knowing instinctively when to move forward, when to fall back, when to grip, to release. They were both incredulous at how naturally and easily they fit together and it shone from their eyes as they drank in the sight of one another.

They looked at one another as they made slow, leisurely love, their glistening eyes mirroring their pleasure. Cathy raised her head and kissed his nipple, then took it into her mouth and sucked it, delighted when it grew erect. A hard little nubbin hidden in a forest of silky golden hair. His entire chest was a soft mass of glistening curls that grew down the flat plane of his stomach and then widened into the V of his pelvis. Muscles rippled beneath the smooth, sun-browned skin, such a contrast to her own pale white body. But they melded together as one, actually seemed to become one as they could have gotten no closer than they were. Her breasts were crushed flat beneath his broad chest, her legs splayed wide and cradlelike to hold him to cushion his pounding weight.

He spoke her name against her lips, whispered he loved her into the wild tangle of her hair, demanded to know if she loved him; but she could not answer for her climax suddenly ripped through her, and she could only moan and writhe and grip him tighter, closer, harder to her heaving breasts. Little, whimpering sobs broke in her parched, tight throat and she felt herself flung up and out of her body to whirl wildly in space and time, to discover a new dimension of herself.

## Chapter Eight

Never had Cathy been so deliriously happy. Falling in love with Marc Monroe had been so wondrous, so unexpected, so blazingly beautiful that it had consumed her like a brush fire, sweeping all thoughts from her mind. They had come together like rockets exploding in space, and it had taken her breath away, dulled her memory of anything ever having happened to her before Marc. She had gone to the studio Monday, dreading seeing Dash but knowing that she must face him and tell him. She wasn't the sort of woman who could juggle two lovers and deceive them both. Besides, she respected Dash too much to ever make him look foolish. She had been almost four hours late as she hadn't been able to pull herself away from Marc's arms, his kisses and sweet words of love. Rushing in just as her secretary was leaving for lunch, she had encountered Dash's secretary, Clare, and had mumbled an embarrassed, "Hi—is Dash around?"

"Mr. Sunderling is at UCLA Medical Center," Clare had said with just the slightest sniff of disapproval in her voice. "His wife has taken a turn for the worse." Her cool eyes behind the rimless glasses had swept Cathy's flushed face, her swollen mouth where Marc had kissed her so wildly. "I rang you several times this morning, at

Mr. Sunderling's request, but received no answer." She waited.

"I, uh, didn't get back from the Valley until just an hour ago," Cathy had said, too quickly. "How is Grace? What happened?"

"Mr. Sunderling left a number where he can be reached. I left it on your desk." She turned back into her own office and Cathy went quickly to call Dash. She told him the same lie, that she had stayed overnight in the Valley—and had been painfully aware of the pause, the slight change in his voice when at last he had spoken, telling her about Grace. In her guilt, Cathy was sure that he knew she was lying, and she was relieved that he was in a public place and could not speak freely. Grace had been taken ill early that morning, he had told her, and was going steadily downhill. It seemed that the end was near.

That had been over a week ago and Cathy (coward that she had suddenly become) had been almost grateful as it meant she wouldn't have to face Dash just yet. She had seen him only briefly at the studio and had held him, comforting him as best she could, listening to the reports on Grace's decline. She told herself it would be cruel to break up with him now and so she had let him believe that nothing had changed. But, oh, it had! Everything had changed.

She was in love for the first time in her life and wanted to shout it to the world! What she felt for Dash had been kid stuff compared to Marc. She had been impressed with Dash's wealth, power and influence—a heady aphrodisiac to be sure. He was also a father figure, someone she could look up to, admire and want to emulate. She was as much in love with KNAB as she was with its president. She knew that Dash could teach her the television business, and she wanted that more than anything. More than anything until she had met

## The Love Game

Marc Monroe. But in that first, dizzying week she did not think once about the studio or her ratings (even though they had soared with her tribute to Kane as she knew they would). Her mind and heart were filled with this new wonder that she had only read about and seen in the movies before now.

She had been amazed at her own sexuality. Never had she been so greedy for sex. She wanted him all the time, would glance at her wristwatch a hundred times a day, willing the day to be over so she could rush home to Marc. She seemed always to be out of breath and panting either from wanting him or from just having had him. She was like a drug addict, dying a little inside until her next fix.

She had given him a key to her apartment and he had brought over his typewriter so he could write his articles while waiting for her to return from the studio. What he told Bitsy, Cathy never thought about. Bitsy Bushore was a piece of yellowing celluloid on a film cutter's floor for all she cared. For the first time in years, she rushed home eagerly, anxious to leave her work behind, easily forgetting it the moment she was in Marc's arms.

Always before she had been the last one to leave the studio and then would take home an armload of work that she would pore over in the evenings. Now, her evenings were spent in bed with Marc or dining at some small, intimate restaurant, gazing lovingly into his eyes across a candlelit table, holding hands and trying to still the pounding of her heart—wanting him, always wanting him.

She had told Maggie and Pamela about this new wonder called love and they had laughed, delighted for her. Pamela had suggested that she and Marc have dinner with her and her lover, Ashley Carrington, but Cathy had declined, not wanting to share her joy with anyone just yet. There was too much to learn about one another, too many childhood stories to chuckle over, too many dreams to dream, plans to make. Nothing interested her but Marc. She had to force herself to listen to Dash when he dutifully related Grace's condition and expressed his regret that he wasn't able to spend much time with her. Guiltily she would assure him that she understood, then hang up the telephone and reach eagerly for Marc. Just as they did not speak of Bitsy, they did not dwell overly long on Dash. They both knew that soon they would have to face it, but for now it was just the two of them—and that's all either of them wanted.

Cathy bloomed, became more beautiful than ever. Her skin glowed, her eyes sparkled, her mouth was always ready to bubble into laughter, and she found herself touching everyone she met, hugging them. Her crew and co-workers basked in her radiant light, became more efficient and eager to do a good job and were as thrilled as Cathy at the show's high ratings.

The "Cathy Curtis Show" was an instant hit and working on a hit show made everyone feel good. When she received the telegram from the Television Academy informing her that her show had been nominated for Outstanding Achievement in Programming, it was the cherry on top of the sundae, and she loved it even more because she shared her joy with her man. She was consumed with wanting to please him, make him proud. She thought about him constantly, letting her mind drift off to the wondrous feel of the touch of his hands on her face and body, the warmth of his arms and mouth, the miraculous passion they shared. She felt sated, smug, complete.

Then Dash called to tell her that Grace had died, and she swallowed her laughter and tried to feel his pain. They met for lunch at The Ginger Man in Beverly Hills,

## The Love Game

where the famous proprietor, Carroll O'Connor, congratulated Cathy on her Emmy nomination.

"I'm sorry darling," Dash said, squeezing her hand. "I forgot to congratulate you, but you know how I feel, don't you?"

"Of course, Dash." She returned the pressure of his fingers and looked into his tired face. "Poor darling, you've been through so much, you can't be expected to remember a silly little award."

She leaned aside for the waiter to fill their glasses with Bordeaux and hand them menus.

"It was sheer hell, Cathy. Christ, you can't imagine what it's like sitting there day after day, watching someone you love die. It's ugly and undignified and so very sad!" He swallowed half his wine and tried to smile, but it looked more like a grimace of pain. "I'll never go that way, by God! It's so damn demeaning, so pathetic. I'd rather put a bullet through my head than to suffer the way Grace did."

"I know, honey." She watched him, not able to find the words to comfort him and knowing that he had to say it all and get it out.

"And she never complained—not once. She hung onto life like a fucking bulldog, not willing to let it go even when she knew there was no hope. God, what guts. I couldn't do that—I'd want to end it." He tossed off the rest of his wine and refilled his glass. Squaring his shoulders, he gave her the old Dash Sunderling smile. "But no more about dying. It's over and today is the first day of the rest of my life and I love you, little Cathy, and have missed you more than you'll ever know."

Guilt made her flush, and she couldn't meet his eyes. "I'm just sorry I wasn't able to be with you, to—you know—help or something."

"You were with me in here." He tapped his heart, his eyes soft with love. "Okay, we go from here. Catch me up. What's been happening at the studio that I should know? How's the show going? I tried to watch it when I could. Loved the thing you did on Kane. Your idea?" He was the old, dynamic Dash, the boss, impatient interest crackling in his voice.

On safe ground, Cathy relaxed and told him all that had been going on. She bragged about her high ratings, gushed with pride about her talented crew, and couldn't conceal her triumph at having conquered the afternoon talk-show audience. "Everyone's been so wonderful to me," she said. "It's even better than I thought it would be having my own show."

"How could anyone be any other way to you, sweetheart. You're so damn beautiful." His pale blue eyes searched her face. "You seem to have gotten even more so if that's possible—or maybe it's because I haven't seen you in so long. God, I missed you!" He brought her hand to his lips and kissed it passionately, urgently, forgetting that they were in a public place or perhaps no longer caring. "I can't wait until tonight, my darling, when I can hold you in my arms and make love to you. It seems like forever—and I need you so!"

Cathy murmured some reply and ducked her head to her glass. She couldn't tell him about Marc like this— here in a public place—seeing the love shining from his eyes. She owed him one last evening, didn't she? Smiling tenderly, she said, "Seven, then. Why don't you stop and pick up some food at Ah Fongs and we'll stay in. Okay?"

They were lying in bed, Cathy with her head cradled on Dash's shoulder, her arm resting across his chest, one leg thrown familiarly over his. She felt warm and comfortable, like slipping into an old and much loved bathrobe and snuggling safely into its worn contours. They were quiet for a long time, listening to Kenny

Rogers's melodious tones drifting to them from the living room, then Dash said, "You've changed, little Cathy. You don't love me like you used to."

She was silent but she tightened her arms around him and pressed her lips against his throat. He stroked her arm, caressed the curve of her hip, then drew her closer still.

"I can't say I'm surprised. I've had you longer than I deserved anyway." He sighed deeply and kissed the tangled blond curls on top of her head. "And I love you, Cathy, with all my heart. That's why I'm able to let you go—to want to see you happy with someone closer to your own age. I know about Marc Monroe, of course." She jerked her head up but he pressed it back to his shoulder and stroked her hair gently. "When I heard, I thought maybe it was just a physical thing, you know, an act of lust. Marc is a hell of a handsome guy—couldn't blame you. That's what I wanted to believe."

"Dash, please let me explain." She raised herself on her elbow and looked earnestly into his face, willing him to understand. "I didn't want this to happen, you must believe me. I tried—I really tried—but—"

"Shh, darling, I know. I do understand sweetheart." He chuckled softly, wryly. "Remember, I told you you'd fall madly in love with Marc Monroe. Maybe now you won't scoff at my crystal ball!"

"But I love *you*!" she wailed, falling forward to wrap her arms about his neck. "I really do, Dash—it's crazy, I know, but I *do* love you."

"And you also love Marc Monroe."

"That's—that's different."

"I know it is, darling. I knew it the moment we made love. That special something that used to be there was missing. Do you hate me for wanting you even when I knew you were in love with another man? Is it terrible to want you one last time? I didn't mean to force you. . . ."

"You didn't force me, Dash. I wanted you—I wanted to see—I had to find out if I still felt the same."

"And you didn't." She shook her head, miserable for having to hurt him, but loving him too much to lie to him. "I'm so attuned to you, my little Cathy, I think I know what you're thinking before you do. So don't worry—nothing will change between us—except we will no longer be lovers. I'll still be your very best friend, darling, and I'll always be here if you need me. I'll help you all I can with your career—but you must know that. I should have kept it that way from the beginning, playing the benevolent Svengali instead of allowing myself the luxury of falling in love with you." He shook his head and his eyes sparkled with mischief and wry humor. "But you seduced me, and I was no longer the master of my own fate."

"I did seduce you, didn't I?" Cathy giggled. "God, I'll never forget that night. How I wanted you!" She grew quiet wondering how this could be happening. She searched his face, taking in the beloved lines and contours she knew so well. How could she look at him now with this warm but detached feeling when she had loved him so desperately and had come to think of him as her hero, the diviner of her destiny? She had spoiled everything by going to bed with Marc and for a moment she hated him.

"You wanted my knowledge as much as you wanted me," Dash chuckled. "You are an almost compulsive achiever, my girl, and you have a gut instinct to go directly to the best source. I love that in you—reminds me of myself when I was your age."

"I guess that's what attracted me so strongly. We're so much alike, Dash, it's really funny."

"I know, and that's why I'll never desert you. It would be like cutting off one of my arms."

"God, Dash, I love you! How can I love you so much

and still be in love with Marc at the same time? It's crazy."

"Not entirely, sweetheart. You love us in two very different ways. You love me because you're used to me and I'm a nice old cocker—but you can't keep your hands off that sexy young stud Monroe!"

"Dash—how tacky!" But she laughed and hugged him close, marveling that they could treat it so lightly, laugh and joke about it. She had expected a much different reaction, a sad and/or angry scenario with hurt feelings and guilt pangs. But they lay together, naked, arms and legs familiarly entwined, as comfortable as any old married couple discussing the day's events. She supposed this was what it meant to love someone so much you wanted only their happiness.

She smiled and touched his cheek tenderly and with infinite love. "Thank you, Dash," she whispered and he understood and brought her fingers to his lips and kissed them. She would always love him, her first passion, her learning love, her beloved mentor. But this thing with Marc had to be played out. Had to reach some climax. Like a dare to ride the world's largest roller coaster. Once you were in the seat there was no turning back. The risk factor was the lure, the danger that lay in all those curves and plunging lows and breathtaking highs. Dash's love was safe and predictable. Marc's love filled her with fearful dread that it might end.

The following night Marc was back in her arms, in her bed and Cathy felt whole again. She unashamedly drank in the beauty of his wonderfully proportioned youthful body, his taut, smooth skin and could not help but compare it to Dash's soft, aging body. She touched him with awe and tingled with pleasure when his own smooth fingers caressed her in return.

They played together, giggled and teased, cooked steaks on the outside grill dressed only in towels, too bold in their love to care if the neighbors saw. They played Scrabble and gin rummy, went for long walks after dinner, sometimes talked all night long. And they made beautiful, heady love.

They worked together, one on either end of the sofa, Cathy studying her script, Marc editing an article. They attended the Emmy Awards and danced until dawn in the Crystal Room of the Beverly Hills Hotel, celebrating Cathy's victory. She had clutched the little gold statuette almost as tightly as she had clutched Marc, and neither of them noticed the photographers madly snapping pictures.

The seasonal rains started in April and they tucked themselves warmly in Cathy's snug apartment, cooking great pots of chili and beef stew, not leaving their love nest for entire weekends. They walked together beneath the same umbrella, dreamily, the misty sidewalk and light drizzle adding to their oneness. They mentioned neither Bitsy nor Dash.

The rain stopped as suddenly as it had begun, and the sun came out, turning Los Angeles into one of those picture-perfect days that only southern California can produce. Like a Hollywood backdrop, the sky stretched endlessly blue. Trees and shrubs sprouted tiny green leaves and pale blossoms, and even in the city the birds trilled and flirted with one another.

"Let's take a drive," Cathy said, slipping her arms about Marc's waist. "It's such a glorious day."

"Great idea. Where shall we go?" He hugged her back and kissed the smile on her lips.

"How about visiting Maggie and Ken? I haven't seen them in ages." She grinned impishly. "Not since I fell in love with you and dropped out of society."

He arched an eyebrow. "Complaining, are you?"

"Never!" she said and kissed him fiercely, then swatted him on the butt. "Come on—let's get out of here." She grabbed his hand, pulled him laughing out the door and breathed deep of the sweet, spring air. "Umm, what a gorgeous day!" She wanted to skip to the car but managed to control herself and allow Marc to open her door. She turned on the stereo and snuggled against him, her hand possessively on his thigh. He was hers, this bright, handsome, witty, charming man and she wanted to laugh with delight and pride. She wanted Maggie and Ken and Pamela and everyone to see her prize. He loved her, desired her and the wonder of it made her shiver with happiness. She wanted to show him off to the world, wanted to shout, "Hey, look what I've got! Isn't he something?"

They arrived at the Rocking K Ranch to find the parking lot near the stables filled to capacity. Ken was mounting a party of five on horses, tightening cinches, straightening bridles, adjusting stirrups. He turned and waved when they got out of the car and called a greeting. The four dogs came charging at Cathy, almost knocking her off balance and she laughed and stooped to pet their shaggy heads, formally introducing them to Marc. Just as formally he shook hands with all four of them, and then laughing and hugging, they went inside to find Maggie.

"Well, this is a surprise!" She came out of the kitchen wiping her hands on a dishtowel. "I thought you two would never surface!" She hugged her sister and took Marc's hand, leading them farther inside. "I'm so darn happy for you, I could cry," she said, then laughed and hugged Cathy again.

"Thanks, Sis, I'm pretty darn happy myself!" She leaned against Marc, eyes shining with love and Maggie looked on, beaming.

"How about a glass of wine?" she asked. "Or something stronger? What would you guys like?"

"Wine will be fine, Mag," Cathy said, sitting down on the sofa and pulling Marc down beside her. "Where's Staci?"

"She went to a birthday party," Maggie called from the kitchen. "I have to pick her up in a couple of hours."

"Wait until you meet her, Marc," Cathy said. "She's the cutest little thing."

"How old is she?" He lit a cigarette almost apologetically, knowing that Cathy hated for him to smoke.

"Four going on forty. God, I'd hate to be her teacher when she starts school. She's so bright and sassy, she'll have the entire class on its ear!" She suddenly wondered what it would be like to have a baby with Marc. Now *there* would be a wonderchild!

Maggie returned with the wine and they sat drinking and talking, catching up on all the news. "Pamela comes out every weekend," Maggie said. "Ken has been boarding her horse for a couple of months now." It was a gentle reminder that Cathy had not visited as often as Maggie would have liked. "Have you met her, uh—Ashley Carrington? That boy she's dating?"

"No, I haven't," Cathy said. "She's invited us over for dinner a couple of times but we, well . . ." She giggled softly, giving Marc an intimate glance. "We haven't been too social lately."

"Tell me about it," Maggie laughed. "I've been trying to get you out here for months! What do you guys do with your time?" Realizing what she had said, she blushed crimson and then all three of them were laughing together.

"Ashley Carrington," Marc said, quickly changing the subject. "What a great name. Sounds like a character from *Gone with the Wind*."

"What's he like, Mag?" Cathy picked up Marc's cigarette from the ashtray and crushed it out. "You're too young and beautiful to die," she said softly.

Marc shrugged in Maggie's direction. "Just my luck to fall for a lady who was raised during the cancer-scare generation." He took a swallow of wine and hugged Cathy close. "So, tell us about Lady Pamela and her royal paramour. Is he a duke or an earl?"

"He's a boy!" Maggie blurted, actually blushing. "God, I couldn't believe it when they came out this morning. He's no more than sixteen or seventeen, and yet they were holding hands and necking and—and everything!"

"You're kidding." Cathy tried to imagine the tall, stately, elegant Pamela with a young man not out of his teens. It was preposterous. "Are you sure they're not, well, just close friends?"

"They couldn't have gotten much closer," Maggie snorted delicately. "Oh, I don't mean to be unkind. I really like Pamela, you know that, but I just can't understand what she sees in such a young—man."

"Well, it's a well-documented fact that women in their late thirties and men in their late teens are better suited sexually than a couple of the same age." Lady Pamela and a teeny-bopper? The thought brought a giggle to Cathy and she shrugged her shoulders. "Whatever turns you on," she said. And an hour later she saw just what had turned Lady Pamela on.

Ashley Carrington was a dream walking. He was tall, slender and dark with sleek hair and big, dreamy brown eyes that rested often on Pamela with undisguised love. He was polite and very mature for his years, with a kind of shy humor that was enchanting. He was a fan of Marc's (Yet another one, Cathy thought with a smile.) and spoke intelligently of Marc's many interviews and articles. That Pamela was totally smitten with the young Mr. Carrington was obvious to all. She hardly took her eyes or hands off him, and for one silly moment Cathy wondered if she were going to cut his meat and feed him when they all sat down to dinner.

"I've had my eye on him for months," Pamela confided to Cathy when they were alone in the kitchen. "But I never dreamed he would feel the same way." She actually giggled and blushed. "Oh, Cath, I'm so damn happy, I keep thinking it's all a dream. Isn't he delicious?" She hugged herself, then Cathy, laughing, her already pretty face becoming beautiful.

"He's gorgeous," Cathy agreed. "And very bright." She couldn't suppress a small grin. "You must be a very good teacher!"

"Ain't I just?" The Lady of Glendorshire leered, then hugged Cathy again. "Be happy for me, luv?"

"Of course I am, Pamela. You know that." She wanted to ask, "But how long do you think this sort of relationship can last?"—but she didn't. She smiled instead and picked up the tray with the brandy snifters and turned toward the living room. "Come on—let's see if your boy can hold his liquor."

"As long as he doesn't stop holding me," Pamela laughed.

They sipped brandy and coffee, talking easily together, this rather unlikely group. Ash questioned Marc about his work, admitting that he had used one of his articles in *National Geographic* for a school assignment. "God, that must be really exciting, traveling all over the world like you do." He leaned forward with boyish eagerness. "What are you doing now? I haven't seen any recent articles by you."

"I have a piece coming out in *Playboy* in a couple of weeks," Marc said. "Then I'm off to Cambodia to do a television special on the conditions there. It's really appalling, all those poor, starving people, the hospitals filled to overflowing with orphans and no one to give them aid."

"You didn't tell me that." Cathy sat up straighter looking squarely at him. "When did this come about?"

"A couple of days ago. My agent talked to a couple of execs at NBC and CBS. They think it's timely as hell, what with all the fuss over the boat people and the civil war still being waged over there. We're just waiting for a clearance from the government."

"I see." Cathy frowned, a little miffed that he hadn't discussed it with her. Of course he would want her to go with him. Like the proverbial light bulb going on in her head, she exclaimed, "Marc! It's perfect—we can do it for my show!"

Surprise flashed in Marc's eyes for a moment, then he laughed and said, patting her knee, "Come on, honey, your show is light entertainment. This is heavy news stuff."

"Come on yourself. My show has covered some pretty serious topics. What's wrong with doing an interview like this? Formats can be changed, you know." She was annoyed that he thought so little of her show.

"You're not serious, darling. You wouldn't have the audience for this type of show. This is prime-time meat—not some afternoon fluff for bored housewives."

Cathy's eyes blazed sudden anger. "I wasn't aware that you were such a snob, Marc. I thought you were proud of me, that you liked my show."

"I am and I do, sweetheart, but you have to admit it isn't exactly "60 Minutes" or "Walter Cronkite." He laughed lightly, ruffling her hair, and she jerked away, hurt and angry.

"That doesn't mean that it couldn't be." She knew her voice sounded sullen. "God, you don't think for a minute that I intend to make this silly talk show my career, do you? I *want* to do heavy new stories like this. Women do, you know. Look at Barbara Walters."

"Yes, look at Barbara Walters," Pamela drawled.

"She's a good twenty years older than you, luv—as well as twenty years more experienced. I don't know much about the world of show biz, but isn't there an unwritten law that one must pay one's dues?"

"I've paid some dues," Cathy mumbled. She knew she was being petulant, but Marc's criticism had stung.

"Oh, Cathy honey, don't be so serious!" Maggie laughed and got to her feet to pour brandy all around.

"What dues?" Ken scoffed good-naturedly. He did not seem to notice the anger in his sister-in-law's eyes. "Hell, you've been damn lucky, and you know it. What other twenty-five-year-old do you know with her own talk show?"

"Twenty-six-and-a-half." Cathy knew she sounded like a spoiled child but didn't give a damn. Let them scoff. Let them think that she had gotten her own show because some old drunk had had the good sense to kill himself. That's what they were all thinking and didn't have the guts to say out loud. Well, let them think that. She'd show them.

"Oh my, shall I run get your rocking chair, ducks?" Pamela teased, and everyone laughed with relief, hoping this was the end of the quarrel.

Ashley threw Cathy a sympathetic smile as if he understood the feeling of being the "youngster" in a crowd of smug, complacent adults. "Well, I like your show, Cathy, and I don't exactly agree with Marc that it's just a piece of fluff." He grinned shyly at Marc. "I saw the one you did on the food industry—you know, flies in the hamburger, insects in the canned goods, mercury in the tuna fish. I thought it was a pretty powerful piece of reporting."

"Thanks, Ash, but I had to fight *every* man in the studio to get it on the air. *They* didn't think that housewives would be interested. *They* told me that women want to relax and be entertained in the afternoon, not be scared to death to buy a hamburger for their kids. Bull!"

"See, that's what I mean, honey. Afternoon television isn't the place for a depressing story like Cambodia."

"Oh, I see. Save the heartstoppers for prime time when the station is guaranteed a hefty profit. God forbid they should lose money as well as inform the American people of what's really going on in the world!" She sipped her brandy, forcing herself to calm down. This wasn't new, this scoffing, this patronizing attitude. She'd been confronted with it ever since she had started work at KNAB. She smiled tightly. Little did they know, those sexist boors, that it was their condescending attitudes that had helped further her career.

Beautiful and sexy—therefore stupid. She had always been underestimated by men and had used it to her advantage. Actually, they had often handed her the advantage by ogling her tits and ass and thereby letting their guard down and becoming negligent. And she had played it for all it was worth, knowing just when to widened her big blue eyes, when to laugh at their corny jokes.

She laid her hand on Marc's thigh and looked properly contrite. "You're right, of course, darling. The situation in Cambodia is too strong for daytime programming, but who says we can't run it in the evening—prime time? You're not tied in with NBC or CBS, are you?"

"No, of course not—it's still in the talking stage." He covered her hand with his, smiling warmly down at her, relieved that she apparently wasn't going to pursue this silly argument.

"Well, how about giving KNAB a shot at it?" Cathy smiled sweetly. "I'm sure Dash would be thrilled with the idea of doing a special on Cambodia. He's an avid fan of yours, you know."

"Is he really?" Marc grinned modestly. "Well, it's not

up to me, you know. My agents handles the business end. I'll have him get in touch with Dash." He tossed off his brandy and looked around at the others. "I'm just a whore at heart," he said. "I go where the best money is." In the ensuing laughter he did not notice the hard, grim expression that had settled over Cathy's face.

## Chapter Nine

"What do you think, Dash? You can preempt that dumb cop show on Friday night in the ten o'clock slot and run Marc's special. I'll wager a month's salary that you'll pull in the highest ratings of the evening. People love to watch other people suffering—and, who knows, maybe we can do some good. Ask for donations or something to help out those poor, homeless kids." She paced his office, excitement in every step. "You know that first-run movies and specials always pump up the network points and we're falling behind the other networks in most of our evening shows. This could put us in the lead again."

Dash smiled as he watched her, wondering if she was aware that she had referred to KNAB several times as "our" network, had been concerned that "we" were falling behind in ratings on some of "our" regular weekly dramatic shows and sitcoms. "Okay, Suzy Silverman," he said, using his nickname for her and referring to NBC's bold president, Fred Silverman. "I'll talk to Earl Brill, Marc's agent, and see if we can work something out."

"Oh, great, Dash! Thanks." She rushed to him, threw her arms around his neck and kissed him soundly. "You won't be sorry—just wait and see, KNAB will take the evening!"

"I wouldn't doubt it. Marc Monroe's name is a big draw and I've always liked his stuff—so has everyone else, it seems." His heart ached as it always did when she so innocently pressed herself against him. Jesus, couldn't she see what she was doing to him with her open, childlike display of affection? He patted her arm and gently drew away. "Maybe we can work out some kind of contractual agreement with him—say, half a dozen specials a year. We're in third place with our news programming, and I'd like to catch up with Silverman for once instead of always getting projects with his fingerprints all over them."

"Oh, Dash, do you mean it? That would really be the coup of the season!" Her mind raced and her pulses soared. To work with Marc at her own studio, to see him every day, maybe even drive to work together, lunch together, discuss their shows at the day's end. They would be a real working team, the Hope and Crosby of television broadcasting. She wondered if she should retain her maiden name after they were married. *Cathy Monroe*, she tried it on for size—then, *Curtis and Monroe*.

"Speaking of the season, we've got another one coming up very soon," Dash said. He stood and moved to the bar and poured himself a Scotch and water. Cathy's closeness had caused a tightness in his chest that only booze could temporarily relax. "Something to drink, sweetheart?"

"God, Dash, it's only eleven in the morning! When did you take to tippling before lunch?"

Since you left me, he wanted to say, but grinned and shrugged instead. "Gotta get the old heart going, you know. Sometimes it needs a jumper cable called Scotch." She wrinkled her pert nose and gave him that saucy little grin that he loved so much.

## The Love Game

It was with great difficulty that he managed to keep his voice normal, keep the love from his eyes. "So, about the new season. I've got a pile of scripts a mile high to go through." (He had always prided himself on reading every new script for every new project.) "How would you like to sit in, so to speak, and help me with the fall schedule?" He kept his face bland, but his pale blue eyes were shrewd as he watched her.

"Are you serious? You mean be in on the early stages of program development?"

"Why not? You've always had a gut instinct about what's good and bad. Your show's hiatus is coming up—can't let you wander about with nothing to do. You might get into trouble." He waited for her to tell him that she had planned to go to Cambodia with Marc, but she said nothing, merely stared at him. "You said you wanted to be a television producer when you grew up—this is your chance, kid!"

"You mean I'd really have a voice in what got on the air?" She still didn't believe him, was still wary of studio brass bearing gifts.

"Sure—the pilots, anyway. Then it's up to the public."

"Not necessarily," Cathy said. "With the right promotion and lead-in, we can almost guarantee a hit. We've got about a 20.9 rating on series programming now with seven solid hits and four old sitcoms that people tune in to out of habit. We carry three made-for-TV movies a week and two theater releases—which are usually good for grabbing the ratings. Now if we had some ballsy, dynamite specials to round out the schedule, we just might catch up with ABC and CBS. We're already ahead of NBC in many areas, even with Silverman at the helm, but I've heard he's planning a really big line-up for the fall, buying options right and left. Hell, half the actors in Hollywood think they're starring in an NBC series next year."

As well as Dash knew her, he was still amazed at how much she knew about the television business. His instinct had been right. With Cathy by his side, they'd own TV Land. "They probably are, but they'll be canceled before the thirteen weeks are up. That's why most studios buy so damn many pilots, so they'll have something to stick on the air mid-season when the flops start coming in. The answer, of course, is to buy only the best pilots, promote the hell out of them and, like you said, make sure they have a good lead-in that will ensure us an audience. Most people are too damn lazy to get up every half hour to change the channel. They want to sit on their asses with a beer and a bowl of popcorn and watch the same network all night."

"Then we don't mess around with the solid hits we already have. No changing the time slot or day of the week where people are used to seeing their favorite shows." Cathy went to the bar and poured herself a cup of coffee, then perched on a bar stool, swinging her leg thoughtfully. "We have to build next season's hits on the solid program base that we already have."

"Providing we do have hits," Dash grunted. "And we'll need *Big* hits to break into first place and stay there. Another "Dallas" or "Little House on the Prairie" would lock us in good." He grinned to himself, his heartbeat quickening that his plan had obviously worked. He had been devastated when Cathy had left him for Marc Monroe and had plotted ways to get her back. He couldn't compete physically with Marc for Cathy's love for obvious reasons, but he had something the younger man did not have and something that Cathy wanted very badly. He had a television network and the power to give her any job she wanted. He pressed his advantage. "Maybe a ninety-minute variety show . . ."

"No," Cathy interrupted. "That's old hat. There hasn't been a successful variety show since Dean Martin got too rich to do television. Singing and dancing only works in Las Vegas, it seems, except for an occasional Frank Sinatra or Liza Minnelli special—and it only works then because they're Las Vegas stars the television audience doesn't get a chance to see very often. No, I'd say go with more first-run movies."

Goddamn, his little Cathy was bright! He beamed at her like a proud father but kept his voice almost bland. "I guess you're right." He faked a sigh. "Christ, I've been around so long I don't even know what sells anymore."

She saw through him and laughed. "That'll be the day! KNAB is successful because you *are* KNAB—and you know it." She sipped her coffee, frowning slightly. "But it could use a small facelift, just a teensy one. Like anything else, it needs a little new blood now and again to keep it fresh."

"Now do you see why I need you to help me select next season's shows?" Dash asked. "You're young enough to know what today's viewers want to see—and smart enough to pick a hit show."

"This is true," she said flippantly. "Well, boss, when do we start?"

He wanted to jump up and dance an Irish jig, throw his arms about her and kiss that sweet little mouth. He'd done it, by God. He'd won. He'd beat Marc Monroe. Almost lazily he said, "Maybe you'd better give it a little more thought. It's a hell of a tough job, sweetheart, with hardly any time to call your own."

"Oh no you don't mister, you're not backing out on me!" She advanced toward him, hands on hips, eyes sparkling with laughter. She put both hands on his shoulders pinning him back in his chair.

"I'm not backing out, little Cathy, but I'm a fair man. I just want you to know what you're getting into. Long, grueling hours poring over scripts, most of them pieces of shit, dealing with neurotic writers and temperamental stars. . . ." He kept his expression innocent but could not control the twitching smile that tugged at his lips.

"You rotten prick," she laughed, bending to kiss him on the forehead. "You just love to torment me, don't you?"

"Cathy, you wound me deeply when you talk like that! I'm merely pointing out certain facts about the job that you may not have thought about . . ."

"Stow it, Sunderling. You don't fool me. We're too much alike, remember? You said so yourself. And you know I'd kill for a chance like this—so, I'll ask you again. When do we start?"

"As soon as your show goes on hiatus. That soon enough for you?" He waited for her to mention Marc and the trip to Cambodia, but she said nothing, only grinned from ear to ear and stooped to kiss him again, this time on the mouth. Jesus, couldn't she see what she did to him?

Later that night, lying beside Marc's sleeping form, she wondered why she hadn't told him about Dash's exciting offer. There's plenty of time, she thought. He isn't even sure when he's leaving for Cambodia. Maybe their schedules would work out so she could accompany him for at least part of the trip. They could be married quietly somewhere, spend a few days together and then, when the actual filming began, she could hurry home and get to work on the fall schedule. She still had two weeks of filming to do on her show, and she knew that Marc had an assignment to interview some professor of anthropology on Indonesia's orangutans for *National Geographic*. So they would both be busy for the next couple of weeks.

She told herself that Marc would be thrilled for her— but a tiny voice deep inside wasn't so sure. There was still a certain amount of jealousy where Dash was concerned even though they had all been so politely civilized about it. She had told Marc about Dash's promise to talk to Earl Brill about the special, and Marc had seemed pleased, saying again that he was a whore and would go where the money was. She did not mention a possible contract for six specials a year, wanting to wait and see how it would fit into the fall schedule. *Her* fall schedule.

She hugged herself under the blankets, too thrilled to sleep, her mind churning with possible new shows, dramas and sitcoms, news magazine programs and game shows. She couldn't wait to get into the fray of network executives, to fight it out toe to toe. She saw herself brilliantly wheeling and dealing, beating older and more experienced network brass at their own game. And if one of them dared to pat her on the ass and tell her not to worry her pretty little head about business, she'd kick him right where it hurt the most—in the Nielsen ratings!

She could barely concentrate on doing her show so anxious was she to get her hands on a stack of scripts. She buzzed Dash's office a dozen times a day, asking if anything good had come in yet, suggesting this or that idea for a special, begging to be reassured that she was actually going to have a say in the fall line-up.

She was so happy even Marc commented on it and she told him it was because she had everything she had ever wanted in life—him. He had accepted this modestly but not without a certain thrill of pride, and she had had a moment's guilt at not telling him about Dash. She told herself she wanted to wait until she was actually working with Dash, and then she would surprise Marc with the news that KNAB wanted to sign him for six specials a year. He had confessed to her that he had always wanted to do such a show, and she wanted more than anything to be the one to give it to him.

She would be twenty-seven years old the day her hiatus began, and Pamela had planned a small birthday dinner for her, inviting Ken and Maggie, and the ever present, ever adoring Ashley Carrington.

Cathy had finally gotten used to seeing Pamela with her young lover and had come to like Ash very much. He seemed much older than his seventeen years and totally devoted to his sophisticated mistress. Cathy had learned that he was the son of Hedy Carrington, a once famous screen siren of the thirties, and had traveled all over the world during his formative years. He was polished in all the social graces, quietly confident, deeply intelligent. He had experienced more than most men twice his age and seemed to Cathy a wise old soul trapped in a boy's freshly magnificent body. She had thought it was merely sex that drew Pamela to young Ashley, but after spending a few evenings with them, she saw that they were deeply in love with one another.

Hedy Carrington, aging and alcoholic, fighting valiantly for a career that no longer existed, had placed Ashley in the Gray Eagle Academy while she sought a comeback on the Broadway stage. His father had died of a heart attack a year ago, and Hedy had thought her "little boy too young" to stay alone in the Beverly Hills family mansion while she toiled in New York. Pamela had hooted with glee when she had related this last bit of information to Cathy. "Wouldn't she have a royal fit if she knew where her 'little boy' spends most of his nights?" she had chuckled. She had met Hedy Carrington on a couple of occasions and had announced her an unadulterated bitch and ballbuster. "She would devour Ash if she could," Pamela had said. "Eat him whole— but I'm not going to let that happen. He belongs to me now."

\* \* \*

## The Love Game

"This is the best birthday I've ever had," Cathy sighed, leaning against Marc's shoulder. She took a sip of her champagne, Louis Roederer, of course, and grinned across at Pamela. "Thanks so much, Lady Pamela."

"My pleasure, luv." Pamela toasted her with her own glass of bubbly.

Cathy glanced fondly about the room, basking in the warm friendship. Pamela and Ashley snuggled together on the striped satin loveseat in front of the fireplace and Maggie, Ken, Marc and Cathy shared the long crushed velvet sofa. Soft music made for a romantic background mood and the dancing flames in the fireplace cast hypnotic shadows swaying up the walls.

Cathy felt full to bursting and thought, "Now I know what it means—my cup runneth over." She had everything. Her own show, a chance to help develop next season's line-up, loving friends and family and her own, fantastic man. Her birthday wish, when she had blown out the candles earlier, had been that everything could stay just as beautiful as it was at this moment. She leaned her head against Marc's shoulder, sipping her champagne, listening to the conversation around her, relaxed and drowsy. It would be a rare treat to sleep-in tomorrow morning instead of busting her butt to get to the studio at five A.M.

She was looking forward to this hiatus, planning a million things she had to do before next fall's shooting started. Of course the trip to Cambodia with Marc came first, then she would return to help Dash and get her own show blocked out. She had several good ideas she wanted to try out, more serious themes than she had done last season. An idea had begun to form in her mind about asking Dash to move her talk show to prime time; an evening news magazine and guest talk show could work very well. Maybe she and Marc could co-host such a show, he covering the news, she, the entertainment. Her attention was drawn back to the conversation when she heard Maggie ask when they were leaving for Cambodia.

"Sometime this week," Marc said. "I'll know for sure tomorrow." He turned to smile at Cathy. "Oh, I forgot to tell you, babe—I made an appointment with my doctor for the shots we'll need. We have to take our passports. Is yours up to date?"

"Oh, gosh, I never thought of that," Cathy said. "I don't even have a passport."

"No problem. I'll take you down town tomorrow morning and get everything rolling. Shouldn't take more than three or four days." He grinned at the others. "Unless, of course, you're wanted for murder or some other unspeakable crime."

"The only crime I'm guilty of is being too happy," Cathy laughed, snuggling closer to him.

"The courts should be filled with more criminals like you," Ashley said.

"Hear, hear, luv," Pamela murmured. "Will you be flying directly to Cambodia, then, or will you stop somewhere along the way for a bit of sightseeing?"

"I'd love to visit Hong Kong," Cathy said. She squeezed Marc's leg and looked adoringly up into his face. "What do you think, darling? Hong Kong would be a fabulous place to start our honeymoon."

"Honeymoon?" Maggie cried. "Oh, Cathy, that's wonderful!" She leaned over to hug her sister a moment, then clasped Marc's hand.

"Hey, that's super," Ashley said. "Congratulations—both of you." He raised his glass in a salute.

"It's about time he made me an honest woman, don't you think?" Cathy beamed with pleasure, hugging Marc's arm as she smiled at her friends.

"This definitely calls for another bottle of champagne," Pamela said, and Ashley hurried to the kitchen to fetch it.

## The Love Game

"Well, it's about time," Ken sighed in mock relief. "I thought you were destined for spinsterhood for sure!" He shook hands with Marc. "Does this mean we're brothers?"

"I'm not sure what it means," Marc said slowly. He stared at Cathy's flushed face, the pure delight in her eyes. God, she was beautiful and he loved her and loved being with her—but where in hell did she get the idea that they were going to be married? It would be a pretty neat trick as he was still very much married to Bitsy!

"A toast," Pamela said, pouring champagne all around. "To Cathy and Marc—may you have a long and happy life together."

Marc grinned foolishly as everyone drank watching him over their glasses, smiling at him. He knew he should say something but what? He sipped his champagne, stalling, and heard Cathy thanking everyone, laughing happily. What a mess! He couldn't very well say anything now. She would be humiliated. How could this have happened? Surely Cathy couldn't have simply *forgotten* that he already had a wife. That was something a woman would *never* forget.

He heard Pamela and Maggie asking what sort of clothes Cathy would be taking, did she plan on getting in some shopping, et cetera, and he was suddenly angry. Forget Bitsy for the moment (as Cathy apparently had), but where had Cathy gotten the idea that he wanted to marry her in the first place? He had never proposed— not that he hadn't thought about it. He was in love with Cathy. It was a feeling he had never had before with a woman, a feeling of finally finding that elusive *something* that had been missing from past affairs. It seemed now that he had always been waiting for love to catch up with him but had been traveling too fast for it to happen. He had thought himself incapable of really falling in love, and when it had happened, it had scared him to death. Shaken him to his shoes. A cautious man, he wanted to feel his way instead of plunging heedlessly into some unknown emotion. He was angry with Cathy for presuming so much. He tossed off the rest of his wine and put a smile on his face.

"Well, thanks all of you. And thanks for the great dinner, Pam, but we have to be going." He stood, pulling Cathy up with him. "I'm expecting a conference call from New York tomorrow morning at nine, their time, which means it'll be six here."

"Oh, darling, can't we stay just a little longer?" Cathy asked, and Pamela urged, "Have another glass of wine, ducks." But Marc shook his head and led Cathy firmly toward the door, apologizing, "I'm sorry. Thanks anyway, but we really have to go. It's past one and by the time we get to Hollywood it'll be two, and I really do have to be reasonably alert tomorrow morning." Everyone followed them to the door, leaning out to call goodnights and congratulations, and Marc gritted his teeth as he slid behind the wheel of his sleek black Masserati.

"What's the matter, darling? Don't you feel well?" Cathy slid next to him gripping his thigh possessively, snuggling herself close. She giggled and moved her hand up to his crotch. "Or were you just in a hurry to get home? God, the way you jerked me out of there—I wonder if Pamela was offended?" She was slightly drunk and too happy to see the dark expression on Marc's face. She caressed him through his tight jeans, but he remained still and unresponsive, staring straight ahead as he drove. "What's the matter, Marc? Are you angry about something?"

"Oh, it's just a small thing, really," he answered sarcastically without glancing at her. "I realize it's petty of me, but when I want to get married I would like to do the asking."

## The Love Game     143

Cathy felt as if she had been slapped hard across the face. She reeled back against the seat, staring at him, stunned.

"As a matter of fact, you didn't even *ask* me," he continued in the same hard voice. "Nor did you bother to give a thought to the fact that I already have a wife."

"Oh, Marc, I—I just thought—" Cathy stammered in embarrassment and humiliation as the cruel words sank into her numb brain. My God, it was true! She had forgotten completely about Bitsy Bushore. How could she have been so stupid? "Oh, God, I'm so sorry, Marc. I feel like such a damn fool—but I just—just assumed . . ."

"You assumed too much." He slammed on the brakes at a red light and angrily lit a cigarette. "Jesus, announcing to everyone that we're getting married—I don't believe it!" He stomped on the gas pedal and the car leapt forward, throwing Cathy hard against the seat.

"I—I don't know what I was thinking," Cathy said weakly. Her hands turned icy and she clasped them together in her lap. "I was so—so happy—thinking about the trip and I know we can't travel together unless we're married, so—so—I just assumed that we'd get married, you know . . ." She glanced up at him, her face flushed with shame, her eyes pleading with him to understand, to still love her and want her.

"Come on, Cathy, you're not that damn naive."

"But, I mean, in a foreign country—different passports and well, we're both pretty well known—and the press will be there . . ." She trailed off helplessly, looking intently up at him, but he refused to meet her eyes. "Marc," she wailed, "don't you want to marry me?"

"You seem to think so." He gripped the steering wheel so hard his knuckles turned white, and for the first time he looked at her. The silver-gray eyes were black and hard, his voice icy with supressed rage. "Speaking of the press, did it ever occur to you that my wife is capable of reading a newspaper? What if Pamela or someone else says something about your—" He chuckled nastily. "—premature announcement? Christ, I'd get buried in divorce court!" He turned back to the road and she saw a muscle jerking angrily in his jaw.

"Oh, Marc, I'm so sorry—I didn't think."

"Didn't think?" he blazed. "Jesus Christ, Cathy, you've lived in this town long enough to know what the wrong kind of publicity can do to a person. Can you even imagine what Bitsy would do if she read about my 'engagement' in the papers?"

"But she knows about us! God, we've practically been living together for months!"

"She knows nothing. Only that I'm away from home a lot." His laugh was mirthless and sent cold chills down Cathy's spine. "On assignments."

"You bastard," Cathy whispered. She stared at him for a long moment then moved to the other side of the car as far away from him as she could. "All this time—I've just been 'an assignment'—another conquest for the hotshot reporter."

Weary, but still angry, he snapped, "Oh, Cathy, it wasn't like that and you know it!"

"Wasn't it? How many other 'assignments' have you lived with since your happy marriage to Bitsy? Did you tell them that your marriage was over—that you wife didn't understand you and you had an 'arrangement,' an open marriage?" She choked back tears, determined not to let him see how he had hurt her.

Marc made a sound of disgust. "Really, Cathy, you sound like a heroine from some Victorian novel. Surely you didn't think I had come to you pure—unsullied by female flesh?" Again the mirthless, cold laugh. "Good God, I can't believe this conversation!"

"Then it's true—you have lived with other women."

She felt suddenly empty, betrayed, and she was colder than she had ever been.

"Not like you mean," Marc said shortly. "There was never anyone like you. I mean, the others weren't this serious."

"I see." She took a deep, shuddering breath and let her head fall back against the smooth leather upholstery. "Bitsy must certainly be inattentive. I think I'd notice if my husband were missing for weeks at a time."

"Don't be cute, Cathy. You know about my relationship with Bitsy. We go our separate ways. She enjoys being the wife of a foreign correspondent; it sounds classy and amuses her jet-set friends. It also leaves her free to lunch at the various studios with her old flames, attend theater openings or premieres with people of a like mind, give little dinner parties. She doesn't embarrass me and I don't embarrass her. We both have entirely different sets of friends and we don't get in each other's way."

"How wonderfully sophisticated and civilized—how very Noel Coward!" She felt cheap and used, just another easy statistic in a long line of conquests by the dashing Marc Monroe. She had been right about him after all. But the knowledge did not make it any less painful. She had been a fool to fall in love with him. She had warned herself against him from the very first, had known it would end this way. But she had believed him—just as she was sure countless other women had. The bastard! The charming, rotten prick! She had been so wrapped up in her love for him that she had let her guard down, let her heart rule her head.

It had seemed so perfect, so wondrous, that it had to be right. They were meant to be together. She had been so busy spinning pretty pictures in her mind about life with Marc, she had forgotten all she knew about him. She had turned her back on her wary instincts, put Bitsy

Bushore out of her mind—and had left herself wide open to getting hurt. Damn him for his expertise with gullible females! She felt like a prize jerk and flushed with shame from her forehead down.

"Right," he said tightly. "So glad you understand." He sped onto the freeway and floorboarded it, wanting to drive the anger out, face the fear of flying down the highway at a hundred miles an hour. He knew his fast driving frightened Cathy, and he drew his lips back in a sneer of a smile. She was such a ballsy chick, let's see how long she could take it without coming unglued. Yeah, that was her all right—tough, shrewd, cocky, wanting to run the whole show. Wanting to show men up and run the whole damn network. Hell, she'd even suckered him into committing himself to KNAB for the Cambodia special when he knew damn well it'd get better coverage on CBS or ABC. And come to think of it, whose idea was it for her to go with him? He didn't recall ever having asked her; she and everyone else had just *assumed* she would go. Just as she had *assumed* they would get married. Conniving little schemer. And he had been so sure that she loved him, really loved him—with or without a silly piece of paper. They were all alike, a coven of ballbusters, voracious, wanting it all. First the marriage license, then the house, Cadillac, maid and charge cards.

"Oh, I understand, all right." Cathy's voice was as tight and cold as Marc's. She crossed her arms over her breasts, hugging herself to keep from trembling. She was icy cold and filled with hate. God damn him to hell for doing this to her! She knew she sounded like a shrew, a jealous fishwife, but she couldn't stop the ugly words. "You and Bitsy are 'roommates'—isn't that what you told me when we first met? Just friends sharing the same house but living separate lives. Tell me, Marc, do you and your *friend* compare notes when your and her various affairs are over? Do you have a good laugh over the little idiosyncrasies of your lovers? What are you anyway, a couple of degenerates? Do you get a kick out of telling each other dirty stories about your sex lives? God, Marc!"

"Stop it, Cathy, you're becoming hysterical." He glanced at her nervously and slowed down a little. He had never seen her this way, and it shocked him. She looked so ugly!

"Or maybe you both find that extramarital affairs keep your marriage fresh and alive," Cathy continued. "Isn't that what all the sex therapists are always spouting on talk shows?" She gave a shrill, ugly laugh. "Marriage in trouble? Go out and get laid, that'll fix things right up! And share your sexual experience with your spouse, that'll keep the old marriage from getting dull!"

"You're being a complete ass, you know." Marc kept his voice even, almost expressionless. He wouldn't give her the satisfaction of fighting back. It was ludicrous. Jesus, where did women come up with such outrageous fantasies? "I explained, in depth, my relationship with Bitsy when we first met. We are merely sharing a house and a marriage in name only. We are good friends and genuinely care about one another, but our personal lives are separate." He spoke slowly, distinctly, as if to a child. "She doesn't give a damn whom I sleep with nor do I care what she does. It's a marriage of convenience only."

"I understand why it's convenient for Bitsy, but what's in it for you, Marc?" He didn't answer and she glared at his perfect profile, saw the muscle jerking in his jaw, the hard grip of his hands on the steering wheel, and she wanted to scream that he had killed her, driven a sword of deceit through her heart. She had given him her most precious gift, her love, and he hadn't seen its value. "What do you get out of this arrangement, Marc? Tell me." She watched the muscle knotting beneath his smooth skin, the lips tight and grim, but still he did not speak. "Oh, come on, darling, surely it can't be all that bad. You must have had *some* reason for staying married all these years."

His voice was icy. "As a matter of fact, I did. It has been a wonderful deterrent for any marriage-minded female who pressed for a commitment the minute the affair started getting comfortable!"

"I see." Her tone matched his, but beneath the icy calm, she shook with emotion and her heart hammered painfully against her ribs. No, she wanted to cry, don't let's do this to one another! We had something so wonderful, so special, let's not throw it away! She wanted to hold him close, beg his forgiveness, promise always to love him. But the hateful jealousy filled her with rage and spite and she sneered, "You fucking macho men make me sick! You all run around talking a good game of equality but it's still the old double standard, isn't it? Married men can fuck around all they like—tell some poor girl he's crazy about her just to get into her bed, then when she wants something closer, he cries that he's already married and runs home to Mommy! I pity your wife—you're too damn insecure to have a meaningful relationship with a real woman! You want some empty-headed little twit who will tell you what a big, wonderful man you are, spread her legs dutifully, and never, *ever* ask any question that's too tough for you to handle!"

"I want a woman who's not afraid of being a female, if that's what you mean!" He turned on her, eyes blazing. "What the hell's wrong with that? Who wants some hard-nosed broad who is hell bent on competing with him, jockeying for top position, calling the shots? I'm so sick of the damn so-called 'career' women who are out to castrate every man they meet, that it's exciting as hell to be with a really feminine woman. And, yes, I'll use

## The Love Game

the old cliché—it makes me feel strong and protective and loving toward her!"

"But not loving enough to make a commitment to her," she shot back.

"That depends on the woman." He slowed for the Hollywood offramp and reached for a cigarette, punching in the car lighter with his clenched fist. "I made a commitment to you, and it doesn't seem to have done a hell of a lot of good." He sped down the dark street he knew so well, remembering the many times he had driven it, anxious to get to Cathy's apartment, impatient with love. Damn it, why had she spoiled it?

"Some commitment," she sneered, hating him. "You'll live with me more or less permanently until you get tired of me. Well, no thanks, Charlie, I deserve better than that. If you really loved me as much as I love you, you'd want to marry me. You wouldn't be able to live apart from me—and you sure as hell wouldn't be able to stay married to Bitsy!"

"I do love you, Cathy! And I am with you all the time. What more do you want, for God's sake?" He was suddenly very weary. The fighting, the bitter, hateful words were all too familiar. How could something, once so beautiful, turn so ugly and painful?

"I want marriage," she heard herself saying and wanted to bite back the words. But she had gone too far. She had to know the answer now if it killed her.

"Jesus Christ," he exploded. "What is it about women that a fucking piece of paper signed by some obscure justice of the peace is so all powerful, so vitally important—so necessary for their happiness? I don't understand it, I swear I don't!"

"It's not just the paper, you jerk!" Cathy screamed and wanted to smash her fists in his face for being so thick-headed. "It's the commitment! The proof of your love!"

"If you have to go around proving your love it can't be built on a very strong foundation. Whatever happened to trust?"

"Marriage is trust, you idiot! When you offer someone marriage, you're asking them to trust their life to you, their happiness."

"Trusting your life to someone is putting a pretty heavy responsibility on him, don't you think? And depending on another person for your happiness is just plain stupid!" He squealed to a halt at the curb in front of Cathy's apartment and reached for another cigarette.

"Then I guess I'm pretty damn stupid." She sat glaring at him, hating him, but hating herself more for ever having become involved with him. She jerked open the car door and jumped out, then slammed the door and ran up the walk before he could say anything else. She heard the loud squeal of his tires and the grinding of gears as he sped away, out of her life. She couldn't help herself and turned and stared at the small red dots of his taillights until they disappeared from sight. Tears filled her eyes, and she fumbled for the lock, missing it and cursing herself, cursing Marc. "Damn him," she cried aloud. "Damn him to hell! I hate him!" She found the keyhole and stumbled inside, crying hard, her stomach in painful knots. Falling face down on the sofa, she clung to a cushion and wept as if her heart would break.

## Chapter Ten

Numerous white-coated waiters, balancing trays, weaved their way efficiently between the many tables that dotted the floor of KNAB's commissary. The vast dining room had been transformed into a softly lit banquet room filled laughter and music. A live band performed at one end of the long room and there was an area cleared for dancing. What had been the sandwich counter yesterday was now a properly stocked and staffed bar with five young bartenders to take care of the customers.

Cathy sat at the head table in the center of the room facing the dancefloor and next to her Dash Sunderling, looking more fit that he had in months. Also seated around the table were other luminaries of KNAB. There was Arthur Berg and his wife Gay, a very successful writing team for afternoon soaps; Solly and Bea Hauser, he being one of the top programmers; Beth Hoffman, producer and creator of the new hit sitcom "The Love Game" and her escort, Monte.

Cathy frowned a little when she looked across at Beth speaking animatedly with Monte. She had been dead set against doing "The Love Game" when Dash had shown her the pilot. Not because of the show—it was surprisingly good and very witty—but because of the star they had chosen to play the lead: Bitsy Bushore.

Cathy had wanted nothing to remind her of Marc, and just thinking of the possibility of having to face Bitsy each day at the studio gave her a migraine headache. But Dash (as well as Beth Hoffman) had persisted and Bitsy had been signed.

Cathy had hoped that the series would fail and be canceled during that first crucial thirteen weeks, but to her chagrin "The Love Game" had been the earliest and biggest hit of the new season and Bitsy Bushore had been mostly responsible. She had tirelessly made the talk-show circuit, hitting even the smallest burgs to plug her new show and flirt and dimple and tease and otherwise enthrall her mostly male interviewers. Film clips shown on the numerous talk shows caught the interest of the viewing public and they couldn't wait to see the debut of "The Love Game." Critics were kind to Bitsy (They had always loved her little-girl openness and she was a damn good interview.), and before the month was out, "The Love Game" was the most talked about new show of the season.

Cathy found little solace in the fact that her own show was also a hit. Moved to prime time in the ten o'clock Friday spot, it followed "The Love Game" and capped the evening for KNAB. A cop show and another sitcom preceded Bitsy's show, both with solid ratings, and the eleven o'clock news was second behind CBS and ABC. The rest of the week looked good as well, and Cathy took a certain pride in having had a hand in the programming.

She raised her eyes to glance idly at the dancers and saw Lon Howland moving suggestively just a few feet from her. She couldn't tell which wildly gyrating young woman was his partner in the moving mass of dancers, but it seemed as if Lon were dancing just for her alone. His skintight black tuxedo trousers shimmered like a sexy, black snake in the muted lights as he bumped and writhed to the erotic beat. He was starring in a Western series called "Tumbleweed" that she had personally picked, just as she had personally picked him over five hundred other hopefuls. He had the sassy sex appeal of a Burt Reynolds. The show, as she had known it would be, was a solid hit and Lon Howland was understandably grateful to Cathy. He had thanked her profusely at the start of the series, still awed at his Big Break, and had, she imagined, fallen a little in love with his beautiful blond benefactress. He had sent roses and perfume and had deluged her with telephone calls asking her to dinner, anywhere, just to be with her. She had refused his offers, not because she wasn't attracted to him, but because she was once again Dash Sunderling's lady, and this time no pretty boy was going to take her for a ride.

With "Tumbleweed" a hit and Lon an instant superstar as only television can manufacture them, he changed toward Cathy, became almost belligerent. He flaunted his numerous "groupies" on the set when he knew Cathy would be there; he managed chance meetings where he would force her to stop and chat a moment, all the while stripping her with his hot, dark eyes. And now tonight, thrusting his crotch at her while he danced, those brooding eyes resting on her near-naked breasts.

She deliberately turned her back on him and tugged at the décolletage of her ice-blue gown. By Monte, of course. He had been "dressing" her for the past few months, and she knew she had never looked lovelier. She was no longer a scatterbrained young talk show co-host too busy pursuing her career to give a thought to her appearance. She was now holding her own in prime-time television with the likes of Barbara Walters, Geraldo Riviera, Rona Barrett and Phil Donahue and had to dress the part. Her show was a combination of show business, big business and monkey business, Dash liked to say with a fond, proud chuckle.

Cathy glanced at him as he spoke with Arthur and Gay Berg, and her eyes softened with love. She wondered, for the hundredth time, what she would have done without him these last six months. When Marc had gone to Cambodia without her, she had been stunned, disbelieving that she obviously meant so little to him. Her ego, as well as her heart, had been badly bruised. She had cried and pouted and fully expected him to call her at the last minute and ask her to meet him. When he did not, the hurt and bewilderment turned to icy fury. She had not thought it possible to hate someone as much as she now hated Marc Monroe.

She had wept on Dash's shoulder one moment, stalked his office and raged against Marc the next—and through it all Dash had remained patient, loving and understanding. He had kept her so busy at the studio that she seldom had an evening to herself to think, so weary was she when she fell into bed at night. He fed her mind and kept her body on the move, knowing that time would heal her heart. And it had, for one night she had asked him to stay with her, and it had been almost as if he had never been away. Almost. His lovemaking no longer thrilled her as it once had, as Marc's *always* had, but it was warm and comfortable and safe.

Now that Dash was a widower it was no longer necessary to sneak around, and Cathy found that she loved the attention she got as Dash's lady: the limousines; the head waiters who remembered her name and her favorite wine or dish; the guards at the studio who deferentially waved her through the big arched gates; the writers, directors and producers who knew that their boss was totally besotted with her. It was well known around KNAB that anyone saying a word against Cathy Curtis would be looking for another job—and anyone foolish enough to make a pass at her would be looking for another head!

Cathy loved it. It gave her an acute streak of pleasure that everyone knew that a man as rich and powerful as Dash wanted her—and it eased the hurt a little when she thought that Marc had not wanted her. Oh, he had wanted her all right, but not the way Dash did—forever. Marc had merely wanted her to be there for him with no ties. Dash had asked often for her to marry him, and she had gently put him off, using the mourning period after Grace's death as an excuse when, in truth, she was afraid to make that final commitment. So afraid that Marc would return and ask her to come to him and she would go.

Marc had returned a little over a month ago with the footage from his Cambodia assignment and had conferred with Dash behind closed doors for the better part of one afternoon, and Cathy had caught only a glimpse of him as he was leaving. But that one tiny glimpse had been enough to set her heart pounding and her stomach fluttering. She had pleaded her period that night when Dash wanted to stay over and had waited by the telephone until almost two in the morning, but Marc did not call. She sneaked a look at Clare's calendar listing Dash's appointments and saw that Marc was meeting with him the following Monday. She had dressed with care that day and found some reason to be in the vicinity of Dash's office when Marc arrived, but he had merely greeted her briefly and had gone into the office, closing the door firmly behind him.

The next meeting was scheduled for Wednesday, and again Cathy found herself waiting in the hall by Dash's office, but Marc did not show up at all. She learned later from Clare that Marc had called and asked that Dash meet him at The Bistro rather than his office. So, Cathy thought, both angry and hurt, he doesn't want to see me at all. She felt humiliated and wanted to hurt him as much as he had hurt her, wanted to wipe that cool smile off his handsome face.

She had approached Dash about the Cambodia special, pretending an interest in the air time KNAB had allotted as well as the date, but he had seen through her and laughed kindly. "I think I'll handle this one alone, little Cathy," he had said. "Love and business don't exactly mix." Then he had laughed again and pulled her close to his side where they lay in bed together. "Neither does hate," he had added.

Cathy had come close to hating Dash that night for seeing through her. She had intended to sabotage Marc's show if she could by putting it up against the other networks' toughest competition. She would love to see him on his ass wondering what in the hell had happened.

She was convinced now that those beautiful, brief months they had spent together had all been a sham as she had first suspected. He hadn't written her once from Cambodia but had written to Bitsy several times, letters that Bitsy delighted in reading aloud to Cathy whenever she saw her. Was the woman really that stupid, Cathy thought, or that devious? She had tried to remain aloof with Bitsy but the bubbly blond was impossible to insult. She always rushed over to chatter excitedly to Cathy whenever they were in the same room, inviting her to dinner or any number of places and smiling brightly when Cathy coolly refused, saying "perhaps another time." And Cathy would grit her teeth and wish to God she had never heard of Bitsy Bushore—or her insufferable husband!

Another thorn in Cathy's already aching side was the fact that Bitsy was very well liked at KNAB so Cathy had to maintain a certain friendliness. Professionalism, Dash had called it. "You can't let private emotions interfere with a successful show," he had said and "The Love

# The Love Game

Game" was clearly the most successful show KNAB had had in years.

Cathy preferred to give Beth Hoffman all the credit for "The Love Game," after all, it had been her creation and she was a well-established producer at KNAB. Before "The Love Game" Beth had produced two soap operas and one evening drama, an hour-long cop show that had held its own these past three years. Now she had another solid hit under her belt, and Cathy was glad for her.

Beth always seemed to reflect some secret, inner sadness. Her big brown eyes always seemed somehow tormented until they settled on Cathy's face, then they would light up with shy friendliness. She wasn't aloof but she held herself apart from most groups, going about her work with professionalism and keeping her private life very much to herself. There were whispers that she was a lesbian as she had never been seen out in public with a man, and Cathy stared at her now wondering if it were true.

Beth was a striking woman in her forties. She wore her sable hair in a long pageboy that would have looked old-fashioned on anyone else but seemed perfectly right and classic with her high cheekbones and wide, soft mouth. Tall, slender, flat-chested and slim-hipped, she moved with the easy grace of one born to money. She was always flawlessly made up and coiffed, elegantly dressed in the slinky fashions of the thirties and forties that seemed made to order for her figure. Monte had been her designer for years, but her fashion statement was clearly hers alone.

Beth raised her eyes and smiled as she felt Cathy's gaze.

"Welcome back," she said in her husky voice. "You've been staring into space for the past hour."

"Counting her rating points, no doubt," Monte laughed,

giving her a wink. He had been drinking freely of the champagne chilling in ice buckets around the table and was more animated than Cathy had ever seen him. She supposed he was celebrating his success as being chosen the designer for "The Love Game" and she felt a twinge of jealousy. Everyone, it seemed, was benefiting in some way from that stupid show—everyone but her.

"Actually, I wasn't even thinking about television," Cathy lied. She extended her champagne glass to Monte, and he refilled it and then his own. "I was wondering who our other dinnermates are," she said quickly. "Those two chairs have been empty all evening." She indicated the places directly across from her and next to Beth and Monte.

"They're for Bitsy and Marc," Beth said, glancing down at her watch. She, too, had been wondering what had happened to their tablemates. They were over an hour late and dinner would soon be served.

"They're probably fucking each other's brains out even as we speak," Monte drawled. "Marc just returned from New York this afternoon, and you know how Bitsy is when she hasn't had a man for awhile!" He glanced meaningfully at Beth but Cathy didn't notice. Her face seemed frozen in a silly half smile and her hand curled around the stem of the champagne glass grew numb.

"Bitsy and Marc are coming here?" she asked stupidly.

"Of course. How could we have a party for the success of the new season without the biggest success of the new season being present?" Monte lifted his glass in a salute then downed the contents and reached again for the bottle. He was becoming quite drunk, his movements and speech more effeminate. "Two successes," he slurred, then giggled. "A two-Emmy family, right, Cathy? You heard that Marc's Cambodia special has been nominated, haven't you? And Bitsy's a sure winner—God, I haven't seen a show take off like that since 'Mork and Mindy.'"

"Bitsy still has it," Beth said. "Whatever 'it' is that sets some actresses apart, makes them so special. The show is a success because of her—because of the special quality she brings to her character. She deserves an Emmy."

Cathy finally raised her glass to her lips and swallowed until it was empty. *She* felt empty. Numb. Marc coming here? My God, he would be seated directly across from her! How could she cope? She was furious with Dash for not telling her, then immediately chastised herself for being so dumb. Of course Bitsy would be very much present at the biggest party of the year honoring KNAB's finest. She had worked on putting Bitsy out of her mind completely and had managed to forget her for entire weeks—now here she was again turning up like the proverbial bad penny. And with Marc. It had not occurred to her that he would attend such an affair—fearless war correspondent and serious news reporter that he was.

Cathy reached for the champagne bottle nearest her and refilled her glass, aware of the conversation around her but not hearing anything that was said. Marc would soon be here. A sharp pain clutched her stomach and tears sprang to her eyes. She ducked her head and blinked them away. Lies, she thought, it was all lies. He was very much married to Bitsy, and everyone seemed to know it but her. There had been no "understanding," no "marriage of convenience" as Marc had told her. She wanted to lower her head to the table and weep with disappointment.

During all the months that Marc had been gone, she had clung to a tiny scrap of hope, had subconsciously believed him, believed that it would all work out and that they would somehow be together again. That's why she hadn't married Dash even though her practical mind had known she should; because she had wanted so desperately for Marc, unable to live without her, to return and sweep her off her feet. Apparently he was living very well without her. "Fucking each other's brains out," Monte had said, and Cathy died inside that he might be right. She tried to force away the unwanted image of Bitsy and Marc together, naked bodies entwined, his familiar husky voice whispering words of love and hers answering. . . .

"Hi, everybody. Sorry we're late, but a thousand last-minute things came up." Bitsy's tinkling laugh splashed over Cathy and she looked up to see the dimpled actress clinging to Marc's arm. "Ohhhh, goodie! Champagne! I'm *dying* of thirst!" She leaned over and stage-whispered, "We smoked a dynamite joint on the way over, and I have cotton-mouth something *awful!* Quick, Monte, save me!"

Bitsy shrugged out of her leopard jacket and wriggled down into her chair, leaning forward so her breasts almost fell out of the white silk dress she wore. A magnificent jade necklace hung to her cleavage and shoulder length jade earrings peeked through the touseled blond curls. She raised the full glass of champagne to her lips and drained it, grinning as she pushed her glass back for another. "Umm, Monte, you're a love, thanks." She dug into her white beaded evening bag and withdrew a joint and handed it to him. "Here, sweetie, go to the sandbox and get stoned. It's lovely grass." She twinkled and dimpled in Cathy's direction and cried, "Cathy! Hi! How are you? You look smashing. Is that Monte's gown?"

"Yes, it is," Cathy answered dryly. "He let me wear it tonight if I promised to have it cleaned before I return it." Everyone laughed, Monte the loudest.

"Oh, what the hell," he said. "You may as well keep it—it looks better on you than it does on me."

## The Love Game

Greetings were exchanged around the table, and Cathy met Marc's eyes briefly as she said hello. Damn those beautiful silver-gray eyes! They seemed to slice right through flesh and bone to pierce her heart.

"God, what a fabulous necklace and earring set," Beth said and reached out to lift the heavy jade in her hand, weighing it.

"Isn't it gorgeous?" Bitsy cried. "Marc brought it back from Hong Kong for me. And I've got a special present for you, sweetie—just wait until you see!" Her bright, round, parrot's gaze lingered lovingly on Beth's face until the older woman flushed and reached quickly for her champagne.

"Oh, Bitsy, you don't have to give me a gift . . ." Beth was clearly embarrassed, and Cathy found herself wondering what was between the two women.

"Oh, but I *do!* Gosh, you made me a star—" She giggled happily. "—all over again! Isn't it just too, too super?" Her bright gaze swept the table and she shivered with excitement and hugged her arms about her bare shoulders. "I mean, who would have believed it? Every ten years I'm a new star all over again and I just *adore* being a star!"

Cathy was aware of animated conversation around the table, but she stared dully at the gleaming jade around Bitsy's smooth throat, wanting to choke her with it. So Marc cared enough to buy his wife an expensive jade necklace. She wondered what other little love gifts he had brought home for her, and knots of anger and pain twisted her stomach. She had to get out of here, she thought wildly, but knew she couldn't. She couldn't embarrass Dash by leaving before dinner was served and obviously he couldn't leave to take her home. There would be speeches and congratulations later, and as president of KNAB, he had to remain for the whole boring affair.

Cathy had drunk a bottle of champagne already and still felt the dull, heavy ache in her temples, the hot tears behind her eyelids. If she got any drunker she would probably make a fool of herself by going on a crying jag, and that certainly would not do. She saw that Monte was still holding the joint, turning it lazily between his fingers as he listened to the conversation at the table. She remembered Pamela giving her a joint when she had been so numb over Kane's suicide and how it had relaxed her, taken her mind off the problem. She leaned over and whispered, "Hey, Monte, let's go smoke that thing, shall we?"

He raised his eyebrows in suprise. "Sure, why not?" He stood and held her chair for her, swaying slightly. "Where shall we go? The men's room or the ladies' room?"

"Where are you guys going?" Bitsy cried, but Cathy turned quickly away pulling Monte after her. They made their way through the packed room and out into the hall where Monte, giggling and still staggering a little, leaned against the water cooler and lit the joint.

"Jesus, Monte, not here!" Cathy said glancing quickly about. "There're guards all over the place. We'll be busted for sure."

He sucked in a lungful of smoke, giggled and chucked her under the chin. "Honey, you could drop your drawers and take a crap right in the middle of KNAB and you wouldn't get busted. You *are* KNAB in a way." Again he giggled. "By injection, anyway."

"How tacky," she said, and then laughed with him. In a way he was right. As Dash's lady she had carte blanche at KNAB. "Give me that thing," she grinned and took a big toke, fighting tears and coughing to keep the smoke down. She took another before passing it back to Monte. Already the warm, swirling rush was seeping into her bloodstream, relaxing her muscles, soothing her brain.

Jeez, pot sure as hell beat booze. She'd have to ask Lady Pamela to score her some.

"Have I told you that you look simply smashing and stunning in that gown?"

"Several times, but tell me again." She felt fine all of a sudden. Happy and bold and sexy. She twirled about and the loose skirt split on one side exposing a shiny stretch of leg in blue-tinted silk stockings, a tint so subtle that it was barely noticeable. Soft folds fell to below her waist in the back leaving her skin bare and just hinting at the dimples there. She wore four-inch heels that were dyed to match her dress, and her only piece of jewelry was a three-carat marquise diamond pendant that Dash had given her for her birthday.

They giggled and whispered together like naughty children as they finished smoking the joint, hiding it behind their backs when someone walked past them in the hall. By the time they returned to the table, dinner was being served, and the conversation was lively. Bitsy winked and said, "I know what you've been doing!" And Dash asked her where in hell she'd been.

"I went to the sandbox with Monte," she giggled sitting down next to him and giving him a hug. "Did you miss me?"

"Always," he answered softly and then cleared his throat as he glanced quickly about the group. As much as he loved Cathy, he tried to keep his dignity when with his colleagues. He knew what they were thinking: Look at that old cocker balling a chick younger than his own daughter.

If only she would marry him and remove some of the stigma. But she was so damn stubborn, his little Cathy. He reached beneath the tablecloth to pat her knee. "Hungry, darling? This roast beef looks great."

"I'm ravenous." She kissed his cheek and leaned back, allowing him to spread her napkin in her lap. She had noticed that about pot. It really made her hungry, but she supposed there must be ways of controlling one's appetite while high since Pamela and Monte were pencil slim. She had not glanced at Marc and projected a sort of studied nonchalance as she ate her salad and talked with the rest of the group. Champagne flowed continuously throughout the meal, and by the time dessert was served, she was fairly flying. Bitsy and Beth excused themselves to go to the ladies' room, and she rushed after them.

"Uh, Bitsy, can I talk to you a minute?" She saw the surprised look that Beth threw her but hurried on in a low voice. "Do you think, that is—do you have any more of those—"

"Pot?" Bitsy asked brightly and reached into her bag and handed Cathy a joint. "Here you go, sugar. Isn't it dynamite?"

"Yes, it's very good." She felt awkward standing in the middle of this rich, successful, elegant crowd scoring pot like some junkie. Exactly how did one go about it, anyway? "Uh, thank you. Shall I pay you—or what?" She palmed the joint and hid her hand beneath a fold of her long skirt.

"Don't be silly! In fact, I'll smoke a doobie with you. Come on to the john with us." She looped her arm through Cathy's and pulled her through the crowd.

"I thought it was the sandbox," Cathy said trying for humor. She felt foolish being dragged along by the giggly, busty blond and felt she had to say *something*.

"Oh, that's only when Monte uses it. He's such a little pussy!" She bent to kiss a balding man on his shiny dome, and Cathy recognized him as a television critic with the *Los Angeles Times;* no wonder one of Bitsy's breasts "accidently" brushed his cheek and she dimpled so prettily. They made their way through the room in this manner, Bitsy squealing with delight whenever she recognized a familiar face and kissing even those who were unfamiliar. Cathy had to grin. Bitsy sure wasn't wasting any time assuring herself of winning the Emmy, and the awards were still at least four months away.

An effort had been made to transform the usually dreary commissary restroom into something more befitting such a posh gathering, and there was a black maid standing ready with towels and assistance.

"Martha!" Bitsy cried flinging her arms about the maid's neck and giving her a kiss on her smooth dark cheek. "How wonderful to see you! I didn't know you were here."

"Hello, Miz Bitsy," Martha grinned, returning the hug with affection. "Yeah, here and anywhere else I can pick up a few extra dollars." She grimaced and rolled her eyes at Cathy and Beth. "With all four kids in school now and my husband out of work, it takes every nickel I earn just to stay alive. I sure do wish the president would do something about this—what's he callin' it this week?—this recession." She shook her head and absently straightened a stack of hand towels with the KNAB logo in gold thread in one corner.

"I don't know what the president is calling it," Beth said. "But it looks a lot like a depression to me." She leaned against the sink next to Bitsy and lit a cigarette.

"Oh, really? Is the country in some kind of finanical trouble?" Bitsy asked innocently, and the other woman laughed. Cathy, remembering the elaborate swan bed and gold and crystal bathroom at Bitsy's house, could only shake her head. The very wealthy were not affected in the least by the current crisis, and she thought it would make a hell of a theme for her show. She would talk to Dash about it, but now she just wanted to get high and try to forget that she had ever loved Bitsy's husband. As if reading her mind, Bitsy took out a joint and said, "Hey, let's get stoned and forget all this depressing stuff, okay, girls?" She lit the joint with her diamond-studded Cartier lighter and passed it to Cathy, who looked quickly at Martha. "Oh, don't worry about Martha, sugar—we've gotten stoned together more times than I can count. Right, sweetie?"

"I should say so," Martha laughed. "Lord, the times I flew home higher than a kite when I was working for you and Mr. Monroe. My husband was always scared to death that I'd get busted and lose my job."

They passed the joint companionably among themselves and Cathy was surprised to see Beth and Martha indulging in the illegal weed. She had thought it was a young person's drug, but then, Bitsy was obviously a devotee and she wasn't exactly a teeny-bopper, either. Almost instantly the now familiar rush filled her, soothed the jagged corners of her mind, filling her body with the lightness of air. Laughing together, exchanging gossip, the three women primped in front of the mirror, combing their hair, straightening the strap of an undergarment and by the time they had consumed another "doobie" as Bitsy called them, Cathy realized that she was having a marvelous time. She had actively fought against liking Bitsy Bushore, for obvious reasons, but now found that the giggly blonde was a lot of fun to be with. She was a wealth of information regarding the comings and goings of the Beautiful People and kept the other women laughing helplessly. As they prepared to leave the restroom, Bitsy said, "I'll leave the tip, girls," and placed a hundred-dollar bill in Martha's silver tray.

"Oh, Miz Bitsy, that's a hundred-dollar bill," Martha cried. "I can't keep that."

"Oh, pooh, of course you can. You know I'm a notoriously big tipper." Bitsy hugged the maid and then held her at arm's length, looking fondly into her face. "Now you give me a call Monday morning, you hear? I'll get you settled some place nice. It's too bad you're not free to live in. Most of my friends want live in help these days it seems. But don't worry, I'll find you something."

"Thank you—thank you so much." Martha grinned but her dark eyes were shiny with unshed tears, and Cathy saw a whole new side to Bitsy. The perennial starlet with the ding-a-ling personality was also a very nice, warm person. Cathy knew that everyone at the studio loved Bitsy, from Dash to the lowliest grip, but she had fought not to be drawn into that charmed circle because of her jealousy over Marc. The prick, she thought, how can he be so rotten to such a sweet person as Bitsy? Poor kid, she probably puts up with his affairs because she loves him too much to leave him. She wondered if Bitsy knew about her affair with Marc, then decided she couldn't possibly. She was much too warm and friendly to suspect anything, and Cathy and Marc *had* been discreet.

As her new affection for Bitsy grew in her fuzzy, drugged brain, she found herself hating Marc even more for the abuse she believed he had inflicted upon Bitsy over the years. And he undoubtedly would have come to treat her the same way had she continued her affair with him. She had been right about him from the start and mentally kicked herself in the ass for being such a fool as to have fallen in love with him. Well, thank God she'd had the good sense to see him for what he really was before things went any further. She was well rid of him. That tiny scrap of hope that she had clung to all these months died, and the pain in her heart left her.

She was able to look at Marc when they returned to their table and not feel anything but the muffled roaring in her head caused by the marijuana and champagne. She felt the beat of the music pulsating through her body and drew Dash onto the dance floor, laughing, loving him. Lon Howland cut in and she was whirled away in his arms and she laughed, loving him too. She gazed up into his handsome face and saw the naked desire in his dark, hot eyes and squirmed closer, laughing. The evening passed in a pleasantly fuzzy haze and she laughed more than she ever had in her life.

She made another trip to the ladies' room with her new best friend, Bitsy, and smoked another doobie and drank more champagne and danced and laughed. "Happiness is a business," she told the group at the table. "You have to work at it like anything else. You have to get rid of those things that make you unhappy—cast them out. You can't depend on anyone else for your happiness—you must make your own happiness." She felt so sage, so spiritual. She had unlocked the door to the universe, discovered the answers that wise men had sought for centuries. She knew it all now.

"I think my little Cathy is stoned." Dash drew her close to his side and patted her arm. He kissed her cheek and looked fondly into her glazed eyes. "I'd better get you home, sweetheart," he said softly.

"Don't wanna go home," Cathy said reaching for the bottle of champagne, which Dash promptly removed from her hand. "Let's stay and dance some more."

"We can dance at home—just the two of us. Come on now, honey." Dash stood and helped her to her feet, and she gave him a dazzling smile and said, "okay," and then almost fell into Marc's lap.

Marc caught her and pressed her back into Dash's arms, and his eyes were dark with emotion. God, how he wanted her! He still loved her. He wished *he* were going home with her instead of that aging old stud, Sunderling. He had never seen her this way, so giggly and gay, smoking pot, drinking and dancing. She had always been so damn serious about her career before. Maybe the past six months had caused her to grow up a little, lighten up. He very much wanted to have a private word with her but knew it was impossible under the circumstances. She was blitzed out of her mind and Dash was holding her up as they said their goodbyes. He would call her tomorrow and ask her to meet him for lunch. Seeing her tonight had brought back such wonderful memories that it was all he could do to keep from telling her so.

He had wanted to tell her he was sorry for being such a stubborn boor, that he still loved her and wanted her back. But every time he had seen her it had been at the studio with Dash just a few feet away, and he hadn't been able to think of a thing to say except an inane greeting. He wanted to believe that she had planned that brief meeting outside Dash's office, but he couldn't be sure. They had said so many hateful things to one another before his Cambodia trip and had hurt one another so much, he wondered if it would ever mend.

As he watched her weaving gracefully through the room on Dash's arm, her hips swaying seductively, he knew he had to find out where she stood. He had done some thinking and changing in the past six months and had discovered that the thought of marriage with Cathy was not all that hard to take. He had almost convinced himself that he would ask Bitsy for a divorce and try to make a go of a "real" marriage when he had returned to find Cathy very much involved with Dash again. He had been hurt and angry and felt betrayed even though he knew it was foolish. They had made no promises to one another—and Marc suddenly wished very much that they had. He drained his champagne and reached for a cigarette, lighting it almost savagely. Tomorrow, he told himself, I'll find out tomorrow if there's a chance for us.

\* \* \*

But when he telephoned the next day, Cathy's answering service said she was out of town and had not left a forwarding number. As he replaced the receiver in its cradle, Marc had a swift premonition of doom and a heavy sadness settled over him like a shroud.

## Chapter Eleven

Every newspaper on both coasts carried a photograph of Cathy and Dash, the stunning young blond and the aging television executive. It was the same photograph: the one of them leaving the Little Chapel of the Flowers in Las Vegas where they had been married. News footage that evening on all networks showed them boarding Dash's private Lear jet on their way to Rome for a two-week honeymoon. They both smiled and chatted with reporters, answering questions easily and unselfconsciously when someone had the bad taste to bring up the age difference. Then they were off, Cathy in a swirl of black sable, Dash looking tanned and Cary Grant-handsome in a topcoat lined in mink.

"Well, it looks like she's gone and done it," Pamela said to Ashley. She lifted her glass in a silent salute to the television screen. "Happiness, luv," she murmured.

"I still can't believe it," Maggie said. "Running off like that without telling any of us anything. It's not like Cathy." She frowned and took a sip of her after-dinner liqueur.

"She looked awfully happy to me," Ken said, drawing his wife against him where they sat on Pamela's striped satin loveseat.

"You'd look bloody happy yourself," Pamela drawled, "if you had just married twenty million dollars!"

"Don't be a cat, Pam," Ashley teased. "You know you're happy for her. She really loves Dash. Gosh, you've seen them together—always necking and stuff."

"She *loves* him, ducks, but she's not *in love* with him—not the way she is with Marc Monroe."

"That's what worries me," Maggie sighed. "I'm so afraid one of them is going to be terribly hurt."

"Wow, doesn't Cathy look beautiful?" Bitsy squealed to Marc. "So old Dash finally caught her, huh? He's been batty about her *forever!* I'm really happy for them aren't you, darling?"

They were sitting in Marc's study, he behind his desk where he had been trying to write an article, she curled up in the big leather chair near the fireplace. She had burst in and switched on the television set, forcing him to watch the newscast with Dash and Cathy even though he had told himself he would not. He had seen their picture in the morning paper and had sat at his desk most of the day in a sort of stupor, not believing it. His heart rejected it even as his brain told him it was true. He had lost her.

"God, will you look at the *size* of that diamond!" Bitsy gasped and leaned forward as the camera moved in for a close-up of Cathy's wedding ring. "And that coat! It's to die over! God, I've never seen her looking so beautiful—or so rich!"

Marc pushed angrily away from his desk and strode to the bar to pour himself a Scotch. Sometimes Bitsy drove him nuts with her incessant, insensitive chatter.

"Mix me one, sweetie, and come sit down and watch this. Dash looks super and his coat is almost as beautiful as hers!" She turned to laugh and saw the dark, pained expression on Marc's face. Sudden realization struck

## The Love Game

her, and she rose and went swiftly to him. "Oh, darling," she said softly. "You loved her, didn't you?"

"Bitsy, please just be quiet for a minute and leave me alone, all right? I've got this article to finish and . . ."

"Marc, sweetie, it's *me*, remember? I *know* you, honey—we're pals, remember?" She laid a hand upon his arm and looked up into his face with compassion. "I'm so sorry, Marc—I didn't know it was serious when you were seeing her. I thought it was just another fling, you know? After all, it lasted about the same length as the others."

"Three months and two weeks to the day," he said dully and scrubbed a weary hand over his face.

"Come sit down, darling, and tell Bitsy all about it." She led him to the sofa and pulled him down beside her. Thankfully, the news had changed scenes, and they were not faced with the smiling newlyweds.

"I don't know, Bits, I don't know what happened. One minute everything was fantastic, beautiful—and the next minute it blew up in my face, and I found myself in Cambodia alone wondering what in the hell had happened. It didn't really register, I guess, that she felt that way about Dash. Oh, I knew she had been seeing him when I first met her, but I thought it was more platonic. I just couldn't imagine . . ."

"You couldn't imagine how a woman could go for a man Dash's age when she could have a sexy young hunk like you, right, babe?" She tickled him, trying to tease him out of his bad mood.

As if he hadn't heard, he went on in the same dull voice. "I guess I just assumed that she would be waiting when I got home and we'd talk it out, come to some understanding—I don't know." He took a swallow of Scotch and stared into the fireplace.

"Did you tell her about us?" Bitsy asked softly. "Did she know that we're married in name only?"

He nodded his head miserably and swallowed more Scotch. "She didn't believe me."

"Did you tell her the other—you know, about me?" She drew his head to her shoulder and stroked the dark hair back from his face.

"Of course not, Bits. You know I wouldn't do that."

"Maybe you should have." She gently massaged his temples, and he sighed and closed his eyes. "It might have helped."

"No, it's too late."

"It's never too late, darling."

"Jesus, will you look at that coat Dash is wearing?" Monte gasped, staring at the television screen. "Fanfuckingtastic! Must be worth at least fifty thousand bucks!"

"Be quiet—I want to hear what they're saying." Beth turned the set up with her remote control and reached for the roach smoldering in the ashtray. She took a hit and passed it to Monte.

"Rome, yet!" he squealed, spluttering on too much smoke too hastily inhaled. "And she didn't ask me to go along. Who's going to dress her for all those marvelous restaurants and clubs on the Via Venato?"

"I know who's going to be *undressing* her," Beth chuckled. "Get a load of the look on his face. That's a man *in love,* honey." She sipped a glass of white wine and leaned back into the comfort of her favorite chair, a big overstuffed lounger.

"Cathy looks happy, too, don't you think?"

"I don't know yet. I'm still trying to figure that one out." She watched Cathy and Dash waving from the ramp leading into his Lear jet, she with arms full of mink and roses, he with arms full of her. "You know about Marc Monroe, of course."

"Who doesn't? It's the worst kept secret in Hollywood."

"I thought they would get married—or at least set up housekeeping together. I wonder what happened?"

"Beats me. Doesn't Bitsy know?"

Beth shook her head and brought the roach clip to her lips, dragging in deep.

"Too bad it didn't work out. Bitsy would make a charming gay divorcee!"

"Indeed she would," Beth chuckled fondly. "Indeed she would!"

Cathy stood looking at the dining room table elegantly set for Christmas dinner. It was so long she had often kidded Dash that she would have to call long distance to speak to the other end. Dozens of bright poinsettias in silver bowls ranged down the center of the snowy lace tablecloth and two silver candelabra holding slender white tapers were set at each end. Boughs of fir and spruce decorated the large room and made soft placemats on the sideboard where dozens of pies, cakes and other holiday goodies mingled their delicious odors indiscriminately. Everything was in excellent order as usual.

Since marrying Dash and moving into his luxurious mansion, everything about Cathy's personal life had been in excellent order as well. She had only to ask and it would be hers, or done for her. Her closets bulged with dozens of silk blouses, designer jeans, tailored slacks and countless shoes and boots. Drawers were filled with lacy lingerie and shelves held a variety of "fun" hats. She had so many robes, hostess gowns and at-home outfits that she knew she would never wear them all, not to mention the coats, jackets and evening capes in every type of fur and fabric imaginable. She shopped on Rodeo Drive in Beverly Hills and Fifth Avenue in New York and had hairdressers and manicurists on call twenty-four hours a day. There were two chauffeur-driven limousines at her disposal at all times as well as a new, baby-blue Mercedes-Benz with her name on the license plate that Dash had just given her for Christmas.

Cathy knew she had never looked better. It's hard to look bad when your every desire is fulfilled instantly. Dash's chef knew her tastes perfectly and always prepared her meals with health and fitness in mind. Her personal maid scrubbed her body with a loofah, and her personal masseuse kept her limber and glowing with vitality. The many private balconies, terraces and courtyards provided excellent nude tanning areas, and she kept her skin peachy beige at all times. She worked out in the Olympic-size pool daily and tried to play a couple of sets of tennis on weekends on her private court.

The lovely formal gardens and multitudes of shrubbery, flowers and trees were kept immaculate by the gardner, and the twenty-three room mansion was always sparkling clean and kept running smoothly by the maids, housekeeper and laundress. There was a butler named Harrison and a chauffeur named Williams who both seemed to Cathy to be wind-up mechanical men for all the emotion they showed. ("They're hired to do a job, not entertain you," Dash had told her.)

Dash protected his young wife almost fiercely, drawing her into the magic circle that only the very wealthy can provide. She had wanted to obliterate Marc by marrying Dash and she had done it. It was as if she had gone to sleep sometime last spring and had awakened in a summer overripe with promise, in a land that she had only dreamed about and could not believe was real. But it *was* real. And it was *hers*.

"Merry Christmas, darling." Dash slipped his arms about her from behind and kissed her neck. "Everything in order?"

"Isn't it always?" She turned in his arms, kissing him and smiling warmly into his eyes.

"Well, it's your first big dinner as an old married woman and I was just wondering if there was anything else you needed." He put his arm about her shoulder, rubbing his hand gently up and down the smooth velvet of her morning robe. His was matching but hip-length, and he wore it with beige silk pajamas and elegant calfskin slippers. He was freshly shaved and wearing Cathy's favorite cologne. She rubbed her face against his, smiling.

"I haven't 'needed' one single thing since marrying you," she said. "And your staff is so well trained they know what I want even before I do. Isn't the table beautiful, darling? It's like something out of a fairy tale."

"I've felt like I'm living in a fairy tale ever since I met you. Just seeing you here makes the room even lovelier."

"Ah, you silver-tongued devil, you," she teased, tickling him, and he trapped her hands in his and brought them to his lips to kiss and hold tightly.

"I'm serious, little Cathy. You've brought a meaning back into my life that's been missing so long I don't remember ever having had it." He glanced about at the beautiful table and decorations. "I can't remember the last time we had a Christmas dinner party in this house. With Grace so ill these last few years and the children away, well . . ."

"Shh." She put her finger to his mouth. "That's yesterday's news, sweetie. Today is for happiness and no looking back—no regrets."

"You don't have any, do you, sweetheart? Regrets, I mean, about marrying me?"

"Are you trying to get rid of me already, Sunderling?" She teased him with her eyes but saw that his were serious.

"Never!" he whispered huskily and drew her into his arms and kissed her urgently, pressing her hard against his body. "Never, ever," he repeated. "God, I love you so much I can't believe I lived my whole life without you!"

"Not your *whole* life, surely!" She cocked a mischievous eyebrow at him. "You must have at least a couple of good years left for me."

A look of anguish passed across Dash's face so suddenly that she wasn't sure she had seen it—then he drew her back into his arms and held her as if he'd never let her go.

It was a new Cathy Curtis Sunderling who returned to the KNAB studios at the beginning of the new year; a smart, chic, more mature Cathy who strode down the corridors with purpose in every step—and pride of ownership in every glance. At twenty-seven she was already a power to be reckoned with, and it didn't take the execs long to discover that she was no longer just a big-breasted, empty-headed little blond chick who was fucking the boss. Now she was married to the boss, and he seemed content to let her have carte blanche in all things.

Her own network show was in the choicest cut of prime time and was easily holding its own. And she had her hand in the rest of KNAB's shows as well. Grudgingly, the network brass admitted that she was "a damn smart little gal," blessed with a talent for interviewing even the hardest subject and as tough and unrelenting as Barbara Walters or Mike Wallace. She might be dressed by Halston and coiffed by Sassoon but she was nobody's pet poodle to be admired and then forgotten. A few producers and writers who had tried to dismiss her as a flash-in-the-pan, the boss's plaything, had found themselves standing outside of the huge arched gates of KNAB their walking papers in their hands.

She had given Greg Bedford the job as her producer so she would have more time to get involved in the

## The Love Game

programming which was still her first love. Her show was now so well established it practically filmed itself, and her crew was more devoted to her than ever after several of them found themselves nominated for Emmys for their efforts on the "Cathy Curtis Show."

She was usually the first one in the office every morning and had the coffee pot on even before Clare arrived—much to the secretary's disapproval. As the president's personal secretary, Clare had always prided herself on running a smooth office and did not like it one bit that his pushy little blond chic seemed to think *she* was now president. She would have quit but where would a fifty-four-year-old woman get another job as cushy and well paid as this one? She set her lips grimly and kept her voice emotionless as she gave Cathy her appointments for the day.

Cathy's day usually began with breakfast with a business associate, and then she would spend a couple of hours watching the rough cuts of the new shows. Later, she attended to her own show with interviews and script readings. A normal day often stretched to seven or seven-thirty when she would rush breathlessly home in time to have dinner with Dash.

He seemed to be spending more and more time on the golf course or at the Beverly Hills Men's Health Club than he did at the studio, but he was always interested in everything Cathy had to say when she returned home. Evenings were spent discussing the day's events, Dash agreeing with almost everything Cathy reported, giving advice only when it was necessary—which wasn't very often. His little Cathy had fulfilled his expectations. She was as good as he had known she would be and it pleased him enormously.

It should have pleased Cathy enormously as well, but there still seemed to be something missing. She was busier than ever—and more miserable. She felt watched and weighed all the time. As if "they" were just biding their time until she made some mistake, slipped up—and then it would all be taken away from her. She drove herself harder, faster, felt the threat of being on top and knowing that she must stay there to prove to herself that she could run a network. To prove to "them" that Dash wasn't a fool for putting his faith in her. She developed a certain brittleness of manner, a brusqueness, a nuance of attitude that stated clearly that she was on top and meant to stay there. She totally abandoned all pretense of being a naive little talk show host and did not waste her precious time looking for anything that power could not provide.

She even closed her heart to Marc Monroe and signed him up for six specials a year because she knew it would make money for the network. She had steeled herself to the softness in those so familiar silver-gray eyes during their contract conference and had surrounded herself with other studio brass so she wouldn't have to face him alone. And she had coolly declined when he had invited her to lunch to celebrate.

In the spring, KNAB swept the Emmys and Cathy collected her second little gold statuette along with Bitsy Bushore and Marc. Beth had been nominated but lost out to some new hotshot producer at CBS, and Monte, also a nominee, had been overlooked. But no one seemed a loser at the gala party that followed at the Beverly Hills Hotel.

Cathy had wanted to have the victory celebration at home, but Dash hadn't been feeling well lately and thought a party at home would be a little too much. Cathy worried about Dash's health (when she took the time to think about him at all) and had insisted that he see a doctor. "Just age, darling," he had reported after his physical examination. "The old body is slowing down." And she had accepted it, realizing with something of a

## The Love Game

start that he would soon be sixty years old. God, had he aged *that* much in just a couple of years? He was still devilishly handsome and had a sexy swagger to his step, but he seemed thicker somehow, grayer, slower.

"Congratulations, sweetie!" Bitsy trilled, stooping to plant a wet kiss on Cathy's cheek. She held up her own Emmy, then placed it on the table next to Cathy's. The large round table held several other Emmys, their proud owners now engaged in animated conversation with one another. Dash sat drinking Bourbon and talking to late arrivals, telling everyone who would listen that Cathy had singlehandedly been responsible for the Emmy sweep at KNAB. "Smartest thing I ever did was marry her," he nodded sagely, more than a little drunk with the network's success as well as several shots of straight Bourbon. "And the second smartest thing I ever did was give her complete control of KNAB."

This statement caused a few raised eyebrows around the table and Cathy, surprised, said, "Since when?"

"Oh, Cathy honey, you're such a tease!" Bitsy laughed and leaned over to squeeze Cathy's arm. "Everyone knows *you* run the network, for heaven's sake! Gosh, I probably wouldn't have my own show if you hadn't gone to bat for me. Now don't look so surprised, you old faker—Dash told me all about how you convinced everyone to take a chance with me in 'The Love Game.' And you were right—it sure paid off!" She lifted her Emmy in the air and giggled happily.

Cathy shot Dash a look and he had the grace to flush and grin sheepishly. "I can't really take the credit, Bitsy," she mumbled, embarrassed. "It was just the right combination—a good property, a name star and a proven track record. Your series have always made money."

"Modest, isn't she?" Bitsy said to Beth who sat next to her moodily sipping a martini. "And I suppose you're going to deny that you were completely responsible for getting Marc his special contract?"

"Uh, Dash handled that deal," Cathy said quickly, wondering where Marc was. She had kept an eye on the door since arriving, knowing that he would show up and take his place next to Bitsy—where a husband rightfully belonged. She had been torn when he had received his Emmy earlier that evening: delighted that he had won and that she had, indeed, been the major force in getting KNAB to carry his Cambodia special and a little miffed that he had turned to hug Bitsy before running up to claim the statuette. For the first time since marrying Dash, she felt the old, familiar pang of yearning, the weakness in her knees, the dull pounding of her heart. I still love the bastard, she had thought, and hated herself for her weakness. The rest of the evening she had studiously ignored him even though he and Bitsy had sat in the same row as she and Dash. She wondered where he had gone after the presentations. Bitsy had arrived with Beth and Monte, saying only that Marc would join them later.

"Pamela! Hello! Sit down—sit down!" Dash stood and held a chair for the Lady of Glendorshire and she slid into it majestically, drawing Ashley down next to her. She looked every inch a queen in her white broadtail suit and low-cut, royal purple silk blouse. Ashley was movie-star handsome in a tux and ruffle-fronted white shirt with diamond studs and cuff links.

"Congratulations, luv," Pamela said to Cathy, leaning over to kiss her cheek. "That's the little bugger there, is it?" She picked up the Emmy and hefted its weight in her hand like a jeweler measuring its worth. "Not a bad looking trinket."

"Fuck you, Lady Pamela," Cathy laughed, delighted to see her friend and relieved that she would now have someone to talk to. She always felt somehow out of it or bored when she was just with the network people, as if they were looking her over and finding her lacking. With Pamela she could be herself. She snatched the Emmy away from her and held it up, admiring it. "This little piece of metal is the most important 'trinket' in television!"

"You better believe it, sweetie," Bitsy said, holding up her own Emmy. "This little baby is going to be my bargaining power when I come in and ask for a raise Monday!" She giggled happily at Dash, and he reached over to pat her hand fondly.

"You just keep 'The Love Game' in the top ten, Bitsy, and you can have anything your little heart desires." Dash smiled expansively as he looked around at "his family" and all the gold statues on the table. They had done it together, he and Cathy; they had put KNAB back in second place, and he was convinced that with Cathy at the helm the next year would see them as number one. He poured himself another Bourbon and raised the glass. "To all of you," he said, his pale blue eyes warm as they swept the table. "Congratulations." He drank and watched them over the rim of his glass as they murmured responses and downed champagne or cocktails.

"Am I late?" a familiar voice asked, and Cathy looked up to see Marc grinning down at Dash, his Emmy stuck casually in the pocket of his tuxedo. He was swaying slightly and she could smell liquor on his breath as he plopped down in the chair between herself and Ashley. "Well, good evening, Mrs. Sunderling! You look ravishing as always." He took her hand and kissed it, the silver eyes darkening as they met hers.

"Thank you." She snatched her hand away and filled it with a glass of champagne. Damn, he always made her feel so utterly foolish even when she hadn't done or said anything.

"Where in the world have you been, Marc?" Bitsy

asked, taking the Emmy from his pocket and placing it next to hers. She leaned closer and sniffed. "At the bar from the smell of it."

"Oh, I had to stop off and say hello to an old friend," he said reaching for the bottle of champagne and filling a water glass to the brim.

"Marc, for Pete's sake, how tacky!" Bitsy reached for the glass, but he held it out of her reach, laughing, then drained it.

"Jesus Christ, will ya get a load of all that gold!" He stared at the many Emmys about the table, then raised his eyes to Cathy's. "You did it, huh?" he said in a low voice. "You whipped the bastards into shape and made 'em winners just like you knew you could." He splashed more champagne into his glass and raised it in a salute, his grin mocking. "Congratulations, Mrs. President."

Cathy opened her mouth to tell him to go to hell, then closed it firmly, and deliberately turned her back on him, not bothering to acknowledge his drunken insults. The creep, showing up drunk and making a fool of himself. She had thought he had more class.

"Do you get out to the ranch much, Pamela?" Cathy asked, ignoring the low-toned voices of Marc and Bitsy as they argued over his behavior. Poor Bitsy, Cathy thought, putting up with that kind of shit. I'd kick the creep out on his ass.

"Just last weekend as a matter of fact, luv," Pamela said. "And Maggie sent you a message: 'answer her phone calls or she's going to turn you over her knee.' "

Cathy laughed. "God, I've got to get out there for a visit, but I've been so damn busy with the awards and everything. I did try to call her a couple of times, but she's never home."

"They've had a busy spring, I gather," Pamela said, leaning toward Ashley for a light. She puffed out smoke and squinted at Cathy. "How about a ride tomorrow, ducks? Ash and myself, you and Dash. He does ride, doesn't he?"

"Are you kidding?" Cathy laughed. "He's allergic to horses—as well as anything else that costs less then a half million dollars! No, I don't think Dash would exactly fit in at the Rocking K Ranch." She chuckled at the thought of the impeccably dressed television executive side-stepping horse manure and getting dust on his fine calfskin shoes.

"I heard that," Dash said, leaning over to join the conversation. "And I resent it. I'm allergic to anything that costs less than *one* million dollars—you always did underestimate me!" He put his arm around Cathy's shoulders, pulling her close for a moment. "Why don't you go ahead, darling. It'll do you good to get out of the city and the studio for a few hours."

"I'd really like to," she said. "But why don't you come with us? You don't have to ride. Maggie would be delighted to entertain you for an afternoon."

"Can't honey. Big golf game tomorrow at the club. But you go ahead with Pam and Ash, and I'll meet you there later. Maybe we can have dinner at that little Mexican place you told me about."

"Great," Pamela said. "Then it's settled. Pick you up about tenish, luv?"

"Sure, I guess so. I should get away every so often—that damn studio tends to become claustrophobic at times." She drained her champagne glass and reached for the bottle at the center of the table—and her fingers encountered Marc's. She raised her eyes to his which were sober with love.

"Allow me," he said huskily, never removing his steady gaze from hers as he refilled her glass.

"Thank you," she said weakly and could not turn her eyes away from his. A small, rational part of her brain heard the easy conversation between Dash, Pamela,

Ashley and Bitsy, and she felt relieved that they did not know what was happening to her inside. She was consumed with desire for Marc Monroe and had to grit her teeth to keep from sighing out loud. God, just one deeply penetrating look from those silver-gray eyes and she was turned to jello all over again! It wasn't fair! She didn't want him in her well-organized life, fucking it all up again. Confusing her, taking her mind off her work.

His voice was a mere whisper and if she hadn't been looking at his wonderfully sensual lips, she would not have heard him murmur, "Cathy, I've got to see you, talk to you—please meet me somewhere."

The softly spoken words brought her out of her momentary spell and she said coldly, "No way, Marc—not ever!" and pushed swiftly out of her chair and grabbed Ashley's arm, "Come on, Ash, let's dance." She saw his surprised look as well as Pamela's but shrugged and laughed, pulling him on to the dance floor. Her knees shook, and her heart was beating so furiously that she had to stop a moment and draw in a shaky breath before slipping into Ashley's arms.

She couldn't believe the overwhelming desire that still pounded savagely through her bloodstream, sending messages to her brain at an alarming rate. She moved against Ashley and felt the hardness of him, the strong shoulders and lean, firm thighs pressed to hers and couldn't help comparing it to the soft, spongy feel of being held in Dash's arms. God, she was so damn shaky! She clung to Ashley, her mind whirling with sexy visions of Marc and herself making love, showering together, walking nonchalantly naked about the house. He had come up behind her one morning when she had been cooking breakfast in the nude and had gently, tenderly slipped into her from behind; they had let the bacon and eggs burn while they made love on the kitchen floor.

## The Love Game 187

Jesus Christ, I'm horny! she thought with some amusement and much amazement. Dash was not exactly frigid, and they usually made love at least once a week, but now she was literally burning up with desire. Her cheeks flamed and her loins pulsated, sending a moistness seeping between her thighs. She wanted to make hard, passionate love, not safe, familiar love. She wanted Marc Monore so much she could taste it, and the knowledge both thrilled and repulsed her. No, it wasn't Marc she wanted, she told herself severely. It was just a young hunk of solid sex that she wanted. She glanced up at Ashley, but one look at his innocent, boyish face and she knew she wouldn't do what her flustered emotions were telling her to do. She couldn't seduce Pamela's young lover. She took deep breaths, trying to still the erratic trembling and quivering of her pulses, her fluttering heartbeat.

"May I cut in?" a deep, intimate voice asked, and she was spun around and into Lon Howland's arms. The touch of his body was searing and she gasped slightly, looking up at him with hot eyes and dry lips. "God, you're the most sultry lady I've ever seen," he whispered hoarsely and gripped her tighter, bringing their groins close together. He undulated against her, pressing his sudden erection urgently to her body. She felt it burning through her clothes, branding her flesh.

"Do you have a joint on you?" Her voice sounded as breathless and hoarse as his, and when he nodded, she pulled him quickly through the packed throng of dancers and out into the hallway.

"Jeez, Cath, I wanna eat you up like a candy bar," Lon said as she opened a hall door and peered inside. It was a utility room with shelves of towels and linens on two walls and stacks of white cloth bags, which obviously held dirty laundry, on the floor. "I mean, hey, man, if you only knew how many times I've beat off, thinkin' about you—wantin' you like shit—but you never gave me a tumble . . ." His voice trailed off as he stumbled into the small room behind her, and she realized that he was stoned on something. She hoped it was just pot.

"Light the joint," she whispered and watched him fumbling with the button on his jacket pocket. "Oh, shit. Here, let me do it." She found the joint and lit it, sucking in deep and gasping on the pungent smoke. "Jesus, what is this stuff?" She toked again, instantly feeling the rush, the warmth, the liquid bones swaying her body as lightly as a willow in a summer breeze.

"Hey, ain't that righteous weed, man? It's Thai stick—stuff'll blow your head off." He giggled as he took a drag, his hot, dark eyes boring into Cathy's. "Hey, why you bein' so nice to me all of a sudden, huh? I thought you hated my guts."

"I do," she said, taking the joint from him and dragging in deep. "But I want to get fucked good and hard, and who better than this year's superstud?" She kept the joint in her mouth as she raised her skirt and stepped out of her shoes and pantyhose. "Hurry, drop your pants, Lon. I can't wait!" Her fingers trembled as they fumbled at his belt buckle.

"Well, I'll be God damned! I never thought I'd hear talk like that from you! I mean, shit, man, you're Miss KNAB, ain't 'cha?" He giggled again, self-consciously, as she tugged down his trousers and shorts. "I mean, I don't give a good God damn *who* you are, you know what I mean? Hell, I've been wantin' to put it to ya ever since I first laid eyes on you. Oh, baby, are you ever in for a treat!"

"Shut up and just fuck me." She fell to the stacks of laundry bags, pulling him on top of her, spreading her legs and drawing him inside. His hard penis filled her, burned her so good she cried out and ground her pelvis

## The Love Game

against his, forcing him deeper and harder inside her. She took one last toke of the Thai stick, holding her breath and closing her eyes, letting the powerful drug fling her up and out of herself. Lon's powerful cock was unleashing her long pent-up sexuality. She writhed beneath him, bucked wildly in time with his almost hurtful strokes and ripped her fingernails down his tuxedoed back. She wanted it harder, faster, deeper. She sank her teeth into his lower lip and heard his muffled groan of pleasure, and he doubled his efforts, pounding her into the very floor it seemed, and she exploded beneath him with a startled cry of pleasure mixed with pain. But he did not stop. He rode her unmercifully, demanding her response, hurting her with his cruel hands and hard lips, and she said, "Yes, yes, yes—more, Lon—don't stop!" and threw her legs wide, circling his narrow waist, her heels forcing him deeper still. Multiple climaxes ripped through her, shivering her very bones, careening madly through her bloodstream, sating her, draining her. She felt his orgasm as he shuddered above her, and then she rolled over, pushing him off her hot, spent body.

She cleaned herself with a towel and stood, swiftly pulling on her pantyhose and stepping into her shoes. She stooped to retrieve the still smoldering roach and smoked it down to nothing in two short drags, then dropped it to the floor and crushed it beneath her heel. Without a backward glance, she opened the door, stepped quickly through it and closed it on Lon's plaintive voice asking where in hell she was going.

She glanced at her wristwatch. The whole thing had taken less than ten minutes and she smiled grimly as she hurried down the hall and into the ballroom, going directly to the ladies' room. She repaired her make-up and hair, straightened her somewhat rumpled gown and rejoined the table. A quick glance showed her that Marc and Bitsy had left, and she let herself relax with an audible sigh.

"Hi, honey. Enjoying yourself?" Dash stood quickly and held her chair for her.

"Umm, yes, thank you, darling." She smiled and patted his hand as he drew his chair close to hers. "Lon Howland is a surprisingly good dancer." She accepted the fresh glass of champagne that Dash handed her and drank thirstily.

"Yes, I imagine he is," Pamela drawled and her green eyes danced knowingly as they met Cathy's stoned blue ones. "He looks as if he would be quite good!"

"Perhaps you'd like him to show you a couple of new steps?" Cathy had to force herself to keep the laughter out of her voice and she lowered her head quickly to her glass.

"Oh, I think not, luv. Ashley is well versed in all the new techniques, as well!" Pamela couldn't keep the grin off her face, and it was all Cathy needed to explode into laughter, thereby releasing some of the tension that had gripped her all evening. Never in her life had she done anything as outrageous as what had just transpired between her and Lon Howland. It both shocked and delighted her. That she could so callously take a man and use him simply for her own selfish physical relief was something new to her. It had been exciting and gratifying and had given her a thrill of power akin to the sexual thrill she had also experienced. Maybe men had something with their casual attitude of "wham bam thank you, ma'am." It certainly seemed easy enough and was less wearing on one's emotions.

She refilled her glass and drank it all down, then turned to Dash. "Shall we call it a night, darling? I'm suddenly quite exhausted." She kicked Pamela under the table when the redhead made a snickering sound in her throat and fought to keep from laughing.

## The Love Game                                                191

"Oh, poor lamb," Pamela crooned, enjoying Cathy's discomfort. "You'd best get to bed and get plenty of rest. I'll pop by at ten to collect you."

"Why, Lady Pamela, how understanding you are," Cathy said broadly and the two women giggled, then quickly sobered when Dash gave them a questioning look.

"Sounds to me like you'd better take your lady home as well, Ash," Dash laughed good-naturedly. "I think they've both been at the champagne bottle a little too often!" He helped Cathy stand, and she met Pamela's eyes, and it sent them off into peals of laughter again. "Come on, you silly baby," he said, shaking Cathy's shoulder as he turned her toward the door. "Say goodnight and let's get you to bed."

"Goodnight." She leaned over to kiss Pamela's cheek and hissed in her ear, "How the hell did you know what I'd been doing, smart ass?"

"Goodnight, luv, wonderful seeing you." Pamela kissed Cathy's cheek and whispered, "I've been in heat like that a few times myself, ducks. Was he terrific?"

"Let's just say he took the edge off!" She kissed Ashley's cheek. "See you guys tomorrow—goodnight." As Dash led her through the crowd, she saw Lon Howland staggering across the dancefloor, a dazed look on his handsome face, and she couldn't surpress a tiny giggle of pure pleasure.

"So tell me, ducks," Pamela said. "What was this thing with Lon Howland last night? Is the honeymoon over already between you and Dash?" She was sitting on a plaid blanket, leaning back against the trunk of a tree, smoking a joint. Her Arabian gelding, Desert Fury, grazed a few feet away and next to him two of Ken's best rental horses also munched fresh grass. Cathy was sprawled next to Pamela, watching Ashley submerging a bottle of Louis Roederer champagne in the creek.

"I don't really know what made me do it," Cathy sighed. She pushed herself into a sitting position and reached for the large picnic basket that Pamela had brought along. The day was perfect for lazing outdoors, sharing a picnic lunch with friends, but Cathy felt restless, unable to relax. To keep her hands busy she began unpacking the lunch and arranging it on the red and white checkered tablecloth that Ashley had already spread beneath the shade of a towering oak tree. "I just felt so—so—" She shrugged and reached into the basket to bring out plates and silverware.

"Horny? Is that the word you're searching for, luv?" Pamela opened a plastic dish of olives and popped one into her mouth. "I saw the way you were looking at Marc Monroe, sweetie, and just thank your lucky stars that your husband didn't! Gawd, you looked as if you could eat him with a spoon!"

Cathy laughed a little sadly. "Yeah, I guess I could have. Jeez, what is it about that man that drives me crazy? I really hate the prick, you know, and yet every time I see him I want him so much it makes me weak—literally weak! Shit, what's the matter with me, anyway?"

"I do believe it's a condition not uncommon among us mortals—this thing called love. You're still in love with him, my girl, and too damn stubborn to admit it or to do anything about it."

"You're crazy, Lady Pamela. I thoroughly dislike the man and everything he stands for!" She busied herself with spreading out fried chicken, sandwiches, a crock of pâté and a wicker basket of crackers. "He's a liar and a cheat. God, just look at the way he treats poor Bitsy!"

"Poor Bitsy?" Pamela's eyebrows arched in surprise. "Since when have you cared a fig for Bitsy Bushore's welfare?"

Cathy flushed slightly. She *had* spoken badly of Bitsy

when she had been seeing Marc and was so jealous of the actress. "Well, I've gotten to know her a lot better since becoming involved in 'The Love Game' series and she's not so bad, really. She's a lot of fun to be around, you know? She's always so up and happy—although how she can be when married to Marc, I'll never understand. He treats her so—I don't know—so casually, as if she were a thing instead of a person."

"Ah, the typical American husband," Pamela chuckled. "Is that what's wrong between you and Dash? He ignoring you already?"

"Nothing's wrong between Dash and me." She said it too quickly, knew it, and sighed. "Oh, Pam, something *is* wrong but I don't know what it is. Dash still treats me like a princess, gives me anything I want. Hell, he practically gave me KNAB for God's sake! I can do anything I want, and he just looks on, rather fondly, like a benevolent uncle. He loves me. I know he does, but it's a strange sort of love. It's like a great artist who creates a masterpiece and loves it wholly, seeing in it all the things that are perhaps missing from his own life."

Cathy rolled over on her stomach and propped her elbows on the soft grass and gazed out across the pretty, tree-shaded meadow. Ashley had unsaddled the horses and slipped their bits from their mouths to allow them to graze freely in the new spring growth of wild flowers and tasty young weeds.

"Love like that can swiftly become an obsession and lead to all sorts of bizarre behavior, such as lopping off one's own ear!" Pamela observed.

"Dash is hardly as mad as Van Gogh—I don't mean that. It's more like a Pygmalion thing, you know? It's like he created me from all his years of experience, molded me to absorb a crash course in television until I became more knowledgeable than men twice my age—then he stuffed it down their throats by putting me in charge of the network. It used to really hurt him, the things the guys said about us when we first started dating and I got my own show. There was a lot of jealousy and I guess I didn't help matters any by telling the execs to go fuck themselves when they hit on me. Dash knew they were giving me a bad time but there wasn't a hell of a lot he could do about it. You can't fire all your producers just because they want to go to bed with your wife. So, instead, he made me more powerful, taught me everything he knows about television—and believe me, he knows plenty! 'Knowledge is more intimidating than a sword,' he used to say."

"It was really fun then, in the beginning. We sometimes sat up all night talking, going over old clippings and publicity—Dash was a 'Boy Wonder' in the early stages of television and built KNAB single-handedly. Gosh, he used to look so—beautiful—yes, that's the word. He looked absolutely beautiful then, a total babe as the kids say." She was silent for a moment, frowning. "He looks so wistful now when he looks at those pictures and I know he can't help comparing that young, virile Dash to himself today. He didn't used to. When we first started our affair he was a great lover and seemed proud of his sexual prowess." She grinned wryly. "Men are such peacocks—no pun intended!"

"Hear, hear," Pamela drawled. She raised herself slightly to gaze across the meadow. "Where has *my* peacock gotten himself off too, I wonder? The champagne should be properly chilled by now surely!"

"What's it like with you, Pam, being with someone so much younger? With Dash it's sort of sad, somehow."

"Sad is the very last thing it is with me, luv! It's totally joyous in *every* way."

"Maybe sad isn't the word I mean. It's just that he seems so grateful to be with me, you know? Like he'll undress me and just stare at me for the longest time; or

## The Love Game 195

he'll just caress me all over, commenting on my smooth, young skin, that sort of thing. He's always telling me how *young* I am, and it just makes me realize how *old* he is! It's awful, Pam, and I don't know what to do."

"You mean there's no sex at all, luv?"

"Not really. Oh, he'll satisfy me, you know, go down on me or use his hand or something, but it's hardly the same. I *like* sex, damn it. Does that make me bad? And I do not want to be treated like some pampered pet to be humored and satisfied. God, I want the man Dash used to be! I want to be a wife and maybe even a mother."

"Then methinks you have chosen the wrong mate. Dash is a bit long in the tooth to be starting a second family—and he obviously isn't 'long' enough in other areas to keep a young bride happy!"

"Pamela, you're awful!" But she laughed too and sat up to gaze for a moment at the peaceful scene of grazing horses and babbling brook. She should be as serene. She certainly had everything she had ever dreamed of and more. Sex didn't used to be so important to her; maybe it shouldn't be now. She loved Dash and was happy working with him and living with him—so what if their sex life wasn't crashing cymbals and fireworks. But it used to be, she told herself, before Marc Monroe had bewitched her, and spoiled her for any other man.

"Awful, perhaps, but correct. Sex is a terribly big part of any relationship. If you aren't happy in the kip, you're not going to be happy in the drawing room, as dear Uncle Percy liked to say." She shaded her eyes with her hand and smiled when she saw Ashley topping a small hill and walking toward them. "Ah, there's me love, now." She ran her fingers through her hair, straightening it, and quickly applied fresh lip gloss. "Have you thought about taking on a lover? Some young stud who'll give you what you need physically?"

"Of course not!" Cathy was clearly shocked. "I wouldn't do that to Dash."

"Oh? Then what was Lon? Were you two having a script conference in the laundry room?"

Cathy laughed and leaned forward, hugging her knees and resting her chin on her hands. "You know, it was really pretty awful. I think I would have felt better if I had just gone home and used the vibrator!"

"I say, old girl, you need a man and quick! Shall I see if Ash has a friend?" She giggled wickedly. "Those young boys are *definitely* all they're cracked up to be!"

"Are they really, Pam?" Cathy asked seriously. "I mean, are you *really* happy with Ash? Don't people look at you funny when you go out together? People are always staring at Dash and me, and I can just hear the whispers: 'She must have married him for his money and it's obvious what he married her for!' It's just so tacky, but it doesn't do any good to get mad."

"No, it doesn't. To become angry with fools is a total waste of time." Her face suddenly grew sad and she turned once more to gaze at Ashley who was now stooped by the creek's edge retrieving the bottle of champagne.

"It hasn't been easy for you, either, has it, my friend?" Cathy asked softly. She reached over to grip Pamela's hand and was startled by the swift pain in her green eyes.

"No, not easy . . ." She gave a short, dry laugh. "Not easy at all."

"Did something happen? Did the school find out?"

"Much worse than that. His mother."

"Oh no! What happened?"

"Well, after she called me every vile and despicable name she could think of, in four languages yet, she threatened to have me arrested for statutory rape! Can you bloody well *believe* it? Me, the Lady of Glendorshire, whose past mates have all gone kicking and screaming, fingernails still digging into the door frame as I booted them out. Me, one hell of a nice broad, who knows how to make a man feel good about himself—arrested for rape? Surely you Americans have better things to do with your tax dollars!" She chuckled but it was hollow, and her eyes went again to Ashley kneeling by the bank of the creek.

"Oh, God, Pamela, I'm so sorry. Is there anything I can do? I mean, I know there's probably nothing anyone can actually *do*, but—" She stopped speaking and just held out her arms and Pamela went into them and they hugged.

"Thanks, ducks. If there is, I'll let you know." She sighed and passed her long fingers slowly across her face, rubbing her eyes hard. "Thus far, she's given him an ultimatum. Either he buckles down to his schoolwork and stops seeing that "old pervert" or she sends him to Boston and a military academy that is tougher than West Point, from what I've heard. And, of course, she makes good her threat and files charges against me for leading a minor astray!"

"A minor? You mean he's just—?"

"Seventeen. Yes, shocking, isn't it?" "But I love him, damn it! I love him so much I know I'd die without him—and he feels the same way! He's told me! I know it!"

"I know it, too, Pam, I know he loves you. God, it's written all over his face every time he looks at you!" She was a little surprised to see such passion and emotion coming from the ordinarily cool and sardonic Lady Pamela. "Well, what does he say? How does Ash feel about his mother's ultimatum? He certainly isn't going for it, is he?"

"Not really. But he still has a couple of months before graduation and four months before his eighteenth birthday so, naturally, he can't make too many waves right now. He wants his diploma, of course, so he's told the old hag that he will bring his grades up to As and he will devote himself to his studies. When she asked what he intended doing with his 'aging mistress,' he told her that how and with whom he satisfied himself was none of her bloody business."

"She grumbled some but was forced to return to New York and her hit play. Quite surprising, that. Lucky for Hedy Carrington that the play's a hit. She was almost all the way down the Scotch bottle when Broadway beckoned, I understand." Pamela busied herself with laying out the rest of the delectable lunch, and Cathy bent to help her.

"But you'll still see each other, won't you? I mean, how in the world could Hedy Carrington ever find out if Ash still saw you?" She carefully unwrapped a dozen deviled eggs topped with black caviar and placed them on a pretty paper plate.

"When you're as rich as Hedy Carrington, luv, you can find out anything you want to know.

"Before all this business with Ashley started, and believe me, luv, I tried to fight it, I really did!—anyway, before I fell in love with him, I was getting rather deeply into reincarnation. I was on the verge of convincing myself that we had indeed lived past lives, known past loves, and would know them again in present and future lives. When I met Ash it was like a blind person seeing for the first time someone they had always known by their smell, touch, laugh, feel—everything but the face. I didn't recognize his face when I first met him, but I recognized *him*—do you understand, Cathy? I knew who he was. He was my man. My love."

"Yes—yes, I do know what you mean. I felt that way once. The first time I saw Marc I recognized him immediately as the man who would cause me the greatest pain—and perhaps the greatest happiness."

"I never saw Ash as a 'boy,'" Pamela went on, her gaze still on her lover who was bent over the task of opening the champagne bottle down by the creek. One day in equestrian class our eyes met—I don't know what I was doing, tightening the girth or something like that, but I looked up and into those incredibly beautiful and soulful brown eyes and I knew! And I also knew that *he* knew. But he was so young, you understand, so inexperienced, that I had to take the initiative." She laughed softly and her already pretty face turned beautiful.

"I invited him for coffee, I remember, and we sat for the better part of two hours, just staring at one another, each of us starting a sentence only to have the other finish it. It was uncanny! We *knew* each other! And we knew we loved one another. We went directly to my place and made love until dawn's early light and, quite frankly, haven't stopped since except to attend our respective classes."

"I do know what you mean, Pamela. I felt that way about Marc. I thought it was for all time. I thought we were pieces of a puzzle that fit perfectly and that it would stay that way." She squinted against the bright spring sunshine. A red halo appeared around Ashley's head as he rose and started toward them. His youthful thighs and legs were sensual in skin-tight jeans, and she could easily discern the bulge of his crotch. God, when had she last seen Dash in a pair of ass-hugging jeans. But she had seen Marc and remembered with a rush of desire how fantastic he had looked.

"Why don't you simply have an affair with Marc?" Pamela asked. "You say you love Dash, and it's obvious that you love what he can do for you and give you, but you still need that physical release that, apparently, Dash cannot provide. Why not Marc? He's a bit of a playboy, isn't he? Surely he wouldn't be any threat to your marriage. Or would he?"

"God, if you only knew how much I wish I could do just that! Simply have an affair with him—use him like he used me, just for sex and nothing else."

"I think it was a bit more than that, luv," Pamela said softly. "I saw you two together, remember? You were very much in love . . ."

"That was a hundred years ago," Cathy interrupted shortly. She turned to watch Ashley's approach, God, he was a handsome boy—but still just a boy—and she needed a man. Why not Marc? He sure as hell turned her on more than any man she had ever had. Why not simply enter into an affair with him, use him when she wanted or needed him? He would undoubtedly go for it—he had been cheating on Bitsy from the start, apparently.

"Good afternoon, ladies. May I interest you in a spot of the bubbly?" Ashley sank down on the plaid blanket next to Pam, kissing her thoroughly before glancing over to grin at Cathy. He was even beginning to sound like Pamela, Cathy thought with a smile.

"It's about time," Pamela laughed, reaching for the champagne. "I was on the verge of losing the habit!" She took out three glasses and began to pour.

"Oh, not for me, Pamela, thanks." Cathy reached into the picnic basket and withdrew a bottle of Perrier water and filled her glass. "I've been drinking too much lately, and after last night I think I'd better cool it for awhile." She exchanged a secret smile with Pamela.

"Whatever you say, ducks." She touched her glass to Ashley's. "To you, darling."

"To *us*," he said and his dark eyes were soft with love—and Cathy felt like crying watching them. She ducked her head quickly to the picnic basket and began serving up the food.

## The Love Game

\* \* \*

Cathy sat in her large, opulent bedroom, a fantasy of silk and velvet, watching television. She wore a Dior dressing gown in the softest satin and white satin mules were on her feet which were propped upon a crushed velvet ottoman. It was just a little after eight o'clock and she was bored and restless at the prospect of an endless evening stretching before her. Dash lay sleeping in his own bedroom across the hall where he had retired after an early dinner, pleading fatigue. "Too much golf," he had said, kissing her goodnight. "I'm sorry about not taking you out to dinner, sweetheart. Maybe tomorrow night, okay?" She had hidden her disappointment and smiled, agreeing to the raincheck. He did look tired, and there was an unhealthy pallor to his face. His jowls seemed to sag as did his body when he eased it wearily into bed. He looked very old, and she felt hot tears stinging behind her eyelids as she bent to kiss him goodnight.

Maybe he's ill, she thought now, watching the antics of "The Love Boat" gang on television but not really paying attention. Men his age were often afflicted with any number of complaints. She would make an appointment with his doctor on Monday and drive him there herself to make sure he kept it. He was just like a kid when it came to doctors and dentists; he had to be prodded into going.

She got to her feet and went to the portable bar in the corner of her bedroom and poured herself a brandy snifter of Courvoisier and went to the sliding glass doors that led to the patio and pool area. It was a gorgeous soft, spring evening, a full moon spreading a blanket of silver over everything below, giving shrubs and buildings an enchanted look. She stepped out onto the patio and lifted her face to the sky, staring at the stars, the moon, shivering a little when the cool breeze touched her bare flesh. Is this all there is? she thought. Is this what it means to be rich and famous and successful? To be alone in a mansion that was the envy of all who saw it? There were two Rolls-Royces in the garage, her own Mercedes-Benz parked in the front of the house—and no where to go. There were twenty-three rooms in her own fabulous home—and no one in them except a sleeping old man.

Maybe I should get a dog, she thought as she strolled along the brick path amid fountains and lacy spills of delicate ferns, or a kitten—or even a baby. She sank down on a stone bench next to goldfish pond and stared into its mirrorlike surface. Even the fish were asleep. She sighed and drank her Courvosier. What would Dash say if she told him she wanted a baby?

"Jesus, I don't want a baby," she said and her voice sounded loud in the still night. "I just want someone to love." She curled her feet under her and leaned back, enjoying the rough hardness of the stone bench. Her life had become too soft. Too easy. Nothing was a challenge anymore. A baby would be a challenge, she supposed. But would it be fair to the child to bring it into her restless world? She had once wanted to have a baby with Marc, but then she had seen it as a completion of their love, not as an object to entertain her and help fill her lonely evenings.

She rose and strolled slowly back toward the house and her empty bedroom. She left the sliding glass doors open so she could feel the cool breeze as she curled up again in her chair in front of the television set. Couples were frolicking gaily on board the *Love Boat*, intently pursuing that week's love interest and Cathy felt a tight, hot knot in her throat. She swallowed more brandy, emptying the glass, and still the burning lump filled her throat, and she couldn't seem to dislodge it.

She went to the bar to refill her brandy snifter and felt

like crying. She supposed this was the way most alcoholics got started—alone and lonely, needing something to replace the yearning in their hearts, something to dull the edges of reality and make the long nights shorter. With Marc it had seemed that the nights were never long enough. There was never enough time to talk and laugh and make love and play.

"Your eyes have shot arrows into my heart." She remembered him saying that to her and tears spilled over and ran down her cheeks, blurring the picture on the television screen, but she did not raise her hand to wipe them away. She sat so still she might have been a fixture in the luxurious room, a porcelain figurine purchased with the rest of the lovely furnishings.

"Your eyes have shot arrows into my heart," he had whispered to her and she had answered, "That's from Dante"—and he had said, "Yes, and for the first time I understand what it means."

"Oh, Marc—God, what happened to us?" She whispered the words, wailed them piteously—and they hung there in the empty room without an answer.

## *Chapter Twelve*

"Well, are you going to tell me now?" Cathy and Dash were in the back seat of the Silver Cloud Rolls, the window that separated them from the chauffeur was closed as were the heavy black velvet curtains on the side windows. She took his arm and shook it gently. "Dash? What did the doctor say?" He seemed not to hear as he leaned forward and opened the small, compact bar on the back of the front seat and poured himself a Bourbon.

"Want something to drink, honey?" He took a pair of tongs and dropped ice cubes into his old-fashioned glass and swirled them around and around with his index finger.

"No, I do not want anything to drink. God, Dash, it's barely noon!"

"It's the cocktail hour in London." He grinned at her and swallowed some of his Bourbon.

"Ha ha, very funny." She frowned at him. He could be so damn exasperating at times she could kick him. "Will you please tell me what the doctor said? God, you rushed me out of his office so fast I thought the place was being raided!"

"I hate doctor's offices—they always smell so sterile." He drank again, choking and coughing, and she shot him a worried look.

## The Love Game 205

"Are you all right, Dash? For God's sake, please tell me what the doctor said! I want to know if I'm going to be a young widow or an old married woman!" She said it lightly but saw the sudden anguish on his face before he turned away. "Dash? Darling, are you all right? Nothing's wrong, is it? Tell me—please."

He knocked back the Bourbon and leaned forward for a refill. When he faced her he was smiling. "Of course I'm all right. I just have a little—what do you girls call it? Female trouble? Well, I have a little male trouble. Seems the old plumbing needs a lube job or something." He laughed and put his arm around her shoulders to draw her close.

"Is it serious? What did Dr. Moss say to do?"

"Oh, the usual. Take it easy. Keep regular hours—and hopefully, bowels. Bland diet. Mild exercise."

"Are you sure? I'm going to call him and ask him."

"Don't be silly, Cath. It's nothing. Just a little constipation. Too much rich food." He took a swallow of Bourbon and grinned at her, but she did not return it.

"And I'm sure that expensive Bourbon is just terrific for you."

"Medicinal purposes only, I assure you!" He sipped again and reached into his vest pocket for a cigar.

"If you light that thing, you can tell Williams to let me out at the next corner." She was angry and didn't exactly know why. She sensed there was something Dash wasn't telling her, and it frightened her. She felt insecure for the first time since marrying him.

"Yes ma'am," he said meekly and replaced the cigar in his pocket. "Is there anything else I can do to make you happy?"

"Yes. You can tell me the truth." She turned in the lush leather seat and faced him squarely. "You're lying, Dash. There *is* something wrong, isn't there?"

"Jesus Christ, woman, what do you want me to do?

Spread my legs so you can frisk me for a death certificate?"

I wish to hell you'd spread *mine* once in a while, she thought savagely, almost hating him. Her nerves were strung tight, and she was getting a headache. It seemed that she had been just one big ache for the past couple of months. "Stop it, Dash. You're not terribly amusing today."

"So it would seem."

They rode in silence for several minutes, then Cathy turned to him and took his hand. "I'm sorry for snapping at you, darling, it's just that I'm so worried about you. If there's anything wrong with you, I want to know so I can help, that's all."

"Then love me," he said hoarsely and gripped her hand so tight the large diamond ring cut painfully into her flesh. "Just love me and stay close by me. That's all the help I'll ever need or want!"

"You know I love you." She stared at him, at the sudden brightness of his pale blue eyes, the depth of love she saw there. It shook her seeing such naked emotion and she was swept with a chill that she would remember in weeks to come.

"Don't go to the studio this afternoon," he said. "Come home with me and we'll—we'll play. Do something crazy."

She looked at him in amazement. "It's Monday. You know how busy Mondays are." He was still gripping her hand and she gently disengaged the hurting fingers.

"Screw Mondays. I want to spend the day with my best girl." Drawing her across his lap, he smothered in her a powerful hug and kissed her soundly, his hands cupping her buttocks. "Don't you want to play with me, my little Cathy?"

"Of course, Dash, it's just that—you know, the studio. . . ."

"Forget the studio for five minutes, can't you?" He kissed her again and lifted her farther onto his lap, snuggling her against his chest like a baby. "Don't forget, I still own that fucking network, and I order you to take the day off, Mrs. Sunderling. Understand?"

"Yes, boss." She leaned happily against him, wanting desperately to believe that now everything was going to be all right. He sounded like the old Dash of their courting days and the hot look in his eyes was wonderfully familiar. She reached down to grip his penis and heard his sigh of pleasure. "Is this what you had in mind, boss?" She stroked him sensually through his trousers and wanted to laugh out loud when she felt his growing response. It *was* going to be all right. He wanted her—and, God, how she wanted and needed him! She had been a mass of raw nerve endings ever since her tawdry encounter with Lon Howland. The awkward, fast coupling had not relieved her as she had hoped but had added to her frustrations.

"That's *exactly* what I had in mind, Mrs. Sunderling—and I'll give you one hour to stop that." He pressed himself against her hand and put his own hand over her breast, caressing it gently. "Unless, of couse, you have some objections to getting laid in the back seat of a Rolls on Wilshire Boulevard!" He slipped his hand inside her blouse and cupped her naked breast, lowering his head to kiss it.

"Sounds terribly exciting," she murmured, "but shouldn't we close the curtains? Williams might have a heart attack." She brought his head up and kissed him, nibbling his lips, her hand still moving expertly, bringing him to full erection.

"That wouldn't do. Poor Williams . . ." He leaned back in the corner of the seat, bringing her over on top of him and pressed himself hard against her, both hands covering her buttocks, holding her firmly against him.

"Yes, poor Williams—he's been much too good a chauffeur to have a heart attack on Wilshire Boulevard." She undulated slowly, up and down, up and down, sliding sensually over his penis, rubbing her breasts across his chest.

"I agree." His voice was a husky whisper. "We mustn't give Williams a heart attack on Wilshire Boulevard." He kissed her, held her closer still. He pulled away, laughed shakily. "Or me either, for that matter!" He straightened up, eased her off his lap and looked hard into her face. "God, Cathy, I love you! If I died this minute, I'd go a happy and fulfilled man for having loved you."

"The only place you're going, mister, is straight to bed! Tell Williams to step on it—I want to make love to my wonderful, sexy husband." She snuggled against him, happy, excited. This was the way it should be. This was the way it *would* be in the future if she had anything to say about it. All she had ever really wanted was Dash until Marc had come along and messed up her plans. Dash had been an exciting and inventive lover in those early days in San Francisco, and he could be again, with her help. She would exorcise Marc completely from her mind and devote herself to making Dash happy. Then, it seemed only logical, she would be happy as well.

Dash leaned forward to tap on the glass. "Break the law, Williams. We have pressing business at home."

"Yes *sir*, Mr. Sunderling." The big silver and black Rolls leapt ahead as Williams maneuvered it expertly through the heavy, noon traffic. He raised his eyes to the rearview mirror and saw his employer in a passionate embrace with his sexy young wife. "Lucky bastard," he muttered under his breath and laid rubber for fifty yards, turning up Sunset Boulevard.

"I'm sorry, Cathy. God, you'll never know how damn sorry I am!" Dash leaned over the huddled form of his wife, awkwardly stroking her shoulder. "Don't cry, baby..."

"I'm not crying." Cathy flung his hand off her shoulder and sat up in bed, moving away from him. The gold satin sheet fell to her waist and she raised it to cover her breasts—then stared defiantly at him and let it fall again.

"Sweetheart, if you'll just give me a little time..." He swallowed and shrugged helplessly, gave her a wavering smile. "It's just that you're so damn sexy, so beautiful, you overwhelm me—make me crazy—I don't know..." He leaned away from her and reached to the nightstand for his glass of brandy.

"Maybe if you'd lay off the booze you'd be able to get it up," she sneered and was instantly sorry when she saw the hurt expression in his eyes. "Oh, the hell with it—drink all you want. Drink yourself to death for all I care. I'm going to get stoned."

Cathy flung herself out of bed and walked naked to the dresser and took out a box of joints, knowing he hated her to smoke pot. Not only was he afraid of her getting busted, but he, like the rest of his generation, believed that marijuana led to heroin and an early grave or a life of sin—whichever came first.

She lit up and went to the window and stood gazing moodily out at the white-hot day. It was cool in her bedroom with the drapes drawn against the sun's glare, and soft music filtered in romantically. She had even lightly sprayed her pillows and sheets with Joy perfume, Dash's favorite. And for what? She turned and stared at him, a crushed-looking heap propped up against her tufted satin headboard, drinking, staring back at her. Fury such as she had never known raged inside her brain, and she gripped the drapes until her knuckles turned white, wanting to bury her fists in his face, to smash that hangdog look to a pulp, to kill him.

As swiftly as it had blazed, her anger died and she was

ashamed of herself for feeling that way about Dash. He was her husband. She had chosen him, and she loved him and she would make it good again between them.

Maybe she could get him high. She knew he'd never tried pot and she also knew that he would do anything she asked him to do. She had read a little about impotence and realized the importance of being patient and relaxed. It was all in the guy's mind, anyway, wasn't it? Well, she'd get him stoned out of his mind and seduce him!

The first hour that they had been home had been beautiful. They had swum together naked, laughing and necking, teasing. They had sat talking as they hadn't talked for some time in the big redwood hot tub, sipping cold champagne. Dash had gotten and lost a dozen erections before they finally got to the bedroom and another dozen during the sizzling foreplay in Cathy's kingsize bed. She had been so hot, she had begged him to make love to her, *now*—and he hadn't been able to. He had tried to satisfy her with his finger, and she had angrily pushed him away, hating him. Hating herself for wanting him.

"Cathy, please come back to bed. We'll just talk, okay? Don't be mad at me, baby. Don't hate me—God, I couldn't stand it if you . . ."

"Oh, Dash, I don't hate you!" She went to him, stooped to kiss his forehead. "I love you, you big dummy, that's the problem!" She took a huge mouthful of smoke and kissed him, blowing the heady stuff into his mouth. "Don't let it out," she cautioned. "Just inhale it like you would a cigarette, only deeper."

"Jesus Christ, I don't want any of that shit!" He sat up, coughing and spluttering, reaching for his brandy.

"Oh no you don't. No more booze until you get high with me." She took the snifter from him and repeated the procedure of blowing smoke into his mouth, this time keeping her lips pressed firmly to his until he had obediently inhaled. She did it again, then said, "Now—don't you feel better? Did you get a buzz?"

"No, I didn't get a damn thing except a tickle in my throat. Hand me my drink."

"Come on, Dash—give it a chance to work." She kissed him again, blowing the smoke slowly and steadily down his throat. He was grinning when she drew away.

"I don't know about the pot," he chuckled, "but I sure like the package it comes in!" He pulled her into his arms and kissed her again.

"No more kisses without the pot," she giggled, toking again and leaning forward. He reached for her eagerly this time, opening his mouth for the smoke and sucking it in as deeply as she had instructed.

"Umm, more," he murmured. He fell back against the pillows, eyes closed, a dreamy smile on his lips.

"Wait, I have to get another one." She hurriedly lit a fresh joint and filled her mouth with smoke. She stretched out fully on top of him and pressed her lips to his, and he held her tightly, readily gulping in the smoke.

"I think I feel it now," he said. "It's warm and fuzzy—like cotton." He giggled and enthusiastically accepted the next kiss. A muffled roar filled his head and his heartbeat slowed, and all he was aware of was Cathy, naked and smooth in his arms. Cathy, kissing him and blowing new life into his body. Lifting him out of the old one that didn't work anymore. Desire coursed through him, setting up an irregular pulse beat in his groin. He felt himself growing hard, and it seemed to be in slow motion, and it was very funny and he laughed.

"Yep, I think you've got it, sweetie!" Cathy laughed too, and kissed him again, this time without the pot. "Now scoot down in bed—there, like that." She propped pillows beneath his head and pulled the gold satin sheet all the way off his body. She took a drink of brandy and bent quickly to take his penis into her mouth. The cold-hot liquor burned and thrilled him, and she swished it around in her mouth, sucking him at the same time, nibbling, teasing, until she had swallowed all the brandy. She writhed up his body like a sexy snake uncoiling and kissed him with her brandy-scented lips. She took another mouthful, bending now to his nipples to kiss and suck and soak them in the expensive Courvoisier. She seemed to unravel, sliding sensuously over his body, nipping him with her sharp little teeth, kissing him with her soft, moist lips. She fondled him tenderly, patiently, urging his response, dipping her shiny blond head to take him in her mouth and draw him out of himself.

All the pain and fear that Dash had been feeling for the past three months vanished, left him as if it had never been. He felt sixteen again and madly, passionately in love with his girl. She was driving him mad, blowing his mind. Forgotten completely was his doctor's warning about no sex. Dissolved like a bad memory was his impotence and the pain he had recently suffered with his erections. All he wanted, all he could think of, was making love to this incredibly beautiful love goddess who was giving him such indescribable joy.

He filled his arms with her, and she straddled him and sank down upon him, and he thought he would surely die from happiness. She leaned forward, her breasts swaying hypnotically in front of his eyes, and he reached out and captured one creamy globe and brought it to his mouth. She moved upon him, whispering, sighing, moaning, her eyes shining in the dim room, gazing at him rapturously. He grasped her by the shoulders and rolled her over, staying solidly inside her, loving her. He filled his whole being with her and together they soared higher than the highest high.

\* \* \*

## The Love Game 213

"But, Dash, I don't want to go to New York without you!" Cathy set her jaw stubbornly and glared across the table at him. They were lunching in the studio commissary and their meal, as well as their conversation, had been interrupted a dozen times by table-hoppers. "Why can't you come, too?"

"I can't, baby. It's a crucial time. The Nielsen ratings are coming out next week, and I've got a hell of a line-up to promote by then." He took a sip of his iced tea and moved a leaf of lettuce around on his plate. The seafood salad he had ordered sat untouched before him. "You know this is the busiest time of the year."

"Then why can't I stay and help? We can send someone else to New York."

"Honey, I've already explained. It's a hell of a big event and a proper representative of KNAB must attend. Not only because of the party—quite a hoopla, I understand—but because we're running a special on the Pope's visit to the United States. Come on, sugar, admit it—you want to see the Pope, don't you?

"Oh, sure, that'll be a real thrill for a Baptist kid from Oklahoma," she said sarcastically. "Well, Dash, quite frankly, you can't *make* me go, you know. Send someone else—Solly Hauser or Arthur Berg. I'm sure they'd be thrilled to represent KNAB."

"No, they aren't important enough." He sighed mightily. "I guess I'll have to go after all." He lowered his eyes, let his shoulders slump. "I don't know what I'll tell Doc Moss, though. He definitely told me, 'no traveling—nothing too strenuous.'" He met her eyes briefly and his were pathetic-looking, his face drawn and ill. It had the effect he intended.

"Oh, Christ, Dash, I'll go." She looked at him anxiously. "Don't worry about it, darling. I just want you to follow the doctor's orders and get well, okay?" She reached across the table to squeeze his hand.

"Thanks, sweetheart, I knew I could count on you." He returned the squeeze. "It won't be long—a few days."

"I'm just going to the party and the press conference—two days, tops." She forked in the last of her rice-stuffed chicken breast and washed it down with coffee. "You're sending a camera crew?"

"Of course. The Pope's visit is one of the biggest events of the year and KNAB will have complete coverage." He scrawled his name on the luncheon check and stood, taking her arm. "Ready, hon? Let's get back to the office and check over your schedule. You should leave tomorrow morning."

"Jeez, are you trying to get rid of me, or something?" She allowed him to steer her through the commissary and outside. "I've never felt so hustled in my life!"

"Don't be silly, sweetie." He laughed but it didn't ring true, and she turned to look sharply at him. What in hell was he up to? He had been acting rather strange all week—and that one love-drenched night had not been repeated. When Cathy had approached him the very next night, expecting a replay, he had gently refused, pleading fatigue and other aches and pains, and she had gone alone to her own bedroom to toss restlessly until her alarm went off.

The efficient Clare had made all the arrangements and a first class, round-trip ticket to New York was waiting on her desk when Cathy and Dash returned from lunch. "Pretty sure of yourself, weren't you, pal?" Cathy said when the door to Dash's private office had closed behind them. She went to the bar for a drink, then changed her mind. She was drinking much too much lately and had sworn to cut down.

Dash hugged her from behind, nuzzling her neck. "If a man can't be sure of his own wife, who can he be sure

## The Love Game

of?" He kissed her neck but she pulled away when he reached for her lips.

"Don't start anything you can't finish," she said shortly, moving away from him. She felt mean and didn't care if she hurt his feelings.

"That was unfair, little Cathy."

"Was it? Sorry." She flipped open the plane ticket and read it without seeing it. She stiffened when he again came up behind her and hugged her.

"Darling, please just bear with me a little longer. I'm going to get straightened out, you'll see." He closed his eyes and murmured a silent prayer that indeed everything would soon be straightened out. He had made an appointment for a biopsy the following day, at Dr. Moss's insistence. "We'll just snip a bit of tissue from the rectum, Dash, and see what's going on in there," he had said. "It certainly isn't normal to feel so much pain during intercourse—probably a blockage of some sort."

Dash had agreed to the twenty-four-hour hospital stay but he had wanted Cathy as far away as possible. Remembering Grace's pathetic form lying in her hospital bed, he had vowed that no one he loved would ever see him that way. The Pope's visit to the States had been just the excuse he needed to get her out of town. By the time she returned, he would be recovered, the irritating "male trouble" taken care of, and he would be able to function again as a man and a husband.

"I sincerely hope so, Dash." Cathy tucked the plane ticket into her purse and walked to the door. "I'd better get home and start packing if I'm leaving tomorrow morning. Will I see you at dinner?"

"Of course, darling. I'll be home around five-thirty. Would you like to go out someplace?"

"No, I think just dinner at home since I have to get up so early." She blew him a kiss. "Bye."

"Bye, my darling." He watched the door close and then went directly to the bar and poured himself a double Bourbon.

The party had indeed been a gala affair as Dash had predicted, but Cathy had not had a ball as he had also predicted. Instead, she had been rather bored and after the usual roast beef dinner had gone back on her promise to cut down on her drinking. She had switched from champagne to stingers and thereafter watched the proceedings with a sort of detached amusement. She had sat at the table with the others from KNAB and had spent most of the evening talking with Byron St. James, Marc's personal manager. "Even talk show hosts need publicity and personal management," he was telling her earnestly. "Or even network heads, for that matter." He blinked at her from behind his glasses and grinned. "If you sign with me I'll make you bigger than Barbara Walters."

"I'm already bigger than Barbara Walters." She motioned to the waiter to bring her another stinger.

"Just on the West Coast, I can get you . . ."

"Look, I'm really not interested, okay, Byron? I already have an agent, Earl Brill, and I don't see any reason to pay an additional fifteen percent for publicity I don't need or want." She flashed a smile at the waiter (a handsome young hunk in skin-tight black pants and open-necked white shirt) when he set a fresh drink before her. He hesitated a moment, seeing the invitation in her eyes, but when she abruptly turned away, he shrugged and went back to his duties.

"You might change your mind. Never know when you might need a good publicity man to sell something—or hush something up!" He raised an eyebrow in the direction of the departing waiter, and Cathy had to smile. Jesus, would the man never give up? She sipped

## The Love Game 217

her stinger and looked at him. Fortyish, bespectacled, boyishly good-looking, Byron St. James was a notorious head-hunter and she supposed she should be flattered. He only went after clients who were "hot," often luring them away from managers whom they had been with since the early days of their careers. She knew that he had handled Bitsy during her first series and that he had signed her up again when "The Love Game" had become a hit. He was responsible too for Marc's success and had presented him to the public as a courageous, modest, war correspondent, worthy of a Pulitzer Prize. Hah! she thought sourly, the only prize he deserved was for "Prick of the Year."

"If I decide to assassinate the Pope, I'll let you know." She gave him a wide-eyed look. "That *is* what you meant about being able to 'hush something up,' wasn't it? I mean, you surely weren't intimating that I have eyes for that sexy, young waiter, were you?"

"What waiter?" he said, equally innocent, eyes wide behind the horn-rimmed glasses.

Cathy had to laugh. "I see what you mean. A personal manager could be very helpful in certain situations. I'll keep that in mind." She sipped again, her eyes wandering restlessly about the big, packed ballroom. Everyone who was anyone was there, it seemed. It was a little after one in the morning, and yet the party showed no signs of ending. There must have been at least two thousand people milling about, drinking, laughing, talking, dancing, making deals, and yet she had never felt more alone in her life. She had been drinking steadily since dinner, hoping to dull the nagging ache in her head, but it hadn't helped. She was completely sober and still alone.

"Would you like another drink?" Byron asked. "Or coffee?"

"No, thanks, I think I'm going to call it a night." She

tossed off the last of her stinger and stood, smiling down at him. "Thanks for being my dinner partner, Byron. I suppose I'll see you tomorrow at the press conference. Goodnight." She made her way through the crowd and outside where she declined the doorman's offer to call a taxi for her. She felt like walking. It was one of those wonderfully cool spring evenings and she turned up the collar of her mink coat, shoving her hands into the pockets. It was only a couple of blocks to her hotel so she figured her chances of getting mugged were small. As she walked, listening to the sounds of the still bustling city, she remembered the words to an old Frank Sinatra song; something about New York being the loneliest city in the world to be alone in.

She nodded to the doorman as she entered the elegant foyer of the Hampshire House hotel and went to the stately elevator, giving the elevator man her floor number. When she opened her door she was surprised to see a light burning and to hear soft music playing. She was sure she had turned everything off before leaving for the party.

"Well, it's about time! That must have been a hell of a party. Maybe I should have gone after all."

She stopped still and stared. Marc Monroe sat on the sofa, a drink in his hand, shoes off and feet upon the coffee table. An open *Newsweek* magazine lay in his lap. She slammed the door behind her and stalked toward him. "What are you doing here? Who in hell let you into my room?"

"Good evening to you too! I'm fine, thanks." He grinned impudently up at her.

"How did you get in here, Marc? And what in hell do you want?" She tossed her purse on the sofa and shrugged out of her mink, dropping it on top of the purse. She wore a floor-length black gown that hugged her figure like a second skin. High-necked and long-sleeved with a slit up one side, it was more revealing than anything Marc had ever seen. He sucked in his breath and just stared at her.

"You are undoubtedly the most beautiful sight I've ever seen," he whispered.

Cathy stared into those silver-gray eyes she loved so well and for a moment she wavered, wanting to believe what she saw there. God, he was so handsome, it almost hurt her eyes to look at him. Lean and sexy and tall and young. His long legs were encased in faded Levis, and his sweatshirt was slightly rumpled, but to her he had never looked better. It seemed like years since she had seen him, and she just stood for a moment, drinking in the sight of him. He kept his eyes steadily on hers and did not speak either. His lips were slightly parted, and she remembered, with a rush of desire, how they had felt on hers. How he had felt in her arms. . . .

She spun away and went quickly to the bar and mixed herself a drink. He had no right to be here! Her hands shook as she brought the glass to her lips and drank. Damn him anyway for barging into her life again, disrupting her thoughts, her security. "What are you doing here, Marc?" she asked, and her voice was as weak as her will. She knew she could not tell him to leave.

"I had to see you, talk to you." He walked to her, stood close by her side, looking down into her face. His was serious and so beautiful it made her legs tremble. "I knew you were at the party, so I came here and waited in the bar for you. When you hadn't come home by midnight, I tipped one of the maids to let me in your room—and here I am. Waiting for you—like I'll always wait for you." He took her by the shoulders and brought his head down, silver eyes still boring into hers, slowly bending toward her until his lips touched hers.

She wrenched her mouth away. "Don't!" she cried, backing away from him. "Don't ever try that again!"

"Cathy, God, don't do this! I love you, damn it! I've always loved you. I've never stopped loving you—not for a second! Not even when you married that old man, Sunderling . . ."

"Don't you *dare* say a word against Dash, you bastard!" Her voice was suddenly steel, and her eyes narrowed angrily. "He's twice the man you'll ever be! At least he's not a liar and a cheat!" She stalked to the sofa and sat down before her rubbery legs gave way beneath her. She drank quickly to still the angry pounding of her heart.

"I'm sorry, Cathy. You're right, that was unfair." He sat down across from her in one of the satin brocade armchairs and leaned forward, both hands wrapped around his glass. "But I meant what I said about loving you. I've never stopped."

"Jesus, Marc, you must think me one hell of a big fool! How can you possibly sit there and give me all that love bullshit when we both know you're a fucking liar! I know your wife, remember? She works at *my* network. I see the bios that go out of the publicity department, and I quote: 'Bitsy Bushore, happily married to Marc Monroe— one of the most successful marriages in Hollywood,' et cetera. Need I say more?" She dug under the soft folds of mink and jerked out her purse and reached into it for a joint. Damn, just looking at him sitting there across from her made her so nervous she felt as if she were coming apart at the seams.

"Yeah, that's right—and Byron St. James wrote it! Damn it, Cathy, you know those network bios are bullshit!"

"Not in this case. I've seen the 'happily married couple' at numerous affairs." She lit the joint, dragging in

# The Love Game

deep and holding the smoke down until tears threatened to fall.

"If you only knew," Marc said quietly and laughed, a sad, empty sound.

"Oh, I know all right—you explained everything to me, remember? I understand completely about your 'marriage of convenience' and I congratulate you. It must take one hell of a stud to keep all those women happy!" She sucked in again, anxious for the calming rush. She was trembling so badly she felt he could surely see it, could see straight into her heart. *Your eyes have shot arrows into my heart.* A sob rose in her throat and she quickly took another toke, praying fervently that the drug would hurry and do its thing; ease her out of her panic, mellow her out so nothing or no one mattered.

"I only want to keep one woman happy." He said so quietly she wasn't sure she heard it.

"Just go away, Marc," she said dully. "You've already had me. I'm last year's fool, remember?" She took a sip of her drink and let her head fall back against the sofa cushions. She was suddenly very weary.

"You were never a fool, Cathy. Don't ever think that for a minute!" He leaned forward, silver eyes growing dark and intense. "I was the fool for ever letting you go."

"Hah! You didn't 'let me go,' Marc—you left me!" She gave a short, harsh laugh.

"Not the way you mean. It was never like that! I wanted to take you to Cambodia with me, but when we got into that stupid argument I thought I'd better let you cool off a bit . . ."

"Stupid argument?" She snorted rudely. "Yes, I guess *you* would think it stupid to want to marry the person you're in love with." She sucked again on the joint.

March went on as if she hadn't interrupted, his voice quiet, his eyes intently on her face. "I thought the separation would give us both a chance to think about our situation, you know. I thought when I got back we'd talk about it, decide what to do, see if we still loved one another as much as . . ."

"Oh, *please*, spare me, will you?" She stood and walked across the room, sucking on the joint as if it were life-giving. "Jesus, you sound like a script for 'The Love Game,' for Christ's sake! Can't you be more original?"

"Okay. How's this for originality?" He got to his feet and walked slowly toward her, his eyes never leaving hers. "I am in love for the first time in my life. With you." He stopped in front of her and took the joint from her hand and dropped it in an ashtray, then held both her hands in his. "I have never been in love before. *Never.* Until I met you, I thought there was something wrong with me. I went through life feeling as if my nerve endings had been cut or my heart had been improperly installed because it didn't work like other people's. Oh, I loved *things*—beautiful summer days, puppies, good food, friends—but I never felt what I was supposed to feel when I was with a woman, what all the magazines and books said you should feel. So I just played at love—until you walked into my life."

"Please, *please,* don't!" She tried to pull her hands free but he held them tighter.

"You going to listen to me, Cathy—just listen to what I have to say, and then you can tell me to go to hell and I'll go—I'll leave you alone, but you're going to listen to me first."

"I don't want to listen to you, damn it! You've played with me ever since I met you. I don't want to listen to you any more! I won't believe you—never again!" She jerked back, and he tightened his grip again, drawing her toward him.

"I love you," he said firmly, and his eyes shone with intensity. "I'm *in love* with you, Cathy, and I want us to be together. You can't possibly love Dash—not the way you loved me. Remember how it was between us, darling? Remember?" He shook her gently, and she moaned and shook her head from side to side. "I told you once that your eyes had shot arrows into my heart. They're still there. I'm mortally wounded, my love, and only you can save me...." He lowered his head, and she sobbed aloud and fell into his arms, and he held her close and kissed her lips and eyes and throat, murmuring, "I love you, darling. I'll always love you—don't cry, sweetheart." He kissed her tears, and she clung to him and sobbed, and he held her close, stroking her heaving shoulders, whispering, "Shh, my love, I'm here. I'll be here as long as you let me stay."

"Oh, Marc—Marc, hold me!" She sobbed harder, cried as if she'd never stop. His arms felt so good. So warm. So strong. She pressed herself fully against him and wondered why she was crying when she was so happy.

"Thank you, God," Marc whispered and then scooped Cathy up into his arms and carried her into the bedroom and lowered her upon the bed.

Dash was waiting at the gate when Cathy stepped off the plane with Marc, and for one panicked moment she thought he knew that she had been unfaithful. She drew a little apart from Marc and rushed quickly ahead into Dash's outstretched arms. No matter what she felt for Marc, she would never deliberately hurt or embarrass Dash. And at this point, she wasn't sure what she felt for Marc. They had had a beautiful two days and nights in New York but had not mentioned what was in the back of Cathy's mind: Bitsy and Dash. Of course they had been so busy simply loving and rediscovering one another that they hadn't exactly gotten into any profound discussions, and Cathy had assumed that they would settle matters when they were home in Los Angeles.

Dash! Hi, darling." She lifted her face for his kiss, then looped her arm through his, smiling up at him. "I missed you."

"Those are the three prettiest words I've ever heard." He kissed her again, then turned to grin at Marc. He stuck out his hand. "Hi, Marc. How was the Big Apple?"

"Dirty, crowded, noisy, loud, crime-ridden—and totally captivating!" He shook Dash's hand warmly. "I just wish I had had a few more days to catch a couple of shows."

"Hell, you should have stayed over. What brought you back to the smoggy city?" He kept his arm around Cathy's shoulders as they walked down the long corridor toward the baggage claim area.

"Work, I'm afraid." He walked on the other side of Cathy, occasionally brushing her arm with his. "I let a friend talk me into doctoring up a script he bought for some little horror flick. You know Bill Berg, don't you? The director? He used to be with Columbia."

"Sure, I know Bill. Haven't heard much from him lately. What's he been up to?" He held the door for Cathy and clapped Marc on the shoulder as they entered the baggage claim area.

"He's an independent now, doing those quickie horror films and making a bundle, apparently. The only trouble is, he doesn't pay his writers enough for a really good script so he's always asking me to 'fix' them." Marc laughed good-naturedly, seemingly completely at ease with the man whose wife he had been ravishing for the past two days. Cathy couldn't help but admire his cool.

They collected their luggage, and Dash asked Marc if he needed a ride into town. "Thanks, but Bitsy said she would meet me." He did not look at Cathy when he said it, but if he had, he would have seen sudden, cold fury in her eyes.

"Give Bitsy my love," she said sweetly, and her eyes blazed hard into his before she spun on her heel and stalked toward the door, a bewildered Dash trotting to keep up.

"God damn it," Marc groaned. "I've done it again." He sighed and shifted his bag in his hand, walking outside to wait for Bitsy.

## Chapter Thirteen

KNAB had gained mightily in the ratings race and was swiftly catching up with KABC and KCBS. KNBC still trailed behind. Cathy felt certain that she could take the network all the way to first in the ratings by the fall of the new year, and Dash had given her free rein to do what she thought best.

Cathy pored long hours over scripts, studied the actors' directory looking for new faces, new talent. Last year's hit shows would continue, of course, and with that solid base to build on, she could afford the luxury of going with an unknown. Her suggestions and choices of stars and shows last year had brought the network's profits up from eighty million per year to a staggering one hundred and twenty million.

"Peanuts," Dash had scoffed, "compared to ABC's profits last year of two hundred and twenty-five million!" Cathy had been ready to sock him one when she had seen that he was teasing. He then had withdrawn a jeweler's black velvet case from his pocket and had handed it to her. "A bonus for a job well done," he had said. It was a wide, gold bracelet set with one hundred and twenty small, perfect diamonds—one for each million the studio had earned.

She sat twisting the bracelet around her wrist now as

## The Love Game      227

she talked to Pamela. "Damn, I sure hope we get the World Series for our network," she said. "That would absolutely guarentee us the number one spot by early fall."

"I thought I read somewhere that NBC had the World Series all tied up." Pamela was stretched out in a brightly flowered chaise next to Cathy, her long, lean body glistening with suntan oil.

"We can still hope. The deal's not firm yet." She swung her foot over the edge of the chaise, bouncing it restlessly. "Ready for another?" She motioned to Pamela's empty glass.

"Not at the moment, ducks, thanks."

"How's Ash?"

"Fine, studying hard for his finals. He graduates next month, you know."

"God, is it June already?"

"It will be—in less than a week." She studied her friend's face from behind her large, dark sunglasses. She looked tired and drawn, her usually healthy, shapely figure much thinner than Pamela had ever seen it. She was restless and bored one moment, filled with nervous energy the next. Today was the first time she had seen her since her trip to New York and the gala even though she had spoken with her several times on the phone. She knew that Cathy was busier than usual with selecting the fall line-up, but there was something else there too; she could feel it. Cathy seemed tougher, more reluctant to laugh as openly as she once had. Several times today Pamela had glanced over to see Cathy sitting quietly, staring off into space, an expression of such infinite sadness on her face that Pamela had wanted to reach out and take her in her arms and comfort her. When she had asked if there were anything wrong, Cathy had said sharply, "What could possibly be wrong with my perfect life? I have everything in the world I've ever wanted."

"God, I don't know where the time goes." A faraway expression came into Cathy's eyes and she sighed, then stood abruptly. "I'm ready for another Margarita—how about you?"

"Oh, why not? We're eating soon, aren't we. I'm famished." She had brought three lovely New York steaks when she had arrived, unannounced, and informed Cathy that she was taking the day off and getting some sun. "You look positively ghastley, luv," she had said. "You have an executive's pallor." When Cathy had protested that she had a stack of scripts to read, Pamela had merely clucked her tongue sympathetically and proceeded to put the steaks in the refrigerator and two bottles of Louis Roederer champagne in the freezer. "I'm inviting myself to dinner and I'm supplying it," she had said, and had dipped into her large shopping bag to bring out salad makings and tuck them into the refrigerator as well. "Steak, salad and champagne, a typical Yankee dinner, what?"

Dash had sat outside with them for a few minutes, then had excused himself to go upstairs and lie down, complaining that the sun was too hot. Pamela had raised a questioning eyebrow at Cathy, but she had ignored it, plunging into a long, detailed description of the ratings race—which had bored Pamela to tears.

Cathy took a pitcher of Margaritas from the fridge under the patio bar and refilled their glasses. "We can eat whenever you'd like. Shall I have the cook prepare everything in the kitchen, or do you want to go all-out Yankee and have a barbeque out here?"

"All-out Yankee, by all means!" Pamela sat up to accept the cool glass. "What a super idea. Now I won't have to change for dinner, and I can get a couple more hours of sun." She glanced down at the tiny scraps of blue silk that served as a swimsuit. "I've been working like mad on my tan so I can show off to the folks back home next month. It's always so bloody wet and gray in London, one can't get a decent tan."

"I didn't know you were going to London." Cathy pulled her chaise into the shade before sinking down and stretching out next to Pamela. She wasn't much of a sun worshipper and preferred to keep her pale, creamy complexion very lightly tanned.

"Actually, we've just decided to go only this past week. Ashley has been dying to see our little place in Gloucestershire, and it's never more beautiful than in the spring."

"I wish I was going with you—or someplace. Anyplace." She sipped her Margarita and began swinging her foot idly.

"Is there anything wrong, ducks? You've been acting quite odd all day. One moment you're crackling with energy, the next you're as droopy as a chastised beagle. Are you on drugs?" She peered at Cathy over the rims of her huge sunglasses, her eyes squinting with concern.

Cathy burst out laughing. "God, that's funny, Pamela—me, on drugs!" Still laughing, she leaned over to hug her friend. "No, not drugs, unless you consider love a drug." She sipped her Margarita and her eyes grew sad again.

"Marc?"

Cathy nodded her head and sighed. "Uh-huh. Jesus, he *is* like a drug, an insidious drug that has no antidote. I've tried to forget him a million times, force myself not to think about him, not to want him or—or remember, you know? Then he shows up and just looks at me—just *looks*—and I'm like a junkie who would do anything for a fix."

"You were with him in New York, weren't you?"

When Cathy nodded, miserably, Pamela went on, "Well, did you talk? Settle anything?"

"No," she said flashing the old, impudent grin. "We were too busy rediscovering one another! God, Pamela, he's so damn sexy, I just can't get enough of him. I've never made love to anyone like Marc—never! He's just so perfect in every way. He knows *exactly* what I like without me saying a word and, oh God, he satisfies me so well! When I'm with him, I feel like I've never known another man before in my life."

"That good, huh, luv?"

"Yes, that good. So what do I do? Chain him to the bedpost and just visit when I'm horny?"

"Why not?" She poured a creamy drop of suntan lotion into her hand and began massaging it into her skin. "I mean, not literally, of course, but why not have an affair with him? If what I've heard about him is true, affairs are his forte." She removed her sunglasses and stroked the cream into her face, then lay back, eyes closed against the slanting afternoon sun. "But you haven't mentioned Dash in all this. What're your feelings there, luv?"

"Jesus, I don't know, Pamela. I'm so confused when it comes to Dash. I love him. I've loved him ever since I first met him when I was still working as a model on that dumb game show, 'Eureka!'—remember? Or did I know you then?" Pamela shook her head and Cathy went on, musingly. "Dash was all I ever wanted. I saw myself in him somehow. I knew I could learn the television business thoroughly from Dash and that I would someday be a force in programming if he was my, well, mentor, I guess you'd call it. But I wanted him sexually, too—he used to be a very sexy man, you know."

"He looks like he still is."

"He just *looks* it, I'm afraid, and doesn't *show* it. God, I don't know what's the matter with him anymore. I

## The Love Game 231

thought he was ill and forced him to go to the doctor, but when he did, he said he was just a little run down and needed some 'male plumbing' or some such dumb thing. I wanted to call his doctor and find out if Dash was telling me everything, but he wouldn't hear of it. And then for a while he did seem to feel better, so I believed him. Now I'm not so sure that everything is all right physically."

"Well, ducks, he's no young stud anymore, and from what I've read in your American women's magazines, men of Dash's age sometimes go through a sort of 'male menopause' and act rather oddly at times."

"Yes, I thought about that, but impotence isn't one of the symptoms of male menopause."

"I *see*. That's the rub, is it?"

"Umm, but he keeps trying, you know, and that's even worse than not doing it at all. It's so—so frustrating and pathetic when he tries and nothing happens. And then, of course, I'm all worked up and it's—oh, shit, it's just hopeless!" She tossed off her drink and rose, going to the bar for another.

"I say, ducks, all that booze you've been ingesting lately isn't going to improve *your* disposition, either!"

"No, but it sure blunts the edges." She sank down on the chaise with a heavy sigh and drank, staring across the tennis court at the slowly sinking sun.

"Let me get all this straight." Pamela sat up and faced Cathy. "You love Dash and want to stay with him, but you're as horny as hell and need to get laid on a regular basis, and he can't supply the ingredients. Right so far?" Cathy grinned and nodded. "Right. Then my advice is to get yourself a nice, steady piece on the side, some dumb young thing built for sex, and use him as one uses a gym or a shrink. It's common knowledge that you executive types need all sorts of releases from your demanding jobs—why not a man to 'blunt the edges' instead of booze which will only ruin your liver and skin and make your brain fuzzy?"

Cathy laughed. "Ah, if it were only that simple."

"It is. You've got a built-in stud already in Marc Monroe. And he's married as well—he would be discreet, I'm sure."

"Yes, he's married as well." She said it so softly, her lips barely moved, and again the sadness filled her big blue eyes. She drew in a ragged breath. "I don't think I'd be able to do that with Marc—just have a casual affair. I still love him. . . ."

"More's the fun."

"No, not really. There's Bitsy to consider. I like her, and I know what she must be going through being married to Marc and him cheating on her all the time. I couldn't add to her troubles like that. I have to see her every day at the studio, and I just know I wouldn't be able to face her knowing I was sleeping with her husband."

"Ah, yes, Bitsy—there's a pistol." Pamela chuckled and lay back down, eyes closed. "I don't think you have any reason to concern yourself about Ms. Bushore from what I've heard."

"What have you heard?"

"Oh, let's just say that she has her own 'secret,' shall we? Your friend, Monte, would be a better one to ask about Bitsy Bushore.

"But Monte's gay. Surely there's nothing between him and Bitsy."

"Gay—what an amusing word. I've often wondered why they call homosexuals 'gay' when they are usually incredibly miserable with their lifestyle."

"I guess he could be bisexual. I remember when I first met him, I thought he and Bitsy were having an affair." Pamela opened her eyes and gave Cathy a look that was so filled with pity that Cathy was sure that she had

## The Love Game    233

misunderstood. Why in the world would anyone pity her?

"I don't know about you, but I'm ravenous. Shouldn't we fire up that big brick monster yonder or whatever you call it?" She sat up again and put on her sunglasses.

"The barbeque? Oh, yes, I suppose we should." Cathy pushed heavily to her feet and went to the bar for another refill, then to the barbeque and stooped down to look for the charcoal. "Dash always keeps briquettes on hand. He loves to barbeque." She found the bag and poured some into the blackened pit and replaced the grill.

"Will he be joining us for dinner? I brought three lovely steaks." She found the lighter fluid and handed it to Cathy, watching as she expertly lit the coals.

"I don't know. I guess I should go up and ask him, but if he's still asleep I'd hate to wake him."

"Umm, that's rather like having an infant about the house, isn't it?" Pamela went to her purse, and took out a joint, lit it and passed it to Cathy. "Here, luv, put an edge on your appetite—you're much too thin."

"You can never be too rich or too thin," Cathy quipped, taking the joint.

"Yes, well, in my opinion, you are both *too* rich and *too* thin! If the riches don't bring you happiness and the thinness doesn't bring you a mate, what good is it?"

"Good point, Lady Pamela." Cathy giggled, feeling the strong drinks and the heady weed, intensified by the hot sun. She went to an intercom next to the patio bar and pressed the button. When the cook answered, she told her to marinate the steaks and prepare the salad. "The usual oil and vinegar dressing, Mrs. Sunderling?" the voice came over the speaker and Pamela called out, "No! Something thick and creamy and terribly fattening!"

"Did you get that, Mrs. Donahue?" Cathy laughed, getting into Pamela's spirit of things. "Good—and we'll also have garlic bread—a whole loaf! Fine, I'll give you a ring when the coals are ready." She flipped off the intercom key and reached again for the joint. "I don't know if I love you or hate you for turning me on to this wanton weed," she said. "I love the way it makes me feel, sort of an 'I don't give a damn' attitude, but it does make me awfully hungry. And I do still feel a little guilty about being a doper."

"Pish! Everyone in Hollywood gets high—on one thing or another."

Cathy laughed. "I know. You can't walk down the hall at the studio without smelling pot wafting from the offices—mostly the writers' offices!"

"Pot is good for creative types or so I've heard." She went to her chaise and stretched out again, wanting to soak up the last bit of the dying sun.

Cathy checked the coals, then went to sit on the edge of her own chaise. "How long will you be staying in London? Maybe I can get away and join you for a few days—if the offer to go boating on your 'mum's' little lake is still open!"

"Of course, luv, you're more than welcome." She rolled over and pushed herself into a sitting position and picked up her glass. "I don't know for sure how long we can stay—possibly a fortnight."

"You crazy limey broad, I don't know what a fortnight is, for God's sake!" She poked Pamela on the shoulder, handing her the joint, laughing. "Speak English!"

"That *is* English, you bloody barbaric American!" She toked on the joint, grinning. "But I suppose I should be kinder—you obviously learned the language from those half-naked savages who originally occupied this wonderful land." She spoke clearly, slowly and distinctly, as to a child: "I imagine we shall stay for two weeks. That, my luv, is a fortnight."

"Smart ass."

"Seriously, luv, do you think you could get away for a few days? It would be wonderful showing you my hometown, and I'd love you to meet my mum and dad."

"I'll promise to come if you promise to introduce me to weird old Uncle Percy."

"I say, you are a strange duck, aren't you? Only perverts and degenerates have ever expressed a desire to meet weird old Uncle Percy!"

"The truth is out at last," Cathy laughed. She leaned back in the chaise, more relaxed than she had been since returning from New York. She could think about Marc now without wanting to kill him and attributed it to the pot, which had always mellowed her so completely. Damn, but she had been furious when Marc had said that Bitsy was meeting him at the airport. Would she never learn? He was a *very* married man and likely to stay that way regardless of whom he was currently having an affair with. Shit, why couldn't *she* be that way? Just take him as casually as he took her and walk away without another thought? And she had almost believed him in New York when he had said he loved her, was *in love* with her. Bullshit.

"I wonder how Ashley will get along with the family?" Pamela mused. "Rather well, I should imagine. He's been brought up in the continental manner after all."

"Have you heard anything more from Hedy Carrington?"

"Ah, yes, I'm sorry to say. She calls regularly to check up on Ash, has long conversations with dear Mr. Fitzsimmons, even checks with Ash's house mother to see what time her young son goes beddy-bye. The old crow!" She chuckled evilly. "But little does she know that I've bribed the good woman, a Mrs. Murphy—marvelous creature and of impeccable character—to look the other way when Ash spends the night away from the dorm. It's fascinating what a bottle of Irish whiskey and a twenty-dollar bill will buy these days!"

"Lady Pamela, you are incorrigible."

"This is true."

"Does the school know anything about you and Ash?"

"I shouldn't wonder. I often put the other boys in the ring with thirty minutes of cantering exercises while Ash and I make love in my office."

"Pam, you don't!"

"Indeed I do."

"But how do you do that?"

"If you don't know how it's done by now, ducks, then you have a bigger problem than your husband!"

"You ass, be serious." But Cathy laughed with Pamela, enjoying the light conversation, the camaraderie that she had so little time for lately.

"All right, *seriously*—yes, the school does suspect, rather heavily, my dalliance with young Master Carrington and I do believe my tenure at the Gray Eagle Academy is shaky at best."

"You mean they might fire you? How can you be so nonchalant about it? I thought you loved your job."

"I do love my job, but it simply doesn't do to let the peasants know you're worried—they may rush the castle!"

"Well, school's almost out and Ashley will be graduating. They'll probably give you another chance. Good riding instructors are hard to find, aren't they?"

"I'm not so sure I want another chance, quite frankly. That's why we're taking the trip to London, to see if we like it enough to live there for a bit. I haven't been back in years and Mum says I won't recognize it." She threw Cathy a grin. "Rude American tourists everywhere, she says."

"Up yours, Lady Pamela." Cathy stood, laughing, and went to the bar for the pitcher of Margaritas. She checked the coals and rejoined Pamela. "So what will you do over there? Have you any ideas?"

"Yes, I thought I'd be the very first female Master of the Horse and work for the Queen giving riding lessons." She tasted her drink, pursing her lips a little at the heavy rim of salt.

"Why not? Surely Women's Lib has reached Britain's shores."

"One would hope." Pamela reached for a thick terry towel and tossed it across her legs. "Umm, I seem to be getting a bit of a burn. Perhaps I've had enough sun for one day." She looked down at herself, pleased. "Good, I'm definitely a shade or two darker. Ash will be envious. Poor baby, stuck in the classroom on such a lovely day."

"What's he doing in school on the weekend?"

"He was naughty—cut three classes last week to be with his 'aging mistress'—and was busted by Fitzsimmons. He's confined to quarters for the weekend."

"Jeez, it sounds as bad as the Army."

"Perhaps even worse. I say, what about those steaks, Cath? Surely the stove is hot enough by now."

"The barbeque, you bloody barbarian," Cathy laughed. "When are you going to learn to speak proper English?"

Pamela flicked the towel at her and went to peer at the white-hot coals of the grill. "They're not flaming, luv, is that good or bad?"

"Good. That's just the way we want them." She rang the kitchen on the intercom and asked Mrs. Donahue to bring out the steaks. She arrived instantly, a short, portly woman with soft lavender hair and rimless glasses perched on her little, turned-up Irish nose. Her blue eyes twinkled with good humor and she greeted Pamela warmly before setting down the large platter of steaks. They were soaking in a brown marinade with green pepper rings, onion slices and whole mushrooms surrounding them.

"Umm, smashing," Pamela said, peering at the other goodies that Mrs. Donahue was setting out on the table. "What's that rather phallic-looking object wrapped in foil?"

Mrs. Donahue blushed and ducked her head, giggling, and Cathy said, "That's the garlic bread, you degenerate."

"Well, bless my bloomers—so that's how it's done." She lifted one edge of the foil wrap and peered in at the buttered and garlic-spread sliced French loaf.

"I think Lady Pamela only pretends not to know our customs, Mrs. Donahue, so she can get out of helping with the cooking," Cathy stage-whispered to the cook.

"Blimey, I've been found out!"

"I *know* you can open champagne, so get to it. These steaks will only take a minute." She forked two large, dripping steaks onto the grill and topped them with onion, green peppers and mushrooms. She looked at the third steak and asked, quietly, "Mrs. Donahue, did you notice if Mr. Sunderling was still resting?"

"Yes, Ma'am, I believe he is. Ginny was just dusting upstairs a few minutes ago and said the master's door was closed."

"I see. Well, just take this steak back to the kitchen, please. He might want it when he wakes up." She smiled down at the tiny woman, one of the few people shorter than herself, and said, "We'll have the salad now, please, and don't worry about setting the table. I'm going to put Lady Pamela to work—teach her how to set a proper *American* table!" She poured some of the marinade from the platter onto the steaks and they sizzled and popped, giving off a delicious fragrance.

Mrs. Donahue laughed and her tiny hands fluttered to

her frilly, aproned bosom. "That Miss Pamela, she's a pip, she is."

"Yes, she's a pip all right," Cathy agreed, laughing, enjoying herself. It had been months since she had cooked, and she found, to her surprise, that she had missed it. The early evening air was warm and still, caressing her bikini-clad body as gently as a lover and for one insane, wistful moment she wanted to call Marc and invite him over for that third, lonely steak in the refrigerator. She wondered what he was doing at this very moment. Wondered if he was thinking of her.

He had telephoned the very next day after their return from New York, and she had been cool, barely listening when he tried to explain about Bitsy picking him up. (She had had to go to the airport anyway, he had said, as she was dropping off Monte who was catching a flight to Las Vegas. There had been only a matter of a few minutes before Monte's departure and Marc's arrival so she had waited to drive him home.)

How very convenient, Cathy had thought, not believing him for an instant. When he had pressed to see her, she had been vague, using her heavy work load as an excuse not to meet him for lunch. As blissfully wonderful as those two days in New York had been, it had frightened her to see what power Marc had over her. He had merely to crook his finger and she fell into his bed and under his spell. And believed him all over again. And got hurt all over again. It was a painful cycle, and one she intended to break. Damn! How she wished she could simply go to bed with him and not let herself get emotionally involved. Why couldn't he be more like Dash—tender, compassionate, a stimulating conversationalist, understanding? The perfect combination, she thought wryly; The ideal husband would be Dash in the parlor and Marc in the bedroom!

Pamela came striding toward her pushing a well-laden

serving cart. "Whew, that Mrs. Donahue really loaded me down, ducks. If I had known I'd have to work for my supper, I would have taken my steaks elsewhere."

"Quit bitching and set the table. These steaks will be ready in three and a half minutes." Pamela grumbled as she laid out brown linen napkins and heavy stoneware plates with matching salad bowls. She placed the silver ice bucket on one end of the table and swirled the bottle of champagne around in it for a couple of minutes, then pressed two glasses into the chipped ice to chill them. "Grab the bread before it burns, Pam, please." Cathy turned the steaks and rearranged the onions, green peppers and mushrooms on the tops. "How do you like yours?"

"Rare, please." She burned her fingers as she opened the foiled-wrapped bread and cursed heartily when Cathy laughed. She put the bread in a napkin-lined straw basket and made an exaggerated courtesy. "Will there be anything else, milady?"

"If I think of anything, I'll let you know." They laughed together, the high, girlish sound drifting up to Dash's bedroom window where he sat watching the dying day. He smiled at their laughter, wishing he could be a part of it, that he could be a part of Cathy's life again. But he didn't feel a part of anything anymore. He felt old and used up. He also felt cheated, betrayed by life. Just when he had found true happiness, fate had reared its ugly head; not to snatch the happiness away—but to snatch *him* away from the happiness. He knew he was going to die.

He gave a sound of disgust and reached for his glass of Bourbon, bringing it to his lips, staring out at the fading sunset. He heard the rise and fall of voices below, the soft laughter, the clink of silverware and glasses. He knew he should go down and join them. It hurt Cathy that he had withdrawn from her life, but he just couldn't bring himself to make small talk and entertain friends when he was racked with fear and dread.

He had gone to the hospital as he had planned while Cathy was in New York and had had the biopsy done. The tumor had been malignant. When Dr. Moss had told him, Dash hadn't grasped it at once, had scoffed at the doctor's insistence that he operate immediately. Dash had wanted a second and third opinion, and during those afternoons when Cathy had thought he was playing golf, he had gotten them from other doctors. Unfortunately, all the doctors had agreed on one thing: Dash should have surgery at once.

He had put them off, still unwilling to accept the fact that he had cancer. That was an old man's disease! He wasn't sure when he had started seeing himself as an old man. It had come over him slowly the past couple of weeks. Thinking about it now, he decided it had probably started that day he had picked Cathy up at the airport and had seen her walking down the ramp with Marc Monroe. He had been struck by their youth, the sheer animalistic beauty of them as they came toward him, energy and life in each confident step. He had thought then that they looked like a matched set; the Ken and Barbie of the eighties, glowing with health and vitality. He had been stunned by the sudden realization that he no longer belonged to their generation, but to a generation long past. It had saddened and frightened him—facing his own mortality. And sadder still, he had no one with whom to share his feelings. His first wife was gone, as were many of his contemporaries. To discuss mortality with Cathy would have been ludicrous as well as futile. The young think they will never grow old and die.

He told himself that he was hiding his illness from Cathy because she wouldn't understand and because it would only make her unhappy. But the truth was that he was humiliated by it. It seemed to him the final indignity. He had always prided himself on his sexual prowess and now to be reduced to impotence, just when he had found and won his own beautiful goddess, was a cruel blow. And he hadn't been able to handle it well at all. He had withdrawn into himself, dropped out of society and filled his space with Cathy. He had forced her to take on his responsibilities at the network even though he knew she wasn't quite ready. But he didn't have time to groom her slowly as he had planned. Jesus, time! What a fickle trick it played on man. As a youth, he had thought clocks a waste of time and had been bewildered when adults had laughed at him, shaking their heads.

The doctors had given him time. He could have up to five years of it if he would agree to their butchery, let them geld him, take away those feelings that had made life so beautiful. That would make life impossible with Cathy. How could he live with her like a neutered house cat when his brain still wanted her so badly he ached every time he looked at her, and his heart swelled with love. She was a lusty young woman, wanting as much back as she gave, and he couldn't give her anything anymore. Except KNAB.

## Chapter Fourteen

It was night. Cathy sat propped up in her kingsize bed, gazing through the window that framed the night like some massive painting. Moonlight had softly filled the room, adding to the silver glow emitted by the television screen, blurring the furnishings into ambiguous forms. The familiar, husky voice of Marc Monroe came to her as softly as the sibilant rustling of the breeze through her window and she turned her eyes back to the screen.

He sat on a huge tree stump, the sprawling wilderness of the North Toutle River Valley in Washington state behind him, as he spoke of volcanoes past and present; of the three hundred volcanoes that ring the Pacific Ocean. But Cathy wasn't listening to what he said. She stared at him, at his lean, sexy body encased in Levis and a red-plaid workman's shirt. He wore a sheepskin-lined vest and rugged mountain-climber's boots. He looked utterly fantastic.

This was his first special of the new season and she had told herself she had to watch it now that she was in charge of KNAB. The truth was that she would have killed anyone who had tried to stop her from turning on the set! Just to see him. To hear his deep, sexy voice. To remember. She watched his lips as he spoke, barely hearing the words as he explained the history of volcanoes. It was a damn good special, fascinating and well researched. It would undoubtedly carry the evening in rating points, but for once in her life, she didn't give a damn about ratings.

She closed her eyes and let Marc's melodious voice wash over her. The sweet fragrance of roses growing outside her open window floated to her, and she breathed in deep, sighing. June—hiatus time in television land. A time to travel, shop, sleep late, visit old friends, spend time with your family. . . .

A blaringly offensive commercial shattered her calm and she said, "Shit!" and opened her eyes, switching the sound off with her remote control. She reached to the white, French Provincial nightstand for her brandy snifter and brought it to her lips. She allowed herself only one glass before bed, but cheated a little and made it a double. Pamela had been right. Boozing every day was not the answer. Nor was mooning around like some lovestruck adolescent. Work had always been her panacea, and she had thrown herself into it with a frenzy.

She began rising early again, arriving at the studio moments after the gates were opened, working until the last guard was ready to leave for the night. Dash was often asleep when she got home but it was just as well. They had little to say to one another these days. When he wasn't incoherent from booze, he was passed out on pain pills. His flesh sagged and took on a sickly, yellowish color and his once bright, blue eyes were off-focus and always bloodshot. He shuffled his feet like an old man when he walked and his hands shook with palsy. Cathy couldn't remember the last time she had heard him laugh.

The disgusting commercial vanished and she turned up the sound to listen to Marc's quietly authoritative voice discussing the 1980 eruption of Mount St. Helen's. God, he was good looking—the definitive macho

## The Love Game

man standing there with the great Northwest sprawled out behind him, one booted foot on a gnarled tree stump, his strong sun-browned hand dwarfing the microphone he held. The camera moved in for a close-up of Marc and his eyes gazed steadily out from the screen directly into hers.

A sharp little cry rose in her throat, and she drowned it with a huge swallow of brandy. Jesus, how had her life gotten in such a mess? She was in love with a man she knew was no damn good for her and married to one who was *too* good to her. She leaned her head against the propped-up pillows, sipping her brandy, trying to shake the old memories that came creeping in. Seeing Marc on television had been disquieting. She hadn't been prepared for the swift rush of emotion that surged through her veins, the weak trembling of her thighs.

The familiar voice of KNAB's anchorman, Tim Wade, caught her attention, and she listened to the news teaser in disbelief. "Hedy Carrington brings charges of statutory rape against schoolteacher who allegedly seduced her young son. This and other stories, next on—"

Cathy sat in stunned silence for one whole minute before her mind absorbed the news. Then she moved swiftly, grabbing the princess phone and dialing KNAB with hands that shook and were ice cold. She spoke tersely to Jeff Landers, head of the evening news. "Take that item off about Hedy Carrington."

"What? Who the hell is this? Cathy? What's the matter?" Jeff spoke just as tersely. He was one of the execs who had tried and failed with Cathy and therefore hated her, especially now that she ran the network.

"Get rid of that bit about Hedy Carrington, Jeff. I don't run slanderous news items that hurt my friends."

"What? Who the fuck do you think you are? You can't just jerk a news item off the air!"

"I'm jerking this one off." She was aware of the pun and smiled grimly.

"You're not doing fuck, lady. I'm still head of this department and I put the news on—*all* the news!"

"I can arrange it so you'll no longer be head of the news department." Her voice grew icy, dipped dangerously low, and she heard his nervous swallow on the other end of the line.

"What the fuck, Cathy, are you drunk or some damn thing? This is a hell of time to kid around—the news goes on in sixty seconds and the Carrington story goes on as scheduled!" His voice grew hard and just slightly weary and patronizing. It made Cathy's blood boil.

"Listen up, shitheel, and listen good. Drop the Carrington spot—now!"

"You're out of your tree, cunt! Where the hell do you get off ordering me around? Who the fuck made you president of KNAB?" He spluttered angrily and his voice rose in a snarl. "Smart ass bitch, think you're so damn smart, fucking old man Sunderling into giving you the power to . . ."

"The power to fire *your* ass, Landers!"

"Don't threaten me, you little bitch! I've got a contract with Dash!"

"And I've got Dash in bed at night." She gave a soft snort of contempt, and it sent shivers down his spine. "Do you want to put your contract up against that?"

"Pussy Power," Jeff spat, and his breathing grew heavier, angrier. "You're bluffing, bitch—you wouldn't . . ."

"Take the Carrington spot off and you'll never have to find out." Her voice was silky smooth and deadly. She could hear his suddenly rapid breathing and smiled, knowing she had won. She replaced the receiver in its cradle and brought the brandy snifter to her mouth and swallowed until the painful palpitations had eased.

God, poor Lady Pamela! She wondered if she had

been served yet or if she even knew about it. She had left for London just this morning; perhaps the news hadn't caught up with her yet. She switched channels, knowing that Jeff Landers wouldn't run the story. He was a gutless bastard and would kiss any ass to keep his job. She felt a small streak of pleasure at having bested the man—and it had been so easy! It was her first *real* taste of power and she savored it as she waited for the Carrington story on Channel Seven. It wasn't long in coming.

Allegedly, (Cathy loved that word.) Hedy Carrington had flown in from New York to surprise her son, Ashley. Upon arriving at the Gray Eagle Academy for Boys, she had been informed that Ashley had left the academy at term's end and she was shown a letter, "allegedly" signed by her, giving the academy and Mr. Fitzsimmons permission to release Ashley, as it were, so he could join her in New York. And there was Mr. Fitzsimmons, looking Clifton Webb-befuddled and righteous, showing reporters the letter of permission. Cathy recognized Pamela's flamboyant scrawl at the bottom of the typewritten page and whispered, "You crazy limey broad."

Hedy Carrington had demanded to see the riding instructor, a Ms. Pamela Winters, and when informed that she had taken a trip to England, the volatile actress had screamed for her manager, her attorney, the cops and her agent—in that order. Her young son had been kidnapped, she cried, and by that degenerate foreigner! Abducted to another country—her baby! And there was a still photograph of Ashley that had been taken at the last Emmy Awards, looking anything but a baby in his smart tuxedo and ruffle-fronted shirt, holding a glass of champagne. It was a clear case of child molestation, of influencing a minor to do your bidding with drugs and alcohol, his mother claimed. But she wouldn't get away with it!

Cathy shook her head, not taking her eyes off the screen. Good God, forgery, statutory rape, kidnapping—that Hedy didn't fool around! Of course, it was total overkill on the actress's part. She knew how her son felt about Pamela. Cathy couldn't understand why someone, a mother, would want to stand in the way of her child's happiness—whatever or whomever it took to make him happy.

The phone rang and Cathy waited until the answering service picked up, then listened in to hear Jeff Landers demanding to speak to Dash. The service told him that the Sunderlings could not be reached, and he swore viciously and slammed down the receiver. Cathy knew that all hell would break loose tomorrow when he did reach Dash, but she didn't care. She knew damn well that Pamela had not coerced Ashley into anything; that they sincerely loved one another, and she was damned if she would be a party to the scandal. She couldn't do anything about the rest of the media, but she sure as hell could see to it that KNAB did not run any of the ugly gossip.

Cathy was reading the *Hollywood Reporter* and drinking her morning coffee on the patio when Mrs. Donahue came out with the telephone. Plugging in the jack near the white wrought iron table, she said, "It's Miss Bitsy Bushore, Ma'am."

"Thanks, Mrs. Donahue." Cathy sighed; God, it's starting already. "Hi, Bitsy—what's up?"

"Oh, you wonderful, far-out lady, you!" Bitsy squealed. "What a super neat thing to do! Gosh, I'm so proud of you I could just scream!"

"Want to run that by me again, Bits. It's still early." Jeez, what was the dippy broad talking about?

"What you did last night—for your friend. You know." She giggled again and squealed with delight and Cathy

## The Love Game    249

could almost see her wrinkling her little, bunny nose. "Gee, Cathy, that took a lot of guts, telling old Landers off and getting him to pull the story."

"How did you hear about it?" She couldn't believe it had gotten around that fast; it was barely seven in the morning.

"Gee, kid, everyone in town is talking about it. Beth said the station received hundreds of calls last night wanting to know what happened to the Hedy Carrington story. You know, it was on the teaser, and when no one reported on it, people started calling in and demanding to know about the schoolteacher and Hedy Carrington." She laughed with pure pleasure. "Talk about a loyal friend! I should be so lucky!"

"Is there anything about it in the papers?" Cathy sipped her coffee and grinned. Well, she was a heroine to Bitsy, anyway.

"Not yet, but you can bet your cute little bippy there will be a *lot* about it in tonight's papers!"

"Yes, I'm sure there will be. Uh, Bitsy—what are they saying, you know, about me?"

"Oh, gosh, just *everything*, kid! The brass think you've flipped out, suppressing news that way. But everyone else thinks you're one hell of a dynamite lady, going to bat for your friends. Of course, Beth and Monte and everyone like that knows the *real* story about Pam and Ash, so they admire you for what you did. And then, there're some middle-of-the-roaders who think you're just some young, smart ass chick throwing your weight around and taking advantage of Dash being sick and all. You know, so you can take over completely, change the policy of the studio—that sort of garbage."

Leave it to Bitsy with her childlike innocence to lay it on the line! She wondered how many "middle-of-the-roaders" worked at KNAB. "Hey, thanks a lot, Bitsy, I really appreciate the call—and the vote of confidence!"

"You've got it, sweetie, and Beth wanted me to tell you that she's behind you all the way. She said she would have done the same thing in your position."

"Well, that's really nice to hear. Listen, I'd better get going—I have a feeling I'm going to have a busy day!"

"I'm sure you will," Bitsy giggled. "Now you be sure and call me and let me know if I can do anything to help, you hear?"

"I will, Bits—and thanks again." She hung up the phone and leaned back in her chair, gazing out across the pool and tennis court. When she had called Jeff Landers last night, it hadn't occurred to her what her impulsive act might provoke. She had only wanted to stop the ugly rumor before it spread any further. Of course, she realized she was being totally foolish; No one could squelch such a rumor. It was too "juicy," too good to pass up. She stood and squared her shoulders and walked back inside the house and toward Dash's bedroom. He should hear it from her first.

She stood by his bed for a moment, looking down at him. In his slumber he looked almost youthful, and the deep lines she had seen in his forehead and around his mouth, were eased. The silver mane of hair was still thick and luxurious, tumbled boyishly upon the pillow now, and the full, sensual mouth she had once loved so much was curved into a soft smile. She bent and kissed him.

He opened his eyes and looked up into hers for a moment, then smiled sleepily and murmured, "I was just dreaming about you—am I still dreaming?"

She bent again to kiss him, then perched on the edge of the bed and laid a hand on his shoulder. "No, you're not dreaming, darling. Good morning—how do you feel?"

"Good—good." He pushed into a sitting position. "I feel good this morning. I think those new pills Doc gave me are working a hell of a lot better than those other ones. They made me woozy as hell, but I don't seem to have any side effects with these new ones."

"Good, I'm glad." She looked at him, then away, wondering how she was going to tell him. How to tell the president of his own network that she had just usurped his power—and publicly, at that, practically in front of millions of viewers. She could almost see the lighted-up switchboard at KNAB. The operators must be going crazy trying to answer all the indignant callers. Hell, she might even have lost some loyal viewers by holding back *all* the news from them. People tended to think they owned you if they watched you every night—and if you varied one iota from the familiar, they felt betrayed. "How about some coffee, honey, and then I'd like to talk to you, okay?"

"Sure, it isn't often I get to have coffee with such a beautiful young blond." He leaned over to look at his slim digital clock on the nightstand. "Why aren't you at the studio?"

"Hiatus, remember?"

"Oh, yeah, I forgot—June already. God, where does the time go?" He slid past her and started toward his bathroom. "Excuse me while I brush my teeth and make myself a little more presentable for you, okay, babe?"

She smiled at him then rang the kitchen on the intercom and ordered a pot of coffee and English muffins. Well, he seemed in a good mood, not vague and disinterested as he had been lately. Maybe the new medication Dr. Moss had put him on was doing some good. She still wasn't sure just what the problem was. Dash kept insisting it was some minor, but irritating "male plumbing" trouble and seemed so embarrassed by it, she hadn't pushed for an explanation. The coffee arrived and she had Ginny arrange it on the small Parsons table near the window. She opened the drapes and morning sunshine spilled into the room, bringing into sharp focus the lovely antique furniture and masculine browns and blacks of the decor. God, it had been weeks since she had been in this room.

"Umm, smells great." Dash came toward her, dressed in a beige silk robe, his hair combed, and bent to kiss her cheek. "This is nice—having coffee together."

"If you weren't such a sleepyhead, we could do it every morning." She grinned at him as she poured the coffee and served him an English muffin with strawberry jam.

He laughed and shook his head. "No, when I turned over the reins of the network to you, I swore I'd never get up at five o'clock in the morning again. God, I don't know how I did it all those years." He sipped his coffee, looking fondly at her over the rim of his cup. "How in the world do *you* do it, babe? Don't you ever want to just turn off the alarm and go back to sleep?"

"Not really. I enjoy getting up early." She spread jam on her muffin and tried to think of a casual way to bring up last night's incident. She couldn't just plunge into it. He may have turned over the reins to her, but he still liked to know where she was guiding the horse! "Even now that we're on hiatus, I can't sleep in. I don't know what I'm going to do with myself this summer."

"You need a vacation, my little Cathy. You're working much too hard, even for an overachiever!"

"Yeah, well, my vacation might be permanent when I tell you what happened last night!" She laughed a little shakily, drew a deep breath and told him everything.

He listened silently until she had finished speaking, then stood and went to her and kissed her soundly on the mouth. He hugged her close for a long moment, then drew away to gaze deeply into her eyes. "I'm very proud of you, little Cathy. Not only do you have loyalty and integrity, you have more damn balls than any man I've ever known!"

"Thank you—I think." She stared at him, surprised at the effusive support. "So, what do I do about Jeff Landers?"

"Fuck Jeff Landers!" he roared in the old Dash Sunderling voice.

"I'd rather not," she murmured, and he laughed and reached across the table to lightly slap her cheek, to tweak and pat it. The fatherly gesture irritated her somehow.

"I love you, babe. God, I wish I could have seen Jeff's face when you told him to pull that spot!" He chuckled as he poured more coffee. "He must have had a stroke—poor bastard!"

"I'm going to have to face him. What shall I say? I—uh, sort of intimated that you were behind me on the Carrington thing."

"And I am, one hundred percent! I'm crazy about that English broad and her young pup. They're nice people. Hell, I would have done the same thing." He buttered another muffin and spread it generously with strawberry jam, surprised at his appetite. His usual breakfast was brandy-laced coffee and three codeine pills. He felt alive for the first time in months, was impatient to get dressed and down to the studio and into the fray of things. He was fighting for his girl, and it felt very, very good. "I can't understand Hedy, though. She must have flipped out completely to pull a fool stunt like this. I heard she's been hitting the booze pretty heavily. A friend of mine is directing that fiasco she's doing on Broadway—and she's going through that aging actress syndrome and I guess it affected her mind."

"It sure must have. Good God, kidnapping! Can you believe it? You'd think Ash was seven years old instead of seventeen!"

"She probably wishes he was—then she'd be ten years younger. Don't worry about Hedy, babe. I'll go talk to her, tell her the way it is with Ash and Pam. Promise her a special if she'll drop the charges."

"I didn't know you knew her."

"Knew her? Had her!" He chuckled and winked, looking like an old but charming rake.

"Dash, you didn't." God, he was full of surprises—still.

"Yep, back in the olden days, my child, before you were born. Hedy was *the* sex symbol of her day and the sexiest broad I'd ever seen. She just oozed sex appeal and in those days it was relatively new to ooze anything on the screen! I helped her out a little in getting her career off the ground. We've kept in touch."

"Why didn't you ever say anything to Ash about knowing her?"

"It's best to let sleeping dogs lie, if you'll pardon the pun. Besides, I was having an affair with her while she was still married to Ash's father."

"Oh." She sipped her coffee, wondering what else there was about this fascinating man that she didn't know. He could still intrigue her. "You wouldn't really give Hedy Carrington a special, would you?"

"Sure, why not? It would be the highest rated show of the season. With free, built-in publicity." He chuckled. "Hedy Carrington doing a special on the very network that had refused to air her press conference regarding her kidnapped son? It's a sure winner."

"But would she do it? Drop the charges against Pamela, I mean. What about all her breast-beating about her poor, molested baby?"

"She's an actress—she'd do anything for a good part! She knows the value of a successful, highly rated network special. Knows she'll reach millions of people in just one night—twice as many as see her on stage or in

## The Love Game 255

the movies. And the publicity is just titilating enough to draw in those hoping to see something out of the ordinary. Maybe she'll surprise the audience by bringing her son and his mistress on camera. Now that would be the ticket! I wonder if I could get her to go for it?"

"Dash, you can't be serious! Pamela wouldn't go for it in a million years. She hates Hedy Carrington—and now probably even more."

"I was kidding about that, babe," Dash laughed, pouring the last of the coffee into his cup. "But I wasn't kidding about people tuning in just in the hope that they *will* see something out of the ordinary. A good, juicy feud between the Beautiful People is always good for high ratings."

"Well, I don't care about the ratings. I just care about Pamela being cleared of those stupid charges. God, how humiliating for her!"

"You're going to be called on the carpet too, you know."

"I know." She stood and walked to the sliding glass doors that led outside to a carpeted balcony overlooking the pool. It was so serene: the lovely formal gardens stretching as far as she could see, the immaculate tennis court and shimmering turquoise pool, all surrounded by huge, thick trees that shut out the rest of the world.

"Well, don't let them come and get you." Dash went to her side and slid his arm around her waist. "You go and meet them head on."

"What do you mean?"

"Call a press conference of your own and explain why you did it. Pamela isn't here to defend herself and someone should tell her and Ash's side of it, don't you think?"

"Yes, I do." She hugged him tightly and kissed his soft cheek. "Thank you, darling. I should have thought of it."

"You would have—given a little more time." He put his other arm around her waist, holding her loosely. "I'm going with you, babe, if there're no objections."

"Oh, Dash, will you?" He nodded and she hugged him again. "Thank you, darling."

"Okay, get out of here so I can pull myself together." He gave her a slap on the fanny. "Ring the gym, will you, babe, and tell Juno to turn the steam on and get ready for the whole works. Massage, everything! If I'm going to be on national television, I want to look my best!"

"You ham," she laughed. "I love you."

"Of course you do—you have impeccable taste!"

"What shall I wear? Am I going to look serious and businesslike or do the glamorous talk show hostess routine?"

"Knock their eyes out, babe! Wear something smashing so there will be no doubt whatsoever who you are."

She played it coy, loving him when he teased like this. "Who am I?"

"The lady in charge of the second highest rated network in television, that's who. And every inch a queen." He chuckled lightly. "A queen with a heart of gold—defending her friend's honor at the cost of her own career!"

"I love it!" Cathy laughed with him, feeling good for the first time in weeks. It was fun being involved in a controversy with Dash by her side. She wanted very much for everyone at KNAB to see that she had his complete support, that she wasn't trying to usurp his power. And she wanted very much to publicly slap Hedy Carrington for her hateful slander against Pamela. She wondered how many other men (not to mention network heads) would stand behind her the way Dash was. She smiled, watching him paw through his closet for his gym clothes. He was still some kind of guy. And still *her* guy. "Hey, Sunderling," she called softly, and when he raised his head to look at her, she said, "You're all right, you know that?"

"Get out of here," he laughed. "We've got a reputation to save."

"The reputation we save may be our own," she quipped and threw him a kiss before disappearing through the door.

"Gee, just look at her, will you? My little sis sitting up there like the queen of the May, telling all those reporters they shouldn't give media coverage to the story about Pam and Ash. Gosh, where does she get her nerve?" Maggie held Staci on her lap while she watched the six o'clock news and Cathy and Dash's press conference. She still couldn't quite believe it when she saw Cathy on something like this. Her baby sister was such a powerful woman in television that she could actually suppress the news if she wanted to. And to think she could influence others not to run the story. She shook her head, wondering for the hundredth time where Cathy got her confidence, her guts, her drive.

"I don't know," Ken laughed, "but she's sure got a pocketful of it! And more power to her. Pam and Ash don't deserve this kind of treatment. They're not hurting a blessed person as far as I can see."

"I agree with you completely, but I can still understand how some people, especially Ashley's mother, would feel about it. Remember how shocked I was when I first met them?"

"*Before* you got to know them. That's the trouble with people, they jump to conclusions too damn fast."

"Well, I just hope everything works out—for everybody! I worry so about Cathy, living such a fast life and all. She looks awfully thin doesn't she, Ken? Look at her—doesn't she look thin and tired?"

"She looks absolutely gorgeous!"

"I wonder if she'll give me a plug?" Monte asked.

"Shhh, I want to listen." Bitsy waved impatiently at him and he shrugged and swung one long, lean leg gracefully over the arm of his chair.

"Well," he pouted, "It *is* my dress."

"And it's *her* press conference so shut up so we can listen to it." Beth lit a fresh joint and held it to Bitsy's lips.

"Oh, all right, but I've already seen it on my cable news channel." He pretended to sulk, but both Beth and Bitsy knew him too well. Cathy did look scrumptious in his creation, however, a vision of ivory. It was very simple and totally devastating. A three-piece suit in ivory silk, it moved with her. Cleanly cut to fall in an embrace of softness from neck to knee, it was one of Monte's most seductive numbers. And Cathy made it a part of herself. Her beige-blonde hair matched it almost perfectly, and she had a morning dawn mink coat flung casually over one shoulder, its hem dragging negligently on the floor.

Monte grinned, loving it. She sure had come a long way, baby! He remembered her when he had first met her, a rather grim little thing, very serious and atrociously dressed in blue jeans and tee shirts. He shuddered delicately and reached for his glass, sipping the cool, dry martini appreciatively. He giggled and Beth shot him a look. Girls could be so dreary.

"I still can't believe it. I'm sitting here hearing it, and I still can't believe it." Beth took a toke of the joint and held it again for Bitsy. "I never thought I'd see the day when a network president actually stood up for what he believed in.

## The Love Game

"It's not exactly the president's who's standing up for his beliefs, sweetie. It's the president's wife!" Bitsy snuggled against Beth and stretched her legs out on the sofa, wiggling her toes.

"She's a ballsy little chick." Beth stroked Bitsy's shoulder and arranged herself into a more comfortable position. "I've always liked her, but she seems kind of stand-offish, or cool, don't you think so?"

"She used to be at first, and sometimes she still is, but I think it's because she's so madly in love with my husband that she feels real uncomfortable around me, you know?" Bitsy giggled and wrinkled her nose when Beth held a glass of wine to her lips. "I mean, she's such an *honorable* person. Gosh, I don't know many people I can say that about. I mean, she's so *straight.*"

"Nobody's straight," Monte drawled.

"Well, Cathy is and so is my stubborn husband. Jeez, they've been going around *forever* being miserable, trying to pretend they don't like each other. I didn't know people still acted that way."

"I never have understood why they didn't get married when they were first seeing each other," Beth said. "One minute you were telling me how much in love they were and that you'd never seen Marc happier, then I see on the news that she married Dash. What happened?"

"I guess she didn't believe Marc when he told her he wasn't *really* married to me, you know, not like *for real.*"

"Didn't he tell her you were gay?"

"No, *he's* too honorable!" Bitsy giggled delightfully and reached up her arms to draw Beth's head down to hers. "Gosh, maybe that's why they make such a perfect pair, huh?" She kissed her softly, slowly, holding Beth's face between her two hands and looking into her eyes almost dreamily. "Almost as perfect as us." She kissed her again, long and sensuously, sliding her body up on Beth's lap and clinging to her long after the kiss had ended. "I wish Marc would divorce me and marry Cathy and, then I could be with you, and everybody would be happy."

"Aren't you forgetting someone, girls?" Monte cocked an amused eyebrow at them. "I believe the lady is currently married."

"Oh, pooh. Dash would do anything to make Cathy happy. He *adores* her. He must realize that he's way too old for her and she's gonna want to get herself a younger guy someday." Bitsy sipped from Beth's wineglass, frowning when Monte threw back his head and laughed. "Well, gee, we all gotta have sex."

"How delicately you put it, my dear," Beth said. "But you do have a point. Lon Howland tells me that the young Mrs. Sunderling is already restless!"

"Wow, is my husband ever stupid! Letting the girl he loves get away just because—just because . . ." She looked at Monte and then up at Beth, so stoned she had forgotten completely what she was saying.

"Just because he's married?" Monte prompted.

"Yeah, just because he's married! That's a shame, too, cause I know he really loves her, and I just love for people to be in love with each other. Specially my real good friends—like Marc and Cathy."

"Then why don't you divorce him so he can marry her?" Monte drawled lazily. He was getting bored with the conversation and felt like doing something. Women could sit around and chatter for hours without *doing* anything.

"Divorce him? Gee, I never thought of it." She took a toke of the fresh joint that Beth held to her lips, and Monte persisted, getting interested in the conversation again. He loved to put Bitsy on. She was so delightfully gullible.

"Sure, divorce the poor guy and let him marry the girl

he loves. You said he was your best friend, didn't you?" He handed her his martini when she started to cough on the pungent smoke. "And Cathy, too."

"And Cathy, too," Bitsy gasped, taking another swallow of martini.

"Well, you should help your very best friends, shouldn't you? Look at what Cathy just did for Pamela and Ashley. Wasn't that nice?" He refilled the martini glass from a pitcher that sat on the coffee table and handed it to her.

"Aw, yeah, that *was* nice—Cathy's such a nice girl, isn't she?" She sipped the martini and toked again on the joint that Beth held for her, giggling, trying to decide which one to sample next.

"She's a very nice girl," Monte said, winking at Beth. "Why don't you do something nice for her?"

"What? What could I do nice?"

"You could divorce Marc so he can be with Cathy and then you could be with Beth. That would be a real nice thing to do, wouldn't it, Beth?"

"What are you up to, you devil?" Beth laughed. "When you get that look in your eye there's bound to be mischief."

"Beth, you wound me deeply when you say such things. I only want to make everybody happy."

"Monte's right." Bitsy banged her tiny fist on the coffee table and stuck out her chin. "I'm going to divorce Marc and marry Beth. Tonight! We'll go to Tijuana—all of us! Monte, you'll be my bridesmaid and Beth's best man all at the same time!"

"What a super idea! Let's do it!" Monte jumped to his feet and paced across the room. Now *this* was more like it! Something to do. He hadn't been to Tijuana in over a year and felt he was due. He loved the sleezy glitter and tackiness of the place—as well as the abundantly available sex! And if he finally managed to get Bitsy and

Beth together, he would have accomplished something. They had been meeting secretly at his place for almost three years, and he thought it was high time they came out of the closet.

"Can we really? Oh, Monte, can we?" Bitsy ran to him and hugged him, laughing. "I mean, can you arrange everything? You know I don't know how to do things like that—planes and hotels and stuff and whoever you need to get a divorce. Oh, I'm so excited!" She turned to Beth. "You want to, don't you?"

"I thought you'd never ask," Beth quipped and Bitsy flung herself back into her arms, hugging and laughing.

"Get on the phone, Monte. We're about to make a lot of people very happy!"

The telephone rang in Marc's study but he sat staring at the television screen, oblivious to the sound, aware only of Cathy Curtis Sunderling. He had never seen her looking lovelier. She was thinner—he had noticed that right away—but it lent her a certain elegance, a maturity that she hadn't had before. And he was so damn proud of her he wanted to stand up and cheer. It took a lot of guts to defy all the news media in Los Angeles, but she was doing it. Speaking quietly and firmly into the mass of microphones clustered in front of her on the long conference table, she explained, simply yet eloquently, the relationship between Pamela and Ashley. She fielded the reporters' questions expertly and graciously, and by the end of the press conference, she had them practically stumbling over themselves, so eager were they to get back to their desks and report every word she had said. ("To set the record straight and right a terrible wrong," one emotional reporter had gushed.)

The telephone rang again, but Marc didn't answer it. The only person he wanted to talk to was now leaving KNAB with her husband, and he wished desperately

## The Love Game 263

that it was he walking by her side instead of the aging mogul who held her arm so possessively. But he had blown it. Not once, but twice. He pushed out of his chair and went to the bar to pour himself a Scotch.

If only he had leveled with her from the beginning, told her about Bitsy's homosexuality, that he had stayed married to her simply because he genuinely liked her as a friend, a pal, a roommate. It had been a marriage of convenience for both of them. Bitsy had needed a cover because she was gay and knew her public would never accept it—not from someone they had seen grow up, first on the silver screen, then, more intimately, on the small screens in their homes. And he had sworn never to marry. He had seen too much bitterness when once happy marriages broke up (like his own parents'), had seen the pain and devastation brought on by divorce and wanted no part of it. He swore he would never do that to children of his own.

But that was before he had met Cathy. He went to the window and stood gazing moodily out at the moonlight shimmering on the pool. It was so quiet. He wanted to hear voices and laughter, feel a part of something—or someone. He guessed he wanted to be a part of a family—or to have his own family. The thought so startled him that he laughed out loud. No one would believe it (least of all, Cathy), but he really wanted, at long last, to be a husband and father.

A tiny smile touched his lips as a plan began forming in his mind.

## Chapter Fifteen

Cathy stood before the small mirror on her closet door, swaying slightly with the motion of the ship. The steward had told her it would be smooth once they were further out to sea. Never having been on a ship before she didn't know if she would get seasick or not. She still couldn't believe she had allowed everyone to talk her into going on this cruise, but here she was, dressing for dinner at the captain's table. She hoped the simple black sheath by Halston (Monte would have a fit) wasn't too severe, but she didn't feel like unpacking the rest of her luggage just yet. Her stateroom was small, even though in First Class, with a narrow bed against one wall and a bathroom the size of a postage stamp. Jeez, fourteen days and nights in this dinky little enclosure? She hoped she could stand it without jumping ship at the first port of call. She sighed and went to sit on the edge of the cot and smoke a joint before dinner. It seemed to be the only thing that gave her an appetite lately, and everyone was always telling her how thin she was. Maybe she could put "the roses back in her cheeks," as they say, on this trip.

When Maggie had first suggested that she go on a vacation, Cathy had said, "No way—I'd go nuts with nothing to do!" But big sister had had that all figured out as well.

"Take one of those glorious Princess cruises to the Caribbean," she had urged. "You can use the trip as a theme for one of your fall shows. You know, take just a skeleton crew, a minicam and a tape recorder—that's all you really need for location stuff, isn't it?"

Cathy had laughed at Maggie's show biz jargon but the more she had thought about it, the more she had wanted to go. She had hated her instant celebrity after the press conference and just wished that everyone would go about their business and stay out of hers. But it wasn't to be. Within the week every tacky tabloid on the newsstands screamed the story in inch-high, bold headlines:

FORBIDDEN SEX AT PRIVATE BOYS' SCHOOL!; HEDY CARRINGTON'S TEENAGE SON GIVEN "PRIVATE" LESSONS IN SEX!; ENGLISH SCHOOLTEACHER FINDS LOVE WITH MOVIE STAR'S YOUNG SON!; KNAB'S CATHY CURTIS PUBLICLY DEFENDS MAY-DECEMBER LOVE!

And the stories themselves had been even worse, if that were possible. Lewd, vulgar, suggestive, they hinted at wild and licentious behavior among all the principals, and Cathy had been stunned that they could get away with such outright lies. They dug into everyone's past, parading old love affairs like banners, and one scandal sheet had had the audacity to suggest that Ashley was Hedy's and Dash's "love child"!

Yes, she had been more than ready for Maggie's suggestion that she go on a vacation and just unwind. She had asked Dash to join her but he had refused, claiming he should stay and keep an eye on things at the network and insisting that she go without him. She had asked Maggie and Ken to go along as traveling companions, but Maggie wouldn't leave Staci for that length of time and Ken couldn't leave his horses and livestock. She had wanted to invite someone to accompany her, but didn't know anyone that she could spend fourteen days and nights with without getting bored.

She had decided not to combine the cruise with work. For once in her life she didn't want to even think about work (But she had brought one whole suitcase filled with nothing but scripts—just in case.) She just wanted to relax and get away from newspapers and telephones and photographers and leering curiosity-seekers. Once she had made up her mind to go, she realized just how much she needed this trip. It had been years since she had had a vacation and never one as luxurious as this. Fourteen days and nights aboard a fabulous luxury liner, cruising to exotic ports of call, stopping in the Caribbean, the Mexican Riviera via the Panama Canal; soft, tropical nights, exquisite cuisine, impeccable service. She would be waited and catered to, allowed to loll on deck with a book or spend the entire day in bed if she wished.

"Just what the doctor ordered, babe," Dash had said— and so she had done it. And she felt lonely already. She finished the joint, checked herself in the mirror again and started for the dining room with mixed feelings. What if it was a total bore and she didn't like anyone on the whole ship? What if everyone knew who she was and stared at her? What if there were newspapers on board? She almost turned back to her cabin but gritted her teeth and kept walking. "I'm gonna relax and have fun if it kills me," she muttered under her breath.

When she reached the dining room doors, she paused a moment, raised her chin, threw back her shoulders, then swept through the doors and into the room with all the regal bearing of a queen. People stopped eating and drinking and turned to stare, and she was suddenly surrounded by several white-uniformed young men anxious to help her. They escorted her to the captain's table where all the gentlemen stood while the introductions were made, and the women stared enviously at her slim figure and enormous, ten-carat diamond ring. It was the only piece of jewelry she wore, and the only one she needed.

She was a jewel herself in the elegantly understated black Halston, her soft blond hair, worn longer this year, brushed back from her ivorylike, cameo face and fluffed out on her bare shoulders. Her blue eyes were enormous in her new, thinner face, and the cheekbones were fashion-model high. She stood easily next to the captain as he introduced her dinnermates and fellow First Class passengers, mentioning each one's occupation as well as their name.

It was a long, wide table covered in snowy linen and lined down the center with beautiful silver candelabra ablaze with tall, slender white candles. There were about two dozen passengers chosen to dine at the captain's table, and all were formally dressed, men in tuxedoes and women in the latest fashion of gowns and jewels and furs. The captain, tall, broad-shouldered, lean-hipped and tanned—a prototype of what Cathy thought all ships' captains should look like—seated her on his right, next to an empty chair.

"Some of our dinner guests are dancing," he explained when Cathy glanced around at the other empty places at the huge table. "Would you like a cocktail before dinner? Or perhaps a glass of champagne?"

"Yes, thank you. Champagne, please." She turned to look around the vast dining room, impressed with the decor. Everything was show biz, glitteringly beautiful, but done in good taste and with fun in mind. There was a live orchestra playing on a raised platform in the far corner and several multicolored, multifaceted bulbs slowly rotated above the dance floor casting everything below in a rainbow of pastels. Dozens of small round tables dotted the floor, draped with white cloths and each boasting its own small silver candlestick and a vase of fresh red roses. Dozens of white-coated waiters seemed to float through the room, balancing large silver trays high over their heads; and chefs in tall, starched hats prepared flambés of everything from beef to ice cream at individual tables.

A young and very handsome waiter in a white coat with gold-braid trim, bowed low as he presented her with a tulip glass of champagne and welcomed her aboard in a clipped, British accent. She smiled and settled back in her chair, sipping her champagne and letting her gaze wander about the room. The orchestra was playing a Glenn Miller, Big Band number and the nostalgic music filled the room with sweet vibrations. Conversation seemed as lilting and musical as the song, and Cathy hummed to herself as she glanced around at her dinner partners. Everyone seemed to be with someone. The hum died on her lips, and she took a sip of champagne and wondered what she could do with her hands until it was time to fill them with a menu.

She always carried a small notebook in her purse, so she took it out and began making notes about what she had already observed of the ship. Might as well block it out for a future show, she thought. Maggie's idea about doing a show on cruises had been a good one, and Cathy told herself that was really why she had taken this trip, to check it out, see if it was worth bringing a crew on location for two weeks.

She hadn't really believed all that Hollywood hype about "love boats" and romance around every corner. Still, it would be nice to have a little male companionship during the cruise. She glanced at the captain, and he smiled at her, his blue eyes bright and blank. She almost giggled, remembering something Marc had once told her about a particularly stupid politician he had interviewed: "His lights were on, but nobody was home!" Stifling the giggle she ducked her head and went back to her notes.

"Don't you *ever* stop working?" Her head jerked up and her eyes opened wide, staring in disbelief. "I believe this is my place." He bent over the empty chair next to hers and read the gold-engraved name card resting next to the artfully folded napkin.

"Marc Monroe," she breathed, looking from him to his name in old English script on the creamy card bearing the ship's logo.

"Cathy Curtis." He stood looking down at her, his silver-gray eyes devouring her face feature by feature.

She couldn't look away from him, and when he reached out his hand to take hers, she gave it to him. He held it gently, turned it over in his hand and bent his head to kiss the palm. Still holding it, he sat down and drew his chair close to hers. She couldn't speak, didn't know what to say if she could.

"Hello. Surprised to see me?" He still held her hand and now rubbed it gently with his other one.

"Surprised is hardly the word," she managed to say. God, this couldn't be happening. It was too good to be true. Fourteen romantic, lazy days—and *nights*—on a tropical cruise with Marc! It was either a reward or a punishment, but she was too glad to see him to figure it out now. "Is this merely a coincidence or did you wrest the information from Maggie?" She grinned at him and leaned a little closer, returning the pressure of his fingers on hers.

"I confess. I forced her at gun point."

"Knowing Maggie, she probably called and told you!" She laughed and leaned against him when the waiter arrived with fresh glasses of champagne.

He caught her close for a moment, kissing her swiftly, softly on the mouth. If you only knew, he thought, and wanted to laugh out loud with pure joy. He'd done it, by God! He'd pulled it off. When he had first thought of the scheme, he had been a little doubtful of its success. Cathy wasn't exactly known for her pliancy, and he hadn't thought it would be so easy to talk her into this trip. But Maggie had done it, bless her heart. Now Cathy was here and the rest was up to him.

"Really, Marc, what *are* you doing here? I can't imagine *you* taking a pleasure cruise alone." She paled and looked quickly around. God, maybe he had brought someone. She knew that Bitsy was in Mexico with Monte, but that wouldn't stop him. What if he had some girl tucked away in his cabin?

"I might ask you the same question." He kept his voice light and his face innocent. If she found out that he had planned this vacation, schemed the whole thing with Maggie to get her away from the studio and Dash, she'd probably throw him overboard.

"Oh, well, I don't really know." She shrugged and laughed nervously. His silver-gray eyes were so unsettling! "Maggie and Dash practically railroaded me into it. I think they were trying to get rid of me." She laughed again and reached for her champagne.

"Then here's to Maggie and Dash." He touched her glass with his, keeping those smoldering gray eyes on her face as she raised her glass to her lips.

"But you haven't told me what you're doing here." She sipped again before replacing the glass on the table and nervously turning it around and around. She warned herself to go easy, keep it light, not fall victim to those magnificent silver eyes or the persuasive, husky voice. She could have two marvelous weeks of casual sex, thoroughly enjoy the cruise as it was meant to be enjoyed, then walk away from him as he had so easily walked away from her. And no way was she going to believe one word he said!

He shrugged and reached into his pocket for a cigarette. A waiter instantly appeared and held a lighter for him. "I just wanted to get away for a few days. I might jump ship at one of the ports and fly home if the cruise proves too boring." He wondered if his voice sounded normal with his heart pounding so wildly. He didn't want to rush her or tip his hand too soon. But she dimpled in the old, familiar way and her eyes lowered flirtatiously.

"I didn't think you were the type for a soft, luxury cruise—macho man that you are!"

He laughed and squeezed her hand. "Would it be more fitting if I grasped the tow rope in my teeth and swam to the Caribbean pulling the ship behind me?"

She laughed with him, leaning in close, placing a hand lightly on his arm. "Now, *that* I'd like to see! We could do a special for the fall season."

"Hey, speaking of specials, did you see the Mount St. Helen's thing last week?"

She nodded happily, marveling at how easily they could talk together, as if all the tears and hateful insults and hurting egos had never been. "Yes, I loved it. However, I didn't like what followed it. That was the night that the Hedy Carrington story broke, remember?"

"Yeah." He leaned over and kissed her hard and long on the mouth. "I've been wanting to do that ever since I saw your press conference. You were dynamite, baby! It was a real class act."

"Thank you." She actually blushed.

"How's Lady Pamela taking it?"

"She thinks it's all a royal hoot and is as happy as a clam—those are her exact words." Cathy laughed, remembering her many conversations with Pamela during the past week. She hadn't been the least bit surprised, had even expected Hedy Carrington to take the action. Ashley, however, had been humiliated by it—not for himself or Pamela, but for his mother.

He had fitted in perfectly with Pam's family and had fallen instantly in love with the cottage in Gloucestershire. In fact, that's where they planned to live after they were married. Lord Peter had grumbled some about the American scandal, but Pam's mum had serenely accepted her daughter's teenage lover, murmuring, "Jolly good, dear. Now you can raise him to suit yourself." They planned to be married in August when Ashley turned eighteen, and Pamela had made Cathy promise that she would be there.

Marc laughed. "That sounds like Lady Pamela. Well, I wish them both happiness. They're good people." His eyes softened with a love he couldn't hide, and he whispered huskily, "And you're a hell of a good friend, going to bat for them the way you did. Not many people would stick their necks out in such a controversial issue."

She shrugged and smiled shyly. "Thanks, but I don't want to talk about it, okay? I came on this cruise to forget it."

"It's forgotten. Let's dance." He pulled her to her feet and led her to the dance floor, drawing her into his arms. Her body moved familiarly against his, molding itself perfectly to his every contour, and he grew instantly erect. Her curly blond head rested just below his chin and her lips were pressed against his throat, soft and warm. He slid his hands down to her buttocks to press her harder against him and heard her little gasp of desire. His erection sank into the softness of her belly and she sighed and wriggled against it, kissing his throat. "Jesus, Cathy, I want you so much!" He bent his head to kiss her and she clung tighter, opening her mouth for his tongue. With a groan, he wrenched his mouth away. "Let's get out of here before I rape you in front of all these nice people."

"My bed or yours?" She looped her arm through his,

## The Love Game                                    273

almost running to keep up with his long, impatient strides. "Jeez, you're not too anxious, are you?"

He grabbed her at the door and kissed her. "Darling, I've never been so anxious for anything in my life!" He pulled her quickly down the long, red-carpeted corridor, and when she said, "Hey, Monroe, slow down!" he scooped her up into his arms and quickly covered the distance to his cabin. A young steward was lounging in the hallway, and Marc called, "Hey, mate, get this door for me, will you?"

"Yes, sir!" He ran quickly forward and held the door for them, grinning and giving Marc a wink. "Have a good evening, sir!"

Marc kicked the door shut and deposited Cathy on the small bed, lowering himself upon her and kissing her as if he'd never stop. His hands roamed urgently over her body, feeling again the softness of her breasts that he loved so much, the firm buttocks, the soft, soft thighs. He raised her long skirt and slipped his hand beneath the sheer silk of her panties and gripped her gently, and she moaned and writhed against him. "God, Cathy— Cathy, I want you!"

"You've got me," she whispered huskily and raised her hips to meet his searching fingers.

"Jesus!" he gasped, sitting up quickly and running a shaky hand through his hair. "I've never been so damn hot in my life! Look at me—I'm shaking like a leaf." He held out his hands and laughed at the heavy trembling of them.

"Me, too." Cathy held out her own hands, and their eyes met and then their fingers touched, trembling together. A silence fell between them as they held hands and continued to gaze into one another's eyes. Cathy felt her cheeks burning and her entire body grew hot and liquid, quivering with desire. They were both stunned by the swift, powerful emotion that had swept through them, leaving them shaken and breathless. Their eyes filled with wonder as they slowly leaned toward one another until only their lips were touching in the softest of kisses. Eyes closed, lips clinging, they kissed deeply, hungrily, as if feeding from one another, nourishing one another.

They drew apart, their breathing ragged, jolted by the kiss. Marc lifted a shaky hand and gently touched her cheek. "I love you, Cathy," he whispered in a husky voice that shook with emotion. He took the thin straps of her gown and slipped them off her shoulders and down, baring her breasts. Bending his dark head he kissed them, one at a time, and she sighed and raised her hips, helping him remove her gown. He peeled off her panties slowly, gazing rapturously at her naked beauty.

"God, baby, you're so beautiful! I've dreamed of you this way a hundred times—a thousand times . . . !" His voice was hoarse, raspy with desire. He let his hot gaze caress her as he swiftly shed his jacket and pants, then she was reaching up for him, pulling him down on top of her, too impatient to wait for him to remove his shirt and tie. She kissed him, wrapping her legs around his waist, and as he sank into the incredible soft heat of her, she heard her own voice moaning, "I love you, Marc!"

It was four the following afternoon before they surfaced and went in search of food. Cathy had never been so ravenous in her life and begged Marc to stop at the first place they came to that was serving a buffet. They had missed breakfast and lunch and were too early for dinner. Holding hands, they wandered through the large, impressive ship until they came to the Kiki Room, a Polynesian wonder with romantic island music and a manmade waterfall tumbling and splashing behind the bar. The bar itself stretched the entire length of the room, and there were at least a dozen long tables laden with food. Huge, silver bowls of tropical fruits, exotic hors d'oeuvres, succulent meats and vegetables, savory native sauces and breads.

"I don't know where to start," Cathy moaned, looking at the feast spread before them. "It all looks so good!"

"Let's start with one of those rum drinks." He nodded in the direction of a couple who were sipping elaborate drinks in pineapple shells topped with chunks of fruit and tiny, colorful parasols. He motioned to the waitress and seconds later the drinks arrived. Cathy watched Marc taste his and giggled.

"There goes your macho image, Monroe. I thought foreign correspondents were strictly Scotch on the rocks men."

"I'll show you macho as soon as I get some nourishment in the old bod." He laughed and pulled her close for a lingering kiss.

"Either I'm out of shape or love is more strenuous than I thought!"

"Ah, there you are, Miss Curtis!" The captain stood at their table, beaming happily down at them as if he had personally made the match. "I rang your cabin several times this morning to let you know that you left your purse at my table last night." He smiled broadly and actually cuffed Marc on the shoulder, man to man.

"Oh, God, I forgot all about it!" Jesus, everything was in her purse—credit cards, money, passport.

"Not to worry, Miss Curtis, it's in the purser's cabin. I'll have someone fetch it at once."

"Oh, thank you, Captain—" She peered at the nameplate on his chest next to all the gold braid and ribbons: Capt. Vernon Dinkel. She almost giggled but kept a straight face. "—uh, Captain Dinkel." She wondered if anyone ever called him Cap'n Twinkle and almost giggled again but caught herself when Marc gave her a warning glance. She could see the laughter in his eyes.

276 *The Love Game*

"I'll run and get it," he said, rising. "I left my camera in my cabin, and I want to take some pictures of my lady on deck before we lose the sun." He kissed Cathy and clapped a hand on Captain Dinkel's shoulder. "Keep her company until I get back?"

"It would be my pleasure." He sat dutifully (and anxiously, Marc thought) in the vacant chair next to Cathy, his bright blue eyes sparkling with interest.

Marc hurried to the purser's cabin and retrieved the purse, found Cathy's cabin key inside and went to her stateroom as stealthily as a thief. He felt his heart pounding as he rummaged through her bathroom until he found her small pink plastic packet of birth control pills. He walked briskly to the ship's doctor's cabin and took a deep breath, hoping the man was mercenary or romantic enough to go for his plan. Luckily, Dr. Travis knew who Marc was and pumped his hand enthusiastically. "What a thrill to meet you," he gushed, still shaking hands and pulling him farther into the room. "I've followed your specials with great interest—great interest."

"Thanks." Marc gently disengaged his hand. "Uh, listen, I'd love to sit and talk with you, but right now I have a lady waiting for me—a very special lady." He grinned, man to man, and Dr. Travis leaned closer. "Not only is she a very special lady, she's a very *stubborn* lady—and that's why I'm here." He withdrew the birth control pills from his pocket along with two one hundred dollar bills. "Would it be too unethical of me to ask if you'll exchange these for something else, like, a placebo of some kind?"

The doctor took the pills, his gaze still on Marc's face, but now he frowned slightly, and Marc rushed quickly on. "See, Doc, it's like this. I'm crazy about the lady but I'm afraid the only way I can get her to slow down long enough to marry me is to get her pregnant, you know?" He laughed intimately and clapped a hand on the doctor's shoulder. Sensing the man was starstruck, he added, confidentially, "It's Cathy Curtis—you know, the hostess of the Cathy Curtis Show on Channel Six?"

"Cathy Curtis! My God, I love her! I never miss her show." He turned the pills over in his hand, not frowning now but smiling. "Christ, that would be the show biz marriage of the year, wouldn't it?"

Marc grinned modestly. "Well, I don't know about that . . ."

"And I would be a part of it—sort of a ship's Cupid, if you will."

"You sure as hell would." Marc knew he had him now and pushed his advantage. "I'll even invite you to the wedding."

"Gee, Cathy Curtis—she's on board now?"

"Yep, waiting for me in the Kiki Room—and no doubt wondering where I am. I'll introduce you later, but this has to be strictly between us, okay?"

Dr. Travis thought for a moment, then grinned broadly and stuck out his hand, shaking Marc's firmly. "Okay. I'll do it." He laughed as he went to his medicine cabinet and took out a large brown bottle of pills. "I probably shouldn't, but what the hell—I'm as romantic as the next guy!" He seemed to take forever to replace the birth control pills with the placebo and Marc felt himself beginning to perspire. Well, he'd done it now. It was out of his hands and in God's, he supposed.

Thanking the doctor profusely and promising an introduction to Cathy, he fled down the long corridor toward Cathy's cabin, replaced the packet, then ran back to the Kiki Room, his heart in his throat.

"What took you so long?" Cathy asked, lifting her face for his kiss as he slid into the chair next to hers. "I was beginning to think you'd jumped ship already."

"You're not going to get rid of me that easily." He laughed and took a large swallow of the rum drink to still the pounding of his heart. "I ran into a fan of yours, the ship's doctor. Says he never misses your show. I promised to introduce you later, okay?"

"Sure I can always use another fan."

"I'm your number one fan—always." He kissed her again, his eyes soft with love and she leaned happily against him. "I love you, darling very much. You know that?"

"Yes, I know." She looked at him steadily for a long moment. "I think I do, anyway." She finished her drink and took a bite of a pineapple chunk, still looking at him.

"But do you still love me—that's the important question." His hand gripped hers, and he kept the intense silver gaze on her face, waiting for an answer.

"Uh, Marc, I don't really think I'm ready for anything heavy, you know? I mean, I don't want to make any decisions any tougher than what I want for dinner for the next two weeks. I came on this cruise to straighten out my head. I had no idea, of course, that you would be on board." She laughed lightly. "You were one of the things I was going to straighten out!"

"Then I won't press you, darling. Take your time." He kissed her again. "Take as long as you need to realize that I'm the only man for you!"

"I see." Cathy laughed and shook her head. "Still modest, huh, Monroe?"

He laughed with her. "Always. Now come on, let's eat. I'm starving." He pulled her to her feet and kept his arm around her waist as they went to the buffet tables. Christ, if she ever found out what he'd just done, she'd probably throw him overboard. He could only hope that he could convince her that he loved her more than anything and wanted to marry her. Maggie had told him that Cathy really wanted a baby, but probably would never admit it, and that was when he had thought of

## The Love Game

switching her pills. Surely she would divorce Dash and marry him when she found she was carrying his child.

It was downright sneaky, and he knew it and didn't care. He wanted her and, by God, he'd get her, one way or another. He would romance her like she'd never been romanced in her life. He would use the soft tropical nights and gently rocking ship to his advantage. He would ply her with exotic rum drinks and keep her in bed or close by his side for the entire two weeks.

Marc wanted to tell her that Bitsy had divorced him in Mexico last week (He'd received a telegram from her when she couldn't reach him by phone.) but was afraid the news would bring on too many questions that he didn't want to answer just yet. He would have to tell her very carefully about Bitsy's homosexuality and the deep, but platonic friendship they shared. He wouldn't hurt Bitsy, and he just hoped that Cathy was compassionate enough to understand.

He wasn't a man given to asking favors of God, but he asked one now: that Cathy would be receptive to his plan, that she would love him enough to forgive him his trickery, although he hoped she never discovered it. He had sworn Maggie to secrecy and knew she would keep her word. She wanted to see Cathy happy as much as Marc did—as much, apparently, as Dash did. Maggie had told him that Dash had been instrumental in talking Cathy into taking the cruise, and Marc wondered why. If she were his wife, he sure as hell wouldn't send her on a romantic cruise for two whole weeks—but he wasn't going to look a gift horse in the mouth. She was here and that's all that mattered for the moment. He had two weeks in which to win her over and didn't want to waste one precious moment worrying about such unpleasantries as a husband waiting at home.

\* \* \*

## The Love Game

It had worked even better than Marc had planned. Never had he seen Cathy so delightful and relaxed as she had been on the cruise, and when it was almost over and they were in Mexico's colorful, teaming port, she had said, wistfully, "Gee, I kind of hate to see it end. I wish we could stay another two weeks."

"Let's do it," Marc had pressed at once. "Let's stay in Mexico for awhile. Neither of us has to get back for anything."

"Oh, Marc, I couldn't. Dash . . ."

"Dash is fine. He *wanted* you to go on this vacation. You told me so yourself."

"Yes, but . . ."

"No buts. You've always wanted to see Mexico—see, I remember everything you've ever told me—and what better time than now? We can fly home from Mexico City after we've done a little sightseeing."

"I don't know." But she had wavered and at last had called Dash to see if she was needed at home or the studio. Dash had assured her everything was under control and had actually urged her to stay over. Again, Marc wondered what the wily old silver fox was up to.

They had made the *turista* rounds during their stay in Mexico, doing all the things that Cathy had read about. They had rented a boat and gone fishing for marlin off the Gulf of Mexico, had exclaimed over the primitive beauty of Veracruz and Guadalajara, tramped through the ruins of Yucatán, craned their necks at the towering volcanoes of Popocatépetl and Ixtacihuatl. They had pawed through the brightly painted pots and artifacts of the ancient Toltec and Aztec Indians, marveling at the strangely beautiful designs of the Zapotec. They bought gifts for everyone and Marc had laughingly moaned that they would have to buy another large suitcase to carry them home.

And they made love. Everywhere. Every day and

every night. Every chance they got—because they both knew it would soon be over. Cathy had stubbornly refused to talk seriously about their situation whenever Marc had tried to bring it up. She wanted nothing to spoil the perfection of the past few weeks. She preferred to think of it as a "shipboard romance" because she wasn't sure they could maintain the same perfection back home on land. Back in Hollywood where a secret is very hard to keep and so many other lives were involved. She slipped into her Scarlett O'Hara "I'll think about it tomorrow" role and gave herself up completely to the first real, selfish pleasure she'd ever known.

And now it was over. They were flying home tomorrow at noon and she couldn't sleep for worrying. She worried that Dash would find out and hate her. She worried that she wouldn't be able to give Marc up once they got home. She sat in front of the open window in their sixth story room in the Maria Isabella Hotel and stared moodily out at the central plaza, the Zócalo. Its rough, cobbled streets were deserted now as the city slept, but they had teamed with life only hours before. She could make out the dusky silhouettes of the cathedral and the National Palace as they stood haughtily apart from the other buildings. A light breeze drifted to her and she breathed deeply, leaning back in her chair and closing her eyes. The muscles in her calves caught, and she grimaced with pain. She and Marc had climbed the pyramids that afternoon, groaning and laughing, finally reaching the summit and standing with arms wrapped about one another, the king and queen of all they surveyed. Too bad it wasn't real life.

But, as the sage said, "All good things must come to an end" and her "queen for a day" was over. It had lasted a month, actually—one entire, glorious month that she wished didn't have to end. Marc had been perfection itself, and when she was in his arms, she allowed herself the luxury of believing every beautiful, seductive, caressing word he whispered to her. But she had told herself so often in the past that he was a convincing liar, that she couldn't completely believe him when he wasn't fogging her senses with passion, with his incredible lovemaking. In her rational moments she thought about taking Pam's advice and keeping Marc around merely as a lover, but she didn't know if she would be capable of deceiving Dash. She owed everything to him and would rather die than deliberately hurt him. She rationalized that the cruise with Marc had not been deliberate as she hadn't known he was going to be on board. A tiny part of her brain wanted to believe that it was fate, that she and Marc were meant to be together, but she was too practical to believe in such romantic nonsense, she firmly told herself.

She walked silently back to the bed and crawled in beside Marc, snuggling against his naked warmth. She would think about the possibilities of kismet later, but right now there was a Mexican moon peeking around the silvery clouds, and she wanted him again. One last time. She curled her body around his from behind, kissing his ear. She didn't think he'd mind being awakened. . . .

## Chapter Sixteen

"I'm what?" Cathy gasped.

"You're pregnant, Mrs. Sunderling," Dr. Moss said. "Quite frankly, I'm a little surprised. I didn't think Dash was still able to, well, perform sexually."

"What do you mean?" Her head spun. Pregnant? Jesus! She had to force herself to listen to the doctor.

"Surely he's told you that he needs surgery?" Cathy nodded and he went on, frowning slightly. "I'm afraid it can't be put off much longer. I've told him repeatedly to set a date and we'd get this trouble taken care of, but he continues to put me off. I can understand his reluctance, of course. A man doesn't want to think of himself as a neuter—but when it's a choice of your sex life or your life, period—I should think the choice would be clear."

"I didn't know it was that serious," she murmured, still in a sort of daze to learn that she was pregnant. How could it have happened, for God's sake?

"Terminal, I'm afraid, even with the surgery."

"Cancer?" Cathy's head snapped up, and she was suddenly ice cold and paying close attention.

Dr. Moss nodded his head sadly. "In the colon now and spreading fast. We can arrest it with surgery and treatment, and Dash could live five to ten years. Of course, he'd have to take it easy—and there would be no sex." He watched Cathy's face turn white and crumble with compassion for her husband and wished there had been an easier way of telling her. But Dash had forced his hand by his constant refusal to cooperate and have the necessary surgery. Saul Moss had been the Sunderling's family doctor for over thirty years and wasn't about to let an old friend slip away without a fight. He knew that Cathy loved Dash and would help him convince her husband to get the much needed treatment. And now it would be more important than ever with the baby on the way. He would have something to live for.

"I—I didn't know. I thought it was—was just something minor, some . . ." She stammered to a halt, swallowing hard. Cancer. God, no, not Dash!

"With treatment he can live out his life as comfortably as we can possibly make it for him. Dash is not a young man, my dear." His voice was gentle, soothing. "He's had a good life." Cathy nodded miserably, afraid she would cry if she tried to speak. "And now he'll have a new baby, a new beginning in a way. I wish I could see his face when you tell him, my dear. He's going to be one happy man."

Tell him. She had to tell him. She twisted her icy hands in her lap and tried to compose herself. It was too much all at once, and she hadn't fully absorbed it. She needed to be alone. She stood and shook hands with the doctor. "Thank you, Dr. Moss, for—for explaining everything to me. I'll see to it that Dash makes an appointment to see the surgeon you recommended."

"Good, good." He came around from behind his desk and walked her to the door. "Stop at the desk on your way out and have Cindy give you Dr. Rod Clifford's number. He's one of the finest gynecologists and obstetricians in Beverly Hills. You'll like him."

She moved in a daze, past Cindy's desk, down the long corridor, outside into the white-hot glare of the

August sun, the two words repeating themselves in her numb brain: Pregnant. Cancer. She paid the parking attendant with a twenty and didn't wait for her change but pulled her Mercedes into the heavy Wilshire Boulevard traffic, oblivious to the honking horns and screeching brakes.

Dash with cancer? It was unthinkable. But it explained the sudden change in him, the heavy drinking, the withdrawal from the network, the moodiness, his pushing her into the seat of power at KNAB. God, how he must love her! And how she had betrayed that love. Pregnant with Marc's baby. That, too, was unthinkable. How in the world had it happened? She took her birth control pills faithfully, never missing a day, not even those love-filled, wonderful days of the cruise and Mexican holiday.

A tiny part of her wanted to crow with delight: "A baby! Marc's baby!" But the frightening news of Dash's illness forced the happiness away. She could never leave him now. Not ever. The thought jolted her and she realized the idea had been forming in the back of her mind ever since the cruise. She had seen Dash differently when she had returned, had seen him as a much loved and cherished father-figure, someone who would always understand her and love her. She had been on the verge of telling him about Marc a dozen times in the past month, but something had always stopped her. She had wanted to wait a little longer and see if their relationship held as it was—completely platonic, but comfortable and friendly. Like roommates, she thought. Like Marc and Bitsy. Good God, how had her life gotten so complicated?

She turned into the long, winding driveway and pulled to a halt near the garage. She would have to find out exactly where Dash stood before she could make any plans or decisions of her own. If he still loved her and wanted her as a wife, she would stay with him, stand by him during his illness. She owed everything to him and wouldn't run out on him. It would mean passing the baby off as his, but she supposed she could handle that. She'd never had much trouble in seducing him when she really wanted to; she just hadn't wanted to in a very long time.

She got out of the car and walked slowly toward the house, dreading the confrontation but knowing it was inevitable. She wondered if Dash's feelings toward her had changed as well. He certainly hadn't seemed interested in sex at all, not for several months, and he seemed to have only her happiness in mind when they talked about the future of the network or her career.

Maybe he would be happy for her, urge her to go to Marc. He had always known how she felt about Marc even though she had never admitted it—even to herself. And they would always be friends, she and Dash, close and loving friends forever. They had always leveled with one another, and that was why she felt so bad about lying to him now. God, it would be so much easier if the baby were his. She could give him that, at least.

Cancer. The word slipped into her mind again and she shuddered and pushed open the heavy mahogany door and stepped into the cool foyer. She heard the sound of a game show coming from the den and went in to find Dash sprawled on the sofa watching "The Hollywood Squares."

"Hi, darling. I'm home." She went to him and bent to kiss the top of his head.

"Hi, babe—sit down and watch this with me." Lately, he had taken to watching game shows, all day, every day, gleefully answering the questions before the contestants could.

"Just a minute, honey. I want to get out of these clothes and make myself a drink. I'm bushed."

"Tough day, sweetie?"

# The Love Game 287

"Umm."

"Auditions always are. See anything worthwhile?"

"A couple—I'll tell you all about it when I get back." She dropped another kiss on the top of his head and hurried toward her bedroom and a much needed joint. She hadn't told him that she had had a doctor's appointment today, letting him believe that she had been kept late at the studio casting the new fall shows. She smoked a joint as she changed into a loose-fitting blue satin robe, Dash's favorite, wondering how she was going to open the subject. Dr. Moss had suggested that she make *him* the heavy and tell Dash that he had called her into the office for a consultation regarding Dash's surgery and the arrangements that must be made, et cetera.

She combed her hair and applied fresh lipstick and perfume, wishing that Pamela were there to talk to. Or Marc. To her surprise (and delight), they had continued their affair on land, discreetly, of course, and had managed to talk on the phone almost nightly. But he was in Ireland now filming a special for KNAB and she had to face Dash alone.

She went downstairs and into the den, smiling brightly when he looked up from the sofa. "I feel much better. Gosh, it was hot today, wasn't it?" She went to the bar and mixed herself a vodka and tonic. "Can I get you anything?"

"No thanks, babe—got one." He raised his glass of Bourbon and smiled. "Come sit down and talk to me. I missed you." He patted a place next to him on the soft leather sofa, and she joined him, turning her cheek for his kiss. They chatted about the studio, the weather and other general subjects with Dash interrupting every so often to answer a question on "The Hollywood Squares." When the program was finally over, Cathy quickly turned off the set.

"Let's have some music, okay? I need to soothe my shattered nerves after a day of listening to cold readings and agents' lies." She went to the stereo near the bar and put on a stack of records, mixed herself a fresh drink and rejoined him. "A funny thing happened at the studio today," she began. "I got a rather disturbing phone call." She placed her hand on his arm and looked steadily into his eyes, at the beloved and familiar face, craggily handsome still, the pale, faded blue eyes still alight with love. She gripped his arm and said quietly, "Dr. Moss called me, Dash, and told me everything."

He nodded his head quietly, meeting her steady gaze, not flinching. "I wondered when he would."

"God, darling, why didn't you tell me? Do you have so little faith in me that you'd hide something like this? Didn't you think I could take it?"

"It's I who can't take it." His voice was so low she barely heard.

"God, Dash, I can't believe you didn't tell me!" She brought his head close to her breast and stroked him like a baby. "Poor darling, you must have gone through hell. But it's over now. I'm going to take care of you. We'll make an appointment first thing tomorrow morning and get the surgery out of the way, and then you can concentrate on getting well. Dr. Moss said with treatment you'll be as good as new."

"*Almost* as good as new. Did he also tell you that there would be a couple of parts of me missing?"

"Yes he did and so what?" She took his face between her two hands, forcing him to look her straight in the eye. "We've made enough love to last us a lifetime, Sunderling, or have you forgotten?" When he tried to pull his face away, she tightened her grip and shook him. "And don't forget, we've still got a little time before you go in for surgery. Remember what the man said, 'make hay while the sun shines'—right?" And maybe a baby, she thought sadly, hating herself, wishing she could just snuggle in his arms and confess everything and that he'd make it all right as he always did.

"God, Cathy, I love you!" He caught her close in a rib-crushing embrace, burying his face in her hair, holding her for a long time. Finally he gave a shuddering sigh and drew away. His eyes were wet, and he grinned sheepishly as he wiped away the tears. "You're one hell of a dame, my little Cathy," he half whispered, half chuckled. His voice was harsh and strangled with tears. "And you've made my life so full and rich I still can't believe my good fortune." He took her hands and kissed them fervently. "Thank you for loving me. It's the greatest gift I've ever known."

"It's I who should thank you," she whispered, fighting back her own tears. She gripped his hands hard. "You've given me so much, Dash, more than I can say—more than I deserve . . ."

"Shhh, little Cathy, be quiet or we'll both be blubbering like an old Bette Davis movie." He patted her cheek lightly. "Get me another drink, woman. You might as well get used to waiting on me."

"Yes, sir!" She jumped to do his bidding, grinning in that old, sassy way he loved so much, and his heart threatened to burst from his chest it swelled so with love. He couldn't tell her that Dr. Moss had called him the moment Cathy had left his office with the news of her pregnancy. Nosy and cantankerous, Moss considered it his right to interfere in his patient's lives if things weren't progressing the way, and with the speed, he thought they should. He had used Cathy's pregnancy as a further incentive to goad Dash into the operation, never suspecting that they no longer slept together—and hadn't for months.

Dash couldn't tell Cathy that he knew all about Marc Monroe. Oh, they had been discreet, but he had known almost from the first. Maggie was not a very good liar and when he had spoken to her a couple of days after Cathy had left on the cruise, she had seemed nervous and guilty. He had checked with the travel bureau and found that Marc Monroe was taking the same cruise. He hadn't been angry. In fact, he'd been glad that his little Cathy would have a brief fling, a shipboard romance. He had urged her to go on the cruise with that very thought in mind. She would undoubtedly meet some handsome stranger, and nature would take its course. He hadn't exactly planned on Marc Monroe, but after he'd considered it, he had thought: why not? Cathy had left Marc for him before and he had every confidence that she would again—if it came to that. He couldn't be sure of another man, a new man. It was safer, dealing with an acknowledged threat. It hadn't bothered him all that much that she would be making love to another man. He wanted her to have a sex life with someone else if he couldn't give her one. But he also wanted her to stay with him. Until he died.

He looked up as she sat down next to him and handed him his drink. God, she was so achingly beautiful, radiant in her first months of pregnancy. He hadn't planned on the baby. It had thrown him for a loop when Dr. Moss had told him. And it called for an entirely new and different way of thinking. He had to sort out his thoughts, get the priorities straight in his head. Better to go along with everything Cathy said for the time being, agree with her, placate her—until he decided what to do.

Dash allowed Cathy to take him to the UCLA Medical Center, from doctor to lab to administration, making the arrangements for the surgery that was scheduled for the following week. (Christ, so *fast*?)

He took her to dinner and sat talking with her far into

## The Love Game

the night, until he could no longer hold his eyes open. He played Scrabble with her and allowed her to seduce him, knowing why she was doing it and loving her all the more for it.

He thought about the baby and knew it would be happier with its own, real father instead of some old cocker who could be its grandfather. He thought about Cathy and knew she'd be a hell of lot happier with Marc than she would be nursing some ancient old relic, wasting her youth, growing to hate him. The more Bourbon he drank, the more maudlin he became until an idea began to crystalize—a brilliant idea.

It was Saturday night, just one day before he was due to check into UCLA. They had eaten at home and were sitting outside on the patio, watching the sunset over the Valley. "I think I'll run out and get some of that champagne that your friend Pamela used to drink," he said suddenly.

"What?" Cathy had been far away in thought but sat up now and faced him. "Champagne? Now?"

"Sure, why not? We'll drink to my health—literally!" He laughed and jumped up from the chaise he had been lying on. "Don't move. I'll be right back." He started toward the house, stopped, turned to look at her, then went to her and knelt by her side. "I love you so much, my little Cathy." He kissed her, held her by the shoulders and gazed into her face a moment longer, finally asking, "What was the name of that stuff?"

"Louis Roederer—but are you sure you want to go? We have plenty of champagne."

"Not the English broad's favorite brand. I learned to like that stuff for some strange reason." He was holding her lightly around the waist, still kneeling, grinning up at her.

"I can't imagine why," Cathy drawled, smiling at the memory of Lady Pamela and her unending supply of

Louis Roederer champagne, "Well, okay, sure, I could go for some—if you're sure you want to go."

"I'm sure." He kissed her again and left quickly, pausing at the bar to gulp down two stiff slugs of Bourbon and to fill a water-glass to take with him in the car. He took the silver and black Rolls, the one with the stocked bar in the back, just in case he lost his nerve and needed a little more liquid courage.

He glanced back only once as he pulled out of the garage and started down the winding lane that led to Mulholland Drive. He drank steadily, not lowering the glass as he maneuvered the sharp, treacherous curves with one hand on the steering wheel, his foot pressing down harder and harder on the accelerator. He had to do this for his little Cathy and her baby. He swallowed the rest of the Bourbon and let the glass fall from his hand, blinking back the tears that suddenly sprang to his eyes and then floor-boarded it, his hands gripped tight, white-knuckled on the wheel, arms straight out and rigid. He got the big, expensive machine up to ninety-three miles an hour before he turned it out into the darkness, away from the road, crashing through the guardrail and plummeting hundreds of feet down into the yawning, dark abyss.

Dash left Cathy fifteen million dollar's worth of municipal bonds on which he had paid the gift tax, the Bel Air mansion and all his stock in KNAB. His death was listed as "accidental," and his life insurance made her richer still. But none of it registered, and it wouldn't have meant anything to her even if it had. Dash was gone; her Daddy who was always there to make everything all better.

She had remained under heavy sedation for three days and was revived by Dr. Moss for the funeral where she had collapsed and had to be carried from the church.

Maggie had tried to persuade her to come to the ranch for a few days, but Cathy refused, begging to be left alone with her grief. She lay curled in her bed, accepting food only when Mrs. Donahue would no longer listen to her protests that she wasn't hungry. Dr. Moss stopped by every afternoon on his way home from the office and simply sat by her bed, sometimes having a drink with her, urging her to talk about Dash and listening patiently.

"It's too bad he couldn't have lived to see the baby," Dr. Moss said one evening four days after Dash's funeral. "He really wanted that baby."

Cathy was lying in bed, propped up by pillows, listlessly sipping a vodka and tonic. She sat straight up and gasped, "What did you say?"

"I said Dash really wanted this child. It's a shame that he . . ."

"He knew? You told him?" Two bright spots of color appeared on her cheeks, and the rest of her face went chalky white.

"Why, uh—I just assumed that *you* had told him, my dear. . . ." Caught, the good doctor flushed and looked away from the distraught young woman.

"*You* told him!" She flung back the sheet and stood, trembling, eyes blazing with anger. "Of all the unethical— God, how could you divulge a patient's confidence! How could you?"

"I, uh, I thought it would help—I thought . . ." He, too, stood, his eyes pleading with her to understand. She had lost a husband, but he had lost a friend of over thirty years.

"Jesus Christ, I don't believe you would do such a thing!" She stalked to the bar and poured straight vodka into her glass and spun around to face him. "Get out of here, Dr. Moss. Please, just get out."

"I—I don't understand why you're so angry, my dear. Surely you told Dash about the baby . . ." He was edging toward the door, staring at the wildness in her face, wondering if he should suggest a shot to calm her down.

"It's none of your damn business whether I told him or not!" she shrieked. "How dare you stick your nose into a husband and wife's personal business? How *dare* you? You had no right to tell him!" She tossed off the vodka in one shuddering swallow and swung around as Dr. Moss started to creep through the door. *"Just a minute."* Her voice was like a whip cracking and the doctor turned, startled. "What did he say when you told him?"

"He—he was happy—overjoyed as a matter of fact—he—" Dr. Moss swallowed nervously, taking another tentative step toward the door and escape from Cathy's blazing blue eyes.

"He was 'happy'—'overjoyed' . . ." She sagged suddenly, catching the edge of the dresser to steady herself and whispered, "Go away, Dr. Moss, and don't come back here again." She turned her face away, heard the door close softly, then sank to the floor, weeping as she hadn't wept since Dash's funeral. Good God, that stupid, stupid man! He had killed Dash as surely as if he had taken a pistol and shot him through the heart. "Oh, my darling, I'm so sorry," she sobbed, beating her fists on the floor. "Oh God, Dash, can you ever forgive me? Oh, my darling, my darling."

There had been a tiny doubt nagging at the back of her mind that Dash's death had not been accidental, and now she knew for sure that it hadn't been. He had killed himself because that stupid jerk of a doctor had told him that his wife was pregnant. And Dash had known damn well it wasn't his. Christ! He wouldn't have been able to handle it, losing his masculinity, being faced daily with a pregnant wife carrying another man's

## The Love Game    295

child—God! He had been humiliated, no doubt, unable to face his peers and hear their whispers and speculations.

Cathy sat up, shuddering, her hands clenched into fists, her eyes streaming. By God, no one had better say a damn word about Dash in her hearing, or she'd kill the bastard! She would never allow Dash's memory to be tarnished, to have him thought of as a fool. She stood, her legs shaking, and poured herself another vodka and tonic—and heard Dash's voice as plain as day: "Don't let them come and get you, babe—go out and meet them head on!"

She went into the den and pawed through a stack of telephone messages, mostly from reporters, columnists and magazine editors wanting a story about her life with Dash. She found the one she was looking for and dialed quickly, taking a long swallow of her drink to still the palpitations. "Miss Rona Barrett," she said, and when the reporter came on the line, she took another deep, shuddering breath and told her she was returning her call.

Cathy listened to her words of sympathy and responded to the stock questions automatically, assuring Rona that KNAB would continue to function as usual, that, yes, it was true that Dash had given her complete control of the company. "There's only one small difference this season," she said, forcing her voice to be light, even managing to chuckle. "There's going to be a pregnant president at the helm of KNAB this year."

"What? Why, that's wonderful news, isn't it?" Rona said and Cathy could almost hear the wheels clicking in the reporter's head.

"Yes, wonderful. Dash was thrilled. He—he was going out to get a bottle of champagne to celebrate, when he—he—" Her voice broke in a sob. "He left half of his stock in the network to the baby. I just wanted to set the record straight. You know everyone keeps saying that I inherited everything, but Dash wanted the child to have half. He was so happy about the baby, and, well, I just wanted you to know, Rona, because I know you're one of the very few reporters I can count on to report the news accurately. I'm probably going to get a lot of flack from the tabloids when I start showing and I'll just feel better knowing you're in my corner."

"I understand completely, Cathy, and you know you can count on me. Those filthy rags should be taken off the newsstands. They make it doubly hard for a legitimate reporter to get an interview with anyone."

"Well, I knew I could trust you, Rona. That's why yours is the only call I returned." They chatted a few more minutes and Rona made Cathy promise that she would call when the baby was born and give her the exclusive.

Cathy was drenched with perspiration when she put the receiver down and stood leaning heavily against Dash's desk, trembling. She was weak and lightheaded from her days spent in bed. She started to take another sip of her drink then set it firmly on the desk and reached for the telephone again, quickly dialing.

"Juno? Hi, Mrs. Sunderling." She listened, nodding impatiently as he expressed his shock and sympathy. "Listen, Juno, I'm going to need you all this week, okay? Let's start tomorrow morning, eight o'clock, all right? Thanks." She hung up, feeling better than she had in weeks. Juno would get her back into shape with his wonderful therapeutic massages and workouts in the gym. She wanted to look nothing less than sensational when she showed up at the studio the following week. Let the curious bastards stare. She'd give them something to stare at! She picked up the telephone again and dialed Monte's number. "Hi, Monte—it's Cathy. I was wondering if you'd be interested in designing a complete maternity wardrobe for a slightly pregnant television executive?"

Lackadaisical as usual, Monte drawled, "Oh? Is Norman Lear pregnant?"

"You nut." Cathy laughed, feeling alive for the first time since the funeral, feeling the new life inside her. It would be Dash's baby, Dash's life, and no one would ever know otherwise. "I'm pregnant! Isn't that a kick in the ass? I still can't quite believe it."

"Nor can I. Gads, a baby. I've never even seen one up close."

"I understand they're relatively harmless. Well, will you do it, Monte? I'm not showing yet but we should probably get started on the fittings soon, don't you think?"

"I should think the sooner the better. By the time I get them made up you'll probably have a belly on you like Dom Deluise! Are you planning on continuing with your talk show?"

"Of course. That's why I want you to do my wardrobe. I want to be the most sensationally fashionable pregnant lady on television!"

"Probably the only pregnant lady on television. Well, I can take you this Tuesday, around noonish."

"Thanks, Monte. You're a love. See you Tuesday." And she rang off before he could ask her any questions.

Cathy had heard about Bitsy's quickie Mexican divorce as soon as she returned from her own Mexican holiday and had been plagued with guilt, fully believing that Bitsy had divorced Marc because she knew about the cruise they had gone on together. She had wanted to talk to Marc about it but they had only had a few nights together before he left for his assignment in Ireland. He had been gone for over a month, and she missed him and needed him. It seemed that he was always gone when she wanted him the most. He had called when he had heard about Dash and asked her if she wanted him to come home and be with her, but she had refused, had still been numb with shock.

She was in a quandary as to what to tell him about the baby. She wanted everyone to believe it was Dash's baby, of course, and had never considered an abortion for even a moment. But what now, now that Dash was dead? Did Marc have a right to know it was his baby? She didn't know. Couldn't think. Her thoughts were so confused and she was so very weary. She would think about it tomorrow, after Juno had worked her out and her mind was clear. There would be no more booze or grass during her pregnancy. She was going to have the most beautiful and perfect baby in the world. Holding that thought, she walked back to her bedroom and crawled between the gold satin sheets and fell instantly asleep.

The shrill jangle of the telephone woke her and she opened her eyes to stare groggily at the clock on her bedside table. The lighted dial showed 11:23. She picked up the receiver and mumbled, "Hello?"

"Cathy, I'm home! I just got in!" Marc's excited voice crackled over the wire, alive, vital, happy. "Why didn't you tell me about the baby? When did you find out?"

"Marc? Is that you?" She sat up, fully awake. "Where are you?"

"I'm here—at the airport. I was having a drink in the bar while I waited for my luggage and heard Rona Barret on the eleven o'clock news. I can't believe it!" He laughed happily. "Are you all right? When did you find out? Hey, listen, I'll be right over. I can't wait to see you, darling!"

Cathy sat with the receiver buzzing dully in her ear, torn between wanting to see Marc and dreading it. Torn between telling him the truth about the baby or going through with the bluff and insisting it was Dash's baby. It was possible. She could have been pregnant before she went on the cruise with Marc. And where did he get off automatically *assuming* it was *his* baby, anyway?

She switched on the light and got out of bed wondering if she should get dressed or just slip into her robe. Not that Marc hadn't seen her in a nightgown before, she just didn't want any rumors about Dash Sunderling's gay, young widow—and servants gossiped, no matter how loyal they were. She splashed cold water on her face and combed her hair and applied lipstick. God, what should she do?

It was very important to her that she retain her position and reputation in the television industry. She wanted no slurs on Dash's memory. She slipped on a pair of jeans, pulled a tee shirt over her head and fluffed out her hair. She would just go for it. Give it the whole shot and tell Marc that it was Dash's baby, that she hadn't known she was pregnant when she had taken the cruise. She didn't care if he believed her or not. She would stick to the same story with everyone and then, maybe later, when things calmed down, she would tell him the truth.

There had been so much ugly publicity with the Pamela-Ashley scandal and when Dash had died, the tabloids had revived it all over again. She couldn't understand how people could be so cruel. She hated seeing her name on the front pages of those awful newspapers accompanied by a fuzzy, close-up photograph sloppily reproduced. She would go to any lengths to stay out of such publications. And she assumed Marc felt the same way. Surely, he would understand. She heard his car pull up in the driveway and took a deep breath and hurried downstairs to let him in before he rang the doorbell and awakened the servants.

"Cathy!" He filled his arms with her, kissing her until she grew dizzy, saying her name over and over again. He lifted her and carried her inside and kicked the door shut and began kissing her again.

She managed to pull her mouth away long enough to gasp, "Marc, please! Wait a minute." She laughed and drew away from him, glancing quickly about in case any of the servants were still up. "Come on, let's go to the den." She pulled him quickly down the hall, and the moment the door was closed behind them he took her into his arms again.

"God, Cathy, I've missed you so much!" He kissed her hard. "I'm so sorry about Dash, honey, and I know you must have gone through hell, but I can't help being happy about the baby. You don't mind, do you? You must be glad about it too, or you wouldn't have told Rona."

"Why should I mind? I think it's—it's very nice of you." She pulled her hands away and went to the bar. "Can I fix you a drink?"

"Sure, I'll have a Scotch." He came up behind her, nuzzled her neck and laughed softly. "Yes, it was very nice, wasn't it? I've thought about that cruise a hundred times, relived it in my mind every day that I was away from you." He patted her stomach and grinned happily. "That little dude in there was sure conceived with one hell of a lot of romantic love, wasn't he, darling?"

She took a deep breath and turned to face him. "Marc, you seem to think that the baby's yours." She handed him the Scotch. "It isn't—I was already pregnant when I went on that cruise."

"Bullshit." He stared at her, silver eyes narrowed. "You're kidding aren't you? You know damn well that's my kid."

She was suddenly angry. "Bullshit, yourself, Monroe!

How the hell do you know so much about my private life?"

"I know that Dash couldn't get it up! You told me on the cruise, remember?"

"I—I was lying." Forgetting her promise not to drink, she turned back to the bar and mixed herself a vodka and tonic.

"Cathy, what the hell's the matter with you? Why are you doing this?" He took her arm and turned her to face him, his expression bewildered, hurt. "I *know* you got pregnant during the cruise, because I paid the ship's doctor two hundred bucks to switch your birth control pills with placebos!" He hadn't meant to say it, and the moment the words were out, he knew he'd blown it. Again.

"You bastard! You despicable bastard! How dare you interfere in my life!" She began pounding his chest with her small fists, cursing him, kicking his shins. "God damn you to hell—you killed him! You killed Dash! God—I hate you!"

He grabbed her hands and held her away from him, shocked at her outburst. "Cathy, stop it! Calm down! You're hysterical, for God's sake!"

She jerked one hand free and took a swing at him, just grazing his chin. "You prick! Dash committed suicide because I was pregnant and he couldn't face it—the embarrassment. How could you do such a stupid thing?" He captured the fist again and she kicked him in the shin, panting, eyes wild.

"Ow! Stop it, you little bitch. Now just calm down—I don't want to hurt you." He half dragged, half carried her to the sofa and pushed her down, still holding her wrists together in one hand. "Listen to me. I'm very sorry about Dash, but I know that he had cancer and was dying. Clare told me before I left for Ireland."

"That's not true! He was going to have an operation, and he would have been fine!" She struggled to free her hands, but he held them in a viselike grip.

"Then why did he commit suicide?"

"Because of you, you prick! Because you had to play macho man and deliberately get me pregnant! Did it ever enter that conceited brain of yours that I might not want a baby? Oh no, you just pull out a couple hundred bucks and decide my future for me!"

"Cathy—darling, I want *your* future to be *my* future. I want to marry you, sweetheart, and now I can."

"You're out of your cage, Charley! Do you think for one minute that I'd marry the man responsible for my husband's death?"

He snorted in disgust and shook her, hurting her wrists. "Don't be a naive little ass, Cathy. You know damn well Dash took a dive off that cliff so you would be free to marry me—and you'd also inherit KNAB!"

"Why, you arrogant son-of-a-bitch! You really believe that, don't you?" She stopped struggling, and he released her.

"You do too, but you're just too damn stubborn to admit it."

"I'm supposed to believe that my husband, who loved me very much, drove his car off a cliff so I could marry *you*? Don't you think a simple divorce would have been a little less painful?"

"Cathy, Cathy, please, let's stop this. I love you, darling, and I was so happy when I heard about the baby. Please, let's not fight anymore." The silver eyes pleaded, and he reached out his arms to her, but she flung herself off the sofa and stood staring down at him, eyes narrowed in cold fury.

"The baby is Dash's," she said evenly. "And you and I have nothing more to say to one another. Get out of

## The Love Game

my house." She turned her back and left the room, walking quickly down the hall and up the stairs, locking her bedroom door behind her. A moment later she heard the front door slam and ran to the window, staring down at him as he slid behind the wheel of his car.

The arrogant bastard! The sneaky son-of-a-bitch! To deliberately get her pregnant when he knew she was married and expect her to be happy about it—fall into his arms and ride off into the sunset with him. The conceit of the man was phenomenal. And he had just naturally *assumed* the baby would be a boy. Well, if it was, it would be David Sunderling, Jr., but she hoped like hell it would be a girl. She wanted nothing to do with males—even very small ones. They always used you, manipulated you, tried to bend you to their will. She was thoroughly fed up with men.

She jerked off her clothes and got into her nightgown, still trembling a little with anger. She took a sleeping pill and got into bed, switching off the light—wishing she could switch off her thoughts as easily. She had never been so furious in her life. The nerve of the man to impregnate her so casually, so thoughtlessly, without even consulting her about her *own* body! Well, she'd have this baby, but it would be hers alone! Let Marc Monroe live with the knowledge that his child bore another man's name—*that* would get the macho prick where he lived!

She punched her pillow into place almost viciously, wishing it was Marc's conceited face. She would show him that he couldn't take her for granted, plan her life. She was no dumb, giggling Bitsy Bushore to be conned and tricked—and he'd better get used to that idea damned quick. She was head of KNAB, by God. She was his boss and she could fire his ass. She would too, just as soon as his contract ran out. She'd show him—she'd show him. A sharp pain pierced her heart, and she drew her legs up, clutching them close to her chest. And she wept hard, her sobs muffled in the gold satin sheets.

## Chapter Seventeen

It was a cold, rainy February afternoon, Friday the thirteenth, and all day Cathy had had the strangest premonition that something was going to happen. She had spent most of the day in the den, reading, her feet propped up, her enormous belly resting on her knees. She wore a flowing silk caftan, by Monte, of course—the only kind of clothing she was comfortable in these days. God, she'd ballooned up like a baby blimp the past two months and could barely squeeze behind the wheel of her Mercedes. Everyone at KNAB was making bets or starting baby pools, and the crew on her talk show had started a contest for her viewers to get in on the fun. The one who correctly predicted her delivery date would get tickets to all the KNAB shows and dinner for two at Chasen's.

She was a little embarrassed about the fuss but had to admit that it felt good. It was like a big, warm family, waiting with her for the birth of her baby. Lucille Ball must have felt this way all those years ago when she and a breathless nation awaited the birth of Desi Arnez, Jr. She smiled at the comparison. It was hardly the same but a nice thought to hold on to.

Everyone had been so supportive since she had opened her fall show wearing a maternity dress. She had explained briefly and simply about her husband's death last summer in an automobile accident and then proceeded to get on with business, not mentioning it again unless one of her guests brought it up.

She captured the public's attention and sympathy with her warm graciousness, her unfailing class. She was the beautiful young widow, pregnant and proud, and the viewers loved it, felt a part of it and cheered her on. Her fan mail tripled, and her show jumped to the top of the ratings and stayed there all season.

She began getting letters from Marc, short, chatty notes at first, mailed from wherever he happened to be on location. Then he began writing her when he was in town, long, wistful letters, reminding her of how much they had loved one another, how much he still loved her. She knew he watched her show every week when he was in town and had caught herself on more than one occasion dressing with him in mind, wondering what he would think about a certain show or guest.

Sometimes, after receiving one of his letters, she would want to see him so badly she would actually ache. But it was too late. She had allowed the chasm to widen between them. It would be too awkward to try and span the distance now. Her pregnancy had mellowed her, and she realized now what a stiff-necked fool she had been—almost as stiff-necked and arrogant as Marc. But she was a romantic by nature, and when the anger had left her and she had felt the baby growing inside her, she was filled with wonder. A peace that she had never known came over her.

She grew complacent and was filled with benevolence. She forgave Marc completely, saw it as an act of love, the highest compliment a man could pay a woman. She was flattered, even a little grateful. She loved being pregnant. She loved thinking about the baby, wondering what it would be, who it would look like. A dozen times over the Christmas holidays she had wanted to call Marc, but what in the world would she say? "Hi there—want to come over and feel your baby kick?"

She giggled at the thought and got heavily to her feet, going to the fireplace to throw on another log. God, it had been such a dreary day, no wonder she was getting nostalgic. Unrelenting rain beat a steady tattoo against the windows and on the roof, and she felt again the uneasiness that had been bugging her all day like the proverbial calm before a storm. And it *was* Friday the thirteenth! She laughed at her silliness and went to the intercom to ring Mrs. Donahue and order her dinner brought into the den. It was too cold in the huge, lofty dining room—and too lonely sitting all by herself at the long table.

She was ravenous and ate a big dinner and then curled up in Dash's soft leather chair in front of the fireplace. She picked up a copy of Judith Krantz's *Princess Daisy* and began reading. Before she had gotten halfway down the page, a cramp sliced through her stomach, doubling her over, causing her to gasp. "My God, what was that?" she said aloud, clutching her stomach. The pain left her as quickly as it had come, and she attributed it to heartburn—the result of the rich dinner she had eaten. It was too soon for the baby by at least two and a half weeks. She made herself more comfortable in Dash's big reclining chair, snuggling into the soft sag left by his body. Mrs. Donahue bustled in bringing her nightly hot toddy, a delicious concoction of milk, Southern Comfort, raw egg and ginger, heated to sipping temperature.

"I'm going to just fetch you a blanket, Mrs. Sunderling if you're going to be reading a while longer. It's nasty out tonight, and I don't want you getting a chill." She added more logs to the already blazing fireplace and took a thick wool blanket from the trunk near the window. She tucked it around Cathy, making sure her feet were covered. "Now you be sure and ring my room if you need anything during the night."

"I will. Thank you, Mrs. Donahue." It had become a regular request the past few days, and Cathy smiled at the woman's concern. Everyone had expected her to be sick or at least grouchy during her pregnancy, but she had never felt better. She settled back to read and sip her hot drink, growing drowsy in the warmth and quiet. The rain beat hypnotically against the window, and the flames in the fireplace swayed seductively, lulling her to sleep.

She dreamed about Marc and in her dream he was kissing her. She stretched and sighed, opening her eyes to gaze into his beautiful silver ones. She thought she was still asleep and opened her mouth for his kiss—then jerked back as if she had been burned. This was no dream! "Marc! For God's sake! What are you doing here?"

"Damned if I know." He shrugged, grinning at her in that old, cocky way of his. "I was driving down Sunset Boulevard and suddenly found myself on your street. I've been getting the strangest vibes all day—I thought I'd see where they led me."

"Me too! I've had the funniest feeling all day." She stared at him, and he stared back at her, then they both started speaking at once. "Oh, Marc, I'm so sorry—I understand now—"

"Cathy, can you ever forgive me for being such a chauvinistic jerk—"

They laughed and fell into one another's arms, kissing, still trying to talk, their hands moving urgently over one another as if they would never get enough of touching and feeling.

"If you had any idea how much nerve it took for me

## The Love Game      309

to walk in here tonight," Marc finally said, "you would offer me a drink at once!"

"Oh, I'm sorry." Cathy jumped to her feet and started to the bar only to stop midway, doubled over with a cramp. Marc was by her side instantly and helped her back to the chair.

"Cathy, it's not the baby?"

"Of course not." She shifted her weight in the chair. "Whew, I'm going to have to cut out Mrs. Donahue's rich hot toddies, I'm afraid. I've had heartburn all evening."

"Are you sure you're all right?"

"Yes, I'm perfectly all right. Now make yourself a drink and add some more wood to the fire. Gosh, I must have slept longer than I thought—it's almost out. What time is it, anyway?" She looked at her watch, feeling suddenly awkward and shy, knowing that she was probably babbling. "Eleven o'clock—I did oversleep. "Who let you in?"

"Dear old Mrs. Donahue, wearing an old-fashioned chenille bathrobe and an honest-to-goodness nightcap on her head!" He poured himself a Scotch and went to sit at her feet, looking adoringly up at her. "I can't believe it—I've been here almost five whole minutes and you haven't kicked me out. Does that mean you forgive me for being such a bumbling fool? It was the only way I could think to get your attention." He shrugged and looked properly contrite, and she laughed, shaking her head.

"Great way to get my attention, Monroe, and terribly original." She laughed and tousled his thick, dark hair, falling for the charm of his smile all over again and not minding one bit. "Jeez, the oldest trick in the book, you bastard!"

"You fell for it—what's that make you?"

"A fool, obviously . . ." She bent down to kiss him.

# 310 *The Love Game*

"A fool over you." A sudden cramp clutched her, fluttered wildly through her stomach and her water broke with a gush of hot wetness, soaking her thighs and gown. "Oh no," she cried, flinching away from the swiftly spreading stain. "Marc—I—think my water just broke!"

"What? Jesus!" He was on his feet in an instant, helping her stand, looking with shocked dismay at the mess in the chair.

"I can't believe it—it's too soon—and I haven't really been in any pain . . ."

"The doctor," Marc shouted, "We've got to call the doctor. Mrs. Donahue—where's Mrs. Donahue? She has to get you ready. Jesus Christ!" He made several dashes toward the door, stopped, ran back into the room and kissed her. "Don't worry, okay? I'll take care of everything—just relax, okay?"

"I will if you will," Cathy laughed, watching him pace, loving him. "Just ring Mrs. Donahue's room there on the intercom, and she will call my doctor. Then *you* sit down and have a drink while I get out of this wet nightgown."

"Are you sure it's all right? I mean, can you walk? Shouldn't you be lying down or something?"

"Really, Marc, you've seen too many old movies. Just get Mrs. Donahue—I'll be back in a minute."

She didn't know how they did it with all the confusion, but finally they were on their way to the hospital, Williams having been roused from his sleep to chauffeur them there in the family Rolls-Royce limousine. "I'd probably run into something, I'm so damned nervous," Marc had laughed. Her pains had started immediately after her water had broken and had come closer and closer together, surprising her with the suddenness of it all. She had no idea it happened so *fast*! She leaned heavily against Marc, and a strange sort of peace settled over her, a warm heaviness that enveloped her, enclosed her in a sweet drowsiness . . .

Sarah Layne Monroe was born in the back seat of a Rolls-Royce limousine and wrapped in her mother's sable coat only seconds before they reached the hospital. "Oh no, she was born on Friday the thirteenth," Cathy murmured, as interns and nurses rushed out to place her on a stretcher.

Marc looked at his watch and leaned down to kiss her, smiling softly. "It's a quarter after midnight, darling—she was born on Valentine's Day."

"How appropriate," Cathy murmured, taking his hand, and they disappeared through the swinging double doors.

**Driven by desire, they would do
anything to possess each other—anything.**

# Passions

Barney Leason, author of *The New York Times*
bestsellers, *Rodeo Drive* and *Scandals*, once again writes about
what he knows best—the shameless sexual odysseys
of the rich, the powerful, the obsessed and the depraved...
the ultra-chic, super-elite trendsetters who will stop
at nothing to satisfy their secret

# Passions

Set against the glamorous milieu of
haute couture designers, foreign correspondents and
political diplomats...rife with the pleasure and pain of the
world's most enviable elite—here is the shocking,
sensuous story of those who live and love
only to indulge their insatiable

# Passions

☐ 41-207-X $3.75

**Buy them at your local bookstore or use this handy coupon
Clip and mail this page with your order**

**PINNACLE BOOKS, INC.—Reader Service Dept
1430 Broadway, New York, NY 10018**

Please send me the book(s) I have checked above. I am enclosing $_____ (please
add 75¢ to cover postage and handling). Send check or money order only—no cash or
C.O.D.'s.
Mr./Mrs./Miss _____

Address _____

City _____ State/Zip _____

Please allow six weeks for delivery. Prices subject to change without notice.